'. . . But you only really knew her when she had lost a lot of her ideals, when she had found that dreams don't often come true. But the girl I knew was a dreamer and an idealist and, in her own way, a romantic.' She smiled at the looks of disbelief on their faces. 'Your mother always said that there were really only three important dates in her life: 1898 when she came to Ireland, went into service, became pregnant and lost her job; 1907 when she renewed her acquaintance with your father, Patrick, and re-met the man who was to become her husband; and 1916, when she lost everything. Incidentally, 1907 was the date when the Crown Jewels were stolen. She was reunited with Dermot Corcoran then because he was investigating their theft. That was also the reason behind her re-acquaintance with Major John Lewis.'

Patrick came to stand before Tilly, his hands folded across his chest. 'Look, perhaps I'm just tired, but let's see, do I have this right? Our mother has fled her house in Mayfair because she fears for her life. You believe she might have been threatened because she is interested in purchasing the Irish Crown Jewels?'

'Exactly.'

'I don't believe it,' Patrick said, turning away in disgust.

Senga looked at her brother, frowning slightly. She turned back to Tilly and attempted to smile. 'Leaving that to one side for the moment, why have you come here to us?'

'I'm looking for help.'

'What sort of help?'

'I would like you both to come back to London with me.'

They both looked at her in amazement.

'I need your help to run your mother's business, and I need help in looking for her.'

'No,' Patrick said firmly. 'She's made her own bed, she can lie in it.'

Season's End

Anna Dillon

This first hardcover edition published in Great Britain 1991 by
SEVERN HOUSE PUBLISHERS LTD of
35 Manor Road, Wallington, Surrey SM6 0BW
by arrangement with Sphere Books Limited,
a division of Macdonald & Co. (Publishers) Ltd

Copyright © Anna Dillon 1990

British Library Cataloguing in Publication Data

Dillon, Anna
  Season's End
  I. Title
  823.914 [F]

  ISBN 0-7278-4180-7

Printed and bound in Great Britain by
Billing and Sons Ltd, Worcester

To the memory of Johanna Dillon,
a woman of all seasons . . .

PROLOGUE

A little after three o'clock on a bitterly cold March morning, Katherine Lundy walked away from her luxurious Mayfair home. She was carrying a small case which held two changes of clothing, a pair of shoes, one thousand pounds in notes and a small silver pistol.

She would be fifty next birthday, and she decided that she hadn't much to show for all those years. True, she was wealthy and enjoyed a standard of living that her parents would never have imagined possible. At the height of her success, Madam Lundy's income had exceeded half a million sterling, and that was not counting the numerous gifts and gratuities she received. Even now, when she had almost – but not quite – retired, her annual income was close to a quarter of a million sterling.

But her great wealth had not brought her happiness. It had cost her her children, and her friends, and much of her humanity.

She glanced back at the house just before she rounded the corner of the park; if things worked out she would be back . . . and if they didn't, well then. . .

Katherine Lundy was going in search of a dream.

She found a nightmare.

CHAPTER ONE

Senga Lundy Corcoran watched the wide-eyed young man weave his way through the ballroom crowd towards her and gritted her teeth. This would be the third time *whatshisname* had asked her to dance, and he was one of those men who refused to take no for an answer. The last time he had asked, she had been positively rude, telling him outright that there was no way she could possibly dance with someone who looked like he did, smelt like he did, and smiled like he did. And it wasn't as if he had good teeth. The young man's smile, which was wide and fixed, revealed a row of yellowed and stained teeth. Like tombstones, Senga thought suddenly, a smile twisting her lips.

She immediately realised her mistake: *whatshisname* thought she was smiling at him. Well he was about to receive a rude awakening.

'So, you will dance?' *whatshisname* said eagerly, standing too close, bathing her in his rancid body odour. Senga knew there was a name for bad breath, she just wasn't sure what it was.

'I have already told you I will not,' she said, a smile fixing itself to her lips. She shifted her gaze past his face, across the large marquee that was filled to overcrowding with Trinity College students, most of them rather the worse for drink. Senga hadn't really wanted to attend the Trinity Ball but, since this was her final year as a Trinity student, she felt she had to attend at least once. However,

9

it was a decision she was regretting more and more as the night wore on.

'Why not?' the young man demanded belligerently.

Senga sighed and turned to look at the young man again, frowning slightly, trying to recall his name. He was tall, thin, balding, and at this particular moment more than a little drunk. Now what was his name . . . Mark . . . yes, it was Mark something or other.

'I don't want to dance with you, Mark,' she said patiently.

'Why not?' he said again. His cheeks were flushed and his eyes were glittering dangerously.

'I do believe we have had this conversation,' she said smiling. 'But let me go through the details again. I will not dance with you because I don't like you. Because you're drunk and because you smell,' Senga said slowly and carefully, reaching up to brush strands of hair from her face.

'Why . . .!' Mark *whatshisname* reached for her suddenly, his fingers curled to grab . . . and Senga's six-inch hatpin slid neatly into the palm of his hand, exiting through the other side with barely a trace of blood. Senga continued to smile. The young man looked at his hand in puzzlement, wondering at the fire that was coursing up his arm, spreading into his chest, racing up into his throat. He opened his mouth to scream – and a figure moved between him and Senga . . . and suddenly he couldn't even breathe, let alone scream. He was dimly aware that someone had kneed him in the groin. He attempted to double up, to curl in around the pain, but iron-hard fingers had latched themselves on to the soft flesh of his jaw. Mark found himself looking into a face carved from stone and about as expressive.

'If you so much as look at my sister again, I'll break your kneecaps.' The hand then closed around his face and shoved him backwards into the milling crowd. He stumbled and went down, the pain claiming him. His scream was lost amidst the laughter.

Senga Lundy looked reprovingly at her older brother. 'Patrick, something a little less dramatic would have been fine. . .' She wiped Mark *whatshisname's* blood from the hatpin with a napkin. 'But I am capable of taking care of myself, you know.'

Patrick Corcoran grinned, the smile taking years off his face. 'I know that.' He watched his younger sister slide the long hatpin back into the thick bun of her hair. 'I'm glad to see you brought that with you.'

'You know I'm never without it,' she said quietly, watching as Mark *whatshisname* was dragged through the crowd by some of his friends. They were all ignoring his cries of pain, laughing at his obvious discomfort. After a terrifying experience in Paris eight years previously, she had sworn that she would never allow any man to dominate or intimidate her, and her reputation in Trinity College, Dublin, was as a straight-talking, no-nonsense 'modern' girl. The last time she had cut a man had been in Paris and he had been attempting to rape her. She had used a comb to devastating effect, and since then she was rarely without her 'defences' – two six-inch straight hatpins woven into her thick hair.

Patrick's hand closed around her elbow and steered her through the crowd. Looking at them one would never have guessed that they were brother and sister, or, more correctly, half-brother and half-sister. Their mother was Katherine Lundy, but Patrick's father had been John Lewis, an English Army officer who had run the British intelligence services in Dublin, while Senga's father had been the crusading journalist, Dermot Corcoran. Patrick more closely resembled his father, having his height and sharp, hard features, with his dark, piercing eyes and thin, sometimes cruel lips. When he had first come to Ireland, fleeing his mother's wrath, he had had his head shaved, and now continued to wear it in that close-cropped style.

Senga had inherited her mother's luxurious mane of jet-black hair, and deep-set dark-brown eyes which gave her oval face a perpetually surprised, innocent expression. Her

11

lips were full and slightly up-tilted, 'smiling lips' Patrick called them, but they could set in the same hard, thin line that was so reminiscent of their mother when she was in one of her foul humours. She was not a great beauty, but her face had character and strength that prevented it from being plain.

A stocky young man stepped in front of them, placing the palm of his hand flat against Patrick's chest. 'My friend said you kicked him in . . .' he glanced at Senga, '. . . kicked him,' he finished belligerently.

'He fell down,' Patrick hissed coldly. 'Now, go away before you fall down too.'

'Just who do you think. . .?' the young man began, and then Patrick took his wrist and twisted sharply, driving the young man to his knees. Patrick leaned forward. 'Don't come near me again,' he murmured, and the smile that curled his lips was anything but pleasant.

'My, we are in an agreeable humour tonight,' Senga said quietly, glancing sidelong at her brother as they passed the Campanile, heading towards the gate. Usually, Patrick would walk away from an argument, knowing full well that he was capable of killing if roused. He had told her something about the time he had spent as an IRA 'operative'. He had never explained in detail what he had had to do, but she had a very good idea. A sudden thought struck her and she turned to Patrick. 'What are you doing here? And how did you get in in the first place. I thought this event was by ticket only.'

'Friends in low places,' he said, gripping her arm tightly as she manoeuvred across the wet cobbles, her low-heeled court shoes slipping on the smooth stones. It had rained earlier that evening, and the sky was clouded with the promise of more rain. There was the smell of thunder in the air. 'Will your date not miss you?' he asked, nearly but not quite managing to keep the sarcasm from his voice.

'I told you I only came with him because it would not have been seemly for a young woman to attend a function like this on her own. But no, he won't miss me; the last

12

time I saw him he was more than a little drunk . . . and so was his companion,' she added.

Patrick glanced sidelong at her. 'Male or female companion?' he asked with a smile.

'Female . . . undoubtedly female,' Senga said, and then laughed, the bright sound echoing across the empty square. 'Oh Patrick, you should have seen him! You should have seen her!' She was still laughing as they walked into the arched entranceway, their footsteps echoing flatly on the wooden floor. 'He will be so ashamed in the morning,' she finishd with a giggle.

'If he remembers,' Patrick suggested.

'He'll have the scars . . . I know the girl,' she confided, slipping her arms through his, and changing the subject deftly, 'And you still haven't told me why you came here tonight.'

'Don't ask me now . . . please,' he added quickly, seeing the stubborn expression drift across his sister's face. 'Give me a few minutes, and all will become clear.'

There was a line of cabs directly across College Green, but Patrick ignored them, as she knew he would, choosing instead to follow the line of Trinity College wall around to the left, heading up towards Grafton Street. The couple walked in silence, Senga on the inside closest to the wall, Patrick close to the edge of the kerb. Senga had lived with her brother for the past eight years now, ever since he had taken her home from Paris, and in that time she had learned to read the nuances of his behaviour and his moods. She knew when something was bothering him. She could read it in the way he moved, the way he hunched his shoulders, as if he were readying himself for a blow. Tonight he seemed even more nervous than usual. His nervousness communicated itself to her, and she felt her good humour of the earlier part of the evening drift away. She found herself watching shadows, looking up and down the dark deserted streets.

'What time is it?' she asked suddenly.

'A little before three,' he muttered.

13

'Feels earlier.'

Senga was expecting Patrick to head up Grafton Street to use the taxi rank at the top of the street or along by the Shelbourne Hotel, but instead he surprised her by continuing to follow the college wall to the left, heading down Nassau Street. The street was deserted, the wan yellow globes of the street light reflecting off the damp cobbles, and the solitary car parked before the bookshop.

Senga noticed that Patrick unbuttoned his coat as he squeezed her elbow, urging her across the street, towards the car. Almost without her noticing he deftly switched places with her, so that he was still on the outside and she was once again away from the kerb. Although there was a thin plume of steel-grey smoke drifting up from the exhaust tainting the sharp clean air with its faintly acrid odour, the engine was idling so quietly that it was virtually inaudible. She wasn't sure what type of car it was, but to be that quiet it must be expensive.

'Patrick . . .?' she asked, as he tapped on the windowpane and then put his hand on the door and pulled it open.

He smiled reassuringly. 'A little surprise for you . . . for both of us,' he murmured.

There was a figure in the back of the car – a woman to judge by the perfume – sitting back into the shadows in the corner. Senga felt her breath catch at the back of her throat, and she looked at her brother in horror, 'P-P-Patrick?'

He reached out and squeezed her hand. 'I know,' he said softly, 'I thought it was our mother too.'

Senga turned to look at the shadowed figure. When she had opened the door of the car and spotted the woman in the shadows, she had immediately thought that their mother had come for them. The thought was always there, always at the back of her mind – and both she and Patrick knew that Katherine Lundy would not give them up without a fight.

But if it wasn't Katherine . . . then who?

Patrick climbed in beside her and the car pulled away, the streetlights casting a flickering light into the interior as the car moved past.

'My God, how you've grown. You're quite the young woman now.'

The voice was familiar, the faintest touch of a Cockney accent, overlain with a broad Dublin accent. Senga frowned, tilting her head sideways, attempting to identify it.

'It must be nearly thirteen years since I last saw you both.'

And suddenly she knew; thirteen years ago had been 1916, when she and Patrick had first left Ireland to take up a new life in England with their mother. 'Aunt Tilly . . .?' she whispered, 'Tilly Cusack?'

'Aaah, but you always were the cleverest of girls, Senga. You must forgive the charade, but I did wonder if you'd remember your old aunt.'

'Oh Tilly, how could I ever forget you?'

In the flickering light it was difficult to make out the woman's features, but from the little she could distinguish, Senga could see that she was still strikingly beautiful despite the fact that she would be a few years older than her mother, her eyes still bright and sparkling, blue against her almost perfect complexion. 'You look marvellous.'

'Thank you, my dear. I must admit I feel marvellous. I haven't felt so good in years.'

'Share your secret, aunty,' Senga laughed.

'Bad living and excess,' Tilly laughed, 'and the love of a good man.'

'Aunt Tilly, you're incorrigible!'

'It's true,' Tilly laughed, knowing the young woman would not believe her, and yet, in a way, it was as close to the truth as she ever came.

In her youth, Tilly Cusack had been one of the most sought-after courtesans on Dublin's streets. She had also been the person responsible for rescuing Katherine Lundy

15

off the streets and introducing her to the Whoremistress of Dublin. When Katherine eventually rose to become the Madam of the house, Tilly had still continued to work, even though Katherine had offered on numerous occasions to set her up in a house on her own. But she had refused. Until she had met Martin Moore, the English army captain sent to Dublin to assist Major John Lewis crack down on the growing revolutionary groups, Tilly Cusack had been contented with her life. Although she was ten years his senior, their love had been immediate, and – much to everyone's surprise, and not a little family opposition – they had married. Although their marriage had, to Tilly's regret, been childless, they were still together, and happy, based in Edinburgh.

'What's wrong?' Senga asked suddenly. 'Something's wrong, isn't it? There must be something wrong to bring you all the way from Scotland.'

Previously, Tilly Cusack's only communication with her 'niece' and 'nephew' had been the occasional letter, and a card at Christmas.

Tilly Cusack nodded. 'There is. About a week ago I received a telegram from Martha Tilke in London.' She watched Senga react at the mention of the woman's name; she had been the girl's governess at one stage. 'Now I know you have had little enough to do with your mother since your last encounter in Paris, but I'm here to tell you that your mother needs you – needs you both.'

Whatever reaction Tilly Cusack had been expecting, it certainly hadn't been the frigid silence that fell over the young man and woman. Eventually Senga spoke, her voice calm and even, giving no indication of the turmoil raging within her.

'You know how things stand between us,' she said carefully. 'What could she possibly want us for?'

'She . . . she needs you,' Tilly repeated. 'But . . .'

'But . . .?' Patrick persisted.

'But she doesn't know I've come here for you!'

'So *you* think she needs us,' Patrick said slowly. 'Does

she? But then, when has she ever needed anyone, eh? Especially her children: she only needed us to possess us, to own us, like objects.' He shook his head flatly. 'We're not interested.'

'You know I wouldn't have come here unless it was important,' Tilly continued determinedly.

'I told you, we're not interested.'

Tilly sighed. 'Is this open to discussion?'

'No!' they both said together.

Tilly Cusack nodded. She had been hoping that the years would have mellowed Katherine's children, perhaps eased some of the bitterness, but obviously not. And, if she were to be absolutely truthful with herself, she couldn't say she blamed them. Katherine had effectively driven Patrick from his home and then hounded him, first by using her own men and then later, when Patrick was on the run, by informing the police of his whereabouts. When Patrick's wife of less than an hour was shot on their wedding day, the blame could be laid squarely at Katherine Lundy's feet. The woman had also alienated her daughter; the girl had only been twelve when she had been sent to an almost prison-like Swiss finishing school. The regime had been so confining that the girl had run away, only to fall into the hands of a notorious and dangerous womaniser. It was only Patrick – and Katherine's – timely arrival that had saved her from rape and possibly death.

Neither Lundy children had any cause to love their mother.

'So, nothing I can say will change your mind? You won't come back to London with me?'

'Under no circumstances,' Senga said quickly.

The car stopped outside the Shelbourne Hotel, and Senga suddenly realised that they had been driving around St Stephen's Green. Even at this late hour the foyer was ablaze with light, the damp pavement outside shimmering with warm reflected light. Patrick stepped out when the car stopped and looked up and down the street before

17

reaching in to take his sister's hand. It was drizzling and she hurried past him to stand under the canopy while he helped Tilly out. Tilly looked at him, catching his eyes, holding his expression; experience had taught her that most men found it difficult to refuse a woman's request when it was accompanied by a direct stare. 'You'll join me for a cup of coffee . . .?'

'The hour . . .' Patrick protested.

'I'm not tired, are you?' she asked, joining Senga under the canopy. A liveried doorman opened the door and touched the brim of his tall hat in salute.

'I was prepared for an all-night party,' Senga said with a smile. 'The night is still young.'

• 'I really must go,' Patrick said, looking at his sister.

Tilly Cusack reached out and touched his arm with the tips of her fingers. 'I need to talk to you both . . .'

'About our mother?' Senga asked.

Tilly nodded.

'We've nothing to talk about,' Patrick said quickly.

'She's disappeared,' Tilly said very quickly. 'Katherine Lundy has vanished without trace!'

CHAPTER TWO

'It has been quite some while since I last saw your mother. As you know we had drifted apart over the past few years. But one day, about a week ago, I got a call from Martha Tilke. I was so disturbed by what I heard that I left Edinburgh immediately and travelled down to London.' Tilly Cusack spoke slowly, choosing her words with care. She hadn't anticipated that the Lundy children would still bear such animosity towards their mother, and she knew that a wrong word would lose her their interest. 'It transpired that she had been acting very strangely of late . . .'

'Define strangely,' Senga interrupted. She didn't look at the woman, preferring to concentrate on the cup of tea on the table before her. On the marble mantelpiece, a small undistinguished clock pinged four o'clock. Beyond the window, the first glimmers of dawn were beginning to lighten the sky.

Tilly Cusack sipped her own tea and looked from the girl sitting in front of her, not meeting her eyes, to Patrick standing beside the window, peering down into the street. Although he was not obviously looking at her, she knew he could see her reflection in the glass before him.

'How much do you know of your mother's past?' she asked suddenly.

'Enough,' Senga said quickly, looking up, her deep, dark eyes hard and challenging.

Tilly met her stare, her own bright-blue eyes now touched with their old, professional cynicism. 'How

19

much?' she whispered.

'We know what she was, what she is,' Senga continued, glancing across at her brother, who hadn't moved, hadn't taken part in the exchange.

'You know what she is now: a hard, sometimes cruel, often unfeeling woman. But do you know what made her that way?' Tilly challenged Senga's hard stare and then twisted in her seat to look at Patrick. 'Do you?'

'I know a little,' he said, his shoulders shifting in a slight shrug. 'But I don't see where this is leading . . .'

'Do you know how your mother and I met?' The woman was speaking principally to Senga now, concentrating all her attention on her, knowing that for her plan to have any real chance of succes she would have to convince her.

'I first met your mother on Christmas Eve, 1898. She had been set upon and beaten by two drunken soldiers out for a night's entertainment. They thought she was one of the many street girls who walked Dublin then, but it was those same women who saved her from a bad beating or possibly worse. I took her and bought her a cup of tea. I discovered that she had been dismissed from her employment a few hours previously, because her mistress had discovered that she had been having an affair with the master of the house.

'And before either of you jump to any conclusions, remember that your mother was a simple girl who had been completely seduced by one of the most dangerous men I ever knew, Major, then Captain, John Lewis.' Tilly's face twisted at the mention of the major's name, and Senga wondered what the man had done to make her hate him so. 'Your mother was pregnant by him at the time . . . pregnant with you Patrick.' She turned to look at him again, and he nodded shortly. 'She was eighteen years old.'

Tilly turned back to Senga. 'So I took your mother to the only safe house I knew, a place where I was certain she would be safe – the house you both grew up in, Number Eighty-Two, Tyrone Street Lower. At that time it was owned and run by one of the most feared women in Dublin, the notorious Bella Cohen, the Whoremistress. You never knew her – although she often bounced you on her knee, Patrick – but she was a terrifying woman who ran many of the brothels and most of the girls in Dublin . . .'

'You mean prostitutes,' Senga interrupted.

'Girls, women, ladies,' Tilly chided, 'prostitute is an ugly word, a label. These women were not labels, they were my friends.'

'*Friends*?' Patrick said, turning to look at her, his mouth opening as understanding dawned.

Tilly nodded her lips twisting in a bitter smile. 'I thought you knew. I was a prostitute. I was one of Bella Cohen's girls; that's how I came to be working the streets on Christmas Eve, that's how I knew the Whoremistress.'

'I never knew,' Patrick confessed. 'I never even suspected.'

'And was our mother a wh . . . one of Bella Cohen's girls?' Senga asked, her voice carefully neutral.

'No. Your mother never worked – at least not in the way I worked. You must remember that she was pregnant at the time and, although there is a certain class of men who like pregnant women, few of them frequented the brothels. A friendship formed between Bella and your mother, a friendship which deepened into something else . . . I'm not sure what, but certainly, in later years, Bella regared Katherine almost as a daughter. Your mother started to work for Bella. She could read and write, manage figures, and so she started keeping the books, ordering the supplies; eventually she began to make suggestions, which Bella followed up . . . and found to her surprise that they were making her money. It turned out that she was a natural businesswoman. Katherine travelled on the Continent, visiting the various European brothels, seeing how they ran their operations, and when she came back to Ireland – and this would have been shortly after you were born, Patrick – she set about making Number

21

Eight-Two one of *the* most – if not *the* most – luxurious brothels in the British Isles.

'And she succeeded. The house became more than a brothel. There was gambling and drinking, of course, and erotic entertainment, but your mother also hosted several literary parties and numerous charity events. She almost – but not quite – made the trade respectable. Why, I can remember numerous representatives of European royalty visiting the house and, on at least three occasions, a certain member of the British royal family visited the house for an evening of special entertainment.

'And of course she made enemies.

'There were hard decisions to be made and she made them, and they in turn made her hard.

'Over the years – and I must admit I'm not sure how it started out, but I suppose it was almost a logical progression from the business she was in – she began to deal in information, buying and selling news, sometimes for a flat fee, often for a percentage of the proceeds her information would bring. It would be fair to say that houses were burgled, consignments stolen or people robbed because of the news she sold. And from dealing in news, she went on to deal in stolen goods – never directly, of course, she merely acted as a middleman, making the right connections, and taking her cut.

'And that, in turn, produced even more enemies.

'In 1907, the year before you were born, Senga, the Irish Crown Jewels were stolen. Patrick would remember it; it happened virtually on the eve of Edward's visit to Ireland. It was a huge scandal at the time, with repercussions that went all the way back to the throne. To this day the jewels have never been recovered and no one knows who stole them – at least not officially.

'But your mother does.

'She received a copy of the lost police report, which detailed how the jewels were stolen and their whereabouts. This report was never made public and was lost soon after it was presented by Inspector John Kane who was

22

investigating the theft. I don't know how your mother got a copy, but I do know she had excellent contacts within both Dublin Castle and police headquarters in Brunswick Street Station.

'Anyway, the jewels vanished. But over the years they have been offered for sale on the black market. I must admit I never had any interest in them, but I do know that your mother made several attempts to buy the stones.'

'What has this got to do with our mother's disappearance?' Senga interrupted.

Tilly nodded quickly. 'Bear with me a moment,' she asked. 'Martha Tilke tells me that shortly before your mother disappeared, she spoke to her about some old Irish jewellery she had been offered and said that she was toying with the idea of buying it. Martha Tilke said that your mother seemed quite excited about the prospect of buying these particular jewels.'

'But they could be anything,' Senga snapped.

Tilly nodded. 'They could. But I made some inquiries with the few contacts I still have in the underworld, and I discovered that several dealers in stolen gems have been approached recently in an attempt to sell various pieces of the Irish Crown Jewels.'

'All right. Perhaps *I'm* being stupid, but tell me what this has to do with my mother's disappearance,' Patrick snapped. Senga nodded in agreement.

'If the jewels were recovered now, it would lead to embarrassment and possibly disgrace in high quarters. Old wounds would be opened, old scandals dragged up.'

Patrick shook his head. 'So . . .?'

'I think your mother's life may have been threatened. She made no secret of her interest in the jewels. I don't know why; their monetary value is limited and some of the pieces are positively ugly. But I think it was something to do with the possibility that a girl from the humblest beginnings could own the Crown Jewels.'

Patrick shook his head. 'I don't believe it. My memories of my mother are of a practical woman with little time for

23

sentiment.'

Tilly shrugged. 'Perhaps. But you only really knew her when she had lost a lot of her ideals, when she had found that dreams don't often come true. But the girl I knew was a dreamer and an idealist and, in her own way, a romantic.' She smiled at the looks of disbelief on their faces. 'Your mother always said that there were really only three important dates in her life: 1898 when she came to Ireland, went into service, became pregnant and lost her job; 1907 when she renewed her acquaintance with your father, Patrick, and re-met the man who was to become her husband; and 1916, when she lost everything. Incidentally, 1907 was the date when the Crown Jewels were stolen. She was reunited with Dermot Corcoran then because he was investigating their theft. That was also the reason behind her re-acquaintance with Major John Lewis.'

Patrick came to stand before Tilly, his hands folded across his chest. 'Look, perhaps I'm just tired, but let's see, do I have this right? Our mother has fled her house in Mayfair because she fears for her life. You believe she might have been threatened because she is interested in purchasing the Irish Crown Jewels?'

'Exactly.'

'I don't believe it,' Patrick said, turning away in disgust.

Senga looked at her brother, frowning slightly. She turned back to Tilly and attempted to smile. 'Leaving that to one side for the moment, why have you come here to us?'

'I'm looking for help.'

'What sort of help?'

'I would like you both to come back to London with me.' They both looked at her in amazement.

'I need your help to run your mother's business, and I need help in looking for her.'

'No,' Patrick said firmly. 'She's made her own bed, she can lie in it.'

'She is your mother,' Tilly reminded him gently.

'No,' Patrick hissed. 'She lost the right to call herself that a long time ago. I'm thirty years of age this year; I've

24

been a widower for the past nine years because of my mother.'

Tilly sighed. 'All right,' she breathed, and suddenly her face and eyes hardened, startling Senga who was staring directly at her. She had seen that same expression on her mother's face, in her mother's eyes. 'There are some other factors to be considered then. If your mother does not reappear, you are the main beneficiaries of her will . . .'

'I want nothing from her,' Patrick snapped.

'Her personal assets, including holdings, property, stock of various kinds, a number of investments both at home and abroad, come close enough to half a million sterling. The vast majority of that money is willed to you both. All you have to do is to claim it.'

'I told you I want none of her money.' Patrick turned away, returning to stand before the window. Without turning around he added, 'I know how she earned it.'

'How do you earn your money now, Patrick?' Tilly asked quietly.

Patrick turned slowly to face the women. Senga was looking at him curiously. Although she lived with her brother, she didn't know what he did for a living. He often worked at night and was sometimes absent for days at a time. He never volunteered information and she never asked, although she was naturally curious.

'I really don't think it's any concern of yours.' Patrick's eyes flickered to his sister.

'Perhaps it's not. But before you contemptuously dismiss your mother's earnings, remember that to throw the first stone you should be without sin. Are you without sin, Patrick?' Without waiting for an answer, she pressed on. 'Another point to consider. If there is an investigation into your mother's disappearance, it would surely lead the police to you both . . . and I'm sure neither of you want that.'

Patrick stared ahead, leaving Senga to do the talking.

'I don't think we'd want that,' she said quietly. 'But then, I don't suppose you want an investigation either.'

'None of us are without skeletons in our closets,' Tilly murmured.

'So what are you suggesting?'

Tilly smiled, realising she had won. 'Come back to London with me. I'll need someone to help me manage the house in Mayfair. Your mother has already committed herself to several large engagements in the coming months. Someone will need to host those parties; if they were to be cancelled, questions would be asked, and, besides, she has already ordered supplies well in advance and these will need to be paid for, whether they are used or not. I would like you to do that, Senga, I would like you to take your mother's place for a few weeks . . . or for as long as it takes Patrick to find your mother.'

The young man turned from the window. 'And how am I supposed to find her?'

'Use your connections. Both legitimate and otherwise.'

'And if we don't find her?'

'Then find her body!'

Although it was still close to six in the morning, none of the early morning tradesmen paid any attention to the couple making their way down the damp cobbled street. All Dublin knew that the Trinity Ball had been held the previous night, and the sight of young women in evening dresses entirely unsuited to the early morning damp and chill, accompanied by young men who might have looked dapper several hours previously, was not uncommon.

Grafton Street was practically deserted, and the few people up and about strode along purposefully. Some of the darkened doorways, however, held bundles that were even now stretching awake. A few of the homeless nodded to Patrick as he passed, their eyes flat and dead in their faces, their very stances radiating hopelessness. Two were women, and although they wished Patrick a good morning, their eyes were on Senga. The young woman shivered at the look – the hunger, the want, the naked greed – in their faces.

26

Senga slipped her arm through her brother's. 'How do you know these people, Patrick?' she whispered, resisting the temptation to look back over her shoulder to where a young couple, with what looked like a child between them, lay huddled in the doorway of Bewley's Cafe.

He shrugged. 'I've spent a lot of time on the streets myself, Senga. I've even lived rough myself.'

'But that was a long time ago . . . wasn't it?' She glanced sidelong at him, attempting to read his expression.

'Not so long, little sister,' he murmured.

'I don't suppose you want to tell me what you do?' she asked, and then continued when he shook his head. 'No, I suppose not. But it cannot be legal,' she added.

'Not entirely. But the victors make the laws.'

Senga's grip tightened on his arm. 'Patrick, Ireland is free, it has its independence. The war is finished.'

'No,' he snapped, the anger in his voice surprising her. 'The war isn't finished. Not while men like me remain alive with our memories. Our greatest weapon is our memories. When you have nothing else, you have your memories, and it is important you keep them alive.'

'Even the bad memories?'

'Especially the bad memories. My mother betrayed me – more than once – and cost me everything, my future, even my bride. I'll never forget what she did to me. I'll never forgive her.'

'Never forget, never forgive,' Senga whispered.

Patrick nodded. 'Aye, something like that. It's a code I live by.'

'It's the same code you'll die by!'

Tilly Cusack stood by the window and watched the couple make their way down towards Grafton Street. Reflected in the glass, she saw the door to the bedroom open and a man step into the room. He came over and pressed himself to her, his large hands encircling her waist and then moving up to touch the bodice of her evening dress.

'You heard?'

27

'You were magnificent,' he said.
'Will it work?'
'It will work,' he said confidently. 'It has to work.'

CHAPTER THREE

It had been eight years since Senga Lundy had last seen her mother, and there had been occasions during that time when she had actually missed her.

Those occasions had been few and far between it was true, but time had softened the image she had created of her mother, and dulled the pain a little, helping to make the woman into something far less fearsome than she had been.

It had been easier in the beginning. Following her last encounter with her in Paris, she had returned to Dublin with Patrick, and it had been very easy then to hate Katherine Lundy. There had been nightmares in the early days, and she had often awoken chilled and shaken from a dream in which a vague and formless creature pursued her across fields of blackened snow. Without ever actually seeing the creature's face, Senga knew instinctively it was her mother.

But no one can hate forever; even Patrick's philosophy *never forgive, never forget*, was impracticable, and eventually Senga found that she could remember the good times, the few happy moments, with great clarity, and that her memories of the bad times became dulled and muted. It wasn't that she had actually forgotten what Katherine Lundy was capable of, it was merely that she chose not to remember it.

And she had had her own life to lead, and that life did not include her mother.

Until now.

And the dreams had returned. Only now she was pursuing the shadowy creature.

Walking back into the house in Mayfair was like walking into some dream. It was at once both strange and hauntingly familiar, and for a single moment she felt as if she had never left it – as if the past eight years and all that had happened had been nothing more than some evil dream. She stood for minutes in the long marbled hallway, just looking around, surprised to find that so little had changed. There were the same pictures on the wall, the same heavily flocked wallpaper, the long hideously-ornate mirror on the wall to the right of the door.

'I thought it would be different,' she said softly, almost to herself.

Tilly turned back to look at her. The older woman had said nothing on the journey from the station to the house, realising that Senga was going to need time to readjust to the life and the city she had left so long ago.

'Your mother did very little with the house in the last eight years or so. Martha Tilke tells me that it was as if she had no reason to do anything, to change anything.'

'You'll be telling me she kept it as a monument,' Senga said sarcastically.

'Indeed, I think she did, Miss Senga.' The woman who stepped out of the dining room was tall and thin, sharp-featured, her lips narrow, barely visible lines. She hadn't visibly aged in the eight years since Senga had last seen her, and the young woman found that her feelings for the woman hadn't changed either. The only difference was that now she didn't have to disguise those feelings. 'Martha Tilke.' She pronounced the name slowly, almost as if she had forgotten it. 'You haven't changed.'

The woman's lips curled in a smile that never reached her eyes. 'It is kind of you to say so . . . even though it cannot be entirely the truth,' she added.

'No, I can truthfully say that you are as I remember you,' Senga said, looking closely at the woman. Still the same sour old witch. Although she had only known the woman briefly, it had been Martha Tilke who had brought her to the school in Switzerland, where she had been 'dumped' by her mother, hidden away from her brother Patrick. During the trip by boat, train and car, the woman had barely spoken to the frightened young girl. Senga Lundy had never forgiven her for it.

'I have prepared your old room for you, Miss Senga. I trust that will be to your satisfaction.'

Senga hadn't actually thought about it until that moment, but the very fact that the woman had gone ahead and prepared the room without consulting her rankled. Surprising herself, she shook her head firmly. 'No, I don't think so. You may prepare my mother's room for me, Miss Tilke. If I am to run this house in her absence, I should at least claim some of the privileges due to me.'

The woman looked at her for a long moment, and then nodded curtly. 'I will see to it immediately.'

Tilly Cusack was waiting for Senga in the family sitting room at the back of the house. Her bright blue eyes were dancing in amusement. 'I can see there's no love lost between you two. Congratulations, you handled her well.'

'Living with my brother has taught me a few unladylike traits and mannerisms,' Senga said, looking around at the cluttered, familiar room. There were two sitting rooms in the house in Mayfair; a pristine, stage-like front room where Katherine would receive her visitors and guests, and the cosy family sitting room at the back of the house opening out on to the long rear garden. It was one of the few rooms in the house without artifice or pretence. Next to her bedroom, it had always been Senga's favourite room.

'Nothing's changed,' she said in a low whisper. She ran her white-gloved finger along the top of the marbled fire-place: the tip of the glove came away black with soot and dirt. She reached out and tugged the ornate, frilled bell-pull that hung beside the fire. The door opened almost immediately and Martha Tilke stepped into the room.

'Madam . . .?' She looked at Tilly Cusack. Tilly turned

31

to look at Senga, and the woman followed her gaze. 'Miss Senga . . .?'

'What is your position in this house, Miss Tilke?' Senga asked.

'Housekeeper.'

'And what staff do we employ at present?'

'There is a cook, two maids and a general handyman who also acts as a gardener. We have had to cut back on staff,' she explained.

Senga ran the flat of her white-gloved hand along the mantelpiece and held up the glove to Martha Tilke. The palm and fingers were black. 'I want this house thoroughly cleaned, top to bottom. My mother insisted on very high standards of cleanliness; because she is not here, I see no reason for those standards to be allowed to slip. You may start with this room.'

The woman blinked rapidly and then she swallowed so hard Senga could see her throat work, 'Very good, Miss Senga.'

'I would like it to be started immediately. Now, is my room prepared?'

'In a few minutes, Miss Senga,' she said and then hurried from the room.

'You know where she's gone,' Tilly said with a smile.

'To clean up my mother's bedroom,' Senga nodded.

'I have the guest room just down the hall. Once you've settled in, we'll set to work. I want you to be thoroughly familiar with your mother's operation before events overtake us. I want you to know her suppliers, their terms, and how their contracts are fulfilled; I want you to be familiar with the merchants who supply the food and drink for her various houses. Katherine Lundy does all her own buying; it is part of her trademark, so some of these people will know Katherine, others will not; you will have to present yourself differently to each group. At all costs, we must prevent any rumours which might suggest that Katherine Lundy is missing.

'Now, the first event we have to take care of is a Grand

Summer Fête towards the end of this month. It is always one of the highlights of the London social scene and will be attended by just about everyone who is anyone. There will be no British royalty in attendance this year, but several minor European royals who will be in the city have been invited and will undoubtedly come. There will be plenty of politicians, with their wives or mistresses as appropriate, numerous high-ranking clergy, various titled folk, as well as the usual mixture of literati and theatre types. The event always receives extensive coverage in the papers, and your mother's absence would be sure to be remarked upon – as would your presence here in her stead. And I'm sure neither of you need that sort of publicity. So . . . let us both pray that we've found her by then,' she added ominously.

A series of deep, oak-panelled wardrobes had been built along one wall of her mother's bedroom, the dark wood conspiring to darken an already dark room. They had all been fitted with tiny locks and Senga had a vivid memory of trying to open them as a child . . . and being caught in the process.

Senga pulled at the first wardrobe, half expecting to find it locked, but it swung open easily.

And then stepped back in astonishment.

The wardrobes were crammed with clothes – many, no, most of which Senga had never seen her mother wear. She opened another door: there must have been at least a hundred – more! – pairs of shoes. She went from door to door, simply opening them, and then moving on, her amazement growing. Finally, leaving the doors swinging open, she sat down on the edge of the bed and looked at the row upon row of gowns, evening dresses, suits, frocks, capes, coats and wraps. Most of it was beautiful, the very best of materials, the finest workmanship, the cut and styling undoubtedly foreign . . . and yet a portion of it was surprisingly out of place: here in one wardrobe were rows of shabby, worn clothes, patched and frayed, and beneath them, heavy brogues or scuffed and broken shoes.

33

But what Senga found even more surprising was that she had very rarely seen her mother wear fashionable clothes. Her earliest memories of the woman were of the black widows' weeds she wore, and she could only remember her mother wearing fine clothes when there was a party or social gathering of some sort. Nor did she ever remember her mother shopping for clothes – although she realised that a woman of her wealth would be in a position to have the clothes brought to her. But that still didn't answer the question – why? Why the vast amount of clothes?

She stood up and crossed to the wardrobes again – they were so deep she could actually step into them – wrinkling her nose at the vague memory of her mother's perfume, overlain with some other, slightly acrid odour, which she took to come from the clothes, although she couldn't immediately identify it. Her fingers hissed along the fine silks, skin-soft leathers and rich furs, were silent as they touched the wools and cottons. There was something amiss though . . . a sudden thought struck her and she suddenly paid more attention to the clothes, examining them now with even greater interest, finally nodding in quiet satisfaction, although her earlier astonishment had now turned to puzzlement. Most of these clothes were not in her mother's size; they were for a younger and certainly a slimmer woman.

'Perhaps they were for you!'

Startled, Senga turned to find Tilly leaning in the open doorway.

'I don't know why she did it either,' the older woman continued, stepping into the room. 'Initially, I thought she was just following the old brothel-keeper's custom of supplying the girls with their costumes and then charging them a fee, but your mother never lent any of these gowns to the girls. They were for her personal use.'

'But some of these would only fit a much smaller woman,' Senga pointed out.

'You're only thinking of your mother in later years as

34

you knew her. But when I first knew her, she was a slim, dark girl, not unlike yourself – not as pretty though. It was only in later years that she began to put on weight, only after she started drinking.'

Senga turned back to the long line of clothes, trying to estimate a value but finding it almost impossible: some of the gowns seemed to be unique creations, while others were sewn with what looked like genuine pearls, or had diamond-encrusted collars and sleeves. There was a fortune here.

'Why did she start drinking, Tilly?' she asked without looking around.

'I used to think it was because of your father's death. She blamed herself for that, you know. I remember her when she only drank wine, but her preferred drink was always tea.

'However, all that changed in the years after 1916. When she first came to England she was drinking heavily. You remember she stayed with me for nearly a month – and I don't think I can remember a single day when I didn't have to put her to bed. But I made excuses; she had lost everything in the Rising; it was her way of coping with the crisis. I kept promising myself that it was a phase that would pass. But it didn't – well, not for a long time anyway. She's nearly cured now though; there are times when she can go for months without drinking, although she still binges occasionally. Miss Tilke can give you all the details.'

'I'm not sure I want them,' Senga said bitterly.

'I think you do,' Tilly said quickly. Senga turned to face her, eyebrows raised in a silent question.

'You must remember that very few people have ever met Madam Lundy. We can use that to our advantage. Your mother has always been a very secretive person. It goes back to the early days when John Lewis was hunting for her once he knew that she was pregnant. She adopted a disguise then, and in Dublin she was known only by the name Madam Kitten, and when she conducted her business she was always swathed in black and veiled.

'When she set up her business in London, she continued with the ploy. Naturally, it would not do for someone to discover that the Society hostess, Katherine Lundy, was running a brothel. Less than half a dozen of her employees know her true identity; when she met people, she always met them dressed in black and veiled. If they were ever to discover that your mother had disappeared, then obviously the entire organisation would begin to fall apart. There is so much tied up in all this, Senga, more than you can ever realise. We must preserve the fiction; Madam Kitten must exist in the minds and certainly in the eyes of her suppliers.'

'I don't think I understand . . .'

'I'm afraid you'll have to trust me and I'll explain as much as I know later.'

'You want me to disguise myself as Madam Kitten?' Senga began, starting to shake her head. 'It will not work.'

'You never met Patrick's wife, did you?' Tilly asked suddenly, startling her. 'I remember Nuala when she worked for us back in Dublin before '16. When your mother and I left Dublin, the house in Tyrone Street was left in her care. To maintain the fiction, to remain credible with her customers and her suppliers, she became Madam Kitten, wearing the same black clothes, the same black veil. No-one ever guessed. If she could do it, so can you.'

Senga pulled out a long, severe, black dress, trimmed in a black braid. 'Where did Madam Kitten come from?'

'I told you; that came early on. When John Lewis was taking Dublin apart looking for your mother she adopted the Kitten disguise. But I think she would have been forced to adopt some sort of disguise anyway because she was dealing with older people, suppliers of food, drink or girls, and she herself was only nineteen or twenty at this time. They would not have respected a young girl, so she assumed the persona of an older woman and the black widow's weeds, complete with veil. She took to meeting people in darkened rooms, or rooms with only one source of light. She developed the character of a mysterious, sinister woman. Rumour and imagination did the rest, and soon Madam Kitten became a name to be feared in Dublin's underworld. If it was necessary, your mother was quite capable of consolidating her reputation with deeds as well as words, and these of course only added to the aura surrounding her. You remember Mickey . . .'

'Uncle Mickey, of course . . .'

'Your Uncle Mickey was a *bully*. That's what they called the thugs who guarded the brothels back in Dublin. And because Number Eighty-Two was the best house on the street, it had the best bully. Your Uncle Mickey once beat me so badly that I couldn't work for nearly a month . . .'

'Why . . .?' Senga whispered.

Tilly smiled, remembering. 'This was before your mother's time of course. The Whoremistress herself was in charge then. I wanted to escape the life, run away, open a little shop of my own. I've since discovered it's every whore's dream, that and marrying into money. I've yet to meet someone from the life who managed to do either . . . except myself, of course,' she added bitterly. 'Anyway, I started to save a little out of my earnings, just a little, I wasn't greedy; I thought I wasn't stupid. But the Whoremistress found out – I still don't know how – and set Mickey on me. He beat me coldly, calmly, marking me, bruising me, cutting me, but not scarring me, no bones were broken. I couldn't work in my condition, and while I was out of work bills were mounting up. At the end of the month, I owed Bella Cohen a fortune. It was her way of making sure it would never happen again.'

Senga shook her head. 'Not Uncle Mickey . . .?'

Tilly looked Senga in the eye. 'Mickey enforced your mother's will. He was a leg-breaker. He had these steel-capped shoes. I once saw him break a man's leg with one kick.'

'Uncle Mickey,' Senga whispered, appalled, remembering only the kindly old man who had bounced her on his knee, and who had died alongside her father Dermot Corcoran in the General Post Office.

'That reputation your mother built up in Dublin carried over to London. Oh, it was not so strong over here, but she worked at it. She found herself a bully to replace Mickey, and started from there.'

'Who?' Senga whispered, although events from her childhood had begun to fall into place now and she already had a very good idea.

'A cruel and evil man named Michael Lee. He disappeared though – no one ever knew what happened to him.'

'Patrick shot him dead,' Senga said slowly. She looked up at Tilly. 'Our mother sent him to Dublin to bring Patrick back to London. I don't know all the details, but I think Mr Lee broke all the rules and made no friends there. Patrick shot him in a struggle in the sitting room of Number Eighty-Two.'

'It was inevitable that he would come to a bloody end,' Tilly said quietly. 'I wish I had it in my heart to say, "God have mercy on his soul" – but I don't. He took too much pleasure in pain. For many bullies, hitting the girls to keep them in line is just part of the job, but Lee went out of his way to hurt. Anyway,' she shrugged and continued, 'your mother bought muscle and know-how and set about rebuilding her Dublin operation. But on a much larger, much more ambitious scale. She also set about catering to two entirely different strata of society. There are now houses which cater to the monied classes, and I believe she runs other, less savoury operations along with these.'

'What could be less savoury than running a brothel?' Senga asked sarcastically.

'Thieving, blackmail, selling drugs,' Tilly intoned. 'Oh yes, there are many stories associated with Madam Kitten's high-class brothels. She has other houses too. Stews we called them in Dublin; cheap – in every way – brothels, selling cheap drink and tobacco, sometimes with a little gambling, catering to the working man. Even I don't know how many houses she runs now, nor how far her tentacles extend into the underworld.

'So that's where Madam Kitten came from, and she still exists, but only a few people – a very few people – know that she and Katherine Lundy are one and the same. So you see,' she added with a thin-lipped smile, 'there is very little danger in you adopting your mother's guise.'

'I won't run any brothels,' Senga said firmly.

Tilly shook her head. 'Of course not. I will do that. In any case, most of the houses have their managers; your mother really only took a personal interest in the house directly across the park. But I'll take care of the day-to-day running of the operation. On the occasions when Madam Kitten will have to appear, you can adopt your mother's disguise and I will accompany you. However, your main function will be to carry on as Madam Lundy's daughter, especially as a Society hostess.'

'And what do we tell people when they ask where she's gone?' Senga asked.

'Your mother is ill and has gone to a clinic in Switzerland to recuperate.'

'Will people believe that?'

Tilly shrugged. 'It happens often enough; they'll believe you.'

'I'm frightened, Tilly,' Senga said suddenly, wrapping her arms around herself, shivering.

Tilly stood and gathered her into her arms. 'There's no need to be,' she said gently. 'You can do this. Believe in yourself. I know you don't have much regard for your mother, but she's made you strong. You will survive and you'll come out of this an even stronger person. You've seen one side of life,' she added with a wry smile, 'now you're about to see a very different side.'

'I'm not sure I want to,' Senga muttered.

'I don't think you've any choice!'

CHAPTER FOUR

'It's as if she has vanished from the face of the earth.' Patrick finished both his report and his toast at the same time and looked from Senga to Tilly Cusack.

'And you've explored every avenue?' Tilly persisted.

'Every avenue,' he said quietly. 'I've spent a lot of money and called in a lot of favours, and all I can say is that if our mother was in London at this moment I would know about it.'

'What do your friends in the movement say?' Senga asked. 'Were they able to give you any help?'

Patrick suddenly looked evasive. His eyes dropped to the remains of his breakfast and he shrugged. 'Not much.'

'I'm not asking you for their names, Patrick,' Senga added with a smile.

'I know,' he smiled. 'I suppose it's just that I have lived too many years with the secrets; keeping those same secrets now is simply second nature to me. I asked certain people – experts – how difficult it would be for someone to disappear completely and without trace.'

'And?' she persisted when he fell silent.

'There are two ways it could be done. Voluntarily and . . .'

'. . . involuntarily,' she finished. 'Tell me the difference,' she said, although she already had a very good idea. She pushed away the remains of her breakfast. Suddenly she didn't feel hungry any more.

'If someone wishes to vanish, then there are certain people in London – as there are in Dublin – who specialise in procuring the proper documents, in any name you wish. There are others who will convert items into cash without asking any awkward questions, and there are others who will change or alter your identity until even . . .' his voice trailed away.

'. . . until even your own mother wouldn't recognise you,' Senga finished with a humourless smile. She remembered Patrick telling her about Eddie, a tiny grey-haired man back in Dublin who had so altered his appearance when he had first fled to Dublin that he hadn't even recognised himself the first time he looked into a mirror. 'Is there any point in talking to some of these people?' she asked.

'Why?' Patrick wondered. He sipped his tea and then grimaced; it had gone cold.

'If we paid them, would they tell us if they had dealt with our mother?'

Patrick shook his head. 'Unlikely. Only the very best last in the business, and one of the reasons they have survived is because they cannot be bought. Not only do you buy a new face, new papers, a new identity, you also buy their secrecy.'

'So we cannot follow that road?' Senga persisted.

'There may be a way and I'm looking into it, but I'll have to go cautiously.'

'And the other alternative?' Tilly asked into the silence that followed. 'You said there were two ways of disappearing: voluntarily and otherwise.' She had listened to the conversation, contributing little, concentrating on her breakfast, thinking how the wheel had turned. She had once been Katherine's closest confidante, then they had drifted apart, and now she was slowly slipping back into her former role with Katherine's children.

Patrick looked at her and shrugged eloquently. 'It is the easiest thing in the world to have someone disposed of without trace. Father Thames holds many secrets,' he added.

'Almost as many as Anna Liffey,' Tilly added. She was

41

sure if either the Thames c. the Liffey were dredged it would reveal too much.

'So have we got anywhere?' Senga demanded forcefully.

'No,' Patrick shook his head.

'Yes,' Tilly contradicted him with a smile. 'At least we have started looking for your mother. We've begun our inquiries as the police would say.'

'I wonder should we go to the police?' Senga asked.

Both Tilly and Patrick turned to look at her in such shocked amazement that she returned to the remnants of her breakfast.

Patrick patted his lips with his napkin and then stood up. 'If you ladies will excuse me, I'm going out; I was given the name of some people who might be able to help.'

'What time will you be back?' Tilly Cusack asked and then immediately apologised. 'I'm sorry, I've no right to ask.'

Patrick smiled. 'My mother always demanded to know where I was going and what time I would return. I resented it then . . . but not now. Sometimes it's nice to know that someone is interested.' He glanced up at the squat, ugly clock on the mantelpiece. It was a few minutes before nine. 'I should be back in the late afternoon. If I'm going to be unduly delayed, then I'll get a message to you. And what will you both be doing today?' he asked, forcing a lighter tone into his voice.

Tilly Cusack smiled and reached across for Senga's hand. 'Today, your sister becomes Madam Kitten.'

Senga Lundy sat before the ornately-carved dressing-table, naked except for a flesh-coloured maillot, brushing her waist-length hair. Her lips moved slightly as she counted the strokes of the brush, and over the years this had become an almost hypnotic ritual. Reflected in the mirror she could see Tilly sorting through her mother's wardrobe, tossing dresses, skirts, hats, veils and gloves on to the bed. The older woman talked incessantly, feeding Senga information in the form of gossip and stories, attempting to relax her

42

and prepare her for the day ahead.

'Today, you will become Madam Kitten . . .'

'I still don't see why,' Senga muttered, but Tilly pressed on, ignoring her, if indeed she had heard her at all.

'I think you need to know what sort of operation your mother ran, I think you should see the houses, the girls, the men, and perhaps then you can begin to appreciate your mother's position. It will certainly help make a little more sense of what I'll tell you. There is also the possibility that we might excite a reaction from one of the people we visit today.'

'What sort of reaction?'

'If someone had hurt your mother, kidnapped her, made her run, well then if you appear as her they might betray themselves. It might force them into acting precipitously.'

'You mean they might come after me?' Senga asked, turning around in her chair, although her brush never missed a stroke.

Tilly's head popped out of the wardrobe. 'It is a possibility.'

'So you're using me as bait?'

Tilly smiled and ducked back into the wardrobe.

'And what happens if someone does come after me?' she demanded.

'You need have no worries. Patrick has borrowed some men from his organisation here in London. They're in position around the house and will remain there until this situation is resolved. Don't worry – no one can come close to you.'

Senga lifted the six-inch hatpin from the dressing-table. The morning sunlight sparkled from its glittering tip. 'And anyone who does come close gets a nasty surprise.'

Tilly stepped out of the wardrobe, a dress of heavy black wool thrown across her arm and a pair of black button boots caught between her fingers. She smiled at the wicked-looking pin. 'You needn't worry, we've thought of that eventuality too.'

Senga looked at her, pencil-sharp eyebrows raised in a silent question.

Tilly smiled hugely. 'We're going to give you a bodyguard.'

'You're not serious!'

Tilly began sorting through the bundle of clothes on the bed. 'I am. We'll be going into some fairly rough places and we need someone to take care of you in case things get out of control. Anyway, the real Madam Kitten went everywhere with her "assistants" – professional bodyguards, who also enforced her will. Now, we don't want to use those bodyguards just in case they were somehow involved in her disappearance, and also because they might recognise you as an imposter.'

Senga shivered suddenly. She turned back to the mirror and continued brushing her hair, her hands moving slowly, hesitantly. She watched Tilly in the glass. 'You know the more I learn about my mother, the more frightened I become. I know I was frightened of her as a child, but it's only now that I realise that she really was a terrifying figure.'

'In Dublin and to a lesser extent in London, she was. She was very successful at what she did because she behaved in a masculine manner. And I don't mean that she behaved like a man. I can think of very few men who would have had the nerve to act as she did. If she perceived a problem, she took care of it immediately – and permanently. There's a lot to be said for her ways. You always knew exactly where you stood with her. There's a marvellously crude American expression that became common during the war, but I think it sums up your mother's attitude and manners exactly – you didn't fuck around with her!' She lifted a black garter belt and a pair of black silk stockings and passed them across to Senga. 'And we're going to make sure that's the way it remains.'

When Senga and Tilly came down the stairs half an hour later, they found Martha Tilke serving tea in the formal sitting room to a tall, broad woman who seemed particularly out of place in the meticulously ordered room. She came to her feet as the two women stepped into the room, her almost colourless eyes suddenly wary before they finally settled on Tilly and she seemed to relax somewhat.

Tilly turned to Martha Tilke, who was standing to one side, looking at Senga with what looked like alarm in her wide eyes. 'Miss Tilke, perhaps you would be good enough to bring us two more cups.'

The woman took one last look at Senga and then nodded, moving quickly from the room. Senga looked at Tilly. 'You look like a younger version of your mother,' Tilly remarked.

Senga smoothed down the heavy black satin dress and wondered whether she was pleased or not.

Tilly reached out and took the newcomer's hand in hers, drawing her closer. 'Senga, I would like you to meet an old friend of mine, a good friend. Miss Willimena Fadden, Senga Lundy.' The two women reached out to shake hands and Senga suddenly realised just how big the other woman's were. Each of the fingers were easily as thick as two of hers, and the skin of her palms and the underside of her fingers were calloused. The woman was a head taller than Senga, her face was broad and a thick net of red hair curled tightly across her head. She was no great beauty and, although her broad cheekbones lent her face character, her almost colourless eyes gave her a slightly vacant expression. Even before she opened her mouth, Senga had guessed she was Scottish.

'Call me Billy,' she said, her hard-soft accent placing her close to Glasgow, and her smile altered her face completely, imparting it with character and life.

'Billy will be looking after you for the next few weeks,' Tilly said and then, catching Senga's surprised expression, continued, 'Billy is one of the best in the business.'

The young woman looked from Tilly Cusack to Billy. 'The best . . .?'

'Minder,' the Scotswoman said with a quirky smile.

45

'I'm usually called a personal assistant or a secretary, but I'm really a bodyguard.'

'Oh . . .'

'Now, you're thinking it's not a woman's job, and perhaps you're right, and perhaps I'm the only one in the whole country, but as Miss Tilly says, I am the best.'

'Oh . . .' Senga said again, and then added quickly, 'I'm sure you're right, it's just I was expecting . . .'

'A man? Aye, well people expect a man, they don't think a woman would do a job like this, but that gives me the advantage of surprise.'

There was a deferential tap on the door and Martha Tilke reappeared, two cups and saucers and a small pot of tea on a silver tray. She looked at Tilly Cusack. 'Will that be all, Ma'am?'

Senga turned quickly. 'That will be all, Martha.'

'Very good, Miss,' Martha said, her voice carefully neutral.

Tilly poured the tea, while Senga arranged the chairs around the occasional table. Senga sat facing Billy, while Tilly was positioned between the two. Senga looked at Billy with something approaching fascination, watching while the red-haired woman loaded four heaped spoonfuls of sugar into her tea. Billy glanced up at her without moving her head. 'I've a sweet tooth,' she said softly, her Scots accent less pronounced.

'I don't take it myself.'

'Probably a good thing.'

Senga drank most of a cup of tea in the silence that followed. 'Has Tilly explained anything to you?' she asked eventually.

The big woman shrugged. 'A little. But I don't need to know a lot. My job is to keep you safe, that's really all I need to know.' She smiled over the rim of her cup. 'I don't ask too many questions, and when you pay me you guarantee my silence.'

'Billy has an excellent reputation in her circle,' Tilly said with a smile. 'She has gone to jail rather than talk.'

46

Senga looked at the big woman and was surprised to find that she actually blushed. 'Have you spent long in jail?' she asked and then immediately apologised, 'I'm sorry, I had no right to ask.'

'I've spent a while,' Billy said shortly.

Tilly took the opportunity to interrupt. 'I know you don't care for the details, Billy, but I think in this case I would rather you were at least aware of the broad outline of events.'

'As you wish,' the woman said, sipping her tea with surprising daintiness.

With her cup and saucer in her hand, Tilly stood up and went to the window, looking down across the park. Without turning around, she said, 'Senga is the daughter of Madam Kitten . . . I'm sure you know the name.'

Billy Fadden glanced at Senga and nodded.

'Until recently, Senga did not know of her mother's life – indeed, relationships between mother and daughter were strained. But now Madam Kitten has disappeared – whether voluntarily or involuntarily, we are attempting to determine. By having Senga act out her mother's part, we are attempting to keep not only the police but also some of her competitors unaware of her disappearance. Both Senga's mother and Madam Kitten have a fairly full calendar of events in the next few weeks and it is important that she appears at them, or at least sends her daughter in her stead. And if, at the same time, we frighten or startle someone into revealing themselves, well then that will be a bonus. And that's why we need you, Billy.'

The Scotswoman nodded.

Tilly Cusack turned and stood with her back to the window. 'I'm going to take Senga around to some of her mother's operations, acquaint her with the details . . . show her off in other words. I'd like you to come along just in case there's trouble.'

Billy nodded.

'And Billy,' Tilly said, crossing the room to stand before

47

the red-haired woman. 'I would prefer us to keep a low profile. If there is any trouble, try not to kill anyone.'

'I'll try.'

Senga started to laugh – until she realised both women were serious.

'This is not a game,' Billy said softly, turning to her, her eyes catching and holding her. 'Now, if I'm to have any chance to do my job properly, I'm going to need your full co-operation. Because if you do something stupid, then both you and I could get hurt, or at the very least end up in police custody – and whereas you'll walk away from a prison sentence, what with your background and money, I'll go to jail, and I don't want that. I can't afford that.'

Senga nodded. 'Tell me what you want me to do.'

'You'll do as I tell you. If I tell you to run, you'll run. If I tell you to stay, you'll stand stock still, as if your life depended on it. As indeed it might. Now the rules are simple. You'll walk behind me and always on my right-hand side. That way, I'll know exactly where you are at all times. If there is trouble, you'll not interfere. And you'll never question my methods. I do what I have to do to keep you safe. Is that understood?'

Senga nodded.

'I'll add one final thing to what Billy has said,' Tilly Cusack said. 'If anything does happen and the police are brought into it, you will see nothing, you will remember nothing.'

'Of course. Why, are you expecting something to happen?'

Tilly smiled coldly. 'I wouldn't have asked Billy to come along if I wasn't expecting trouble!'

CHAPTER FIVE

The car arrived as the clock in the sitting room was chiming four. Seconds later the grandfather clock in the hallway began tolling the hour with its rather more stately chimes. Billy moved away from the window and smiled reassuringly at Senga. 'Nervous?' she asked.

Senga nodded. 'Should I be?'

'There'd be something wrong if you weren't. But don't worry; it won't be so bad. You don't have to say anything; all you have to do is look impressive.' She reached out and adjusted the veil down across Senga's face with a surprisingly delicate touch. 'Can you see?'

Senga nodded. 'I can see perfectly, but I feel . . . strange.'

Billy patted the extra padding that had been added to Senga's bust, stomach and hips beneath the ankle-length, high-necked, black funeral dress. 'So you should.'

The door opened and Tilly Cusack appeared, wearing her coat and tugging on her gloves. Martha Tilke followed her, carrying two coats across her arm. She stopped when she saw the veiled figure in black and her mouth opened in surprise. 'Madam!'

Senga peeled back the veil, astounded by the woman's reaction.

Tilly laughed. 'Well, you've passed your first test. The rest should be easy.'

Martha Tilke looked from Senga to Tilly and then back to Senga again, something like accusation in her eyes. 'I thought . . .'

'I know what you thought, Miss Tilke, and that is what you were meant to think. Mrs Katherine Lundy may be out of town, but Madam Kitten has returned.'

The woman nodded silently and then held out a slightly antiquated, surprisingly shabby, black coat for Senga to slide her arms into the sleeves. Billy reached for her own coat, a cheap-looking, greyish cloth that might once have been white, and shrugged into it. She looked from Senga to Tilly. 'All set?' Both women nodded. 'Then let's go.'

With Tilly walking alongside, her left arm looped through her right, and Billy walking in front and to her left, Senga felt a curious air of unreality settle over her. This was a dream – she was quite convinced of it – and she would awaken shortly. She had experienced this same feeling a couple of times in the past few days, but never as strongly as this. From the moment she had agreed to Tilly Cusack's outrageous suggestion in Dublin last week, events had been gradually slipping out of her control, and she seemed to be having increasingly less say in them. How, for example, had she allowed herself to be manoeuvred into the position of posing as her own mother? Because it had been put to her in a perfectly logical and reasonable manner . . . and now, here she was, pretending to be her own mother – whom she didn't even like – and with a huge Scottish woman as a bodyguard. The unreality of it made her laugh aloud.

'What's so funny?' Tilly asked quietly.

'Everything. You, me, Billy . . . everything.'

'This is not a game, Senga,' Tilly said seriously as they walked down the scrubbed stone steps towards the car. Billy was standing by the rear door, holding it open.

'What is it then, Tilly? Tell me what it is?'

'We're talking about your mother's life here. Her life and your future, yours and Patrick's.'

'I told you, we're not interested in her money.'

Tilly made a disgusted face. 'I'm afraid I cannot see either of you turning down an inheritance which comes close to a quarter of a million apiece.'

'Well then, you really don't know us,' Senga snapped. She bent and ducked into the car.

Tilly leaned forward, looking in. 'No, I don't think I do.' She straightened and spoke briefly to Billy before climbing in beside Senga. The Scotswoman moved around the front of the car and climbed in beside the driver, a short, stout white-haired man who had looked neither to right nor left while his passengers had climbed into the car.

Senga went to lift the veil, but Tilly's hand closed in an iron-hard grip around her fingers. She glanced in the direction of the glass partition separating her from the driver and Billy. It was closed but she still lowered her voice to little more than a whisper. 'Never remove the veil – not while we're out of the house. And remember, Senga, neither you nor Patrick want or need a police investigation into your lives at the moment. I really am doing this for your own good. You might not believe that, but it is true.'

Senga nodded and sighed. 'I know. I know, Aunt Tilly, and I am grateful – we both are. Thank you.' She looked away, concentrating on the parkland directly across from the house. 'Where are we going?'

Tilly's lips twisted in a wry smile. 'Not far.'

Senga leaned forward, looking out of the window as the car pulled smoothly away from the kerb and then made two complete circuits of the park before coming to a stop almost directly across from her home. Dumbfounded, Senga turned to Tilly, but the older woman simply shook her head. 'Speak only if you have to and only then in a hoarse whisper. Look, listen and learn.'

Billy came around and opened the door on Senga's side, allowing her to step directly on to the pavement. Through the enveloping veil, Senga looked in astonishment at the exclusive Mayfair house that was almost the image of her mother's. Surely this couldn't be a brothel?

Tilly slipped her arm through the young woman's and urged her forward, following Billy. 'This was your mother's first London house,' she said softly. 'I think she

51

wanted to establish herself in the wealthy market – hence the setting. There are twelve working girls here, and the house is managed by a woman called Elizabeth Miller. She orginally worked for your mother when the house was first opened. She was a popular, vivacious girl, one of the few working girls whom you could say had a great future ahead of her. However, that was before the accident. A minor nobleman's son, who had ideas far above his station, wanted Lizzie to marry him. She refused. There was a fight and she was slashed across the face with a broken bottle. She didn't want to work again, although she could have – there are some men who are attracted to scars and blemishes – but Lizzie knew the life, and so, when Michael Lee vanished some years ago, Lizzie became the Madam of the house. She's hot-tempered and arrogant and there were numerous arguments with your mother, and now, with Katherine out of the way, she is in complete and absolute charge of the house. She wouldn't be shedding too many tears if your mother were to disappear permanently.'

Tilly finished quickly as the door opened and Billy stepped inside, only to reappear almost immediately to stand beside the door, one hand resting on the jamb while she looked up and down the street. Senga noticed how her pleasant face had turned hard, almost masculine, the eyes stony and bitter.

It was dark and gloomy inside the house after the bright daylight, the servant who had opened the door standing so far back into the shadows as to be almost completely invisible. And it was silent. After the muted traffic noises of the street, the stillness seemed almost unnatural and was more than a little unnerving. There were the faint odours of tobacco smoke and stale alcohol and there was another, slightly bitter, faintly antiseptic smell lurking in the background.

Senga followed Tilly down the short hallway towards the sitting room. Tilly's hand was actually reaching for the handle when it turned and the door opened. A small, pleasant-faced woman stood framed in the opening. Pleasant-faced that was, until she turned her head slightly, allowing the light to fall across the left side of her face. It took all Senga's self-control to repress her horror at the damage that had been done to the woman's face. The flesh was seamed and goughed, deep scars running from above her eyebrow down to the edge of her lips, the corner of which was drawn back in a rictus. An embroidered eye-patch covered her left eye. The woman nodded to Tilly, but kept her eyes fixed on Senga.

'Madam. What a pleasure to see you again!' She reached out with both hands – and Billy's large blunt-fingered hands gently pushed her arms down. The big Scotswoman shook her head slightly, but said nothing.

'Madam?' Lizzie Miller asked, her face darkening, the scars standing out lividly.

'Your receipts for the last four weeks are down,' Tilly snapped. 'The Madam would like an explanation.'

Lizzie turned on the older woman, her ruined face twisted into a snarl. 'Business has not been good. And by what right . . .?'

'Do you know who I am?' Tilly hissed. 'Do you know what I am?'

Lizzie Miller's expression faltered. 'You're a friend . . .' she looked at Senga. 'What is she?' she demanded, her voice harsher than she had intended.

Senga Lundy suddenly strode forward, brushing past the two older women, striding into the large sitting room. 'Obey her,' she hissed, her voice low and harsh, rasping against the silk of her veil. She faltered momentarily when she suddenly discovered that she was faced by twelve very beautiful women, who were staring at her with a mixture of fear and trepidation on their faces. Regaining her composure she crossed to the empty fireplace and sat back into the large, leather, easy chair, the wings of which cast some shadows over her face. All the faces turned like flowers following the sunlight to stare at her again.

Senga looked at the woman closely, glad of the

53

enveloping veil. It allowed her the privacy to look at the women without them being aware that they were being scrutinised. What sort of women, she wondered, would sell themselves for money? Surely they would be different, there would be something in their faces that would betray them.

She was almost disappointed to discover that they seemed quite ordinary women. They were all pretty – some of them were even beautiful – well dressed, all of them wearing the minimum of make-up and no jewellery. If any one thing distinguished them, it was their eyes; looking at them, Senga thought that their eyes seemed almost weary. Perhaps it was that same world-weariness that was the badge of their profession.

Senga looked for Tilly and found she was still standing in the doorway with Lizzie. Billy had taken up a position just behind her own chair. The voices from the doorway were becoming heated, and from what she overheard Senga gathered that the takings for the house had fallen quite dramatically over the past month, although the decline had apparently started some weeks earlier. She did a quick calculation and realised that that would have been about the same time that her mother disappeared.

She tilted her head back looking upwards and Billy immediately lowered her head alongside hers. 'Ask the girls if there is anything wrong. Tell them if there is I will fix it immediately and that I'll ensure that no harm will come to them.'

Billy nodded briefly, and then lifted her head to look from woman to woman, before finally fixing on a slender blonde-haired woman with startling black eyebrows sitting across and a little to Senga's right. 'The Madam would like you to tell her what is wrong,' she stated flatly.

The blonde-haired woman's eyes widened and she looked quickly from Senga to Lizzie, before finally returning to Billy. And, although she spoke to the Scotswoman, her eyes were on the veiled Madam. 'There is nothing wrong,' she said in a breathy whisper.

54

Billy folded her arms across her bosom. 'The Madam knows that there is something wrong. Do you wish to lie to her?' Her voice, which had been couched in a rasping gravel that accentuated her Scottish burr, now turned stone cold.

The blonde-haired woman shook her head.

'Then tell the truth, woman,' Billy snapped.

'What's going on? How dare you question my girls . . .' As soon as she had spoken, Lizzie Miller realised she had gone too far. Tilly stepped into the room behind her and closed the door with her foot.

'*Your* girls Lizzie? Surely not *your* girls . . .?'

'I meant . . .'

'Perhaps that was why the takings have been down for the past few weeks, eh?' Perhaps you have been treating this place as your own house, treating these as your own girls . . . and the takings as yours also.'

As Tilly was speaking, Senga was watching the girls' faces closely. She could see the almost imperceptible nods and the loosening of tension-filled shoulders and neck muscles. It seemed as if Tilly had indeed hit on the truth, and if this woman, this Lizzie Miller, had been creaming off her take almost from the moment of her mother's disappearance, then surely that meant that she knew something about it, or was aware of it? She was about to speak, when Tilly looked first at Billy and then turned to the girl sitting closest to her. 'Find Miss Miller's coat, she's coming with us.'

'No . . .' Lizzie began.

'Shut up,' Billy snarled, and the implicit threat in the two words sent a shiver down Senga's spine.

Tilly then turned to look at the blonde-haired woman. 'Who has worked here longest?' she demanded.

Without saying a word, the woman turned to look at a tall, vaguely exotic-looking, raven-haired beauty standing behind her.

'You're in charge here for the moment. We will return later.'

The tall woman spoke, the vaguest hint of a Spanish or Italian accent barely audible in her voice. 'Will you be bringing Miss Miller back with you?'

Tilly smiled humourlessly. 'That depends.'

'On what?' Lizzie Miller demanded, the tremble in her voice clearly audible.

'That is not my decision.'

'Oh,' the woman whispered and turned to look at the veiled figure in the high-backed chair.

Senga Lundy walked home with Billy. She was beginning to enjoy the security of the veil, and she found it amusing when gentlemen tipped their hats to her, obviously thinking her recently bereaved. They had cut through the small park that separated the brothel from her home and the air was fresh and damp, the promise of spring very much evident, the faint chill in the air not unpleasant, although she guessed that the night would be cold. Almost in the centre of the park, along one of the winding gravelled walks that bisected it, Senga spotted a wooden seat and detoured across to it.

'Is this wise?' Billy asked carefully. She tilted her head slightly. 'We're not far from home.'

'I know . . . but these boots are killing me. I didn't know my mother had such small feet. Give me a few moments.' She sank down on to the wooden seat and then waited while Billy prowled around it a couple of times before finally coming to sit beside her. She noticed that the Scotswoman's eyes were constantly moving, and although she seemed perfectly relaxed the tension in the veins of her neck and the taut muscles of her jaw betrayed her.

'Don't you ever relax?' she asked gently.

'Not while I'm working,' Billy said seriously, glancing sidelong at her charge. 'I'm here to keep you safe, remember.'

'But we're not even sure if there's anything to keep me safe from.'

Billy shrugged. 'That woman, that Lizzie Miller – she

56

was trouble. Dangerous too. I know the type,' she added.

'Do you think she had anything to do with my mother's disappearance?' Senga asked.

The woman's lips pursed, and then drew into a thin, white line. 'Hard to say. She didn't act as if she was surprised to see you – or the woman she thought you were, but I'd certainly say that she was aware of your mother's absence at least. The very fact that she was withholding money would indicate that.'

'Where has Tilly taken her?'

Billy Fadden shrugged. 'None of my business, none of yours either.'

'What will happen to her?'

'You don't want to know that,' Billy said firmly. She stood up and reached out her hand for Senga. 'I think it's time we went. The cold is starting to get to me.'

Senga reached for the woman's hand and came gingerly to her feet, wincing as the high-ankled button-boots bit into her soft flesh, crushing her toes. She stumbled and Billy's hand shot out, catching her elbow, supporting her. 'These boots,' Senga muttered.

'Nearly there,' Billy said soothingly.

'I'll never make it,' Senga said grimly.

The two women strolled through the park gate that was almost directly facing their door. Traffic had increased a little and cabs and carriages competed for the slim stretch of cobbled roadway. With the onset of dusk, however, there were few pedestrians about and the footpath was almost deserted. The two women stood by the side of the road, waiting for a break in the traffic, Billy aware of her surroundings, Senga looking at the brightly-lit houses on either side of her own, wondering if they had any inkling of what went on behind their neighbour's solid oak door, with its brass lion's-head knocker. And if they did know, she wondered, would they care? But yes, they would care: this wasn't Dublin, where attitudes were much more relaxed; this was London, and having a Madam as a neighbour and a brothel across the street would certainly lower the tone of the neighbourhood. But . . . just supposing one of them had discovered her mother's true identity, would they have arranged her disappearance . . .?

Stop it!

She shook her head quickly. If she went on like this, she would start seeing enemies everywhere; she would become – what was that word – paranoid.

Billy's tight grip on her elbow brought her back to reality as the big woman urged her across the street, her smooth-soled boots slipping on the slick cobbles. 'Not so fast,' she muttered.

Once they gained the pavement on the opposite side, Senga stopped, leaning against the pillar, lifting one foot slightly, while Billy went up the steps to open the door. The boots were far too small and her feet were burning, her heels, ankles and toes feeling as if they had been scorched. She swore softly, using the profanity she had picked up in college.

'Madam?'

Senga straightened automatically, turning towards the voice . . . and then realised that the man was coming at her far too quickly, and the fixed expression on his face was terrifying.

'*Bitch*!'

His fingers hooked into claws as he reached for her and Senga had the momentary impression of something glittering in the palm of his hand.

Dimly, vaguely, almost unconsciously, she was aware of figures on the opposite side of the road moving towards her.

And then something brushed past her and she felt – rather than saw – the arm that shot past her face, striking the man before her on the forehead with a dull, flat crack. He stopped as if he had run into a wall. Senga looked at him and her mouth opened in a scream: there was blood streaming from a semi-circular gash in his forehead. He dropped to his knees and then continued falling forward without a sound.

Billy's hand tightened around Senga's shoulder, and she

dragged her back away from the man, almost pushing her up the steps in front of her. As soon as she had reached the door, Billy pushed her inside. 'Upstairs to your room. Lock the door.'

Ignoring the pain of her throbbing feet, Senga staggered for the stairs, only to stop as the hall door opened again and the two men she had seen on the opposite side of the road dragged the unconscious man into the hallway and dumped him there.

Billy was crouched over the man, her fingers at his coat. She pulled out a long slim blade from a concealed pocket and handed it to one of the men who, Senga noticed, was already holding a knife. She looked around for the second man, finally catching sight of him in the sitting room, peering out into the street. There was a gun in his hand.

Billy Fadden looked up and caught sight of the pale-faced girl standing on the bottom stair.

'For Christ's sake, get to your bedroom now. Lock the door. There may be more than just one!'

CHAPTER SIX

Billy Fadden walked into Senga's room without bothering to knock on the door.

And stopped.

Senga Lundy was standing directly opposite the door with her back to the wall, a large heavy-looking pistol clutched in both hands. She stared at Billy, wide-eyed and grim faced, and then released a breath and lowered the pistol, easing down the hammer at the same time.

'I didn't know you had that,' Billy said evenly, although her heart was pounding. She crossed the room and reached out her hand for the gun. 'May I? Where did you get it?'

'It was a present from my brother,' Senga said, handing it across.

Billy opened the cylinder and was surprised to find five copper-coloured rounds in the chambers. Snapping it shut, she handed it back to the young woman without a word. She would have to revise her opinion of this young Irish girl, she decided.

Senga crossed to the window, limping slightly. Standing well back from the glass, she touched the edge of the lace curtain with the fingertips of her right hand, the gun still clutched tightly in her left hand. 'There are people in the park,' she said, without turning around. 'I think they're watching the house.'

Billy stood on the opposite side of the window and peered out. 'They are. But they're all right; they're ours.'

'Ours?' Senga asked.

'Well, your brother's really.'

Senga moved back from the window. 'Would you mind telling me what happened today – and what's happening now,' she asked quietly.

'I think *I* can do that,' Tilly Cusack said, stepping into the room and closing the door behind her.

'I think I have a right to know,' Senga muttered.

Tilly Cusack sat down on the small chair before the dressing table, while Senga crossed the room to sit on the edge of the bed. Billy Fadden remained standing by the window, alternatively glancing out into the street and watching the two women.

Tilly spoke slowly, choosing her words with care, realising that a slip now would frighten the young woman, and possibly drive her away, and if she left them now then everything would be lost. 'We knew that you were in some danger today – I did warn you of that – and that was why we hired Billy. Today is the first day that Madam Kitten has appeared in public for the past four weeks, and yes, I'll admit, we hoped that your appearance might help flush the rats into the open.'

'You used me as bait,' Senga stated flatly.

'We used you as a catalyst. But you knew that when you came over here, you would be standing in for your mother, so remember, it wasn't you – it wasn't Senga Lundy – they were after, it was Katherine. However, we certainly didn't think they would move so quickly . . . obviously their plans were laid some time ago and they've been watching either this house or the brothel across the park. Probably the latter. The man who attacked you was nothing – a hired thug. Billy took care of him.'

'What did you hit him with?' Senga turned to ask the Scotswoman.

The big woman smiled thinly and then shook her right arm, moving her wrist slightly; then, with her fingers cupped, she held up her palm for Senga's inspection. There was a flat, roughly oval-shaped, metal pad nestling in the palm of her hand. There were two loops on either end and, even as Senga watched, Billy slipped the loops

61

over her thumb and little finger, so that the metal now covered most of her palm. Senga remembered the curious way Billy had struck the man – with the flat of her hand, her fingers curled slightly – and the immediate effects of the single blow.

'I've never seen anything like it,' she said.

Billy shrugged. 'Nor had I. It was given to me by an . . . an acquaintance I met in jail in Glasgow. She worked for a jeweller . . . until she made some for herself that is.' Billy brought both her hands together with a sharp clap. 'She made me a pair; I've one for the left hand too.'

'You could kill a man with those,' Senga remarked, looking at the fixed expression on the woman's face. There was a blankness there which frightened her.

'You could,' she agreed.

Realising she would get nothing further from the woman, Senga said to Tilly. 'And how is the man?'

'What man?' the older woman asked, sounding almost surprised.

'The man Billy stopped so dramatically.' She giggled suddenly, surprising herself, and was then annoyed that she sounded so hysterical. 'He looked as if he had run into a wall.'

'He had,' Billy grunted.

'The man is "helping" with our inquiries,' Tilly said carefully.

'But I thought you said he was only a hired thug; he'd know nothing.'

Tilly nodded. 'He wouldn't know anything of consequence. But he'd have been contacted by someone, and he would have their name. And that person would have another name . . .' She shrugged. 'It's a simple enough matter to trace back.'

'Provided he tells you the name.'

Tilly's expression was carefully neutral. 'Oh, he'll tell us the name all right. There's no question of that.'

'I don't suppose I want to know how you'll ask him,' Senga said.

'You're right. You don't.'

'Will they try again?'

Tilly shrugged and looked at Billy. 'What do you think?'

'I would almost guarantee it; but it really depends how badly they want Madam Lundy. I think today's attack tells us something though . . .'

'What?' Tilly frowned.

Billy turned to look at Tilly. 'Whoever "they" are, they don't have the Madam. If they did, they wouldn't have mounted an attack today, there wouldn't have been any need.' She shrugged her broad shoulders and smiled almost sheepishly at the expression on Tilly's and Senga's faces. 'Simple,' she said, turning back to the window.

Senga looked at the Scotswoman in a new light. Although she hadn't consciously thought about it, she had classified the big woman as nothing more than a thug – a female thug – and she had been reasonably dubious as to her effectiveness. But in the light of the day's events and the woman's incisive assessment of the situation, she had been forced to revise her opinion. She looked over at Tilly Cusack and realised that her aunt might very possibly have made the same mistake of underestimating the woman.

'So you think that it looks as if Senga's mother simply vanished of her own accord?'

'Aye.'

Tilly's bright-blue eyes flashed in excitement. 'And if she's out there, hiding someplace, laying low, I'll warrant that she's keeping an eye on the house either directly or indirectly, and, if she is, then I think it's only a matter of time before she becomes aware that we're here.'

'How do you know she's still in London?' Senga asked innocently. 'Why shouldn't she have fled to the Continent, for example?'

'Because the house is here; this is the heart of her operation; her banks and contacts are here, as well as the few friends she has whom she might – although it's unlikely – call upon for help if she needed to. No, you may rest assured, she won't stray too far from London.'

63

Billy sat down on the Ottoman at the end of the bed. Looking from Senga to Tilly, she asked, 'The Madam is English, isn't she?' Both women nodded. 'Does she have any family here?' she asked, looking at Senga.

The young woman shook her head, looking at Tilly. 'I don't really know. She rarely spoke of her childhood and family,' she said.

But Tilly was nodding slowly, attempting to contain her excitement. The fading light had washed some of the lines and age from her face, allowing Senga a glimpse of what she must have looked like when she was a young woman. 'Yes, yes, she came from a large family as far as I can remember,' she said quickly. 'They were from Yorkshire, I think. I'm not sure, but I can find out.'

'Would she have gone back?' Billy asked.

Tilly shrugged. 'It's unlikely. I still think she would need to stay here in London.'

'Would she have made contact with them?' the Scotswoman persisted.

'Possibly. I'll ask Patrick to use his connections to see if he can find out.'

'Would any of her family now be living here in London? Would she have anyone else she could stay with? What about friends?'

Tilly raised both hands to still the barrage of questions. 'I'll pursue that line of inquiry and see what happens.' She stood up quickly. 'At least we know a little more now than we did. If your line of reasoning is correct, then she is in London and free.'

'And in danger,' Billy added, looking at Senga.

'I know that,' she whispered, surprised to find tears in her eyes.

Senga spent the rest of the afternoon touring the house, wandering from room to room, surprised to find that her childhood memories remained sharp and clear, even after the passage of so many years.

She had left this house just after Christmas 1921 on the

64

first leg of a journey that was to take her through France and into Switzerland to a finishing school that her mother considered appropriate.

But the school had turned out to be little more than a prison. And the sole reason she had been sent there, Senga was convinced, was to ensure that Patrick would not be able to find her. Something like a smile touched her lips, as she remembered how she had finally run away from the school. Her memories of that period were, particularly vivid: it was the first time in her life that she had experienced true freedom, and her few weeks of freedom had been an exhilarating – and terrifying – experience.

And although her adventure had nearly ended in disaster, it had been an education she would not have forgone. It had taught her many things – including independence. And it had finally cut the ties her mother had wrapped around her. In the years that followed, when she lived with Patrick in Dublin, she had never really missed her mother, and the image that had seared itself on to her mind was that of a domineering, cruel and spiteful old woman. That image of her mother had changed radically over the past few days, helped along by the few insights she had been given into the woman's character. She wondered, if she had known *then* what she knew about her mother *now*, would things have been different between them?

Probably not, she decided ruefully.

Her tour of the house ended back in her mother's bedroom, and it seemed suddenly full of her presence. She stood in the centre of the rather gloomy bedroom and breathed deeply. There were traces of her mother's perfume still lingering on the air, the dry odour vaguely oppressive and unpleasant . . . an old woman's perfume. Senga suddenly found herself wondering what her mother looked like now. Had she changed – obviously she had, but how? The thought that she might not recognise her own mother if she stood in front of her was almost frightening.

She stepped into the bathroom which adjoined the bedroom. As a child it had always seemed enormous, and the passage of years had done nothing to make her revise that opinion. It had always had an eerie feel to it and, as a child, she could remember that the place had given her nightmares. It was all glass and mirrors and cold silver taps, and the bath, sink and toilet were a pale, icy-looking shade of blue. One wall – the wall above the bath – was covered by one large mirror, and the back of the door was also sheathed in mirrored glass. The ceiling had been painted a deep indigo, while a pale sapphire carpet covered the floor. Even on the hottest summer's day, the room felt cold.

Senga turned, catching her reflection in the glass over the bath – and stopped. The blues from the ceiling and carpet leeched the colours from everything, rendering the reds dark, almost black, robbing the bloom from her cheeks and lips, deadening her eyes. She looked like something from Mr Stoker's novel, like something long dead. The atmosphere in the room was oppressive, depressing. The combination of the cold colours, the hard metals and the mirrors robbed it of all warmth and character. She couldn't imagine herself spending any length of time here and wondered what her mother must have felt coming into this room every morning. Obviously it didn't affect her in the same way, or she would have changed it. She tried to imagine herself standing naked before the long cold glass . . . and abruptly stepped out of the room, images of dead flesh behind her eyes.

After the chill of the bathroom, the bedroom felt warm, almost comfortable. It was still dark and gloomy, and although the carpet, was a little faded and the wallpaper beginning to look a bit grey, her overall impression of the room was gentler, more welcoming. It was easier to imagine her mother in this room; soft, slightly shabby, worn – it seemed suited to her nature. And then she remembered the cold, hard bathroom, and realised that that too was part of her mother's personality. She remembered from her earlier childhood how loving and caring her mother had been – and then she recalled with equal clarity how terrifyingly cold-hearted she had been when Patrick had left with one of the servants, and how she had ordered one of her henchmen, the vicious Michael Lee, to follow them to Dublin and bring him home.

And she remembered how her mother had caused the death of Patrick's wife and very nearly had him killed too.

Were there two different personalities living in the one body? Both Freud and Jung had done work on the personality and she had read a paper in college in Dublin about multiple personalities. It would certainly account for her mother's curious, often irrational behaviour.

She sat down at the dressing-table and looked into the speckled glass, seeing not herself but the image of her mother's face as she remembered it superimposed over her own. She wanted to believe that her mother was ill, perhaps suffering from some mental illness, but she knew, deep in her heart and soul, that she wasn't. The woman was simply cruel and heartless. But was it any wonder, considering what she did for a living; could she have afforded to be otherwise to have survived so long and thrived in her evil profession?

Senga smiled humourlessly, realising that she was beginning to make excuses for Katherine Lundy. The woman wasn't ill, and while her 'career' might have moulded some of her characteristics, Senga realised that they must have been there in the first place. People did not become cruel overnight, and people had to learn not to care. Her mother had been trained to be a Madam by Bella Cohen – obviously she had had a good tutor . . . she stopped herself: there she was again, making excuses. Hadn't Tilly told her that Katherine had gone to the brothels in Europe and returned to Dublin with ideas? Obviously the seeds of the present day Madam Kitten had existed way back then: if Bella Cohen, the Whoremistress, was to blame, it was that she had sparked those seeds into growth.

But the potential had been there.

67

And Senga couldn't help wondering what it would have been like if things had been different. Where would she be now – what would she be doing – if her mother had been a simple middle-class housewife? Staring into the mirror, she realised that there was no way she could even conceive of a 'normal' life now . . . in fact, she wasn't even sure what was 'normal' any more. Normal girls did not have brothers who gave them loaded pistols to carry, normal girls did not have bodyguards, and normal girls did not have mothers who were Madams of brothels.

And where was her mother now?

Was she on the streets, wandering lost and dazed, not knowing her own name? Or had she been taken, kidnapped by someone or some organisation she had offended?

Or was she dead?

No. Not dead. Senga reached out and rubbed her hand down the mirror, leaving long dust-marked streaks in the glass. She rubbed her two hands together, brushing off the dust, reluctant to return to the bathroom to wash it off.

Her mother was alive, she had to believe that. Billy had said so, and surely she would know. She found herself wanting – desperately – to see her mother again. There were questions she wanted to ask, answers she needed.

A tap on her door snapped her from her reverie, and she turned to find a pale-faced Martha Tilke staring at her. 'Miss . . . it's the police! They want to speak to you!'

CHAPTER SEVEN

Billy appeared behind Miss Tilke and pushed the smaller women unceremoniously to one side. 'Police,' she snapped, her Scottish accent harsher, more pronounced.

Senga took a deep breath, forcing herself to be calm. 'What should I do,' she asked, 'speak to them or say I'm not in?'

'I'll say you're not here . . .' Martha Tilke said and began to move away – when Billy's iron-hard fingers closed around her upper arm. 'You'll stay here. An' you'll do what you're told.' She turned back to Senga. 'Speak to them. There's no point in lying to them and possibly arousing their suspicions. There's a chance they've had someone watching the house, so they'll know you're here. If you refuse, they can always come back with a warrant. See them now, allay their suspicions.'

Senga nodded quickly. 'You're right, of course. I suppose I had better appear as myself.'

Billy nodded. She glanced down at Martha Tilke. 'Go down and tell the police that Miss Lundy is just finishing her bath; she will be down shortly. Make them some tea.' And as the woman turned to go, she added ominously, 'And try not to tell them anything, Miss Tilke.'

The woman's lips closed into a thin, white line as she bit off a reply and then hurried back down the corridor towards the stairs.

'I wish Tilly was here,' Billy said quickly, 'she'd know how much to tell the police.'

'We will stick to the truth as much as possible,' Senga

said, reaching a decision. She undid the buttons down along the side of her dress, allowing it to slide to the floor before stepping out of it. 'I had better appear in something simple . . .'

'Something youthful, fashionable, revealing if you have it. Make yourself as young-looking as possible – let's have them looking at you, rather than asking you questions.' The Scotswoman was watching Senga intently as she rummaged through the wardrobe, looking for something to wear. 'If they ask you anything, answer as simply as possibly – let them think you're dumb, there's no shame in that. It takes brains to be able to pass yourself off as really stupid. The only problem is,' she added softly, 'is that you don't look stupid.'

Senga glanced back over her shoulder, her eyes wide and surprised. 'I think that was a compliment.'

Billy tilted her head slightly, considering. 'So do I.'

The two men waiting for her in the drawing room were obviously surprised by her youth, but the older of the two managed better to conceal his shock. They both came to their feet as Martha Tilke opened the door and Senga entered the room, crossing to stand before the fire without a word. She was wearing a knee-length saffron-coloured dress that was almost – but not quite – out of fashion, and the pearls around her neck were real. Billy had wanted to do something with her hair, but Senga had insisted that she leave it alone, and it now flowed down her back, like a long shawl, curling at the base of her spine. She had wrapped a yellow ribbon around her head, and the whole effect emphasised her youthfulness, making her look little more than a teenager.

'Good afternoon, Gentlemen.' She spoke slowly and distinctly, adopting the vaguest of lisps. She looked at the two men, before finally settling on the older. 'I do apologise for keeping you.'

'Miss,' he nodded. 'It's good of you to see us at such short notice, without an appointment. But I was

70

expecting . . .' he smiled and was about to rephrase his question, when Senga said innocently, 'Expecting someone older?' He nodded. 'But that would be my mother, Mrs Katherine Lundy. I am Senga.'

'You must forgive my rudeness, Miss Lundy; I am Inspector Colin Holdstock and this is Constable Thinn.' The younger man nodded politely, smiling vaguely, his grey eyes wide and curious.

'The constable looks like a constable,' Senga said innocently, gazing steadily at the broadly-built young man, bringing a blush to his cheeks. Although he was out of uniform, his stance alone betrayed his profession.

The inspector looked at his constable and smiled slightly. 'Ah well, perhaps he does at that . . .'

'But you do not look like an inspector,' Senga continued, deliberately interrupting him, re-enforcing the image of a naive, slightly immature, young woman.

'And what do I look like, Miss?' the inspector asked.

Senga looked at him just long enough to embarrass him. He stood slightly short of six feet, and although he was broad across the chest and shoulders his waist was thin, and Senga wondered if he had been a sports enthusiast in his youth. And that begged the question of his age. She looked at him quickly . . . and decided that he was in his late forties, if that. His face was long, as was his nose, although it was not out of proportion in his long face, and she imagined that it had been broken at one stage. His eyes were perhaps set a little too far apart, and were an indeterminate woody colour, and both the corners of his eyes and his rather full lips were crinkled with laughter lines.

'You look like a favourite uncle,' she said eventually.

Inspector Colin Holdstock laughed delightedly. 'I've been called worse, Miss, I can assure you; I've even been mistaken for a bank manager.'

'Heaven forbid,' she smiled. 'Has Miss Tilke brought you in tea? She has . . . well, you will have some more, I think?' And before either man could speak, she had

71

tugged on the bellrope that hung down by the fire. The door opened almost immediately and Martha Tilke appeared. 'Martha, some more tea for our guests, and I will take a cup with them.'

'*Ja*, Very good, Miss,' she said, in a strong German accent.

Senga took the seat furthest away from the inspector and closest to the fire. It was her mother's accustomed seat and Senga imagined she could feel her mother's presence enfold her as she sank into the soft, worn leather. Leaning back, she caught the faintest wisp of her mother's perfume. 'Now, Gentlemen,' she said, speaking to both men but actually concentrating on the inspector, 'what can I do for you?'

But it was the constable who spoke, and Senga realised with a start that it was an Irish accent she was hearing. 'Miss, we're investigating a report of a disturbance here earlier today. Would you be able to assist us in any way?'

'Yes,' Senga said, surprising them both.

The constable immediately produced a notebook and a tiny stub of a pencil. 'For our records, Miss, could I have your full name?'

'Senga Corcoran-Lundy,' she said, suddenly wondering when last she had used that version of her name.

'And your address, Miss Corcoran-Lundy?' he stumbled.

'It's one or the other,' she said gently, and then continued at his puzzled expression. 'It's either Corcoran or Lundy; I rarely use both.'

'Ah,' he nodded, and then said, 'And the address . . .?'

'Why – here!' she laughed.

'Yes, yes, of course.' His cheeks flushed bright red and he bent his head over the page. 'Now, would you care to tell us in your own words what happened earlier today?'

Senga was opening her mouth to speak when Martha Tilke appeared with a large, silver tray. Constable Thinn immediately stood and took it from her, obviously surprising her. When Martha had left the room, Senga

72

busied herself for a few moments pouring three cups of strong, black tea. Colin Holdstock took his black with no sugar; the constable took milk and two sugars. Senga drank half of her own cup quickly, grimacing at the strong, sharp taste, and then continued, 'I was returning from a walk through the park opposite when I was accosted by a ruffian. I think he was drunk,' she confided, lowering her voice. 'He was certainly unsteady on his feet. He was loud and abusive, and my companion simply pushed him away and he stumbled on the bottom step.' She shrugged. 'That's really all there is to it.'

'We have a report that he was taken inside here,' Holdstock said suddenly.

'That is correct,' Senga said without pausing. 'When he stumbled on the step, he struck his head and there was some blood. We took him in, washed his wound – which was little more than a graze – gave him a cup of tea and sent him on his way.'

'And that was all?' Holdstock said.

'Well, I think he may have been given a few shillings. But it was an accident,' she added quickly, continuing to play the innocent.

'Was this incident reported to the police?' Thinn asked.

Senga hesitated. 'Well no, we didn't think . . . I hope we haven't done anything wrong?'

'No, no, nothing at all,' Holdstock said casually, and yet his gaze was fixed on Senga and she knew instinctively that he didn't believe her story. Which meant that they had to have someone watching the house. 'We got a report that there were three men involved.'

'Some men – passers-by – came to our assistance.'

'I would like to speak to your companion,' Colin Holdstock said, fully expecting the answer he received.

'Well, I'm afraid that she is out at the moment, but I will have her call upon you, if you wish.'

He shook his head. 'You're very kind, but it probably will not be necessary. If we're passing, we might call in. But you know how we have to check up on these reports.'

'Of course,' she said, realising that they would be back, again and again, until they finally spoke to Billy. Senga wondered just what her mother had done to warrant such attention. What had she got herself involved in?

'Is your mother away?' Holdstock asked casually.

Senga nodded. 'On holiday.'

'Somewhere nice?'

'Ireland,' Senga said and immediately regretted it. Anyone who knew her mother well would know that she detested the country. Belatedly she remembered that Tilly had told her to say that her mother was in Switzerland recovering from an illness.

Thinn's face brightened up. 'I'm from Ireland,' he said, his Irish accent seeming almost to deepen as he said it.

Senga smiled slightly. 'I thought I recognised the accent. I'm just home from Ireland myself,' she added, and then immediately regretted it. There was no point in volunteering information to these people.

'What part?' Thinn asked, his broad face cracked in a smile.

'Dublin.'

He nodded. 'I was in Dublin a couple of times. Always reminded me of London. Did it not remind you of London?'

Senga thought about the cold and impersonal sprawling metropolis of London, comparing it with the almost village-like atmosphere of Dublin, and shook her head slightly. 'No, I'm afraid it didn't.'

'Aaah.' He nodded. 'I'll wager you weren't born in London then,' he asked innocently and Senga's estimation of the man went up. She had initially decided he was a simple police officer, the inspector's note-keeper, but she realised now that he was obviously something more. She supposed she should have guessed that the very fact he was assigned to Holdstock meant that he wasn't just some country bobby.

'I was born in Dublin,' she said, unable to avoid answering the question, annoyed that he had extracted the information so easily.

'You don't have the accent for it,' he said innocently.

'I lived in London for a long time, and I finished school in Switzerland.'

'Aaah well, that would account for it. I don't think I'll ever lose my Limerick accent. Have you ever been to Limerick, Miss?'

'Never,' she admitted.

'Lovely place. Close to County Clare and the Cliffs of Moher. Have you ever seen the Cliffs of Moher?' He continued when she shook her head. 'Magnificent. You must make a point of visiting them when you're next in Ireland. Do you go back often?'

'Yes . . . I . . . I live there. I'm in college in Dublin. I'm not long back in London. It's here I come to holiday.' If the police had been watching the house, they would have realised that Senga was not one of the usual occupants.

'When will your mother be back?' Colin Holdstock asked suddenly, his voice soft and gentle.

Senga looked at him and smiled. 'I must admit I'm not sure. She hasn't been well recently,' she confided, 'she thought the break would do her good. She did say a couple of weeks, but her social diary is not full at the moment, and I'm sure if the weather is clement she might even extend it for an extra week or so.'

'I thought your mother was organising some grand ball later this month,' he said, still smiling easily.

'All the arrangements have been made,' Senga said, staring him straight in the face. 'I will be hosting the Grand Spring Fête myself.'

He bowed slightly. 'I'm sure it will be a marvellous success.'

'I hope so,' Senga said, with more feeling than she had intended.

'I'm sure I will read about it in the papers,' Colin Holdstock said easily.

'Why not come, Inspector?' she said suddenly.

He looked at her quickly, and something behind his eyes betrayed him; Senga realised then that she had walked into a trap of sorts.

'Bring your wife,' she added.

'I have no wife,' he said quietly, although Senga noticed that there was a wedding band on his finger. Widower, she guessed.

'Will I have the invitations passed to your home or office . . .?' she asked.

He reached into his vest pocket and pulled out a slim, ivory-coloured card. 'Perhaps to my home; at least I shall be sure of receiving them. You really are most kind, Miss.'

'Please, think nothing of it. I would be honoured to have you . . . and a companion too, if you care to bring one.'

Holdstock stood up suddenly, catching Thinn by surprise, who scrambled to his feet. 'Well now, I think we have taken up far too much of your time. I would imagine you would rather be out and about. I'm sure a pretty young lady like yourself must have plenty of gentlemen callers, eh?'

'Not in London,' Senga said diplomatically.

'Only a matter of time though, I suppose.' He was moving towards the door as he spoke, the constable following behind. 'If we get a chance, we might call back to talk to your companion, but if I do not see you before the Fête, goodbye Miss Lundy and thank you again. Thank you for the tea.'

'You're welcome, Inspector Holdstock.'

He turned suddenly, catching her hand so suddenly that she attempted to snatch it back, and pressed it to his lips, his soft, brown eyes on her face. 'Until then,' he said.

Moments later, Senga heard the front door close and Billy stepped into the room. 'You were good,' she said quickly.

'But they were better,' Senga admitted.

Billy nodded. She crossed to the window and peered out through the lace curtains.

'Aye, too good for what should be a routine investigation into an incident. They've obviously had the house under observation.' She turned to look at Senga, her eyes like chilled water. 'Be careful of that inspector, he is dangerous, and that constable was no fool either.'

'I know that,' Senga murmured.

'I think Tilly owes us some sort of explanation,' Billy Fadden said quietly. 'There's a lot going on that we don't know about. I think she's got us involved in something far more serious than she says.'

'How serious?' Senga asked.

'Deadly!'

CHAPTER EIGHT

Senga's eyes snapped open, wide with alarm, limbs flailing: there was a hand pressed over her mouth, a face inches from hers.

'She's back,' Billy's breathy, warm whisper was harsh, her accent pronounced.

Senga struggled into a sitting position. She ran her fingers through her hair, brushing it back off her eyes, blinking hard. 'What time is it?'

'A little after three.'

'Where is she now?' she asked, throwing back the covers and swinging her legs out of bed.

'Still downstairs,' Billy said. She handed Senga a black, silk dressing-gown that matched the black, silk pyjamas she was wearing. In another age both had once belonged to her mother.

'Let's go and see her then,' Senga yawned, sliding her feet into soft, Persian-style slippers.

When Billy opened the bedroom door and stepped out on to the landing, Senga realised that the other woman was barefooted, wearing a man's short jacket over a cream-coloured shift. One of the coat pockets bulged suspiciously. She deliberately tapped it as she drew level with her bodyguard. It felt like a short stick. 'Don't you ever rest?' she murmured.

Billy dipped her hand into her pocket and took out a short leather sap. There was a wrist thong at one end and the head of the sap bulged slightly. 'Lead-filled,' she remarked simply. 'And no, I never rest.'

They descended the stairs in silence, the ticking of the clock in the hall below sounding very loud indeed. The hallway was in darkness, but a bar of light was visible beneath the sitting-room door. When they reached the bottom step, Billy stopped Senga by placing an arm across her chest, and then she pointed first to her own bare feet and then to Senga's. The young woman nodded in understanding and stooped to pull the slippers off her feet. Barefooted and silent, both women crossed the hall and stopped before the door, listening. There was no sound from within.

Senga looked at Billy, her face a pale blur into the night, and her eyebrows rose in a silent question. The Scotswoman caught the movement and her shoulders rose and fell in a shrug. Abruptly she reached forward and pushed the door open.

Tilly Cusack was sitting in Katherine's deep, leather chair, a heavy glass in her hand, the decanter of Scotch on the occasional table beside the chair. She looked up as the two women burst into the room – and the expression of absolute weariness on her face stopped them both in their tracks, questions and accusations dying on their lips.

Eventually Senga whispered. 'What's wrong?'

Tilly drank deeply and then reached out and poured herself another. 'Find yourselves a glass and sit. I think you're going to need it.'

'Tilly?' Senga demanded. Billy's fingers closed around her arm, just above the elbow, and she shook her head slightly. Pulling her short coat closed she padded off to find glasses. Senga sank into the chair facing Tilly and looked at the older woman. She looked haggard, her face was the colour of old ashes, and her eyes, usually so bright, seemed dead in her head. Her clothing was rumpled and there was mud on her boots. She reached for her drink and Senga caught the faintest hint of the odour of salt and smoke.

'You've been to Dublin!'

Billy turned to look at her in surprise, but Tilly merely

79

smiled. 'Oh, you're sharp. You're your mother's daughter all right. How did you guess?'

'You look so tired . . . there's mud on your boots, your clothes are the same ones you were wearing when you left, and there's a definite odour of sea-brine about you.'

'Very good,' Tilly whispered. 'Yes, I've been to Dublin.' She lifted her glass as Billy lifted the decanter, and watched while she poured a generous amount of the deep, amber liquid into it.

'There's no ice,' the Scotswoman muttered. She reached over and handed Senga a small Scotch and soda and then sat down on a high-backed chair almost directly across from Tilly, where she could watch both women but where it was difficult for Tilly to see her. Billy Fadden had taken her first bodyguard job when she was twenty; she had always been a big, strong girl, and even then she could take down most men. She had been fifteen years in the business, and one of the reasons she had survived so long – and stayed reasonably intact – was because she believed that everything that affected her client affected her.

'I think some sort of explanation is called for,' Senga said quietly, but with very real authority in her voice. 'I want to know what happened the day before yesterday, shortly after you left with Lizzie Miller . . .' She paused and added, 'What happened to that lady, by the way?'

Tilly smiled coldly. 'I thought you didn't want to know . . .'

'I didn't then; I do now,' Senga snapped. 'You used me as bait on that occasion, well I think I have a right to know what sort of fish we hooked.'

'We hooked a greedy woman, that's all,' Tilly sighed. 'Your mother had been watching her for some months now. Lizzie was a greedy woman. She had problems coping with the idea that she was making money for your mother while she herself was on a fixed salary, admittedly with a generous bonus thrown in. She wanted a bigger slice.' She smiled thinly. 'Most working girls get that idea into their heads at some time during their working lives. A beating or two usually takes it out of them,' she added grimly.

'Personal experience speaking there?' Billy said suddenly.

Something flickered behind Tilly's eyes. 'Oh, I've tried it twice in my life. I got away with it once. The second time my Madam damn near had me beaten to a pulp.'

'And where is Lizzie now?' Senga persisted.

'Lizzie has retired.'

Senga stared at the older woman and then said slowly and clearly, 'Have you killed her?'

'Would it matter if I had?'

'It would matter to me,' Senga said, her voice a chilling whisper.

Billy found herself looking at the young woman with even greater respect.

Tilly sighed. 'No,' she said finally, 'she's not dead.'

Something in her voice betrayed her.

'But . . .?' Senga persisted.

'She was beaten,' Tilly said quickly, 'she'll spend some time in hospital, and when she's up and about again, she'll be told to leave London.'

In the long silence that followed, Senga asked, 'Why?'

Tilly shrugged and a ghost of a smile flickered across her lips. 'What do you want me to tell you. That it's traditional? Or that it's a necessity?'

'I want you to tell me the truth.'

'Well now, that's a slightly different matter altogether. It was done because it was how your mother would have done it. The Madam – your mother – is a hard, cruel woman, Senga. If you're to take her part in public, you'll have to learn to act like her.'

'I have no intention of taking her part.'

Tilly looked up, and her eyes were shadowed. 'You already have, my dear.'

Senga glanced at Billy. 'Don't you think it's time you told us the truth?'

Tilly twisted in her seat to look at the Scotswoman. Billy

81

Fadden's expression was closed, but she nodded once. 'I agree with Senga. We need the truth here.'

'I have told you what you need to know,' Tilly said, still looking at Billy, but they knew the statement was directed to both of them.

'Enough!' Senga hissed. 'Enough of this "need to know" nonsense. I want to know what you know. I want the truth, or I'm on the next boat back to Dublin in the morning.'

'I told you before,' Billy said quietly, 'what affects my charge affects me. Now, you can either tell me the truth, or I'll be gone in the morning also.'

'The police were here,' Senga said quietly, watching the older woman carefully. 'They said they had called because they had received a report of the incident which took place on the steps of this house, but there was more to it than that, much more. It's my opinion that this house is being watched.'

Surprisingly, Tilly Cusack nodded. 'Yes, I think you're right.' She finished her drink in one, long swallow and then shook her head when Billy indicated the decanter. 'I suppose this story begins nearly twenty-two years ago, in 1907 . . .'

'The Crown Jewels,' Senga breathed, and then continued, seeing Tilly nod and Billy Fadden shake her head in puzzlement. 'In 1907, the Irish Crown Jewels were stolen by person or persons unknown. They have never been recovered. Tilly told me that my mother wanted those jewels, but . . .' she looked back at Tilly, 'I thought she had no involvement in the theft.'

'She didn't. But she knows who stole them.'

'How?' Billy asked.

'There was a police investigation into the theft – which was an obvious inside job. And there was the almost inevitable cover-up.'

'Why should it have been covered up?' Billy asked, puzzled. She had never heard of the theft of the Irish Crown Jewels.

'Too many important names were mentioned,' Tilly smiled, 'too many inflated reputations might have been damaged. There were allegations of a homosexual scandal, orgies, wild parties, gambling debts. Anyway, a Chief Inspector John Kane was sent over from Scotland Yard to investigate . . . which he did with admirable thoroughness. And after four or five days, he produced a report which named the culprit. The report was read by four people in Ireland: Lord Aberdeen, the Viceroy; Sir John Ross of Bladensburg, the Chief Commissioner of the Dublin Metropolitan Police; Mr W.V. Harrel, the Assistant Commissioner . . . and Madam Kitten. It then vanished completely.'

'How did my mother get a copy of the report?'

Tilly smiled. 'Your mother's connections were second to none. You must remember that she ran one of the most successful brothels in the British Isles – a notorious brothel, which was frequented by heads of state and by royalty on at least three occasions that I know of. The fame of Number Eighty-Two was not a light that was kept under a bushel.'

Senga frowned and shook her head slightly. 'I'm not sure I understand . . .'

'I think Tilly is trying to tell us that your mother either paid someone or blackmailed them for a copy of the report for herself,' Billy supplied.

'Exactly. And at a very high level at that.'

'Fine. But I'm not sure what all this has got to do with . . .'

Tilly raised both hands, palm upwards. 'Bear with me. In 1919, your mother was given the opportunity of purchasing the jewels, but nothing ever came of it. Earlier this year, she was once again offered the jewels . . . and this time I think she went hunting them.'

'You're still not answering my question,' Senga snapped.

'Your mother wants those stones; they have come to mean something to her . . . I'm not sure what. It's something to do with the idea of a simple country girl owning the Crown Jewels, even if they are only the Irish Crown Jewels. She has become obsessed with them, and she will have them at all costs . . . and no matter what the cost, either in cash or reputation or suffering. There is even the possibility – although it is only a possibility – that she may be blackmailing the thief!' She looked from Senga to Billy and then back to Senga. 'And you must remember that this affair has connections going all the way back to the throne!'

'Sweet Jesus,' Billy breathed.

'She wouldn't . . .?' Senga asked hopefully.

Tilly nodded her head. 'Your mother is no longer a simple whoremistress or a fence, she's moved on to greater things. Now, she's threatening minor royalty, threatening to rake up an old scandal that our present king would prefer to forget: remember, the jewels were stolen practically on the eve of his visit to Ireland. He was to have worn them throughout his stay; the various dignatories there were to have worn their jewels which were also part of the haul.'

'It would explain the police interest,' Senga said quietly.

'It would explain a lot of things,' Billy added. 'Someone who threatens the throne – no matter how vaguely or obliquely – either has to be very brave or very confident of their sources and back-ups.' She looked at Senga. 'And if you are masquerading as your mother, then all you've done is inherit her problems. And the risks.'

'There is real danger here, isn't there?' Senga asked, her eyes locked on Tilly's. 'My mother has fled in fear of her life, hasn't she?'

'I've already told you that much.'

'Who is she running from? The authorities or her underworld partners in crime?'

'Both.'

In the long silence that followed Senga's gaze remained locked on Tilly's face, memorising every detail of it – here was the face of . . . of what? Greed, stupidity, or that of a very cunning woman.

'Whose idea was this whole charade?' Billy asked suddenly.

'Yes,' Senga breathed, as something cold settled into the pit of her stomach. 'Whose idea was it? Who sent you to Dublin for Patrick and I?'

Tilly smiled bitterly. 'Don't presume too much on your mother's cunning. This wasn't her idea; only I can claim the credit.' She twisted to look at Billy. 'And if you're asking me whether I knew what I was doing, then the answer was yes.' She turned back to look at Senga. 'I knew I was bringing you into danger – but in truth, I wasn't aware just how much trouble your mother was in.'

'Time to get out,' Billy said to Senga.

'I've a horrible feeling it's too late for that,' Senga muttered. She looked back to Tilly, 'You might as well continue.'

'Your mother approached me a few weeks ago – not Martha Tilke as I told you. She was obviously under a great deal of strain – initially I thought she had been drinking again. She told me that there had been several attempts on her life. Now, while she wasn't specific, I did discover that there had been two separate occasions which, while they could have been accidental, could equally have been murder attempts. Katherine told me she was going away for a while to try and sort things out. She thought if she were able to buy the jewels, she might use them as a bargaining tool to purchase some immunity. She asked me to run her London operation. I refused. And then she suggested that I could masquerade as Madam Kitten. I said I'd think about it, but your mother never gave me the chance. She simply disappeared. The idea to bring you to London was mine. I thought you could legitimately be in the house as Katherine's daughter, while also adopting the disguise of Madam Kitten.'

'I suppose it never occurred to you that I had my own life to lead, and that life certainly never included operating in some shadowy criminal world.'

'Your brother Patrick operates in that same world, and

has done so for the past ten years. It's in your blood, Senga Lundy, in the same way that whoring is in mine, or violence is in Billy's!'

Senga stood up suddenly. 'Make other plans, I'm leaving in the morning.' She turned and had her hand on the handle of the door when Tilly's voice stopped her in her tracks.

'Don't be a fool. Don't you realise you cannot leave now? You told me yourself the police had been here. Who was it – Holdstock, I'll wager?' She continued quickly, seeing Senga's eyes widen slightly. 'Holdstock leads a special crime squad which is attached to the court. It deals with cases which threaten, either directly or indirectly, the Crown.'

Senga turned back to the room, looking at Tilly in mounting horror.

'Holdstock is a cunning and dangerous man, ruthless too in his own way. Your mother said he reminded her of John Lewis, Patrick's father. He doesn't deal with ordinary cases, but he always gets results. If you attempt to leave now, they'll want to know why, and you had better have a very good answer for them. I'll guarantee you'll never even make it to the boat. They'll arrest you on some trumped-up charge . . .'

'I don't believe it. This is England!'

'Grow up, Senga. In an ideal world there wouldn't be people like your mother, there wouldn't be people like Billy, there wouldn't be people like me . . . or Holdstock for that matter. This time your mother has overstepped herself. She's struck at the very fabric of this society . . . and it will crush her.'

'And what about me?' Senga asked, and her voice sounded very small.

'If you make a mistake, it will crush you too.'

Senga began to shake . . .

CHAPTER NINE

'Anything?'

The man standing before the window of the house directly across from Katherine Lundy's Mayfair residence lowered the binoculars and squeezed his eyes shut, pinching the bridge of his nose between forefinger and thumb. He tapped the single sheet of paper with the back of his hand. 'Someone arrived at 3:05 a.m. in a cab. A woman.' He smiled at his companion's start of interest. 'No, not who you think, although I think I know who it was. I can't swear to it – and until we get the cabby's report I'm certainly not going to include any name in my report.'

'But . . .?'

'It looked like the woman, Tilly Cusack.'

'And?'

'A light went on in the bedroom – Katherine Lundy's bedroom – almost immediately afterwards; it went off again seconds later. It's just gone on again now . . .' He checked his watch and made a note on the sheet of paper. It's 4.32 a.m. precisely.'

Billy led Senga back up to her bedroom. The young woman was still shivering as the realisation of just how much trouble she was in struck home with devastating effect.

Once again her mother had managed to exert control over her actions like some foul witch from a folktale weaving the threads of destiny. When she had made her decision between her brother and her mother in Paris back in 1921, she had sworn she would have nothing further to do with her. That period of her life was over; she was starting afresh, mistress of her own fate. For the first time in her life she had felt truly free. It was as if a great suffocating weight had been lifted from her, and she swore that no one – no man, no woman, no circumstance – would ever bind her again.

Well, she had broken that rule when Tilly had come with her vaguely threatening story . . . and now look at the mess she was in. But there was a way out – there had to be a way out!

The burning at the back of her throat and behind her eyes finally disappeared and she heard herself sobbing out her frustration and rage. She suddenly grew furiously angry with herself for allowing her emotions to take control of her like this . . . for allowing her mother to retain that amount of control over her.

And then Billy's arms went round her shoulders, turning her around to face her. Senga buried her head in the big woman's shoulder and sobbed against the rough material of the coat she was wearing. The Scotswoman's big hard hands went to Senga's back, tracing her spine, and she held her close, whispering softly in her hair, murmuring as an adult would soothe a child.

'Come on now, let's get you to bed. We'll work this out in the morning.'

'It was a trap . . .'

'Maybe not in the beginning, but it is now. We'll get a message to your brother in the morning; maybe he might be able to shed some light on it.'

Mention of Patrick's name reassured her. He had always been her hero; he had stood up to their mother when everyone else was terrified of her; he had walked away from her when she had threatened and railed, and had even survived the men she had sent to bring him back; and when Senga had experienced her darkest moments, trapped in that apartment in Paris, he had arrived to save her. And he had contacts both in England and Ireland, legitimate and otherwise. He would know someone, he would do something . . .

'Bed,' Billy said decisively. She reached down and undid the belt of Senga's black, silk dressing-gown, and then eased it off her shoulders, tossing it over the end of the bed. The Scotswoman, her arm still around Senga's waist, brought her over to the bed and turned back the covers. Senga obediently sat on the edge of the bed and pulled her legs in and over the sheets. Billy ran her fingers through the young woman's hair, and then leaned forward and kissed her on the forehead. 'Sleep. You'll need a clear head for the morning.'

'Billy,' Senga whispered, 'you'll stay with me, won't you? I mean, whatever deal Tilly did with you – whatever your fees are – I'll meet. I do have some money of my own.'

Billy pressed her index finger to Senga's lips. 'Sssh now. I'll stay with you, don't you worry about that. She may have tricked you – but she's also tricked me as well. I'm now involved in this, and if the police are watching this house they'll certainly have my description, and from there, it's a short step to discovering my identity. I'm as much a prisoner here as you.'

'What can we do, Billy?'

Billy Fadden sat on the edge of the bed, holding Senga's hand in both of hers.

'We're trapped, good and proper. If that attack hadn't taken place, we might have been able to walk away, and no one any the wiser. But it's too late for that: we know the police are watching the house, and we know it's under observation by your mother's mysterious enemies. All we can do now is to play the game, their way.' She glanced down at Senga and smiled humourlessly. 'For the moment, anyway.'

'And then?'

'I'd lay the blame for this situation at Tilly's door. She

was less than honest with us.' Billy said quietly. 'I'm a great believer in revenge.'

'Billy,' Senga whispered, 'would you stay with me tonight . . . I mean just for a little while?'

Billy looked at her curiously. 'What's wrong?'

'I feel . . . I don't know. Betrayed.'

'That's hardly surprising. You have been betrayed.'

'I know, but it's more than that. Lost. Lonely. Alone.' She nodded. 'Alone. I trusted Tilly Cusack. My brother and I called her Aunt Tilly. I only came over here because she asked me and because I thought I was helping my mother. I trusted her.'

Billy shrugged off her short coat and slipped into the bed beside Senga. She put her left arm around the young woman's neck and drew her close. 'How old are you now, Senga – twenty, twenty-one?'

'Twenty-one.'

'Well, I'll be thirty-four or -five next birthday, and I haven't trusted anyone since I was fifteen.'

Senga, her head resting on the Scotswoman's breast, twisted to look upwards into her face. 'You must be very lonely.' Billy stared straight ahead at the ceiling, her eyes lost in the wan morning light that seeped in through the curtained windows. 'Sometimes.' She lifted her head slightly, twisting her right arm so that it was beneath her head. 'I'm not really in a business which lends itself to friendships.' A wry smile twisted her lips. 'You don't get to meet a nice class of people either. And if you don't trust people, you'll find they won't disappoint you. If you don't have friends, they can't betray you.' She lifted her head to look down at Senga and squeezed her shoulders slightly. 'Now, you counted Tilly Cusack as a friend and you trusted her; so she's disappointed you on two counts, but you learned your lesson, and I'll wager you won't be so trusting next time.'

'It's not easy.'

'Never is.'

'Why do you do what you do, Billy?'

The big woman grunted. 'I did what I had to do, Senga; we all do what we have to do.'

'That's not what I asked you.'

'No, I suppose it's not. Why do you want to know?'

'Just curious.'

Billy yawned. 'Curiosity can be dangerous – didn't your mother ever tell you that?'

'No. She was too busy running her brothels to look after her children. Patrick maintains that we became objects to her – like her house and fine clothes and jewellery. We were objects to be trotted out on special occasions, like trained animals. When Patrick rebelled she didn't know how to handle him, and she reacted towards him as I suppose she would with one of her employees. She sent someone out to hurt him or the girl he was with. When that didn't work, she gave instructions for him to be brought back dead or alive.' Senga's voice was level, barely above a whisper, the words sounding casual, almost detached, and yet Billy could feel the tension in the young woman's shoulder, feel it thrumming along her taut muscles. 'The first man my brother ever killed was the killer my mother had sent after him. When that didn't work, she sent a whole team of killers after him: they too failed, although they were responsible for the death of Patrick's wife. Shortly after that she brought a four-man team armed with machine-guns from London to take care of him. But before she did that, she sent me away to a prison-like school in Switzerland where I would be out of the way . . . one less nuisance to look after, just another little detail taken care of.'

'She sounds like a really nice woman,' Billy murmured, amazed by the quiet, almost resigned way Senga told the terrifying story. 'She reminds me – in a roundabout way – of my father.'

'Tell me,' Senga breathed.

'It's not a particularly pleasant story,' Billy muttered. 'He was, what they call in Glasgow, a hard man.' Without closing her eyes, she could see him now: big and broad, with a perpetual stubble on his chin that never seemed to develop into a beard, grizzled, grey hair and eyes that looked like dirty water. 'He was a violent, dangerous man, but he wasn't subtle like your mother. He was a rent collector, and while some collectors went around with a minder my dad didn't need one. Thirty years he was a collector, and he never lost a penny once. Oh, there were a few tries apparently, but once the word got around that Big Billy Fadden was not a man to be messed with there were no further tries. He was quick with his hands, and he had boxed in the army, and often boxed in some of the illegal bare-knuckled bouts in the "clubs" in the city. He rarely lost. But he used his hands just as easily and as frequently at home.' Her lips compressed themselves into a thin line, and Senga could feel the Scotswoman's hand tighten into a fist alongside her shoulder. 'My sister Moira became pregnant,' she said slowly. 'She had been seeing the boy for years and they had even set the date for the wedding. It was a terrible disgrace, of course, we being a good Catholic family and all that. Moira told us all over tea one night . . . and then we waited for the explosion. But nothing happened. My father said nothing, refused even to discuss it with my mother, and went out immediately after tea. We thought he was going to the pub as usual. He arrived back at his normal time, had his supper and went to bed.' Billy took a deep ragged breath. 'The body of Moira's young man was discovered the following morning. He had been beaten to death. The police report said that there were few unbroken bones in his body. Now just about everyone in Glasgow knew who did the killing, but no one said anything. Word travelled – and, if anything, his reputation improved: here was a man who looked after his family, a man of high morals . . .' The deep solid thrum of Billy's heart began to quicken, and Senga imagined that she could feel the woman's flesh begin to quiver with the sound.

'And then my sister "went away" – or at least that's what my mother and I were told. She would return when the baby was born, my father said. Two days later my mother opened the door to our tenement and found her lying on the landing in a pool of blood. She had gone to an abortionist and he had bungled the job.' Billy's voice began to thicken, the words coming slower and slower, while the thundering in her breast grew louder. 'She had crawled back through the streets and managed to climb the steps to our top-floor tenement, but she hadn't the strength even to knock. It wasn't difficult to discover which quack doctor had done the job; while Glasgow may be a city, the tenements were like a small town. I went to the man and talked to him, and he finally admitted that my father had taken Moira to him.'

'Why would he admit that to you?' Senga asked softly.

'I was a big girl, even then,' Billy said, and Senga could almost imagine the smile on her lips. 'And by that time I had broken four of his fingers with a hammer. He wasn't going to lie to me. When I returned home, I confronted my father. He admitted it, openly, brazenly. My mother screamed at him; I screamed at him. And he hit me – an open-handed blow across the side of the face. He punched my mother.' She stopped suddenly.

Senga raised her head and moved up in the bed to look down into the woman's face. In the dim, pre-dawn light, the unshed tears sat on her eyes like quicksilver. 'You don't have to . . .' Senga began, but Billy continued as if she hadn't heard her.

'When I got up off the floor, he was standing over my mother kicking her. So I picked up a kitchen knife and stabbed him in the back. The knife penetrated his heart and he was dead before he hit the floor.

'I was fifteen years old.'

Senga awoke with the early morning light grey against the windows. She was still lying beside Billy in the crook of her arm, her head now resting just below the woman's muscular shoulder. She wondered briefly what it must have been like to live in a house where beatings were the rule rather than the exception. Her own father had never laid a hand on her, and even her mother, for all her cruelty, had never beaten her. But was there a difference between physical and mental cruelty? Was it worse to beat a child or to ignore it? She moved out of the comforting circle of the sleeping woman's arms, and rolled to the far side of the bed, before throwing back the covers and coming to her feet. She looked back at Billy, watching her sleep, her hard face now relaxed, the tightness around her eyes and lips now gone, lending her face an ephemeral, transient beauty.

The woman was a product of her background; a hard, seemingly uncaring woman, capable of violence, and yet beneath the surface lurked great pain and a terrible hurt.

And how did she differ from the sleeping woman? She too was a product of her own background, and did that not mean that she was capable of the same cruelty and cunning her mother was infamous for? Surely she had proven that when she had organised and planned her escape from the Chateau; surely she had proven that again, when she had survived on the road to Paris and eventually defended her honour – and her life – from that terrifying Frenchman. And when she had looked at his bullet-torn corpse, she had been able to do so without a flicker of disgust or the least pang of conscience.

She was her mother's daughter, then, no doubt about that. Perhaps she had certain advantages that her mother lacked – a certain gloss of education and some breeding. But beneath the skin she was a brothel-keeper's daughter. Scratch a saint and find a sinner. She wondered what people would find if they scratched her surface.

She wasn't sure she wanted to find out herself.

Senga looked down at Billy Fadden again. At least Billy knew what she was; she knew where she came from and, very probably, had a fairly good idea where she was going.

However, she herself was only beginning to discover where she came from. And she didn't think she wanted to know where she was going.

Billy's pale, colourless eyes flickered open. Her lips twisted in a smile and she reached up to catch Senga's fingers with her hand.

'Stay with me,' Senga said suddenly. 'Teach me what you know. Show me how to defend myself. Will you do that?'

'I will.'

'Make me hard, like you.'

'You don't need me to make you hard. That comes from within.'

'I think I could learn a lot from you,' Senga said shyly.

Billy's eyes clouded. 'There are some things I could teach you that you don't want to learn,' she said, and it sounded almost like a threat.

CHAPTER TEN

Senga and Billy were finishing breakfast when Tilly Cusack arrived downstairs. The few hours' sleep had done little to restore her and she still looked haggard, purplish bags beneath deep-sunk eyes, her skin waxy and sagging. She nodded a silent good morning to the two women and then sat to the table. Martha Tilke appeared almost immediately behind her with a thick bundle of letters in her hand. With her eyes fixed on Senga's face, she set the letters down on the table in front of Tilly and then moved away to lift the coffee pot from the sideboard which was spread with the breakfast dishes. She poured Tilly a large cup of strong, black coffee.

'Will that be all, Ma'am?'

Tilly nodded, without saying anything.

The housekeeper's hard, cold eyes drifted across Billy – whom she had already dismissed as a nothing – and settled on Senga. 'Will that be all, Miss?' There was a tiny pause before the title.

Senga caught her gaze and held it. 'Just the post, Miss Tilke,' she said with the barest flicker of a smile.

The woman's eyes went to the pile of letters to the left of Tilly's cup, and then went back to Senga's face. Finding nothing there, she turned back to Tilly Cusack and was about to appeal to her when Senga snapped. 'The letters – please!'

'They are all for Mrs Moore . . .'

It took Senga a moment to realise that Moore was Tilly's

married name. She had married Captain Martin Moore, John Lewis's second-in-command, in 1916, and Senga suddenly felt ashamed that she hadn't so much as inquired into his health since she had encountered Tilly Cusack in Dublin nearly two weeks previously.

'I think you should give Miss Senga the letters,' Tilly said softly, her voice barely above a whisper.

The woman took them from Tilly's hand and passed them across the table with as little grace as she could muster. 'That will be all; thank you Miss Tilke,' Senga said without looking up.

The woman stalked from the room without so much as a backward glance.

'Don't be too hard on her,' Tilly advised, looking at Senga, 'she would be difficult to replace, and because she is aware of your mother's type of operation she is both invaluable to us – and dangerous.'

'Once you start to fear your employees, then it's time to let them go,' Billy rumbled. 'Smacks too much of blackmail for my liking.'

'I'd be inclined to agree with you – and in normal circumstances I would not see Katherine allowing the woman to get so close. But I'd like to try and keep to the normal routine of the house – especially now, especially with the police watching us. If she walks away, there's a good chance the police will pick her up "to assist them in their enquiries" as they say. And, much as I trust her, I don't want that happening.'

Senga looked up and caught Billy's eye. The Scotswoman nodded. 'It's sound advice, Senga.'

Senga nodded sharply once, although neither woman was aware whether it related to her in particular. She turned her attention to the post, sorting through the letters and papers. The vast majority of them were addressed to Madam Katherine Lundy, in a variety of fine handwriting on good-quality paper.

'Most of them will be replies to the Grand Spring Fête invitations that were sent out some weeks ago. A few have trickled in to date, but the next few days should bring a flood.'

Senga slit open the first envelope with her bread-knife and – as Tilly had predicted – found it contained an embossed acceptance card. She could tell by the feel of the second envelope that it too contained an acceptance card. 'How many people have been invited to this Grand Spring Ball?' she asked without looking up.

'Fête,' Tilly corrected, 'fête, not a ball. One hundred and fifty invitations went out,' she continued over the rim of her coffee cup. 'Most of those invitations would have been for couples, a few for families and a very few for individuals. If this were a normal ball, one would expect fifteen or twenty per cent to make their excuses, but this is Madam Lundy's masked fête. I dare say you will find nearly one hundred per cent acceptance . . .'

'How many people?'

'Upwards of four hundred, give or take.'

'I've invited Inspector Holdstock,' Senga said without looking at Tilly.

'She was tricked into it,' Billy added quickly.

'No matter; he would have had people there in any case and at least we know what he looks like. Now, there are still some arrangements left to be made – minor ones, it is true, but Madam Lundy would normally make them herself. What's wrong?' she asked suddenly, realising that the young woman was no longer listening to her. She reached for the single page in Senga's hand, taking it from her numb fingers. Holding up the sheet of cheap writing-paper, she adjusted a pair of gold pince-nez on to her nose.

' "YOU WILL DIE, YOU BITCH",' she read aloud. The five words had been gouged deeply on to the page with a soft, leaded pencil. In some places, it had actually torn through the paper. She added unnecessarily. 'It's not signed.'

'They never are,' Billy remarked, reaching for the paper, taking the envelope from the table. 'Posted locally,' she said, looking at the envelope. She passed both back to Tilly.

'This makes three,' Tilly sighed. 'The same message, the same postal district. Your mother was here for the first message only, but I got the impression from her that there had been others.'

Senga tapped the back of the letter with the blunt end of a butter-knife. 'Any idea who this is from?'

'Your guess is as good as mine. She had a lot of enemies.'

'Any friends?'

Tilly's eyes locked with Senga's. 'Damn few. But they are loyal.'

'I hope she treats them with greater respect than she treats her children,' the younger woman said evenly.

'Anything else in the post?' Billy asked quickly, attempting to ease the situation.

Almost reluctantly, Senga lowered her gaze and began to sort through the remainder of the post. Close to the bottom of the pile there was a small yellow envelope. There was no stamp on it, and there was something familiar about the writing. There was a perceptible tremble in her fingers as she carefully slit open the envelope, unfolded the single sheet of paper and smoothed it flat on the table.

My dearest Senga,

You must believe me when I tell you that it was not my idea to bring you here. I didn't want you involved, you were the last person I was thinking of when I looked for a substitute while I went into hiding. You must believe me when I tell you that I would never knowingly bring you into danger.

But do not be too harsh on Tilly. She did what she thought was right, and she has been right so often in the past, who is to say that she is not right again this time?

I am doing everything in my power to bring this whole affair to a conclusion.

The house is under constant supervision, so do nothing to

draw their attention to you, and try not to venture outside the house. But on the night of the Fête, all will be confusion and it should be possible for you to flee back to Dublin where at least Patrick's organisation should be able to keep you safe.

Trust Billy, I know her reputation, she will protect you.

Trust Tilly, she has my best interests at heart.

Forgive me.

Your mother.

Senga looked up to find both Tilly and Billy looking at her, and she got the impression that they were waiting for her to say something. 'I'm sorry, I was reading.'

'Anything important?' Tilly asked, watching her closely, and in that instant Senga knew that Tilly was aware of what was in the letter. It also explained why there had been no stamp on the envelope. The letter had been planted.

'Nothing important,' she said evenly.

Tilly stared at her a moment longer than was necessary before finally looking away. 'I don't want you going outside the house,' Tilly said, echoing what Katherine Lundy had written in the letter. 'So, I think you should go through your mother's clothes and look for a ball-gown for this masked ball . . .'

'Even if I find one, it'll never fit me!' Senga exclaimed.

'Probably not. But we'll find one that comes close, we can have it altered. Unfortunately there's no time to have one made for you.'

'I take it then that I'm to appear as myself?'

Tilly nodded. 'Madam Lundy will, unfortunately, take ill at the crucial moment and so you will have to act the gracious hostess.'

'I don't think I want to go to this party. I hate parties.'

'This is one of the most important social events of the Season.'

'That is not particularly relevant to me, now is it?'

'Perhaps not. But it is necessary for you – as a representative of the Lundy family – to appear, if we are to keep up the pretence.'

'And are you any nearer to finding my mother?'

Tilly shook her head. 'No. I'm hoping Patrick might be able to assist us. He has made inquiries in places which would normally be closed to me. He will be back in a day or two.'

Senga's eyes dropped to the yellow envelope on her lap, the sheet of paper still clutched tightly in her fingers. She was surprised to find that she cared and even more surprised to discover how deeply she still cared for her mother.

'Sir!' The man surged to his feet and snapped to attention, betraying his previous occupation.

'Stand easy, men.' Inspector Colin Holdstock crossed to the window and stared across the small parkland towards Madam Lundy's Mayfair home. He tapped the report on the window ledge with his gloves. 'Anything?' he asked the two men.

'Nothing unusual, Sir,' the second man said quickly. 'Only the postman – no other callers.'

'Very good then. Stay on it.'

'Yes, Sir.'

'Very good, Sir.'

The empty house echoed to his footsteps as he thundered down the stairs, stamping out his frustration into the wood. What was happening in that house – or, more correctly, was nothing happening? Finally, becoming conscious of what he was doing, he stopped and leaned against the jamb of the kitchen door, looking out into a weed-choked garden while he smoked a cigarette. The thin, dark, Egyptian cigarette tasted like perfume to him, but it was better than nothing, and it stole the dust from the air.

This case was getting out of hand, he decided, and if he'd any sense he'd pass it on to one of his highly-paid superiors and let them earn their salaries. But he couldn't let it go: Madam Lundy had become something of an obsession.

Scotland Yard's suspicions about Madam Lundy had been fired by a routine report from Dublin Castle. The report had been ignored until, almost by chance, it had landed on his desk. He was investigating the reappearance of the organised brothel trade in London. There had always been flash houses and gambling dens which offered other services, but now the street girls were beginning to talk about being recruited into an organisation which looked after its girls, took them off the streets, fed and clothed them, ensured they had the best of medical attention. And only the very best girls – or those with special talents – were recruited.

This had been back in 1916, close to the end of the year – shortly after the mysterious Madam Kitten had disappeared from Dublin. It needed no great stretch of the imagination to realise that the woman had shut up shop in Dublin – undoubtedly the uprising there had been bad for business – and moved her base to London. Colin Holdstock began the investigation into the woman known as Madam Kitten . . . and that had been thirteen years ago.

And he was still no nearer to catching the woman.

Sherlock Holmes had once said that Moriarty was behind every crime in London; well, over the years he had become convinced that Madam Kitten's hand could be seen in many seemingly unrelated crimes. Ten years ago, he had come as close to catching her as he was ever likely to, and her escape then, although nothing short of miraculous, was to be one of many. Other cases had intervened and were given prominence, and the case of the brothel-keeper was filed away. Every so often, when Holdstock felt that another case was relevant, he would pull out the file and update it, and what had started out as a simple four-page report from Dublin now ran to many hundreds of pages. All it lacked was the woman's true identity.

And now he had that.

Everyone makes mistakes; more crimes are solved by

the criminal's errors than by any other means. Recently, Holdstock's man had been watching a jeweller – a known dealer in stolen gems. Following a series of daring jewel robberies across London, the man had been picked up on the Dover night-train. He was carrying a suitcase, whose contents were later valued at something close to half a million.

But the man was co-operative and, in an attempt to lessen what would otherwise have been a heavy sentence, he provided a detailed listing of the various illegal dealings he had been involved in. He spoke of acting as an agent for the sale of the Irish Crown Jewels, and one of the women who had expressed a more than passing interest in the stones was Madam Kitten . . . and also a certain Katherine Lundy. Curious as to why a cultured socialite was interested in stolen property, Holdstock had ordered a full investigation into the woman and her background . . . only to discover that she had no background.

Madam Katherine Lundy had appeared complete on the London social scene in 1916. Widowed and obviously wealthy, no one had been inclined to ask too many questions of the woman and she had volunteered little herself.

And Madam Kitten had disappeared from the Dublin scene in 1916.

Coincidence?

Colin Holdstock didn't believe in coincidence.

However, it still required an extraordinary leap of the imagination to envision this rather plump and plain old woman with the terrifying tales of the infamous Whoremistress of Dublin. But his initial scepticism had gradually disappeared before the mounting evidence, and the deeper he delved into Katherine Lundy's background the less he liked it. Details of her life in Dublin were scarce and the report from the Dubin Metropolitan Police was so inconclusive that he had actually travelled to Dublin to investigate. The new Irish government and administration had been somewhat reluctant to help. With that door firmly shut before him, he decided to try other – slightly more dramatic – means of acquiring his information.

Colin Holdstock took to wandering through the notorious Monto district – the red-light area of Dublin. He was propositioned numerous times by the street girls, but these weren't the women he had come to find. On his third night down Tyrone Street, he had been accosted by three, very well-dressed and well-spoken women, who had berated him for walking the mean streets and preying upon the fallen women. The women were Members of the Legion of Mary, a staunchly Catholic organisation, who had as one of their chief aims the destruction of the Monto scene, the closure of the houses and the rehabilitation of the women. These were the women he had been looking for. Quietly, and without fuss, he showed them his identification and informed them that he was attempting to imprison one of the famous Madams, and that he needed their help.

Holdstock had accompanied them back to the house they kept on the very fringes of the red-light district, and he was then introduced to several of the women who were living in the house, having come off the streets in an attempt to give up the 'life'. Some were obviously ill, others frighteningly young. And all of them knew Madam Kitten, or the Madam as she was more simply known.

What he had learned then had frightened him. This woman – this mysterious Madam Kitten – had virtually ruled Dublin's underworld for twelve or thirteen years. Armed with information gleaned from the girls' clients, she had made a fortune financing robberies, taking a cut from the proceeds, and then organising the disposal of the goods. She had dealt in information, buying what she considered useful and selling packages to certain interested parties. She had also been involved with the Easter Rising, although no one could decide exactly how – the most popular rumour was that she was running arms. Certainly she had disappeared immediately after the ill-fated uprising.

No one had ever seen the mysterious Madam – who went clothed and veiled in black, 'like a widow' he had been told – but Holdstock did discover that she had a son and a daughter.

Pursuing this line of inquiry, Holdstock went to the register of births, marriages and deaths, and demanded a list of all births, marriages and deaths associated with either the Lundy or Corcoran names. Three days later he had his reply.

On the 7th July, 1899, a son, Patrick Montgomery Lundy, mother Katherine Lundy, 19, domestic, father unknown.

On 28th April, 1908, a daughter, Senga Lundy Corcoran, mother Katherine Lundy-Corcoran, 28, housekeeper, father, Dermot Corcoran, journalist.

And Katherine Lundy, Mayfair socialite, had two children, a boy and girl, Patrick and Senga.

On a separate sheet of paper, there was a note of the wedding, on the 1st of May, 1908, of Katherine Lundy to Dermot Corcoran.

Both children, Holdstock had noted, had been born out of wedlock. He wondered how a woman, who described herself as a housekeeper, could appear with all the mannerisms and money of a socialite? Where had the money come from . . . but then he knew where the money had come from; he was only surprised that she seemed to be so wealthy. Obviously crime did pay. But it wasn't just the money; to carry off such a charade, she would have had to practice: adopting the airs and graces of an upper-class widow was not something that someone could do overnight.

Madam Kitten's brothel was reputed to be one of the most exclusive in the British Isles, whose clients included men from the armed forces, the church, various titled families and – if the rumours were to be believed – from the royal family itself. The woman who ran that house would have to be a cultured lady, he reasoned.

Delving deeper into the woman's background, he discovered that her son, Patrick, had been involved in the proscribed Irish Republican Brotherhood, and her late husband would seem to have been one of the prime movers in it.

When the Irish Crown Jewels had been stolen in 1907, suspicion had immediately fallen on the mysterious Madam as the person most likely to fence the stones. And her involvement was taken so seriously that Major John Lewis had actually investigated her himself. Lewis, who had been killed in the fighting in 1916, was one of the men who ran the British intelligence operation in Dublin at that time, and his reports often mentioned the woman. She seemed to be a true mercenary, and he discovered that she had even sold out the rebellion in the early months of 1916. And possibly that was the reason she had left Dublin so precipitously, Holdstock thought excitedly; she had sold out the revolutionaries and they had discovered the fact, and, no matter how powerful a position she would have occupied in the Dublin underworld, no one would protect a traitor. So, she had fled to London and operated under the name of Katherine Lundy, reasonably secure in the knowledge that no one in Dublin knew her real name.

Holdstock stubbed out his cigarette on the bare floorboards. He had been very close to taking the woman in the past. He knew a lot about her operation – certainly enough to put her away, but he supposed he was being greedy; he wanted it all. Not only the house in Mayfair, but the houses in Edinburgh, Glasgow and Manchester. He wanted her network of informants and her girls, both those she ran in the brothels and the street girls; he wanted the bullies, the men who kept the girls in line; he wanted the thieves who operated on her instructions; and he wanted her suppliers of alcohol and cocaine. He wanted her son, who was a brutal killer, and her business manageress, Tilly Cusack.

And the girl, Senga Lundy?

He didn't know what to make of Senga Lundy. His investigations had turned up very little about her. Katherine had protected the girl very well, and had seemed determined to keep her away from the life. She had been sent to a finishing school in 1921, from which she had run away, and since then had lived with her brother in Dublin. She pursued an academic career in Trinity College Dublin and seemed to have no association with her brother's illegal organisation or outlawed friends. But it was certainly a case of guilt by association, and, in any case, what was she doing here and now?

But even more importantly, where was Katherine Lundy? All the indications were that she had simply upped and left – no-one seemed to know whether it was voluntarily or not, although he was inclined to believe it was.

Colin Holdstock shrugged as he opened the hall door and stepped out into the quiet street. No matter, he would have her . . . sooner or later he would have her.

And her family.

CHAPTER ELEVEN

'And if I don't want to go to this ball?' Senga demanded belligerently.

The two women ignored her, and in truth she hadn't really been expecting an answer.

Senga took a step back from the mirror and turned to admire the dress Tilly Cusack had chosen for her from amongst the enormous collection in the wardrobes. She was wearing a Chanel-designed, crepe-de-chine, black dress, with long, close-fitting sleeves, and even though the waist had been taken in to accommodate Senga's slim figure and the sleeves had been adjusted slightly, it looked as if it had been made for her. Although it was three years old, like most of Coco Chanel's creations, it possessed a certain fashion timelessness.

'It's too late even to think about changing your mind now,' Tilly said mildly, not looking at the younger woman. She undid the ribbon on a circular hat box and removed a tissue-wrapped bundle. There was a simple, black leather, helmet-type hat inside, which she passed to Senga without a word. From a second package, she removed a pair of short, white gloves.

'Nice,' Billy commented. She was standing to one side of the mirror, arms folded across her chest, her eyes on Senga. 'It needs something around the neck, though . . .' she added thoughtfully.

Tilly came to stand behind Senga, staring past her to look at her reflection in the mirror. 'Pearls,' she said decisively, 'a single string.' She turned away to rummage through Katherine's enormous jewellery box and returned a few moments later with a string of large, yellow-white pearls, which she fastened around Senga's neck herself.

'Now, let's have a look at you.'

The final effect was quite stunning. The simple black dress, which ended just below her knees, accentuated her slender, almost boyish figure, while highlighting her clear complexion and long, slender neck. The black helmet framed her oval face, emphasising her deep, dark eyes, and her hair flowed out from beneath her hat in a wrist-thick braid that concluded at the base of her spine.

'Well, what do you think?' Tilly asked her.

'It's not too severe?' Senga asked doubtfully.

'It's perfect,' Billy assured her.

'And your mother wore black,' Tilly added, 'so it's natural that you should dress in her style. Although,' she added wryly, 'I doubt if this dress ever looked as good on her as it does on you.'

A knock on the door made all three of them turn. Martha Tilke stepped into the room and looked from Tilly to Senga. 'It's Master Patrick.'

'Where?' Senga asked, surprised. She hadn't seen or heard from her brother in nearly a week.

'He's downstairs, Miss, and he said to tell you he's in a hurry.'

Patrick was waiting in the sitting room, standing close to the window, a short telescope pressed to his eye.

'Patrick!' Senga exclaimed.

Patrick Lundy turned with a smile which broadened when he saw his sister's outfit. 'I wouldn't have recognised you,' he confessed. 'Is that what you're wearing tonight?'

'What do you think?' she asked, crossing to kiss his cheek. Patrick gently eased her to one side, away from the window.

'I think it's grand,' he admitted, 'you look very impressive, very chic. You'll be turning heads tonight, I imagine, and breaking a few hearts too. Although,' he added slowly, looking past his sister to Tilly, 'I'm not sure if it's a good idea for Senga to go tonight.'

'What!'

'I've done some digging and I've discovered that our dear mother has upset far too many people on both sides of the law. The word is on the street: ten thousand pounds to the person who ensures that Katherine Lundy has a fatal accident! The money had been pooled together by several of our mother's competitors.'

Tilly Cusack nodded. 'I thought as much.'

'I also have it on very good authority that there'll be an undercover police presence here tonight, with orders to arrest Mrs Katherine Lundy, also known as Katherine Lundy-Corcoran, also known as The Madam or Madam Kitten!'

'They know?' Tilly breathed. Colour drained from her face and she sank into the nearest chair. 'How? Less than half a dozen people know . . .'

Patrick shook his head. 'I don't know. Inspector Colin Holdstock is in charge of the operation . . .'

'He was here a few days ago,' Senga said quietly.

'What did he want?'

'He said he was investigating the report of a fracas outside this house.'

'What sort of fracas?' Patrick asked, looking at each of the three women in turn.

'There was an attempt on your sister's life,' Billy said shortly.

'Billy saved my life,' Senga said quickly.

'Your people were on the scene very quickly,' Billy added. 'They took care of the body.'

'You didn't kill him?' Patrick asked in alarm.

'Not quite,' she smiled.

'Where is he now?'

Billy shrugged. 'I don't know. I would imagine your people still have him.'

'I'll look into it. But what's this about Holdstock?'

'He said they had received a report from the neighbours, and he came here to take a statement. He said he'd be back.'

'He will be. He is a dangerous man; a brilliant officer who has come up through the ranks solely on merit and results. Be very careful of him.' Patrick turned back to the window and used the small telescope to peer at the house opposite. 'You do know you're under observation, don't you?' he remarked conversationally. 'Was there anyone with him?' he continued, glancing back into the room.

'A young Irish policeman, named Tims . . .'

'Thinn,' Tilly corrected.

Senga nodded. 'That's it. I thought at first he was a bit of a fool, but later, I wasn't so sure.'

Patrick grimaced. 'Malachi Thinn spent three years infiltrating our organisation in Dublin; he was responsible for the capture of nearly thirty of our men and, even now, we still don't know how much information he managed to pass back to the authorities. When his cover was finally blown, he was sent from Dublin to London to assist the police in their surveillance of the organisation over here. He's been here about six months and already we've lost eight men to him. He plays the fool – the innocent Irishman, the gombeen – but he's anything but.'

'I also invited Holdstock to the ball tonight,' Senga said quietly, watching her brother closely.

Patrick rounded on her, his eyes wide with surprise. 'You invited him . . .?' he said in astonishment.

'She was tricked, manoeuvred by Holdstock,' Billy said, coming to her defence.

Patrick nodded. 'Well, I could see him doing that, all right. And at least if he's coming tonight, we'll be able to keep an eye on him. However, while he'll be a visible presence, there will be others not so visible.'

Tilly looked up at Patrick. 'This party is by invitation only. There should be no unknown faces there.'

'And what about the hotel you've booked? What about its staff, the waiters, the caterers, the musicians, the entertainers? And what about the guests; how many of them have you *actually* met; how many of them do you know? No event of this nature is ever completely secure. If the police want to infiltrate people into it, then they'll be able to do it with relative ease. But it's not the police I'm worried about,' he added ominously. He looked at Billy as he continued, speaking directly to her, 'Katherine Lundy's cover is blown. If the police have discovered her identity, then it is only a matter of time before it becomes "public" knowledge. There are certain people whom our dear mother upset in her quest to become what she is today. And while they were not able to move against her, because her identity was a closely-guarded secret, now that it has become common knowledge . . .'

'An assassination attempt?' Billy interrupted, her Scottish accent sounding very hard and uncompromising.

'I believe so.'

'Is there danger?' Senga asked quietly.

'I believe so,' Patrick repeated softly, wrapping his arm around his sister's shoulders. 'If our mother isn't available, then they may strike at you as a way of getting to her.'

'Kidnap,' Billy grunted.

Patrick nodded. 'That is also a possibility.'

Shaking her head, Tilly stood up and crossed to the drinks cabinet. 'But how have these various people discovered Katherine's identity? She operated in Dublin for sixteen years and no one even suspected.'

'Then she was a big fish in a small pond, and she was careful, so careful. Here, her operation is so much more open, and she obviously has been careless. She's become greedy, pushed her prices up, squeezed her competitors, bankrupted some, disposed – and I do mean disposed – of others. You know that adage about honour amongst thieves? Well, it's not entirely true, but there is a live-and-let-live attitude, which the various London crime families adhered to. Unfortunately our mother didn't, and managed to alienate them in the process.

'I've also discovered that she added blackmail to her various crimes, and we're not talking about clients' whispered indiscretions to her working girls. Katherine Lundy always aimed high . . .'

112

'What did she do, Patrick?' Senga asked softly.

'It's bad business to attempt to blackmail one of the titled families, especially one so close to the Crown. It's very unhealthy and very, very dangerous.'

'But what would she have to blackmail them with?' Senga wondered.

'A twenty-two-year-old scandal.'

'The Crown Jewels?' Tilly asked shrewdly.

'The same.' He slipped the small telescope into his pocket and smiled ruefully at Senga. 'I don't think she realised the attention that would be focused on her once she started to move in exalted circles. No secret is ever completely safe, and once the finest police force in the world begins to look into your background, then you really don't have a chance. I also have a theory that her identity was deliberately leaked to the crime families,' Patrick said quietly.

'But why?' Senga whispered. 'Why would the police do that?'

'I'm suggesting that if our mother were to meet with an accident, no one, on either side of the law, would shed too many tears.'

Inspector Colin Holdstock strode into his office, closely followed by Malachi Thinn. 'Now, Gentlemen, if I may have your full attention.'

There were twelve officers crowded into the small office on the first floor of Scotland Yard. They had all been drafted in from suburban police stations and, for most of them, this was the first time they had been in the Yard; for some, it was the first time they had been to London.

'I know some of you have been wondering why you were asked here; apparently my explanation did not meet with your approval.'

Most of the officers managed to look embarrassed; they *had* found it difficult to believe that they were to take part in a police-training exercise.

'Well, perhaps I was somewhat economical with the

truth,' Colin Holdstock smiled, 'but with very good reason. We are mounting an operation tonight at a social function in which secrecy is of the essence. You have all been brought here for a couple of reasons, but one in particular. You are virtually unknown to the central London criminal world. You also have the advantage that none of you look like policemen, and all of your backgrounds are such that you will be able to mix with this type of social gathering without too much difficulty. I should add that if this operation is successful, then a commendation will undoubtedly follow, and a request for transfer to the city will be looked upon very favourably.' He looked from man to man. 'And I have that on the very best authority.'

Malachi Thinn stepped forward. 'Take your seats, Gentlemen.'

Colin Holdstock moved around to sit behind his desk, while his constable stood behind him, arms folded across his chest. 'Now, Gentlemen, this is, in many respects, quite a straightforward operation: tonight the Dorchester hosts an event known as the Grand Spring Fête, and we will be there in an attempt to arrest the organiser of this Fête, Madam Katherine Lundy.

'For those of you who may not be familiar with this affair – this is the largest social event of its type on the London calendar,' Holdstock said slowly, looking at each face in turn. 'There will be representatives of just about every wealthy or titled family in the land there, as well as several minor European princes and other assorted royalty. There was to have been a representative from our own royal family present, but we . . . we persuaded him to cancel. We thought it advisable in the circumstances. There will be a lot of money there, tonight – although probably not a lot of it in cash – but I dare say the total value of the jewellery these people will be wearing would pay off the German war debt. But that is not our concern, even if you see wholesale theft, leave it be, resist the temptation to make the arrest. This event has its own

114

security officers, and they'll earn more for the night than you will earn for the week; let them earn their wage.

'Your job will be to look out for – and arrest – the hostess of this party, a woman named Katherine Lundy, or sometimes simply known as the Madam. She is a very wealthy, sophisticated and respected Society lady who has even been to the Palace . . . she is also a brothel-keeper. We want to question her in connection with that and several other associated crimes, including murder, theft, dealing in stolen goods and blackmail. If we can arrest her tonight, then we will have removed a major criminal from the London streets.'

One officer raised his hand and looked at Holdstock.

'Yes?' the inspector snapped, irritated at the interruption.

'Begging your pardon, Sir, but surely this isn't really our department. Or yours either. I mean, brothel-keepers and whores are . . .'

Holdstock nodded. 'Ordinarily, you would be correct. But there are ramifications to this case which need not concern you. Suffice it to say that we want this woman very badly. That is why an operation of this type is being mounted.'

The men all looked at one another. None of them had any idea of what the *ramifications* might be, but they could all imagine the worst.

Holdstock covered his mouth and coughed to conceal a smile. 'Shall we say, Gentlemen, that this is a matter of national security, and leave it at that.'

Some of the men in the group nodded; they had guessed as much.

'Now, the woman herself disappeared some weeks ago. She hasn't been seen or heard from since. But there is every possibility that she will be there tonight. If she is, then our job will be to go in and arrest her. And I should point out that there will be bodyguards – brothel bullies, probably – so there might be a bit of a fracas. And there is a complication.' He smiled tightly. 'It appears this lady

115

has been targeted by some of her former allies. She has become an embarrassment, an inconvenience, and they have decided that things would be better all around if she had an accident. To this end, they have brought in people to attempt to arrange that; we don't know who and we don't know how many. Our job, needless to say, will be to take the lady out of there in one piece and then ensure that she remains in one piece.' Holdstock finished and looked at Thinn.

The young-looking Irishman turned to face the assembled officers. The lazy manner and seemingly vacuous expression he had exhibited before Senga Lundy was not in evidence now. 'We have a slight problem with Madam Lundy,' he said with an easy smile, 'because we do not possess a photograph of the woman. She would seem to have an aversion to being photographed – understandably so in her circumstances. I have here the latest description which we drew up from statements from known associates.' He handed a bundle of leaflets to the nearest officer. 'Perhaps you would be so good as to pass these around.' Lifting his own sheet, he began to read. 'Katherine Lundy, born Lancashire, 1880, which makes her forty-nine, although we understand that she now looks older than her actual years. She came to Dublin in 1898 to go into service, but she was dismissed seven months later when it was discovered that she was pregnant. From this point on Katherine Lundy has effectively disappeared, and we are now talking about a woman known as the Madam or Madam Kitten. It was only recently that we discovered they were one and the same.

'We do not know what happened after the young woman left service, but it appears she set up or was taken into an existing brothel, and certainly from about 1902 or 1903 her name – Madam Kitten – crops up in association with a woman called Bella Cohen, an infamous Dublin brothel-keeper. She has two children, a son, Patrick, born 7th July, 1899, now aged thirty, and a daughter Senga,

116

born 28th April, 1908, now aged twenty-one. She married in 1908, husband now deceased. Her son is a member of the Irish Republican Army and is a known and wanted killer.' He paused and looked up from the page. 'I know this man, by reputation only,' he added, with a wry smile. 'He is a ruthless killer, quite high now in the organisation, and there is every possibility that he will be there tonight.' He turned back to his notes. 'We also know that Katherine Lundy's daughter has returned for this night's event. We can find no connection between Senga Lundy and either her mother's business or her brother's organisation, but, leaving that aside, I think we should remember that she is a member of the Lundy family and that should be enough.

'The description we have is as follows: Katherine Lundy is forty-nine, as I've said, but looks older. She is tall – heights vary, but close enough to five-foot-eleven seems to be the consensus of opinion. An oval face, square chin, wide-set brown eyes. Wears glasses. Thick, black hair, now greying, swept back off her face. I'll just add an aside,' he looked up, 'her daughter would seem to have inherited her mother's hair, and she too wears it swept back off her face and loose down her back. She should be easy enough to recognise. The mother has put on a lot of weight over the past few years, and she is now described as stout, plump or well-built . . . take your choice. All we can add is that she usually appears in public dressed in black, although this being a special occasion, she may not.'

Holdstock leaned forward, his elbows on the desk. 'Any questions?'

'Yes, Sir.'

Holdstock looked towards the back of the room.

'What do we do if we see the woman?'

'Find a companion or two and arrest her.'

'On what charge?'

'Keeping a bawdy house, living off immoral earnings, receiving stolen goods, accessory before the fact, accessory after the fact, organising and financing theft . . . the list runs for several pages.'

'What do we do about the son and daughter?' another officer asked.

'It's unlikely you will actually see the son; he is wanted by too many people. But I would imagine the daughter will be at the door to greet the guests. We have nothing on her at the moment. However, if you arrest the mother, we'll take the daughter along with us. It'll do no harm to ask her a few questions. One final thing,' he looked at each of the men in turn, 'another reason you've been assigned to me is because you have all had firearms training. You will all be armed tonight.'

Alone with Senga at last, Patrick reached into his coat and took out a tiny silver pistol, its two barrels sitting one atop the other, making it look like a child's toy. 'This is a .22 derringer,' he said softly. 'There's no way you would be able to bring that big revolver with you, but you could carry this without too much difficulty.' He snapped the catch and folded down the barrels, showing her the two bullets already loaded into it. 'You'll have to be reasonably close to do any real damage.'

Senga turned the weapon over in her hands, surprised at its size and weight. 'Where am I going to carry it?'

'Well, women of a certain type usually carry them in their garter.'

'Do you think I'll need it?' she asked seriously.

'I'm afraid you might.'

CHAPTER TWELVE

As the first guests began to arrive, Senga Lundy started to shake. Billy's grip tightened around her arm, squeezing reassuringly. 'What's wrong? Nerves?'

Senga nodded. 'All these people,' she hissed.

'Breathe deeply. Don't think about them; concentrate on each person as they are presented to you. All you have to do is to say hello to the first two dozen couples and then Tilly will take over.' The big woman turned around and looked down the length of the huge ballroom, which had been hung with pennants and flags and festooned with flowers. At the far end of the room a small orchestra tuned up. White-jacketed, white-gloved waiters moved across the empty floor. Billy found herself wondering how many of them were police.

'I think I'm going to be sick.'

'No you're not. I haven't got all dressed up like this just to have to go back home again. And didn't I tell you that I hate dressing up; it'll be extra on your bill.'

Senga smiled wanly. 'You look lovely.'

'Thank you. Green is supposed to suit redheads, isn't it?'

'Well, it certainly suits you.'

Billy was wearing a similar outfit to Senga's – also courtesy of Katherine's extensive wardrobe. Originally the big woman had set her eye on a stunning Molyneux evening-gown in white satin, but even she had to admit that it was a size or two too small for her, and, while that in itself would not have been a problem, the fact that she wouldn't have been able to breathe, never mind move, might be. On Tilly's advice, she had chosen a Chanel design, although, unlike Senga's which had a high, straight neck, this was scooped and emphasised her bust, and also had slightly fuller sleeves, which allowed her to wear the metal-studded, leather wrist-greeves. Although her shoes had a short, square heel she was still a few inches taller than Senga who was wearing high heels.

And then the guests began to arrive.

Tilly Cusack met them at the door, wearing a stunning tulle, Sciaparelli evening-gown, which was high-waisted and fitted to the knees before it flared out below. Some of the guests actually mistook her for Madam Lundy, and there were a few embarrassed moments before they were passed on to Madam Lundy's daughter – Madam Lundy being indisposed and unable to attend.

'Tilly Cusack?'

Tilly turned, an automatic smile twisting her lips, although she had already recognised the voice.

'Inspector Colin Holdstock.'

'Well, what a surprise,' he lied.

'Mutual, I'm sure.'

The Inspector was wearing a simple black evening-suit in a slightly old-fashioned cut that looked crisp enough to be new, although Tilly somehow doubted that it was. It was offset with a dove-grey, double-breasted waistcoat, and there was a heavy, gold watch-chain stretching across his stomach. She wondered if he was armed – and decided that he was a fool if he wasn't.

'You're a little off your beat, aren't you?' he asked. He had last encountered Tilly Cusack in Glasgow when he had been investigating the murder of a number of prostitutes in the city. During his investigations, he had discovered that she was the manageress of a house of dubious reputation that was owned by the mysterious London Madam. However, all his attempts to delve further into the woman's background had come to naught and, at one stage, he had even had the suspicion that his investigation was being

120

blocked at some higher level.

'Surely you're also a little off your own beat, Inspector?' Tilly asked without missing a beat.

'My night off, isn't it?' he said with a smile.

'Of course, Inspector,' Tilly said, in a tone which indicated that she certainly didn't believe him. 'I didn't know you knew Mrs Lundy?' she said expressionlessly.

'I have not had that pleasure,' Colin Holdstock replied smoothly. 'However, I hope to have that pleasure soon.'

'Well, I'm afraid it will not be tonight. Unfortunately our hostess is ill and cannot be with us, but her daughter is here in her place.' She stepped away from the door and walked up to Senga. Touching her lightly on the arm, distracting her from the last couple, she introduced the inspector, 'Senga, I'd like you to meet an old acquaintance of mine, Inspector Colin Holdstock of Scotland Yard. Inspector Holdstock, I'd like you to meet Katherine Lundy's daughter, Miss Senga Lundy-Corcoran.'

'I have already made the inspector's acquaintance,' Senga said shyly.

'Oh, of course you have, dear. Pardon me, I was completely forgetting about that. Now, if you will both excuse me, I have some guests to attend to.'

The inspector turned back to Senga. 'You see, I accepted your kind invitation. A great pleasure to meet you again.'

'I'm delighted you could come. I was told you would.'

'I understand that your mother is unwell?'

'Yes, yes,' Senga said, launching into the story Tilly had prepared earlier that day. 'She was away for a few weeks recuperating from a dreadful cold – and as you know her health has never been robust – but she did so hope to get up to town for the ball tonight.'

'Aaah, what a pity,' he said insincerely, his eyes drifting off Senga's face to fall on Billy's. A tiny frown creased his forehead. 'And who might this charming young lady be?'

Senga bit back a smile. 'This is my good friend, Miss Willimena Fadden.'

'Delighted . . .' he murmured. Billy reached out to accept the man's outstretched hand, and Holdstock immediately decided he had touched smoother stone walls. His eyes drifted over her face, memorising the details. He didn't recognise the woman and, although he had never encountered a female of the species before, he knew the type: a minder. And that begged the question: whom was she minding, Tilly Cusack or Senga Lundy? The latter, he decided, noting the way the big woman kept protectively close to the young woman.

'But you did not bring a companion, Inspector?' Senga asked, distracting him.

'Colin, please. Inspector sounds so formal; I always think it makes me sound as if I work on the omnibuses or the trains.'

Senga smiled. 'Well, Colin it shall be – when you're off-duty, of course. You *are* off-duty?' she asked quickly.

Holdstock glanced at her sharply. 'I am. But why should you ask?'

But instead of replying, Senga turned to Billy, resting her slender fingers on the woman's arm. 'Would you be a dear and fetch me a drink, and the inspe . . . Colin too, if he would like one.'

Billy Fadden nodded and moved away without a word, her face expressionless.

'Talkative,' Holdstock murmured, watching her move smoothly through the crowd.

'Why did you come tonight, Inspector?' Senga asked, deliberately stressing the title.

Her question took him by surprise and it took him a second or two before he answered. 'Because you asked me,' he said eventually.

'Do I look like a fool to you, Inspector?' she snapped, the smile fixed to her face, the words hard.

Completely off balance now, Holdstock could only stare at the young woman. From her position by the open doors, Tilly watched the couple curiously, aware that something was happening, but not sure what.

'You tricked me into issuing you your invitation. Now, don't insult me further by pretending to have come here for reasons other than those of duty. I can save you the trouble, Inspector. My mother isn't here. I don't know where she is, and, do you know something else, I really don't care!' She was turning away when Billy reappeared, the glass of white wine and the tall glass of what looked like orange juice almost lost in her large hands. 'Give the inspector his drink!' she snapped.

Billy handed the tall glass to the bemused inspector. 'I didn't think you'd want alcohol while on duty,' she said with a sly smile, and walked away, following Senga.

'Wonder why I bothered!' Colin Holdstock said to no one in particular.

Getting into the ball had been easy enough. Too many people, not enough invitations, and a hostess who didn't know all the faces made it child's play. He had hired himself a standard evening dress-suit, complete with bow-tie, top hat, white gloves and cane, and had then simply walked into the hotel as if he had every right in the world to be there, and strolled into the ballroom. As soon as he had stepped into the doorway, he had raised his right hand and waved at someone across the room, a broad smile fixing itself to his face.

To the casual observer, it looked as if he were greeting an old friend or the hostess. In reality, he knew no one there, or, to put it more correctly, no one there knew him. But then he didn't mix socially with this class of people, and this class of people didn't mix with his social class at all.

And he knew that all he had to do was to open his mouth, and his East End accent would betray him.

He spotted the girl quickly enough. The crowd were circulating around her, like bees around a hive, and she was easily identifiable with that long, long hair of hers in any case.

He began to move through the crowd towards her, the

long flat blade of the knife cool against his skin, beneath his closed coat. He didn't know who she was, didn't know what she'd done. He didn't ask those kind of questions. He had a job to do.

'Graf Rutgar von Mann, at your service!' The tall, young man snatched Senga's hand, pressed it to his lips, while bowing stiffly over it, his heels clicking audibly together and all before she had time to react.

'Senga Lundy,' she said a little breathlessly.

'I was expecting someone a little . . .' he paused and looked away, almost in embarrassment, and then said quickly, '. . . a little more mature.'

'I am sorry if I disappoint you,' Senga said with a smile.

'Oh, but you do not. That is . . .' he floundered, colour touching his cheeks.

'You must forgive me,' Senga said easily, 'I did not mean to tease. You were expecting my mother, I would imagine?'

'Aaah,' he nodded, visibly relieved to have had the confusion sorted out. 'Perhaps I could begin from the beginning, eh?'

Senga nodded.

'I am Graf Rutgar von Mann,' he said formally, bowing again, and almost, but not quite, clicking his heels. He didn't offer to kiss her hand this time.

'Senga Lundy,' she repeated. 'Katherine Lundy's daughter,' she added, looking closely at the young man.

He was in his early twenties and stood a little over six feet, but his almost unnatural thinness made him seem taller. He had a shock of wavy, blond hair which parted in the middle over his forehead and flowed down to his ears, and his eyes were the deepest blue she had ever seen, beneath almost invisible eyebrows. His nose was sharp, his lips thin and bloodless, and his chin was square. Even if she hadn't been told his name, she would have guessed he was a Prussian Junker.

'I have never met your illustrious mother,' he said in

124

perfect English, his accent, Senga noted, sounding more French than German, 'but she knew my father, and an invitation arrived some days ago. My father unfortunately is tied up with business, and could not come.' He suddenly made a disgusted face. 'But listen to me prattle on like an old woman! Your good mother is not here . . .?'

'She is indisposed,' Senga said gently.

'Aaah, it is not serious, I hope.'

'I don't think so.'

'I will inform my father. I feel sure he will call upon your mother . . .'

'She is recuperating in a private hospital,' Senga said with a smile, 'and we may have to send her to Switzerland.'

'Aaah, Switzerland,' he said, nodding.

Suddenly, Senga recognised the accent. 'Swiss. Your accent in Swiss!'

'But yes,' he said in surprise. 'You know the Swiss accent?'

'I finished my schooling in Switzerland,' Senga said with a curious smile. 'I will never forget the accent.'

The young man looked at her shrewdly, and abruptly some of the rather naive exterior fell away. 'It was a not a pleasant experience, I take it?'

Surprised by his change of tone and demeanour, she shook her head. 'No, it wasn't particularly pleasant.'

'Would I know the school?' he asked gently.

She smiled. 'It's unlikely. It's a girl's school, simply called the Chateau.'

Von Mann frowned in puzzlement. 'I know the place by reputation. Not what I would call a suitable finishing school for a young lady such as yourself.'

'I ran away,' she confided, surprising herself.

'Good for you!'

Senga found herself warming to this rather boyish young man.

'Perhaps you would dance?' he said a little stiffly, touches of colour on his cheeks.

125

Senga glanced at Billy, who was standing a few feet behind her, and then looked back at the young man. 'Perhaps I would.' Resting her hand on his, she stepped out on to the dance floor.

Perfect!

He had her now. She was dancing with a blond-haired young man, who looked either foreign or effeminate or both. All he had to do now was to give her a minute or two and then cut in, take her partner's place, manoeuvre her around until he was close enough to the door, and then do the business. In the confusion, he would be able to slip away without too much bother.

Humming along with the bars of the waltz, he began to cut across the dance floor towards her.

Colin Holdstock didn't know the man but he recognised the determination with which he was moving towards Senga Lundy. Instinct, combined with too many years of following hunches, sent him out across the floor at an angle that would bring him in close to the man.

Billy Fadden recognised the type immediately. The expressionless dead eyes, the *stillness* about him. He was moving in on Senga, his eyes like cold, flat stones, fixed on her, regarding her dispassionately, an object to be disposed of. She had seen too many like him down through the years. And sometimes when she looked in a mirror, she recognised the type.

There was another disturbance in the flow of the dancers and she spotted Holdstock cutting through the whirling couples, also moving towards the man. Something cold clutched at her spine and, ignoring the dancing couples in front of her, she tucked her head down and dashed towards the white-faced man.

The game was blown!

His own instincts – honed on the meaner streets of

126

London. Paris and Lisbon – advised him to get the hell out of there. He could see two people – man and woman – moving towards him, and, while he didn't know what they were, he sure as hell didn't want to find out. But there was a lot of money riding on this one; four times the normal fee. And he was only a few feet from the girl. Gone was all hope of subtlety. He would have to try a straight slash and run.

Opening his coat with his right hand, he reached in for the smooth knife.

She really was a charming girl, von Mann decided, with a directness and a wry sense of humour which he found more than appealing. As the waltz descended into its final, few whirling bars, he decided he would ask her to dance again. Spinning her around, he spotted the pale-faced man moving towards them.

– *They spun* –

The man was closer, pale-faced, hard-eyed, lips peeled back from yellow, discoloured teeth.

– *They spun* –

His hand was under his coat.

The dance finished and the dancing couples turned towards the stage, applauding, and the man came in fast, the knife blade gleaming wanly in the chandeliers' sparkling light. It slashed at Senga, a quick movement that sliced through the pearl necklace, scattering the large, yellow-white beads everywhere.

Rutgar von Mann struck at the man, a quick, left-handed blow that caught him high in the chest, staggering him. Recovering, he stabbed at Rutgar, who lashed out at him with his left hand. His punch missed, but the knife opened a long cut along the inside of his arm.

And then Billy loomed up behind the assassin, both hands locked together as she swung at the back of his head, the metal-studded greeves she was wearing on her forearms beneath her dress cracking into the back of his skull, propelling him forward . . . into the tiny pistol that

127

Senga had produced. The man toppled against Senga as she pulled the trigger, the force of the blow punching him away . . . and Colin Holdstock put two bullets into his crumpling body.

In the long second's silence that followed the two tremendous explosions, before the screams began, before the waiters, members of the band and even some of the guests produced weapons, Colin Holdstock looked down at the body on the floor, the back of its skull caved in, the bullet hole high in its chest and the two larger holes directly below it, and murmured into the unnatural stillness, 'Christ, what a mess!'

CHAPTER THIRTEEN

It was close to dawn before Colin Holdstock concluded that there was nothing to be gained by holding the guests for further questioning. Everyone present, including the hotel staff and management, had been questioned, but with little success. No one had seen the young man enter, no one knew who he was. Senga Lundy, Tilly Cusack and Billy Fadden had all been questioned at length, but with equally little success, and they had been allowed to leave just as the first glimmers of dawn were breaking over the city. On the drive back to the house in Mayfair they were accompanied by Rutgar von Mann, who had had the long gash in his arm inexpertly bound with a torn tablecloth but who had refused medical aid. The cloth was now stained a deep, purplish red and the young man was ashen-faced and in obvious pain, although he attempted to make light of the wound.

'I was scratched once in a duel when I was younger, and it hurt far worse than this.'

'Where were you wounded?' Senga asked without interest, looking out into the grey dawn, still shaken by the night's events.

Von Mann hesitated. 'Well, I'm not sure I should tell a lady . . .'

'I'm not feeling very ladylike tonight . . . today . . . this morning,' she said wearily.

'In the posterior.'

'I beg your pardon?' she asked, looking at him in surprise, wondering if she had heard correctly.

The German nodded again. 'In the posterior.' He looked affronted as Senga, followed by the two older women, burst into laughter. 'It was very painful.'

'I'm sure it was.' She leaned forward in the back of the Daimler until her face was quite close to his. 'But tell me, how did you manage to be wounded in the . . . well, where you were wounded?'

'I sat on a glass,' he said solemnly.

Senga burst out laughing again. 'But I thought you were duelling?'

'We were. In a tavern, in the Black Forest. It was raining outside so we chose to fight indoors. My adversary forced me back and I sat down on a table . . . but there was a glass under me. It broke . . .' he grimaced. 'Removing the glass splinters was most painful.'

'Who won the duel?' she asked, eyes sparkling.

'My opponent. He drew first blood!'

'Patrick!'

Patrick Lundy came forward and wrapped his arms around his sister, squeezing her tightly, without saying anything. He didn't need to.

When von Mann stepped into the sitting room, Patrick gently disentangled himself from his sister and held out his hand to the German. 'You saved my sister's life tonight,' he said quietly. 'I am indebted to you, Sir.'

'Your sister seemed perfectly capable of saving her own life,' von Mann said easily.

'I was there,' Patrick said firmly. 'I saw you move to block the first blow. If you hadn't been there, she wouldn't have had the time to get off her shot.' He turned to Billy as she stepped into the room, talking quietly to Tilly Cusack. 'And you, Billy, you were magnificent.'

But the big Scotswoman made a disgusted face. 'No, I wasn't. If I'd been doing my job right, I'd never have allowed him to get close.'

While they were speaking, Tilly crossed to the fireplace and pulled the long, tasselled cord. Moments later, Martha

Tilke appeared. 'Ma'am?'

'Tea for everyone . . .?' she looked around the room for confirmation and, when no one contradicted her, nodded at the woman again, 'Tea . . . and then some breakfast in a little while.'

'And some bandages, and whatever else you have in the way of a medicine chest,' Patrick added, touching von Mann's wounded arm gently. He looked at the German. 'I'll clean it for you; I've had a little experience with wounds.' He looked quickly at Martha Tilke. 'If you would be so kind as to send whatever you have up to the bathroom as quickly as possible.'

'Immediately, Master Patrick.'

'You are related to Senga . . .?' the German asked cautiously, looking at Patrick. Although the man had called Senga his sister, there didn't seem to be a family resemblance between the two, and the man looked to be about the right age for a husband. Perhaps his poor understanding of the language . . .?

'I am Senga's brother . . . well, half-brother would be more the truth.' And then he smiled quickly. 'But of course, I have not introduced myself. I am Patrick Lundy.'

'Rutgar von Mann at your service,' the German said quickly.

'Well, you certainly were tonight.' He indicated the open door with his right hand. 'Shall we? I want to take a look at that arm of yours before you lose too much blood. It must be painful.'

'It is a little,' the younger man confessed. He followed Patrick out into the hall, leaving the three women staring after them. 'I would like to know what is going on,' he said quietly to Patrick's retreating back.

Patrick glanced over his shoulder, but said nothing. He moved resolutely towards the stairs and hurried up them, shrugging slightly. The German followed.

Patrick led him down the first-floor landing to the bathroom at the end of the corridor. This was Katherine

Lundy's guest bathroom, incorporating the latest in design and convenience, including a French bidet which either amused or scandalised. The windowless bathroom had been decorated in simple white and silver and one wall was entirely mirrored. The overall impression was of space, but with the electric lights sparkling off the tiles and mirrors the room was chill. Patrick found he still preferred the older, slightly antiquated bathroom that he and Senga had used which was on the next floor up.

In the cold, reflected light, Rutgar's face looked even paler, the blood on the bandage on his arm sharper. Patrick came around behind him and eased off his ruined dinner-jacket. As he surveyed the shredded sleeve, Patrick murmured. 'We shall, of course, replace the suit – and the shirt,' he added, clucking as he quickly undid von Mann's bow-tie and proceeded to slip open the buttons on his silk shirt. Rutgar's left forearm was completely bloodied, and as he had held the arm across his chest the silk had sponged up the blood with the result that the front of his shirt was completely sodden.

There was a tap on the door and Miss Tilke stepped in. She gasped when she saw the ragged wound along Rutgar's forearm, which ran almost from the wristbone to elbow. The skin was puffy and swollen, the edges of the wound already purpling.

'It's nasty, but not fatal,' Patrick said almost absently, turning Rutgar's arm slightly to examine the wound in a better light.

'I've brought some bandages and gauze, some alcohol, and iodine. That's all we have in the house.'

'It's enough. I've treated worse with less. I'll need some towels,' he added. When Martha Tilke disappeared, Patrick looked into von Mann's eyes. 'Now, I could lie to you and say this would not hurt . . .'

'I know it's going to hurt,' the German said with a smile.

'I'm going to clean out the wound, first with hot water, then with alcohol – and that will hurt – and then I'm going to dress it. All right?'

'On one condition.'

Patrick looked up at him.

'I would like to know the reason why someone should attempt to stab your charming sister.'

'It's a long story,' Patrick said tiredly.

'I'm not going anywhere.'

'This has changed everything,' Tilly said forcefully. 'I knew there was danger. I mean, we were expecting danger, but not this, not this way; an open attack like this is absolute madness.'

Billy sipped her whisky. 'It wasn't meant to be an attack in the open. If it hadn't been for that German, you'd be dead or badly wounded now,' she said, looking at Senga who was sitting huddled before the unlit fire, a wave of reaction having left her suddenly exhausted. 'When I spotted the man, he was moving through the crowd towards Senga and von Mann. I think he was going to try and cut in on the dance, and then sweep Senga around to some dark or secluded spot, stab her, possibly even call out that she had fainted and then slip away in the darkness.'

'How did he get in?' Senga asked numbly. 'I thought this event was by invitation only.'

'That's something we will need to look at,' Tilly said, 'but there were so many people there tonight it would not have been too difficult. We're just blessed that he failed.' She looked at Billy. 'What went wrong; how did he slip up?'

Billy shrugged. 'I don't know. I don't think he was used to working in that type of crowd. Although he was dressed in suitable clothes. I looked at his hands and they were the hands of a working man. When I spotted him, he looked just a little too determined, a little too fixed on his target as he moved through the crowd. On a street that sort of determination might have gone unnoticed, but not in a crowded ballroom. I fancy Holdstock spotted him in the same way. But whatever happened, only the German was there to give us the few seconds we needed to get to him.'

'Did I kill him?' Senga asked suddenly.

'Does it matter?' Billy shrugged.

'It does to me.'

'I fancy that I killed him,' Billy said gently. She rolled back the sleeves of her gown and then undid the buckles on the metal-studded, leather greeves on her forearms. Beneath the greeve on the left arm, her flesh was bruised black and blue. 'I hit him hard enough to hurt. The back of his head was like jelly when I was finished. I fancy he was dead before he fell on to that little gun of yours. But, whatever the case, Holdstock certainly finished him off with his two shots.'

'What will happen now?' Senga asked.

Billy shrugged. 'I don't know. It's a case for the lawyers at this stage. We have witnesses – including the police themselves – who will swear that he attacked you. You will have to answer how you came to be in the possession of a gun, but we can claim that you had been receiving death threats and we can cite the attack the other day as an example. They may try to pin a manslaughter charge on you or me, but it will not stick.

'The police will interview you,' Billy continued, watching Senga intently, 'and I don't mean a repetition of the questions they asked this evening, I'm talking about an intensive series of interrogations by a number of officers. This is the opportunity they have been waiting for. They will probably interview you here in the first place, and then bring you down to the station and interview you there also. You are entitled to take your lawyer with you, and I would suggest you do. I imagine a woman like your mother has a tame laywer somewhere. I think it would be best to contact him now and acquaint him with the facts. They will ask you the same questions again and again, in a hundred different ways. All you have to do is to ensure that you give them the same answer every time.'

'Will there be another attempt?' Senga asked softly.

'I can almost guarantee that.'

Less than two miles away, in a quiet French restaurant off

134

Curzon Street, a waiter handed a note to a small party of grim-faced men who had eaten their expensive meal without any obvious enjoyment. There was an air of respectability about the seven men, and the waiter, who often amused himself by attempting to guess the occupations or positions of the diners, had decided that these were bankers or stockbrokers. One, the small, ill-shaven man at the end of the table, was a police officer; he knew that for a certainty.

The head of the table, who had the demeanour and manners of a statesman, read the note, folded it and dropped it into the ashtray. He touched the edge with the tip of his glowing cigar and then waited until the single page blackened and snapped into flames. When it was completely consumed, he broke up the pieces with the end of a burnt-out match.

The six men sitting around the table regarded him with various expressions of expectation or dread. When he spoke, his voice was low, scarcely above a whisper, his intonation correct and precise.

'Failure,' he said simply, and then looked at the ill-shaven man. 'We will have to speak more of this. Some of your men were involved in the incident; it is a pity I was not informed, we might have been able to use our contact.' He looked at the other men around the table. 'This matter has now assumed a certain urgency.'

'Patrick, we've got to get Senga away from here,' Tilly said when the two men returned to the room.

Patrick nodded. 'I know. I've just been discussing it with Rutgar.'

Tilly stopped and looked at the German. Patrick smiled at the expression on her face. 'I've told him,' he said.

'Everything?' she asked in astonishment.

'I think that the man has a right to know why he's been wounded, don't you?'

Tilly could only nod dumbly.

'I am not a fool, Madam,' von Mann said quietly. 'I

guessed there was something awry when the police appeared in such numbers, and armed too.'

'You don't seem to be too shocked to find your hostess is wanted by the police,' Senga murmured.

Von Mann bowed slightly. 'Your mother and my father were once acquainted. I must admit that he told me a little of their infrequent association down through the years, both in Dublin and here, and what he did not tell me I guessed or inferred. So, I am not surprised. I am surprised,' he added in a slightly different tone of voice, looking at Senga, 'why these people should want to kill *you*. Patently, you have no association with your mother, you are not involved in her business, or her machinations.'

But it was Billy who answered. 'They want to kill Senga as a warning to her mother, a way of frightening her.'

Rutgar von Mann shook his head. 'The logic of it escapes me. Surely if they kill the daughter, the mother will be all the more determined to avenge herself on them?'

Patrick slapped him lightly on the back. 'People like these don't think so logically.'

The window exploded inwards.

Billy launched herself across the room, toppling Senga and chair on to the floor. Patrick's shove sent von Mann staggering to the carpet, and he caught Tilly around the waist, tumbling her to the carpet beside von Mann. The young German's eyes were sparkling. 'I haven't had this much fun since my student days.'

In the long silence that followed, the sounds of a scuffle outside were clearly audible. Patrick crept to the window and stood up with his back flush to the wall, a large pistol in his hand. He risked a quick glance outside. Three shadowed figures were grappling with a fourth. As Patrick watched, another figure came up out of the shadows and joined the fray, wielding a short stick. Seconds later the four men dragged off a comatose figure, heading towards the park. Patrick guessed they were members of the London branch of the Irish Republican Army posted there to keep a watchful eye on the house.

He turned back to the room to find Tilly unwrapping a sheet of paper from around a half-brick. 'What does it say?' he asked, tucking the gun back into the waistband of his trousers, ' "Death to all" or "You are going to die"? This type of message is usually unimaginative and to the point.'

' "We will kill you",' Tilly read slowly. 'It's been written in heavy, black pencil.'

Patrick took the crumpled sheet from her and tilted it slightly. 'The writing is crude, but the letters are properly formed.' He looked at his sister and attempted a smile, which failed. Billy had her arm wrapped around the young woman's shoulders, and Patrick guessed that that was the only reason she was standing. Too much had happened too soon. Sometimes he forgot that she was still only a young woman, wise perhaps beyond her years, self-possessed and confident most of the time, capable of putting up a brave front and staring down even the most lecherous of her fellow students back in Dublin. But this wasn't some drunken lout with lust on his mind. Those she could deal with. But a faceless, formless foe, threatening her for no good reason, except she was Katherine Lundy's daughter, this was out of his hands.

'You're taking a holiday, little sister. Starting immediately. Go upstairs and pack. You too, Billy, if you're still interested in working with us.'

'I don't quit just because things get a little rough.'

Patrick looked back at his sister. 'I'll arrange tickets for the two of you as soon as the station opens. You're for Dover and then Calais, and then perhaps Rome . . .'

'Paris,' von Mann said quickly.

Everyone turned to look at him. The German blushed slightly. 'I was to go to Paris at the end of the week. I could always bring it forward slightly. You could be my guests . . .'

'We couldn't think of it,' Senga said quickly. 'It is a kind and generous offer, but because of me you were very nearly killed tonight.'

'Don't be so hasty, Senga,' Patrick murmured.

'We cannot intrude,' she protested firmly.

'But it is not an intrusion. I would be honoured. I insist.'

Senga shook her head.

'I would take it as the gravest insult if you were to refuse. You said yourself you were in my debt this evening. Let me – what is the phrase? – call in that debt. I insist that you accompany me to Paris.'

Senga looked at both Patrick and Billy and they nodded. Only Tilly looked doubtful. 'Well, if you insist.'

CHAPTER FOURTEEN

It was a few minutes to seven when Tilly Cusack leaned forward and tapped on the glass partition separating her from the driver of the gleaming silver-and-black Daimler. Without turning around, he indicated to the left and pulled in against the kerb of Parliament Square. The man deliberately looked to the right, towards the Houses of Parliament, grey, damp and indistinct in the early morning mist. It was none of his business whom his passenger was meeting. He saw a vague shape materialise out of the misty air and moments later the back door opened and closed again almost immediately. Even through the partition that separated him from his passengers, he could smell the heavy, faintly cloying odour of damp clothes and unwashed humanity. There was a tap on the window and he obediently turned the long car around by the Guildhall, and drove sedately down an almost deserted Victoria Street.

Maybe it was time he started to look for another position. Working for Mrs Lundy had been peculiar enough, what with her strange rules and regulations and her curious visiting hours, but this new woman, Mrs Cusack, now she was a rum cove altogether. He had done a few funny runs for her at odd hours and to even odder places, but he drew the line at picking up what smelt like a tramp at seven o'clock in the morning.

But good positions were hard to find . . . and anyway, what did you expect from your upper classes; they were all mad as hatters.

'Everything has gone sour,' Tilly Cusack said, breathing through her mouth, the stench catching at the back of her throat, making her eyes water. 'I think you had better come back.'

The figure in the foul rags sitting beside her – incongruous on the leather seats – stirred angrily. 'That is impossible,' Katherine Lundy spat.

'There was an attempt on Senga's life last night,' Tilly said evenly. 'An assassin – a professional we think – with a knife. Only blind chance saved her.'

'She has Billy,' Katherine snapped.

'She has, but last night it nearly wasn't enough.'

Katherine turned to glare at Tilly. 'Let that Scotswoman know that if anything happens to Senga, I'll personally cut her throat! She's costing enough; let her earn her keep.'

'I see your humour hasn't improved any,' Tilly remarked.

'Nor would yours, living as I've been.' Katherine huddled deeper into the rags, seemingly inured to the foul odour. She was living off the streets, one of the countless thousands of homeless Britons who had congregated in London in the years following the last months of the Great War. The industry that had serviced the war effort had provided many jobs, taking many from the unemployment lists – and giving them back again when the war was done. Jobs were now scarce again, and many thousands of men and women and not a few children lived beneath the London bridges or along the Embankment or huddled in the parks or cemeteries, coming out during the day to scavenge and beg for food or money. Katherine Lundy had become part of this impoverished and homeless army of nameless people. And, although she did not lack for money, she had been forced to use what she had sparingly, since opportunities for contact with Tilly Cusack were becoming fewer and fewer, especially since the house in Mayfair was under such scrutiny. She had thought about presenting herself at one of her brothels, but she guessed –

140

rightly as she had discovered – that they too were under observation. Also, because she had always operated in disguise, no one in the houses – with the exception of the managers – actually knew her face. And she had little reason to trust them in any case.

Almost as if she had been reading her thoughts, Tilly passed her across another bundle of coins. 'I don't know when I'm going to get the chance to speak to you again.'

'Well, I'll be at the square about this time every morning. If you're not there by the time the clock strikes the hour, I'll head on.'

'How do you feel?'

Katherine shrugged. 'How do you think I feel? I'm filthy and I'd kill for a dry bed. Why, how do I look?' she asked bitterly.

'Actually, aside for a little dirt, you look to be in good shape.'

Katherine Lundy snorted rudely and wiped her nose across her sleeve. The weeks on the street had stripped Katherine of a lot of her excess flesh. The purpling bags were gone from beneath her eyes, revealing her strong, high cheekbones. The lines around her eyes and mouth were still there, etched deep now and ingrained with dirt, but without the puffy flesh around them they lent a certain character to her face, and Tilly saw for the first time in many years a hint of the beauty she had recognised when she had first encountered the pregnant servant girl on Christmas Eve a lifetime ago.

'I'm sending Senga away,' Tilly said evenly, watching Katherine hiding the money about her person.

Katherine Lundy pulled strands of ragged, filthy hair off her face and stared at her, but said nothing.

'It's become too dangerous here,' Tilly continued quickly. 'The Fête last night was a disaster, and I'm sure the newspapers will be full of the attack and its consequences.'

'What happened to the would-be assassin?'

Tilly's teeth flashed in a flicker of a smile. 'Billy stove

141

his head in and Senga shot him – and then the police shot him again for good measure.'

Katherine's thin lips curled in a smile. 'So he's dead.'

'Very.'

'They'll try again,' she said.

'So they've told us.' She smiled at Katherine's expression. 'A brick through the front window this morning, with a message: "We will kill you." There was another attempt a few days ago on the steps of the house. You've crossed them, Katherine, and now they're going to make you pay for it.' She looked out the window for a moment and then turned to look back at Katherine. 'Is there any way you could . . . apologise?' she suggested diffidently.

Katherine laughed delightedly. 'None. And even if I wanted to, I think it's too late for that in any case. All I can do now is to lie low and attempt to get the jewels. Once I have them I can use them as a bargaining lever with . . . well, with a lot of people on both sides of the legal fence. Once I have the stones all this will stop.'

'How do you know? How can you guarantee that?' Tilly asked bitterly.

'There is a series of letters and a signed confession which goes with the jewels. Once certain people know I have that, I'll guarantee that they will lose interest in me.'

'You're talking about blackmail,' Tilly said coldly.

'No. I'm talking about speaking to certain influential people and asking them simply as a favour to me to do something about this constant police harassment, and especially Holdstock. Once that thorn in my side has been removed, I might suggest that these same influential people might like to look more closely at some of my competitors. By the time I'm finished with them, they'll be so busy fighting for their lives that they'll have little enough time left to annoy me.'

After this tirade both women sat in silence, before Tilly finally asked, 'How long, Katherine? How much longer do we have to keep up this charade?'

'As long as is necessary,' Katherine snapped.

142

'You're playing with your daughter's life here,' Tilly reminded her.

'I'm playing with my own life too,' Katherine muttered.

'At least you had a choice.'

Katherine smiled coldly. 'That's where you're wrong, Tilly Cusack. I had no choice at all.'

Senga Lundy sank deeper into the too-hot bath, gritting her teeth against the sting of the water, breathing in the hot, damp air, sweat beading her face. She rested her head against a towel and closed her eyes, willing herself to relax but failing. The events of the past few hours were far too vivid.

The reaction and resultant fear and doubts were gone now, replaced by a cold anger. It was primarily directed towards her mother, but she knew that she herself should bear her share of the responsibility. She had been stupid. She had broken her own cardinal rule: she had been trusting.

She had come to England voluntarily, and while she hadn't known the degree of danger she had been in she should have suspected a trap. But she had allowed herself to be lulled into a false sense of security; had allowed herself to think that her mother had changed, that the years had mellowed her. For a while there, Senga had actually felt sorry for the woman, felt guilty for her own feelings towards her mother.

And Tilly too was guilty. Tilly Cusack had been the lure that had brought both Patrick and herself from Dublin, and Senga couldn't believe that the woman didn't know the true extent of the danger.

She wasn't a coward; she had learned to rely on her own resources at an early age, and she wasn't stupid. There was no point in staying in London; she was pragmatic enough to realise that if *they* – the invisible they – wanted her dead badly enough, then there was absolutely nothing she could do to prevent it. And no amount of bodyguards would be able to protect her. So, she would run away and possibly live to fight another . . .

She was going to Paris, a city that held nothing but evil memories for her, where she would wait until either the authorities or her former colleagues had caught up with Katherine Lundy. Or her mother had sorted out the mess she was in. She wondered how long she'd have to stay in Paris.

Senga sat up suddenly, water cascading off her shoulders and breasts. She suddenly realised that she would probably only be able to return home when her mother was dead!

Inspector Colin Holdstock read through the type-written report on his desk. Taking into account that less than ten hours had elapsed since the attack and killing, the report was susbstantial enough.

He skimmed through the reports of the twelve officers who had been present; Thinn had provided a synopsis of all their reports on a single sheet of paper, and Holdstock read through this slowly. But in effect it said nothing. Three of the men had seen the man making his way towards Katherine Lundy's daughter, and of those only one of them had actually seen him produce the knife. Holdstock slipped his own report in along with the rest. At least his evidence was unequivocal. He had clearly seen the assassin produce the knife and stab at the young woman.

He turned to the report on the dead man. But that told him nothing. He was a wharf-rat, an East End boy, twenty-seven years old. The man was a known leg-breaker, with a long list of previous convictions for assault, robbery with violence, extracting money with menaces; two manslaughter charges against him had been dropped because of lack of evidence – in both cases the witnesses had either changed their testimony or disappeared. His preferred weapon was a knife.

The autopsy report was much more interesting. Holdstock had seen the big, red-haired Scottish woman strike the man from behind, driving him forward into

144

Senga Lundy. He had initially thought that she had some-how managed to push him off her, and then he had shot him. That's what it had looked like. However, the truth was rather different. The man's skull had been crushed by a blow from a blunt object . . . Holdstock frowned. He didn't think the Scottish woman had been holding any-thing, but obviously she had. A baton, an iron bar perhaps? That blow had been enough to kill him. Then there was the single .22 bullet wound in the man's chest. Fired at very close quarters, the man's clothing and flesh had been scorched by the powder burns. He made a note to question Senga Lundy about possessing the weapon; owning the gun was not, in itself, illegal, nor was the manner of its use – self-defence – but the very fact that she had brought a gun to such an event made him curious. He looked back to his report; there were his own two bullet wounds in the man.

He smiled mirthlessly. A slight case of overkill.

Well, at least he had the evidence now to bring both women in on charges of manslaughter; it could be claimed – successfully too – that it was nothing more than self-defence, but it would be enough for him to hold them, and perhaps enough for him to get a warrant to search the house. So the night hadn't been wasted after all.

Colin Holdstock glanced up at the clock: not quite half-past eight. Time for a little breakfast and then he'd apply for that warrant.

Senga dressed in the black outfit that had been altered to fit her and then sat on the edge of the bed sorting through the remainder of the clothes, trying to decide what she was going to need. A single suitcase was all Billy and Patrick had advised. The tiny Derringer her brother had given her was tucked inside her garter and the larger pistol which she had brought over with her from Ireland was on the bed beside her. Two hat pins, one six inches, the other nine, had been stabbed into the rim of her hat. What every best-dressed young woman was wearing this year, she mused. She should be out enjoying her youth, dancing, partying, drinking, smoking – not armed to the teeth and prepared to flee for her life.

There was a tap on the door and Billy ducked her head in. 'All set, lass?' She sounded in such good humour that Senga had to smile.

'As ready as I'll ever be, I suppose.'

'Take only what you need for the crossing and the journey to Paris. You can buy what you need there.'

Senga stood and began to fold a few items of underwear into the suitcase. 'Have you ever been to Paris?' she asked, looking at Billy.

The big woman crossed the room and began to fold the clothes, handing them to Senga to pack. 'I've been there on three occasions,' she said with a grin. 'And I loved it. It is a marvellous city, a beautiful city.'

'Were you on business?'

'Of course.' Billy looked surprised that anyone would have thought that she would have gone to Paris for any other reason. 'All three occasions were bodyguard jobs; two occasions I was minding children – I was a sort of extreme nanny, I suppose, and the last time, four years ago, I was looking after a young lady, not dissimilar to yourself.'

'I hope her predicament wasn't as serious as mine,' Senga said, closing the suitcase and struggling to snap the locks.

Billy leaned over and put her weight on the case. The locks closed with ease. 'No, nothing so serious. She had rejected the advances of a young man whom the family found to be entirely unsuitable – and I must admit, I found him somewhat distasteful myself. Anyway, he had made threatening noises about what he would do to the girl, and because he had something of an evil reputation it was decided she should have a little holiday in Paris. They asked me to go with her. We had a delightful time,' she said, smiling fondly. 'She was a lovely girl. Married now, with two small children. I'm godmother to her youngest,' she added in an aside.

'But did the ex-beau come looking for her?' Senga asked quickly.

'Oh yes.' Billy stood up, swinging the heavy suitcase with ease.

'And?' Senga demanded.

'And I broke his legs,' Billy said with a humourless smile. 'Both of them. Well, he was running around after us, and ruining a very pleasant holiday,' she added, by way of explanation.

There were six men waiting in the sitting room when Senga, followed by Billy, entered. They all came to their feet together, and she was reaching for the heavy pistol in her handbag when Patrick looked up from his chair by the unlit fire. 'It's all right, they're with me. Or you, rather.' He stood up, stretching, and Senga could see the lines of exhaustion in his face. 'Meet your guard of honour, sister.' He looked over at Billy. 'No offence intended.'

'None taken. I'm glad they're here. I was wondering how we were going to make it to the station.'

'Well now, these lads'll take care of you. I won't give you their names, for obvious reasons, and I know they have no interest in yours.'

'Good morning, Gentleman,' Senga said, stepping forward. 'Thank you for agreeing to look after me,' she said simply.

The six men wished her good morning in turn, and she thought she identified at least two Irish accents, although the rest were London, and one was disconcertingly Italian. Patrick handed Billy a large envelope. 'Tickets for the train and boat, and then tickets to Paris. There're some francs – it's all I could raise at such short notice, but I'll wire you some more as soon as I can.' He looked at Senga. 'If you need to get in contact with me, you can send a message to the bookshop on the Charing Cross Road. You know the one.'

'I do.'

Patrick kissed his sister quickly on the cheek and then held her closely. 'Take care, my love. I'll sort out this

147

mess, or better still, find our mother and get *her* to sort it out. I'll have you home as quickly as possible.'

'You take care of yourself. This isn't Ireland, you haven't got the contacts you have over there.'

'I know. I'll take care, I always do. I've survived this long.'

'But then you knew what you were up against. Our beloved mother has managed to turn every hand against her. Be careful.'

Patrick gently eased Senga towards Billy. 'Take care of her for me.'

'I will.'

'Now,' he looked around the room, 'Gentlemen, if you're all ready.'

Guns appeared – pistols and sawn-off shot-guns – and then vanished again just as quickly.

'I think we'll use the back door, if you don't mind. We don't want to startle the neighbours, do we?'

'Where's Tilly?' Senga asked suddenly, realising that she hadn't seen the woman.

Patrick shrugged. 'She went out when we had finished speaking earlier this morning. She was going to take Rutgar back to his hotel. Perhaps she stayed for breakfast.'

'Then she doesn't know I'm leaving right now?'

Patrick smiled coldly. 'I don't think she imagined events would move along with such rapidity.'

Billy's smile echoed Patrick's. 'Perhaps that's not such a bad thing, eh?'

'Perhaps not,' Patrick agreed.

The six men, with the two women in their midst, had been gone about ten minutes when a solid hammering on the front door brought Martha Tilke scurrying down the long, polished hall. Although she had a very good idea just whom she would be opening it to, she still managed to feign surprise when she discovered that it was Colin Holdstock and Malachi Thinn, along with a half-dozen uniformed police officers.

He handed her a single sheet of heavy paper. 'We have a warrant to search this house and to arrest Miss Senga Lundy and Miss Willimena Fadden for questioning.'

'I fear they're both in bed, officer,' Martha Tilke said in a thick, German accent. 'They had a rather late night last night.'

Holdstock looked at her closely, catching the hint of mockery in her voice even through the accent. He himself hadn't been to bed for the past twenty-four hours – and looked it.

'Well then, bring them down. We'll wait,' he snapped.

Martha Tilke turned away to hide the smile.

Across the road, beneath the shelter of the dripping trees, Patrick Lundy smiled broadly and then, tucking his hands into his pockets, turned to stroll down to Park Lane. Martha Tilke would keep them waiting as long as possible before she announced that the two women had vanished and that their beds hadn't been slept in. She would also discover the ransom note pinned to Senga's pillow. If it did nothing else it would help confuse the police. Patrick chuckled; he wondered what Holdstock's expression would be when he discovered that the birds had flown the coop.

CHAPTER FIFTEEN

'I love Paris,' Billy said enthusiastically. She leaned both elbows on the balcony and looked down over the bustling street. It was a bright, sunny day with just the faintest nip in the air. High, fleecy clouds scudded across the Parisian sky, and the horizon was smudged with darker clouds, promising rain later. The occasional breeze was damp and chill, but in the sunshine, it felt more like summer than late March.

Senga joined her at the wrought-iron rail, smiling at the woman's obvious good humour. 'I think you must have fallen in love here,' she said slyly.

'Oh, but I did,' Billy said seriously. 'It must be – what? – ten years ago now. But you know something,' she glanced sidelong at Senga, 'I still remember it as if it was yesterday. And I don't think I was ever happier.'

'What happened?'

'My business here finished abruptly and I returned to London. Oh, we corresponded for a while . . . and then that petered out. You know how it is.'

Senga nodded sympathically, although she didn't 'know how it was'. She was twenty-one now, and she had never been in love. Ironically, the closest she had come had been in Paris, back in 1921, when she had been courted by Jean Michel Hugo. She had been thirteen years old at the time, innocent and naive to an almost frightening degree, having run away from that terrible school in Switzerland. Looking back on it, she realised she had been flattered by the attention this worldly, suave man had paid her. He had taken her to the best restaurants, bought her fine clothes, taken her to the theatre . . . but of course, he had wanted payment in return. And when she had refused, his rage had been terrible. Patrick had saved her then, but it had taught her a valuable lesson about men, and even now in college in Dublin she had a reputation for being stand-offish. In truth, Senga Lundy was a little afraid of men.

'Do you know Paris well?' she asked.

'I know Paris well,' Billy smiled, 'and I know the sleezy parts particularly well.'

Senga slipped her arm through Billy's. 'Why don't you show me Paris then?'

'Well . . ,' Billy hedged. Patrick's instructions had been explicit: not to leave the hotel room until Graf Rutgar von Mann arrived to take them under his wing. 'Your brother did say . . .' she began, unenthusiastically.

'My brother is in London now, and Patrick – contrary to what you might think – is not my keeper. The last time I was in this city, I was thirteen, hardly old enough to appreciate it, and my companion's idea of the sights included numerous bars, restaurants and music halls. As it turned out, all he was interested in was me.'

'You win,' Billy grinned. 'You tell me about your last visit here, and I'll tell you about Paris.' She crossed the room into the small, adjoining bedroom she was using. Senga leaned in the doorway and watched her strap the studded, leather greeves on to her forearms and then slide the metal plates over the palms of her hands. A pair of soft, leather gloves concealed the cupped plates. She tucked a cosh – a flexible leather strap, weighted at one end with a ball of lead – into her waistband, and then stood up, smiling broadly, reaching for her coat. 'I'm ready.'

Shaking her head, Senga stepped away from the door and reached for her own coat and bag. The bulk of the pistol was a comforting weight in the bag. But what she found even more terrifying was that she didn't even think it peculiar any more.

Her mother had a lot to answer for.

*

'When were you last in Paris?' Senga asked, as they made their way out through the ornate foyer of the small hotel off the Rue de l'Odeon.

'Two years ago,' Billy said, surprising her. 'I was here in May 1927 when Charles Lindbergh, the aviator, landed out at Le Bourget.'

Senga's eyes widened in astonishment. 'But I read about that! Did you meet him?' she asked excitedly.

Billy patted her hand and gently turned her to the right. She stopped outside a bookshop. 'I only saw him briefly when he appeared on the balcony of the Hotel de Ville . . .' Billy said, and then suddenly realised that Senga was no longer paying any attention to her. The young woman was staring intently into the cluttered window of the bookshop, and then she suddenly stepped back into the street, and craned upwards to look at the name over the high windows.

'Number Twelve, Rue de l'Odeon, Shakespeare & Co,' she said excitedly. 'I knew it.'

'It is a very famous bookshop,' Billy said, with a smile. 'I believe I once saw Mr James Joyce here,' she added, and then laughed aloud at Senga's astonished expression. 'I told a lie, I didn't. I just wondered if you would recognise the name.'

Senga leaned forward and lowered her voice. 'I saw a copy of *Ulysses* in Dublin. It had been bought here in Paris – in this very shop I shouldn't wonder – and smuggled back into the country.'

Billy reached over and caught her arm, bringing her closer to the window. She tapped the glass with her blunt fingers. 'And what's that, eh?' she asked, pointing to a large, fat, blue, paper-covered book.

'*Ulysses*,' Senga whispered. 'I must have a copy.'

'As you wish. I know Miss Beach slightly,' Billy added, 'I helped eject a difficult customer the last time I was here.'

'Was it someone I'd know, a name I'd recognise?' Senga asked, as Billy opened the door, the bell jangling. 'An author?'

'It was,' Billy said with a wry grin, but would say nothing more.

'They've gone.' Malachi Thinn dropped the large envelope on to Holdstock's scarred desk.

'All of them?' Colin Holdstock looked up wearily.

Thinn hooked his foot around the leg of a chair and dragged it over. 'We've questioned the housekeeper again. Her English is abominable but, you know, I fancy that's an act. I'm getting a constable from down Whitechapel way who speaks German, and I'll have him question her.'

'Have you got anything from her?'

Thinn smiled tightly, his broad face hard. 'She was the housekeeper, that's all, nothing more. She paid no heed to the goings on upstairs – and if that's true, she's unique amongst all the servants I've known.'

Holdstock nodded. 'Usually they've more of a handle on what's going on upstairs than the family.'

'We've a positive identification of the young woman Senga Lundy and the Scottish woman Willimena Fadden on the boat-train to Le Havre. I've contacted the French authorities, but you know where that's going to get us, don't you?'

'Nowhere,' Holdstock said glumly.

Thinn nodded. 'We also have Fadden's record, and a report on her from the Glasgow police.'

'She's a leg-breaker?'

Thinn looked at him in astonishment. 'How did you know?'

Colin Holdstock shrugged. 'I know the type. Male or female, I suppose they're all the same.'

'Never met a female minder before,' Thinn remarked.

'I suppose few people have. That gives her a great advantage.'

Thinn tapped the report with the back of his hand. 'Well worth having a look at her record. The next time I meet her, I'm bringing company.'

Holdstock leafed through the twenty-two-page report.

153

'Now,' he murmured, 'I wonder why someone like Senga Lundy should warrant heavyweight protection like this.' He looked up at Thinn. 'This woman is more than just a minder – this Fadden woman is a bodyguard. And expensive too, I shouldn't wonder.'

'With a couple of killings laid at her door already,' Thinn added.

'Nothing proved though.'

'Evidence is strong.'

'Any word on the whereabouts of the Cusack woman?'

'Nothing. We suspect she may have gone home to Glasgow, or possibly back to Dublin. We're investigating both possibilities.'

'The brother, Patrick Lundy?'

Thinn smiled coldly. 'Now him I wouldn't mind getting my hands on. He's the sort who gets shot escaping from police custody,' he added ominously. Ignoring Holdstock's sharp expression, he continued, 'He's a cold-blooded killer, nothing more.'

'And nothing on the mother, I suppose?'

'Vanished from the face of the earth. I've asked just about everyone I know. If she's on the streets she's keeping a very low profile. But you see, she has the advantage that so few people know what she looks like.'

'Anything on the Crown Jewels?'

'Nothing. If they have been offered for sale it hasn't been through the usual channels.'

Holdstock sighed and ran his fingers through his fine, brown hair. 'This case is getting out of control.' He looked at his assistant. 'I've been asked to send a copy of my report – incorporating all the latest news – to my immediate superior, and I have a feeling that it won't stop with him.' He sank his head. 'It's got more twists than the Ripper case. Do we have any leads?'

The Irish policeman shook his head. 'All the birds have flown.'

'What about that German fellow, what's he doing? No . . . don't tell me, he's vanished too.'

Thinn smiled sardonically. 'Graf Rutgar von Mann has also vanished. He cut short a two-month stay to return home on urgent business. However, we do know that his destination is Paris.'

'I not a gambling man, Thinn, but I'll wager a year's salary that when you find him, you'll find Senga Lundy. She is now a material witness in a crime, who has fled the scene in suspicious circumstances; we have legitimate reason for hauling her back. Can you get us both to Paris on the next train? I think it's time I renewed my acquaintance with Miss Senga Lundy.'

'And I suppose I'm the chump who has to deal with the girlfriend?'

The first time Senga Lundy saw two men walking arm-in-arm she was shocked, and had just about convinced herself that it was nothing more than an accident when she saw another couple, and then a third, only this time one of the men was dressed as a woman! She immediately thought of a fancy-dress ball or a similar event, but her instinct told her that it was otherwise. She was sitting at a roadside café in Montparnasse with Billy, drinking *café-au-lait* and watching the world go by. A copy of *Ulysses* lay wrapped in Shakespeare & Co's discreet brown wrapper on the table beside her. She leaned over and murmured in Billy's ear. 'They *are* two men?'

Billy nodded. 'Aye, and there's two more over there, and if you look over to your left you'll see two women sitting together.'

Senga glanced around quickly and then looked away. 'Well, I don't see anything wrong with that . . .' she began, and then realised that one of the women was rubbing the other's breast with the back of her hand where it brushed against the table.

'This is the Bohemian corner,' Billy explained. 'Most of the people around her are artists of one sort or another, writers, musicians, singers, dancers, models, whatever. People almost expect them to be different, and therefore most of them are. The visitors would be most disappointed if they found only ordinary everyday folk up here. The people who live here are tolerant of others, accepting them for what they are, not what they look like, or how they act. Here, you will often find couples composed of just men or women, and it is quite accepted. No one passes any comment on it.'

'But I don't understand . . .' she whispered, glancing covertly at the two women, whose heads were now so close together that their foreheads were actually touching. She found it easy to accept the two women sitting closely together – that was fine, but there was something not quite right about the two men sitting at the table opposite, hand in hand, gazing into one another's eyes. She found it just a little disturbing.

'They are lovers,' Billy said, shocking her. 'The women are what are called Sapphic lovers – lesbian is the correct term, I believe – and the men are homosexuals.'

'I think that's dis . . .' Senga began in a shocked whisper, but Billy held up a gloved hand, silencing her.

'Judge not, lest you too be judged. Let he who is without sin cast the first stone. You're only condemning what you don't understand.'

'Do you?'

Billy stared at her with an intensity that Senga found discomforting. 'Yes,' she said very quietly, 'I think I do.'

'But do they sleep together?' she asked.

'They live together, they sleep together, they make love together,' Billy shrugged. 'Their relationship is much the same as any ordinary couple, except that here the couple is made up of two women – or two men – in a situation normally taken by a man and a woman.'

'I can understand men living with other men, or women sharing rooms or a house with other women, and I can even accept sleeping with another woman, but actually making love to another woman . . . I'm not sure I can accept that.'

'Why not?' Billy asked, her eyes on Senga's face, her gaze challenging.

'I just . . . I just cannot comprehend it.'

'You mean you don't understand it,' Billy gently corrected her.

'Yes, I suppose so.'

Billy sipped her cold coffee, her eyes shifting through the crowds, picking out the cruising sharks, the thieves, the pickpockets, the prostitutes – both male and female – the pimps. She was looking for someone doing anything out of the ordinary, someone perhaps paying them too much attention. 'The vast majority of men and women are born with a liking for the opposite sex; some have a liking for their own, and then there are some poor souls who are born trapped in the wrong body . . . a man who only feels comfortable whilst dressed as a woman, a woman who dresses as a man and prefers the company of shy, submissive females. These people are attracted towards their own sex by nature; it is something they can do little about, and often when they deny their natures it destroys them.

'And then there are others – women especially – who feel more comfortable, and therefore safer, associating with other women.'

'Why?' Senga asked, an idea beginning to form at the back of her mind.

'Mostly because they have had a bad experience with a man or men. It might have been a father, a brother, boyfriend, husband . . . but whatever happened, their trust in men has been shaken or destroyed, and for them women are the safe alternative.'

'Was that what happened to you?' Senga asked, her voice a gentle whisper.

'Yes,' Billy said without hesitation. Her colourless eyes settled briefly on Senga's face, and then moved away. 'I saw my father beat my mother, abuse her so badly that she couldn't leave the flat for days afterwards. And I lived in a tenement where men like him were commonplace, the rule rather than the exception. When I left home I swore I would never become involved with a man.' She laughed bitterly. 'And of course, I did, almost as soon as I had arrived in London. Och, but he was a sweet talker, a charmer. He took my virginity in a dirty, little room in a cheap lodging-house off the Old Kent Road. I'd been told that the act between a man and a woman was beautiful. Well, not for me it wasn't. It was dirty and painful.' She paused, and then continued in a different voice, a softer, gentler, sadder voice. 'And when I went back to him some weeks later and told him I was pregnant, he laughed at me, and asked me what I wanted him to do about it.' Her humour abruptly changed and she laughed, but it was a sound completely devoid of humour. 'Well, I made sure he'd never father another child . . . and I made sure that every step he'd take until they laid him in a box would remind him of me.'

'What did you do?'

'I shattered his kneecaps, and then broke a bottle into his groin.' She spoke in such a matter-of-fact tone that it took Senga several seconds to realise what she had said.

'I didn't know you had a child?' Senga said.

'I don't. The pregnancy never made it the full way. Probably just as well,' she added. The big woman stood up and dabbed at her mouth with a napkin. They had no sooner moved away from the seats than they were taken up by a Negro couple, who both spoke French with beautiful, lifting accents.

'We better go,' Billy said, dragging Senga away. 'Von Mann will have a car waiting. And we don't want to keep him waiting, do we?'

CHAPTER SIXTEEN

Senga lay on her bed in her slip, her head resting on her arms, listening to the sounds of Paris through the open window. Her dark eyes were wide and unseeing, the pupils gradually dilating as the evening drew on, the pale ceiling overhead darkening, assuming a gritty greyness and then fading into grainy dusk. With the onset of night, the voices drifting up from the street below changed also, becoming softer, as if couples were now strolling the boulevard rather than the workers and shoppers of earlier in the day. The copy of *Ulysses* she had bought lay on the floor beside the bed. She had read the first page at least three times without making any real sense of it, but she wasn't sure if that was the book's fault or her own sense of unreality. Billy's confession had confused and vaguely upset her – although she couldn't say why. She was bewildered by the whole concept. The term lesbian was one she was only vaguely aware of, having heard it once or twice during her term in finishing school in Switzerland, and even then she hadn't understood it and had been too embarrassed to ask.

Senga sat up in the bed and stared out into the Parisian night. Billy Fadden was a lesbian . . . or was she, she thought suddenly. She had said that she preferred the company of other women, but she didn't say that she slept with them and, given her circumstances, her history and her background, was it any wonder? Perhaps she was reading too much into Billy's statement, reading inferences that weren't there. And she didn't seem to hate men; it was almost as if she had no time for them. In Billy Fadden's world, men occupied a very minor place in the scheme of things.

Had they any place in her own world?

The question left her chilled and shaken.

She threw her legs over the side of the bed and crossed the room to stand in the shadows looking down into the street. She attempted to answer the question as calmly and logically as possible.

She had never had a serious relationship with any man; the only male she was really close to was Patrick, and, even there, their relationship was more like father–daughter than brother–sister. So, there was an obvious lack of reference material. Balanced against that, of course, was her own disinterest in men. Oh, Rutgar was fine; he was an interesting young man, but her feelings went no deeper than that.

Was she, like Billy, a product of her background? She had been brought up in an unnatural environment, surrounded by women, some of whom, she realised now, would have shared Billy's inclination. She had been brought up in a world where men were objects, without personalities, without faces; men who used women and were, in turn, used by them. And surely those same women would have turned to their own kind for solace? What would have been more natural? Of course, she had been very carefully protected from this world, but she had lived in the environment, so surely she would have absorbed some of the attitudes and opinions of the dozen or so women who lived in the house. Surely that would have been inevitable?

Was it any wonder that that world – the twilight world of the brothels and their attendant vices – had claimed both of Katherine Lundy's children. Even Patrick, when he had escaped from their mother, had returned to Dublin and had ended up immersed in that world. Why, he had even married his mother's successor in the Dubin brothel, a women at least ten years older than himself. Was he not, in some strange way, marrying someone who – in his eyes – represented his mother? She smiled savagely; how he would have loved that! Whilst in Trinity College, she had read something of the works of Freud, and, while there was much of his work that she either did not understand or found difficult to accept, she found that a lot of his theories made a strange sort of sense.

Senga smiled into the gloom, wondering what the good doctor would make of the present mess.

It was close to eight when Billy tapped on the door. Senga had slipped into a light doze, in which vague, half-remembered dreams disturbed her. They vanished when she awoke, leaving only an unpleasant memory behind.

'Are you hungry?' Billy asked.

Senga sat up slowly, suddenly self-conscious of her undress, although she had never been so in Billy's presence before. But before she could reply, Billy sat down on the edge of the bed and looked straight into her eyes.

'I'm sorry if what I told you today upset you. It's not something I tell everyone . . . in fact, I think I've only told two other people before this. I just wanted you to know, and to hear it from me rather than from someone else. I need you to trust me; if you learned what I told you from someone else at some later date, it might have destroyed your trust in me, eh?'

Senga nodded dumbly.

'I was employed to take care of you, and that was fine, but I've come to like you . . . and to respect you. And you needn't look so worried: I'm not about to do or say anything that might embarrass either of us. I just wanted to let you know how things stood between us.'

'Thank you. I appreciate it. I'd like to say it won't change our relationship, but I don't know whether it will.'

'That's up to you,' Billy said carefully. 'But I don't think it will, I don't think it should. I think you're a lot

161

like me in many respects,' she said. She stood up and patted Senga's bare leg. 'Now, come on, get dressed; we'll get something to eat, and then I'll show you some of the night-life this city is famous for.'

'I thought we were waiting for Rutgar?' Senga asked.

'We were,' Billy said with a smile, 'but he's late. And you'll learn that you never wait for a man, my dear; make him wait for you.'

'I must say that living rough seems to agree with you.' Tilly Cusack appraised the woman who had sidled up to her on the bridge.

'I suppose that's meant to be a compliment,' Katherine Lundy muttered with a wry smile. Fog drifting up from the Thames below wreathed its tendrils around both women, leaving them nothing more than ghostly and indistinct shadows against the metalwork of Westminster Bridge.

'Well, I must say that you are looking rather well. Except for the smell,' she added.

'You get used to the smell,' Katherine laughed softly. 'I suppose, if the truth were known, I haven't felt so good in a long time. I don't drink and, without the temptation of all the rich food, I've lost quite a lot of weight. I feel good too,' she added, sounding almost surprised.

'You've no worries,' Tilly remarked.

'True.'

'But I have,' Tilly Cusack added maliciously. 'When you return to the real world, I think I'm going to hide out for a spell living rough in London.'

'Oh, I'm not living rough any longer,' Katherine remarked. 'I decided that was unnecessary. I've got myself a room now.'

'Well, there's no need to sound so cheerful about it,' Tilly snapped, irritated by Katherine's show of nonchalance. No wonder she looked so well without any worries. She had passed all her worries on to Tilly and promptly disappeared.

'Anything to report?' Katherine asked, staring down into

162

the dark, dank water below. The first few days after she had been forced to leave the house in Mayfair had been the hardest, and she remembered standing on this bridge, close enough to this very spot, staring down into the waters, wondering if it would not be simpler to let Father Thames sort out her problems. The feeling had only lasted a short time – seconds – but it had left her shaken.

'Have you any word on the jewels?' Tilly asked.

Katherine nodded. 'A little. I believe I know where they are. I also know who wants them so badly that he is willing to kill for them.'

'Who?'

Katherine smiled enigmatically. 'Well, let us say that there would be a lot of embarrassed faces if the stones were ever found. Certain people – certain, very-highly-placed people – want those jewels and the story behind their theft lost forever. And they are prepared to kill to ensure it stays that way. What about Senga and Patrick?'

'Senga is in Paris, with Billy as a bodyguard. Even I don't know where they've gone; they left without telling me. They left a ransom note on her pillow, obviously intending to throw the police off the track, but I disposed of it: it would have drawn even more attention on to us. Patrick had gone back to Dublin – the situation over there demanded his attention, he said, and besides I think he was getting a little worried about the attention a certain Colin Holdstock was paying him.'

'A dangerous man,' Katherine remarked.

'Very.'

'So my children are safe now?' Katherine glanced sidelong at Tilly.

'They would have been safer if they hadn't been dragged into this in the first place. But yes, I suppose they are safe after a fashion. I don't think anyone will try anything against Senga in Paris, and Holdstock will probably lose interest now that everyone has vanished.'

She was wrong on both counts.

*

163

Holdstock's investigation began with the house in Mayfair. Armed with a search warrant and a score of officers, he proceeded to search the house from attic to cellars, confiscating Katherine Lundy's huge collection of letters and files, most of which he had found neatly boxed and labelled in the attic, a vast array of receipts, some going back to 1916 when she had arrived in London, and a series of coded ledgers. With the exception of Martha Tilke, he was convinced that the staff knew nothing of their mistress's affairs; as far as they were concerned, she was simply an eccentric woman and, as such, a not uncommon phenomenon. The Tilke women, however, despite her heavy European accent which she assumed at will, and her seeming obtuseness, was obviously aware and possibly even a part of Katherine Lundy's organisation. But what part she played was extremely difficult to determine.

However, what did come through from his reading of the papers and letters – many of them to Tilly Cusack – was the woman's overriding interest in the Irish Crown Jewels, and her children's lack of involvement in her affairs. Indeed, she seemed to have gone out of her way to keep her children unaware of her activities. That son of hers had obviously gone bad on his own accord, but the daughter seemed to have avoided any involvement with her mother's murky dealings.

Until now.

However, the more he investigated the theft of the Crown Jewels, exploring that angle of Katherine's background, the more confused he became. It seemed more than likely that the woman had been somehow involved in the theft – certainly it was not unlike certain other thefts which she had been involved in, one way or another, in Dublin about that period. He had been a policeman too long not to catch the whiff of scandal surrounding the theft, and when he went looking for the report of the officer from Scotland Yard, John Kane, who had been sent to investigate the crime, and found that the report was missing – with no evidence that it had ever existed in the first place – he began to suspect a cover-up. His own investigations within Scotland Yard hit a blank wall of bureaucratic silence, until eventually, one of his friends in the Yard took him to one side and suggested that it would be better if he were not to continue this investigation.

And that, if anything, only redoubled Holdstock's determination to discover the truth about the theft of the Irish Crown Jewels and Katherine Lundy's disappearance, both of which, he was sure, were connected.

'Billy – you're cruel!'

Billy Fadden stood back, smiling delightedly as Rutgar von Mann rose up from the canopied table directly in front of the two women.

'You knew he was here!' Senga accused.

Billy managed to look innocent, and then she nodded happily. 'Let's say I had a good idea.'

Rutgar von Mann had been waiting for the two women at a roadside café in Montmartre for the past fifteen minutes. He had watched them walk down the cobbled streets, noting how they moved, their mannerisms, their walks. Rutgar was somewhat short-sighted and distant people and places tended to lose their sharp edges and become fuzzy. Therefore he tended to identify people by their walk, their gait, the tilt of their heads. Senga Lundy walked confidently down the slick cobbles, looking left and right with darting interest, taking in the people, the places. Her head was erect, her shoulders straight, her posture perfect. Billy Fadden, however, moved far more cautiously; it showed in the hunch of her shoulders, the quick, constantly oscillating movement of her head. She was walking two paces behind Senga, and Rutgar had no doubt that anyone who came even close to the young woman would not fare too well against the big Scotswoman. Even from a distance she radiated an almost palpable aura of menace.

165

Billy spotted Rutgar sitting beneath the blue-and-white-striped parasol, and gently eased Senga towards it, speaking to her at the same time, catching and holding her attention, allowing Rutgar von Mann to come to his feet.

When Senga turned around – vaguely aware that someone was standing before her – he bowed gravely and said in his almost-perfect English. 'A pleasure to renew your acquaintance, Miss Lundy.' He attempted to keep a straight face, but a smile creased the corner of his lips.

'So that's why she brought me down here!' Senga exclaimed. 'Billy – you're cruel!' She turned back to the German. 'How long have you been in Paris.'

He shrugged. 'A few hours, no more. I made contact with Billy the moment I arrived and arranged to meet you here.'

'I'm flattered,' Senga said, colour touching her cheeks. She allowed him to pull out a chair and she slid into it beneath the parasol. Billy sat herself down beside the young woman, manoeuvring her chair around at an angle where she could watch the other patrons of the café.

'But . . .' Senga began and stopped when von Mann held up his hand. 'Food first. Let us eat and then we can talk. Talk on an empty stomach always leads to trouble,' he said solemnly. 'At least, that's what my father always says.'

'What does your father do?' Senga asked. Although she knew that Rutgar's father knew her mother, she knew nothing else about the von Manns.

A curiously vague look drifted across the young man's face. 'He is a businessman; we have some factories in the Ruhr. They make parts for machines,' he said casually. 'Now, let's eat!'

The food was delicious – if a trifle greasy – although Senga found the all-pervading taste and smell of garlic offensive. Once she started eating, however, she found she was hungry, and after her initial uneasiness about eating in the street, she found herself actually enjoying the pavement table, watching the people strolling by. She was astonished at the mix of nationalities and although she wasn't as surprised as she had been back in 1921, when she had first seen a coloured person, she found the numbers of Negroes astonishing.

'There are so many,' she murmured to Rutgar, 'and so many shades of colour.'

He nodded noncommitally, his deep, blue eyes flicking across a Negro couple who were strolling arm-in-arm down the street. The woman caught his look and smiled openly at him, white teeth flashing against the purple of her lips. Von Mann looked deliberately away.

Having missed the brief interchange, Senga continued on, looking around her in wide-eyed astonishment. 'You don't see many coloured people in Dublin, and in London I only saw a few and they were mostly Indian. These are American, I believe,' she asked, looking at Rutgar.

'So I believe,' he said shortly.

'Musicians,' Billy said, glancing sharply at von Mann. 'Jazz mostly, but a lot would be performers at La Revue Negre. Some would be Josephine Baker's musicians or dancers.'

'Who is Josephine Baker?' Senga asked innocently.

Billy laughed aloud, a harsh, man-like bray which drew several good-humoured comments from the diners surrounding them. 'Do you mean to tell me that you've never heard of Josephine Baker, the Black Aphrodite, the Ebony Venus?'

Senga shook her head, smiling at Billy's enthusiasm.

'She is a singer, a dancer, a *comédienne*, and more . . . she is magnificent, but she must be seen to be believed. Before you leave Paris, we'll take you to the Casino, and you can judge for yourself.' She looked at Rutgar for confirmation.

'I don't think I will be able to spare the time,' he said stiffly.

'Would the lady's colour have anything to do with it?' Billy asked shrewdly.

Rutgar looked at her with hooded eyes. 'I'm not sure I

167

know what you're talking about.' Senga too was looking at Billy.

The Scotswoman held von Mann's gaze for several moments before breaking contact, unwilling to precipitate an argument. It wasn't her place to comment if he disliked blacks; and she was aware that it was probably nothing more than his upbringing and background. She was sure if she asked him, he would be unable to supply her with an answer, other than a vague catalogue of dislikes and racial slurs. She found it difficult to comprehend such unwarranted hatreds; although her own job was often brutal, she rarely had any feelings either way for her 'victims'. She didn't hate them, didn't even dislike them; for her it was merely a job. Some minders took a certain pleasure in handing out a beating, but that wasn't her way. She was tolerant of all colours and beliefs, but then she was in a minority – two minorities in fact – she was a woman doing a man's job in a man's world and she was a woman attracted to her own sex.

'I take it you don't approve of this Josephine Baker?' Senga asked Rutgar.

'She has appeared near naked on the stage, dancing in a lewd and animalistic fashion,' Rutgar said quickly.

'Sounds fascinating,' Senga persisted. 'So . . .?'

'So this just proves the truth that the black races are sub-human, near beasts . . .'

The hand that fell on Rutgar von Mann's shoulder was coal black, the fingers long and thin, perfect nails gleaming in the café light.

'I take exception to that remark.' The voice was American, and the Southern drawl held no amusement in it.

Rutgar twisted in his seat to look up into a hard, black face, the eyes narrowed, nose flaring, the lips in a thin, straight line. An elegant, black woman stood behind him, her face creased in concern, and another well-dressed black couple stood to the left of the tall, thin man.

Von Mann attempted to shrug the man's hand off his

168

shoulder, but the fingers bit deeply into his muscle, causing the German to grimace in pain. The man had him at a disadvantage, but even allowing for that the man still held him in the chair with surprising strength.

'How dare you touch me?' Rutgar hissed, his German accent suddenly more pronounced.

'Why – are you afraid you'll catch something?'

Rutgar glanced at Billy, his eyes wide with appeal, but unwilling to ask. The black man caught the look and glanced across at Billy, immediately transferring his attention to her, recognising the type. But his fingers never left von Mann's shoulder.

'Do you have a problem with this?' he asked softly, squeezing von Mann's shoulder for effect.

Billy met the man's large brown eyes easily. 'I don't hold with his views, and, while normally I don't stand between a man and his just deserts, if you hurt him now it would be something of an inconvenience for us at this time.' She smiled to take the sting from her remark.

The big man turned to look at Senga. 'And you, Miss, do you have any problem with this?'

'I don't think you should hurt him. I don't agree with what he was saying, but I think everyone is welcome to their views, as long as they don't harm someone else.'

'You've said a mouthful there, little sister. But this man's opinions are harmful and hateful.' He glanced from Senga to Billy, his gaze finally falling back on Rutgar. 'But I think you should give me a reason why I shouldn't thump him some.'

The man's three companions immediately began to protest, and the woman came up and begged him to leave it be.

'Touch me, Negro, and I'll kill you,' Rutgar spat, his voice trembling with rage.

'I am touching you,' the man hissed, with a wide smile.

'You can beat him,' Billy said easily, 'and I wouldn't even blame you, wouldn't even stop you. But I'd break your hands afterwards. Both hands,' she added, almost as an afterthought.

The big man looked at her for a few moments and then he threw back his head and laughed. 'I believe you'd try anyway.'

'Believe me, I would.'

He turned to Senga. 'And I suppose you'd have something to say about it too?'

Senga nodded, and inclined her head, indicating that the man should come closer. When his face was level with hers, she whispered something in his ear, smiling all the while. His eyes dropped, and when he looked into her face again a broad grin split his face. He straightened up and patted Rutgar on the shoulder. 'You're a lucky man to have such vixens for companions. You certainly owe them for saving your neck tonight.' He looked at the two women and bowed slightly to them both. 'You're too good for him,' he said, and then, taking his companion's arm and slipping it through his, he sauntered down the street as if nothing had happened.

Rutgar watched him go through slitted, hate-filled eyes. 'An animal, nothing more than an animal. The primate should still be in the jungle where he belongs,' he snarled, but he kept his voice low as he massaged his bruised shoulder.

They left the café moments later, their encounter having drawn a little too much attention to them for Billy's liking. As Rutgar settled the bill, Billy and Senga stood on the pavement outside, waiting for the German's car to appear.

'Tell me,' Billy said, 'just what did you say to that man?'

Senga lifted her purse and clicked it open so Billy could look down into it. The small, silver Derringer lay atop the tiny vials of perfume and the handkerchiefs.

'I told him to look down. When he did he discovered that I was holding this pointing directly at his groin. I think that's what changed his mind.'

Billy Fadden nodded solemnly. 'It would change most men's minds.'

170

CHAPTER SEVENTEEN

The two men met in the shadow of Marble Arch, vague and anonymous in the milling crowds. They went unnoticed amongst all the workers heading home at the end of their day and, even if anyone had paid any particular attention to them, they would have observed nothing unusual about them, except perhaps that the older man seemed perhaps a little too well-dressed to be meeting with a man dressed in casual workingman's clothes. In the background two plainclothes police officers kept a close watch on the older man. They had followed – or perhaps escorted would be a better word – him from a cab which had dropped him off in Bryanston Street, and when he had finished his business they would accompany him at a discreet distance until the same cab picked him up at the same corner where it had deposited him. Although neither officer mentioned it, they had both pulled enough embassy and ceremonial duty to recognise the older man. But both officers were men of long standing and noted for their discretion; it wasn't in their nature to be curious.

The younger man, who was dressed in workingman's clothes, a slightly shabby overcoat, heavy trousers, greasy hat and working-man's boots, handed the older man a folded white envelope. 'They've all gone to Paris,' he said, his face expressionless, not meeting the older man's unswerving gaze. 'So's your Inspector Holdstock,' he added maliciously, and took a certain small satisfaction in watching the expression change on the older man's face.

'This complicates matters. My . . . my principal will

not be pleased. And the Lundy woman?'

'Still no trace of her. We have a team of men watching Tilly Cusack around the clock. I still think our best chance of finding Lundy is through Cusack.'

'And the boy?'

'Back to Dublin. We've lost him, but we had a feeling that might happen when he returned there. It's his city.' The man touched the envelope with grubby fingers. 'I've made a recommendation here,' he said quickly.

'Which is?'

'We bring Senga Lundy back from Paris, and then simply let it filter through into the underworld that she's being held for ransom. Surely that would bring the mother out?'

'I wouldn't be too sure of that. But the plan has merit.' The older man half-turned and then glanced back. 'I take it that Scottish harridan is with her?'

'She is.'

'Hmmm. Fine; bring her back then, but I don't think it is necessary to bring the Scotswoman back also.'

'Yes, Sir!' the man said quietly. A thin smile curled his lips. He might just take this job himself, that Scottish bitch deserved to be taught a lesson.

'Billy?'

The Scotswoman, who had been leaning against the iron-rail that surrounded the balcony of their room, looked back over her shoulder. 'Aye?'

'Would you have let that black man beat Rutgar?'

'I would,' she said shortly, turning back to stare down into the street below. Directly across from her she could see two street girls plying their trade. She felt nothing for them, no pity, no anger, no shame. They were doing what they had to do and she could find nothing wrong with that. Everyone did what they had to do. In a way she was no worse than those women.

'Why?' Senga asked simply. She was sitting in a large wicker chair in a corner of the room. A thin, cold breeze, touched with the myriad odours of the city, wafted into the room through the open window, helping to dispel the oppressive heat from the hotel's antiquated heating system, which only worked intermittently, and when it did turned the rooms into saunas.

Billy shrugged. 'I'm paid to protect you,' she said simply.

'That's not an answer. And I don't think that's the reason,' Senga said from the shadows.

Billy turned around and moved away from the rail. She stepped into the room and leaned back against the wall, her arms folded across her breasts. Squinting into the gloomy interior she could barely make out Senga's face – pale and grainy – in the corner. 'If the man had touched you, I would have broken his arm. I threatened him because he was beginning to attract attention, and that might have brought the *gendarmes*. And we don't need that sort of attention, do we?'

'They don't know me here,' Senga said mildly.

'The French police have long memories. Even if they did not associate a certain Miss Senga Lundy with the late Monsieur Jean-Paul Hugo, they might have had some communication with the police in London. There is always the possibility that they have been asked to look out for us. Besides,' she added with a grin that was lost in the darkness, 'they would certainly have me on their files.'

'What did you do?' Senga whispered.

But Billy simply shook her head. 'You don't want to know,' she murmured. 'Tell me,' she asked, changing the subject, 'did you not find Rutgar's remarks in bad taste?'

'He doesn't like black people,' she stated simply.

'I think it was more than that,' Billy said mildly.

Senga nodded reluctantly. Much as she liked Rutgar von Mann, she wasn't blind to his faults. 'It was almost as if he despised them.'

'Aye.'

'But why?'

'He's a German,' Billy said, as if that explained everything.

'What's that got to do with it?'

'He's a German, a pure-blooded German. I've done a lot of work in Germany, and over the past few years there has been a growing interest in the idea of the purity of the German race, the Aryan stock. Coloureds, half-breeds, gypsies and the like are despised as a lower race, little better than animals.'

'But's that's ridiculous – no one would pay any heed to something like that.'

'But they do. In a few years' time, it could become a very real problem there.'

'And Rutgar would be one of these people who would subscribe to the idea of a pure race?'

'Most assuredly. He is pure-bred Aryan, blond-haired, blue-eyed. He's the perfect example of the new German race . . . of course he's going to subscribe to the idea. It probably does wonders for his self-esteem. Mind you, I'm not sure they'd look too happily on you though,' she added slyly.

'What do you mean?'

'Well, what with your colouring, your black hair, large black eyes, you've the appearance of a gypsy about you.'

'Thanks,' Senga said sarcastically.

'We could pass you off as a Spaniard,' Billy mused, using the darkness to conceal her smile, 'but then, I'm not sure they're too keen on Spaniards either.'

'Who are they keen on?'

'Themselves, their own type.'

'Are you trying to warn me off Rutgar?' Senga asked shrewdly.

'No,' Billy said emphatically, her accent suddenly pronounced. 'I'd never do that. I'm merely suggesting that you remain aware of what he is, who he is and where he's from. His attitudes towards many things – including women – will be very different from your own.' The big woman shrugged and her outline shifted in the gloom. 'But you're a clever girl, you know how to take care of yourself. Tell me,' she asked suddenly, 'would you have pulled the trigger when you were holding the gun on that man?'

'I'm not sure. I'd like to think I would. I came very close to – but I suppose that would have been a mistake,' she smiled.

'It would. One of the reasons I don't like working with guns. Too easy to make a mistake. And if you make a mistake with a gun, well then, there's very little going back, is there? My way may not be as neat as yours, but at least it's "safer". If you know what I mean?'

Senga nodded in the darkness.

She had been thirteen years old when she had seen her first man gunned down – by her mother's hired assassin and her brother, less than a mile from this room. A couple of days ago she had watched another man killed before her eyes – and then she had actually pulled the trigger herself. It had been a purely instinctive reaction, and if the truth were known she had felt absolutely no remorse about it. Indeed, she hadn't even thought about the dead man. After her initial pangs of conscience, she felt nothing for him, no remorse, no regrets at what she'd done. Nothing.

A shudder ran through her body that left her chilled to the core. She knew what Billy meant. She could so easily have shot that man tonight – killed him in cold blood – and the terrifying realisation was that she wouldn't have even thought twice about it.

'What's wrong?' Billy asked into the lengthening silence.

'Nothing. A feeling.'

'The realisation of how close you had come to murder?' Billy asked gently, moving away from the window, coming to kneel before Senga, taking her long, soft hand into hers.

'Something like that.'

'And perhaps the realisation that you would have done it unthinkingly?' She heard Senga catch her breath.

'How did you know?'

'I recognise the signs.' Her voice fell to a whisper. 'There was a girl I knew. Someone like you, intelligent,

175

pretty, self-willed, independent. She killed her husband. Took a twelve-inch, curved, Indian dagger and stabbed him in the chest. She then stabbed him again just to make sure. And she thought nothing of it. Felt no remorse, no shame, and I don't think she ever regretted it. But she did it unthinkingly, impulsively and for all the wrong reasons.'

'What happened to her?'

Billy's teeth flashed in a smile. 'She's married to a clergyman in the north of England.' She smiled again at Senga's obvious confusion. 'When she realised what she'd done, she called me and I sorted out her problem. Oh, later she acknowledged that what she'd done was stupid, but she never regretted it. I suppose you'd have been somewhat the same. You would have admitted that you've done something stupid, but I don't think you would have ever admitted to a mistake. Would you?'

Senga shook her head. She looked at Billy, her eyes wide, trembling with liquid. 'Is there something wrong with me?' she murmured. 'Should I not feel ashamed or remorseful?'

'I can't answer that, and I'm probably the worst person in the world to ask.'

'Dear God, Billy,' Senga whispered as sudden realisation sank in. 'I am like my mother!' The shout was like a cry for help.

The big Scotswoman took her into her arms, murmuring to her like a child, rubbing her hard hands against the thick, black hair. Senga was trembling violently, not crying but wishing that the tears would come, knowing they would bring release. But they refused to come. She clung tightly to Billy, her head against her breasts, taking comfort from the woman's size and solidity.

'What's wrong with me?' she mumbled. 'I was going to shoot him. I was going to kill him. I was going to shoot him. And for what? For nothing. For no good reason. And that's what my mother would have done,' she continued, aghast, '*she* would have acted in exactly the same way, I'm convinced of it.'

'There's nothing wrong with you,' Billy said firmly. 'You were reacting to a situation. People react differently, some back away, others stand their ground, others attack. You're one of those who attacks; unfortunately your method is a little more extreme than most.' She made to pull away from the young woman, but Senga clutched her tighter. 'Please, don't go, don't leave me, not just yet. I need someone to talk to.'

'Get ready for bed,' Billy ordered, 'and I'll sit with you until you sleep.'

Senga nodded wordlessly.

Billy went and stood on the balcony staring down into the street below, while Senga went into the bedroom to prepare for bed. Night had fallen and it must have rained whilst they had been talking. The cobbled streets were slick with moisture, reflecting back the streetlights in circular, rainbow-hued pools. Directly across from her – so close that she could have leapt from her own balcony on to the next – an elderly couple were eating their evening meal at a plain, wooden table. There seemed to be no conversation taking place between the two, and yet, they were completely relaxed in each other's company, and she found herself envying them their simplicity. Almost directly below her, in the deep shadows of the doorways, Billy heard the unmistakable sounds of lovemaking and, looking up and down the street, realised that the street girls had all vanished. There was a long grunting moan from below and she guessed that one of them would be back on the street soon enough.

The Scotswoman was troubled and uneasy. Senga's eagerness to use the gun was disquieting. Perhaps eagerness was the wrong word – it wasn't eagerness, it was the ease with which she produced it, and her apparent unthinking willingness to use it which frightened Billy. She had known people who would kill without rhyme or reason, who would kill on a whim and with never a second

177

thought. Cold, sick and usually evil people, who usually destroyed those around them before destroying themselves. And she hated the very idea that Senga Lundy might be one of them.

With a deepening sense of foreboding, she turned away from the Parisian night and headed back into the bedroom.

Senga was sitting before the dressing-table in her long, silk nightdress, combing her hair. Billy stopped in the doorway and watched the young woman for a few moments. The peach-coloured silk shifted and moved against the pale smoothness of her skin, blending in the gloom to become part of her flesh, making it seem as if she were naked. Billy watched the muscles shift and move in her shoulders, the taut lines of her neck as she lifted her head, tilting it slightly to drag the heavy brush through the shimmering mass. Billy Fadden found it hard to reconcile this suddenly vulnerable girl with the hard-eyed, thin-lipped woman of earlier. Perhaps there was more of her mother in her than either of them wanted to admit.

Aware that Senga could see her in the mirror, Billy stepped into the room and came up behind the younger woman. Without a word she took the brush from her hand and began to run it in long, even strokes through her mane of hair. The brush hissed through the thick, night-black hair, the sound like silk upon silk. Senga gripped the edges of the chair and tilted her head back, her eyes fixed on the ceiling, exposing the long column of her throat, allowing her hair to fall straight to the floor. Billy continued brushing, her strokes even, moving outwards from the crown. It was a curiously intimate moment; neither woman spoke, and Senga realised that she could never remember her mother brushing her hair. It had always been done by a maid or sometimes by Patrick, and in more recent years by herself. There was something very sensuous about the sound – raw, hissing, whispering – and there was a warm tingling in her scalp where her hair was being gently pulled. Senga's dark eyes moved to the pale blur of Billy's face, and as her eyes began to drift closed she saw the older woman's head move downwards.

Even though she was expecting the kiss, when Billy Fadden's lips touched hers, she felt as if she had been stabbed with something endless and ice-cold. A long, intensely powerful shiver spasmed through her entire body, curling her toes, locking her fingers into fists. With her eyes still closed she opened her lips, responding to Billy's kiss, and was shocked when the woman's tongue touched hers. Something fell to the floor, which a portion of her mind distantly recognised as being the brush, and then she felt Billy's hard hands on her hair, stroking the flesh-soft strands, moving gently across until they rested on her shoulders, fingers gently working to ease the knotted tension around her neck. Her fingers splayed and began to slide downwards, along the line of her throat on to her chest. They both knew that Senga could stop everything with a word, but she allowed the questing fingers to touch the soft flesh of her breasts through the silk nightdress and then slide down to cup them. Billy kissed Senga again, this time more forcefully, and now Senga responded, her arms coming up to wrap themselves around Billy's head, pulling it closer, leaning back into the bigger woman's body, her head against her stomach.

Billy took away her hands and moved around to stand before Senga, stepping close to her, standing between her open legs. With her eyes still locked on to Senga's face, Billy undid the two large buttons on her skirt and allowed it to fall to the floor. She then began unbuttoning the plain man's shirt she wore. Beneath it she wore no slip, no chemise or girdle and, with the exception of a pair of surprisingly feminine French silk knickers she was naked. Her breasts looked very white in the wan light from the street, the nipples very dark, seeming almost black. Without a word, she knelt between Senga's legs, and slid her silk dressing-gown upwards, the cloth hissing like a struck match.

Senga's heart was now pounding so painfully that she

was finding it difficult to catch her breath. She was intensely aware of what the older woman was doing, how she was touching her, where, and she was also acutely aware of her own reactions. She could feel, almost with a sense of awe, her own body responding in ways it had never reacted before, could feel the heat in her loins, the almost painful fullness of her breasts. She leaned forward and took Billy's face in both her hands, pressing her lips against hers, kissing her savagely, and the woman's hands moved down, across her belly. She brushed the shirt off Billy's shoulders and then her hands moved down on to the Scotswoman's body, tentatively touching her full breasts, marvelling at their smoothness, at the stiffness of the nipples . . .

Something rippled through her like a physical blow. Her back arched, her head snapped away from Billy's, her mouth opening in a silent scream. An intense warmth flooded through her, leaving her bathed in sweat. And then the reaction set in and she began to tremble.

'What . . . what did you do?' she gasped, her hands on Billy's shoulders, fingers digging painfully into the flesh.

'I'm sorry,' Billy began, but Senga shook her head savagely.

'Don't be. Show me what you did. Teach me how to do it!'

There was a moment of stunned silence and then Billy Fadden threw back her head and laughed. 'By Christ, but you're a strange one, Senga Lundy.' She suddenly swept Senga up in her arms and, lifting her like a child, carried her to the bed, where she laid her down gently on to the coverlet.

'Teach me, Billy,' Senga said eagerly. Propping herself up on her elbows, she watched Billy Fadden intently, taking in the details of her body, marvelling at the woman's hard muscles. Senga reached for her, opening her arms. 'Teach me everything.'

'What do you want to know?' Billy murmured, her Scots accent thicker, more pronounced now.

'Teach me how to make love.' She stopped and then asked seriously, 'Is there much difference between making love to a man and a woman?'

Billy bent her head to hide a smile. 'A world of a difference,' she murmured.

CHAPTER EIGHTEEN

The two men moved down the darkened corridor, counting the doors, reluctant to strike another light unless it was absolutely necessary. The taller of the two – who spoke no French – tapped his smaller companion – who spoke very bad English – on the shoulder and pointed to a pale-coloured door at the end of the corridor. The small, swarthy man nodded almost angrily.

He had no objection to taking the English money, which was unusually generous for such a ridiculously simple task, but he certainly didn't have to take the Englishman's assumption that he was stupid. And if he knew enough of the barbaric language he would have told him so himself. As it was, he contented himself with ignoring everything the Englishman said or did, and pretending to know even less of the language than he did. He took some small satisfaction from the Englishman's growing fury.

The small Frenchman stopped outside the pale rectangle of the door, and traced the metallic numerals with his fingertips, and then tutted in annoyance when his companion struck a match, the sulphur hissing loudly and its smell tainting the warm air. The wavering yellow light washed over the shabby metallic *twelve*. The Englishman grunted in satisfaction before dropping the match with a gasp when it burned his fingertips.

'Silence!' the Frenchman hissed. He gripped the Englishman's arm just above the elbow and, exerting just enough pressure to cause pain – a subject upon which the Frenchman was an expert – dragged him back from the door. 'Now, you are sure that there is *deux femmes* – two women only in the room.'

'Yes,' the other man murmured, shaking his arm free.

'And we will take the *jeunne femme*, the young woman?'

'Young woman, long black hair.'

'And the other?'

'Silence her, stop her, kill her if necessary.'

The Frenchman nodded. He thought it might be necessary.

The door opened silently inwards and the Frenchman stood back, pocketing the key he had 'hired' from the concierge. When he removed his hand from the pocket he was holding a slender, double-edged, Italian stiletto.

The interior of the room was silent, warm and close, a faint, not unpleasant odour in the air. The Frenchman sniffed carefully, attempting to identify the almost-familiar scent, but without success. Both men moved carefully into the apartment, one on either side on the tiny hall, pressed flat against the walls. They knew the layout of the suite, two bedrooms on either side of a small hallway which led down into a larger sitting room. There was a small bathroom off the larger bedroom.

The first bedroom, on the left-hand side of the hall, was empty, and the Frenchman stopped, puzzled. Were both women in their rooms or had they gone out for the night? The concierge had said that she had not seen either of them leave . . . and if she hadn't seen them leave, then they certainly hadn't left.

A soft hiss from the Englishman brought him across the corridor to the other bedroom. Pressing himself flat to the wall, he risked a quick glance inside . . . and then stopped. Vague light from the street filtered into the room, lending it a grainy illumination. He suddenly knew why the other bedroom had been empty; the two women were asleep in the one bed, wrapped in each other's arms, and he abruptly recognised the curiously familiar odour he had smelt when he walked into the apartments: it was the scent of sex. He turned to say something to his companion, and

183

stopped when he saw the curious expression on his face, the rictus of a smile fixed to his lips. With a mental shrug the Frenchman stepped into the room, the knife held flat against his leg, and crossed quickly to the bed. It made no difference to him if the two women slept together, but then, perhaps they did not have women like these in England? The two women were so intertwined and the light was so poor that he couldn't distinguish the younger from the older woman, although he had an idea that the woman lying flat on her back might be the Scottish bodyguard. Taking the sheet gently between finger and thumb, he carefully peeled it back, completely uncovering the two women. They were both naked, the younger woman lying cradled in the older woman's arm, her head on her ample breasts, one of her legs raised high, folded across the older woman's groin. The Frenchman smiled: they were as pretty a picture as he'd seen in a long time. However, it did raise certain problems. He would have to kill the older woman first – a single knife thrust would do it – and then he would be able to disentangle the younger woman. The throat then, he would cut her throat. A quick expression of disgust crossed his face; there was going to be blood everywhere, especially over the younger woman, and then she would have to be washed before they took her . . . And he had thought this was going to be a straightforward job. Shifting the knife, he bent over the two sleeping women.

One hand locked around his wrist, the second dug iron-hard fingers into his throat!

With a roar Billy Fadden surged upwards, tumbling Senga out of the bed on to the floor. Billy stared into the wide eyes of the Frenchman and then slammed her head forward with all her might, striking him across the bridge of the nose, breaking it. Bones popped in his wrist as she continued to squeeze, and he couldn't cry out because of the fingers on his throat. The woman smashed her head into his face again, opening a gash over his eyebrow. Through a blood-haze he saw her rising up like some ancient heathen goddess. She swung her feet out of the bed and rammed her knee into his groin. He attempted to vomit, but couldn't, and then, with a sudden savage twist, she had plunged the knife – his nerveless fingers still wrapped around the hilt – into his stomach. Blood jetted across her stomach and thighs. Before the pain hit him, she had dragged the razor-sharp blade up almost to his breastbone, and then tossed him away like a broken doll. He was dead before he hit the ground.

'That will be quite enough, thank you.'

Billy turned to find that a second man – taller, older – had wrapped his arm around Senga's neck, and was holding a small revolver against her temple.

'You are quite the savage, aren't you?' he remarked, looking at the woman's blood-smeared naked body, his expression a mixture of admiration and disgust.

'Who are you? What do you want?' she demanded.

'I have what I want.' He moved the barrel of the pistol against Senga's face for emphasis. 'But you present me with a problem. Not a very great problem, you understand. I cannot take you with me, and I cannot leave you alive – you might decide to come after me, and I certainly don't want that.'

'Doesn't leave you much choice, does it?' Billy asked.

'No, it doesn't.' The man extended the pistol, pointed it at Billy's head and thumbed back the hammer.

Senga bent her head, not struggling, merely moving her face out of the way of the explosion. The man ignored her. And then she abruptly straightened. The back of her head smashed into his mouth, splitting his lips, breaking one of his perfect teeth. The gun went off as he tumbled backwards, the bullet lodging itself in the ceiling, raining plaster down on them. Senga fell backwards on to the man, ramming her elbows into his stomach, attempting to wind him. He shouted, spraying her naked back with bloody saliva, and threw her off him. He shifted the gun in his grip and brought it up – and Billy's heel, with her full weight behind it, struck him between the eyes. He dropped

185

without a sound.

Billy was reaching for Senga when the lights in the hallway flared and the figure of a man was silhouetted in the doorway. The pistol in his hand looked very large.

'Ladies, we will have to stop meeting over dead bodies like this. People will talk!' Inspector Colin Holdstock stepped into the room.

'The Frenchman was a gangster, an enforcer. He had done some brothel work,' he added, looking at Senga, 'but he worked for anyone who'd pay. I would have liked to have asked him a few questions.' He looked at Billy and smiled.

'I'm sorry. The next time I awake in the middle of the night with a knife at my throat, I'll ask the holder if he minds answering a few questions first.'

Colin Holdstock bent his head over his teacup to hide a smile. Less than two hours ago both these women had been fighting for their lives, and yet here they were, with dawn breaking over Paris, having breakfast as if nothing had happened.

'What about the Englishman?' Senga asked calmly.

'Oh, he'll recover. He'll have a hell of a headache; he's going to need some dental work and a few stitches in his lips, but he'll recover.'

'I mean, did you find out anything about him?' Senga persisted.

'Nothing. He wouldn't tell us his name, and he was carrying nothing that might identify him.'

'His accent was cultured and upper-class,' Billy added.

'I would imagine so. His clothes were tailor-made and his shoes hand-made.'

'Not quite the type you'd expect to engage in a little kidnapping?' Billy remarked.

'No.'

'He wanted Senga. He said that he had got what he had come for.'

Colin Holdstock carefully buttered a slice of toast. 'I have a feeling, ladies, that you two have not been entirely

186

honest with me. And I'll ignore the fact that you've fled the scene of a crime. That, in itself, would be reason enough for me to bring you back to London; you are, if you recall, implicated in a death by unnatural causes. A .22 revolver bullet from a Derringer pistol being an unnatural cause.' He looked at Senga, who met his gaze directly. 'Since you've come over from Dublin, bodies have been dropping like flies around you. Now, I'm not blaming you for it, but you're obviously a catalyst. From what I can determine, you've been manoeuvred into a situation where you are the target for whatever enemies your charming mother has stirred up.'

'You're a very astute man, Inspector Holdstock,' Senga said softly.

'Call me Colin. I'm off-duty.'

'But the *gendarmes* . . .' Senga began.

'Did I forget to tell them I was on holiday? Dear me.' He smiled.

'How much do you know inspe . . . Colin?' Senga asked.

'Not enough.'

'How much do you want to know?'

'Everything.'

Senga smiled and shook her head. 'Even I don't know everything.'

'But I have parts of the story. You have other parts. Between us we might be able to put it together and perhaps solve this riddle of why so many people seem to want you dead or captured.'

Senga walked to the window and stared out across the rooftops. She wrapped her arms tightly around her body and shivered; even though she was wearing a heavy, satin dressing-gown over cream, silk pyjamas, she was still chilled. But this coldness came from within. Twice they – the mysterious they – had tried to take her life, and on both occasions they had failed. And what was it about third time lucky? Unless this situation was sorted out quickly, she was going to die. She suddenly shook her head savagely. Was there any point in lying to this man? He seemed genuine; seemed genuinely interested. What was the point in making another enemy; right now, she needed friends and allies. But she had been advised not to speak to him, to be careful of him, by both Tilly and her brother. But she was tired of people making decisions for her; right now she was making a decision of her own.

'This is all somehow tied in with the theft of the Irish Crown Jewels in 1907,' she began fiercely, not looking at him. 'My mother wanted them, perhaps she was even involved in the theft, and over the years she's made numerous attempts to trace them. It seems that they were recently offered to her again, and it's about the same time that all this trouble started.' Senga watched a flock of pigeons wheel and turn across the roofs opposite and then vanish in through a hole in the red slates. 'A couple of weeks ago, a woman called Tilly Cusack came to see Patrick and myself in Dublin. We had grown up with Tilly, we had called her aunty, although she was no relation; we trusted her. She told us both that our mother had disappeared; she had simply walked out of the house in Mayfair and disappeared. Martha Tilke – the housekeeper – told Tilly that our mother had been talking about the jewels before she disappeared.'

'I think I met Martha Tilke,' Colin Holdstock said with a wry smile. 'I didn't know she spoke much English.'

'She speaks six languages fluently,' Senga glanced over her shoulder and smiled.

'Why did your mother leave?'

Senga turned back to the window. She breathed in the early morning air, winced at its sour chilliness, and then she shrugged. 'I believe that she fled in fear of her life. But whether the threat came from the underworld because they were jealous of her wealth and angry with the attention the police were paying them, or whether the threat came from another source, we just don't know. You see, there is always that possibility that my mother intended to use the Crown Jewels to blackmail the thief, if he were still alive. The theft of the jewels caused a great scandal at the time, and this would be brought back into the public's notice once again.' She turned away from the window. 'But it's another reason for someone wanting her out of the way.'

'Is she still alive?' Holdstock wondered, and then immediately apologised to Senga. 'I'm sorry; I didn't mean the remark to sound so insensitive . . .'

Senga shook her head. 'No, she's alive. She wrote to me just before the Fête last week . . .' She crossed the room and disappeared into the bedroom, reappearing a moment later with a single sheet of paper which had been folded into her notebook. Without opening it, she passed it across to Colin Holdstock.

'There was no stamp and no postmark on the envelope, so I guessed that either Tilly Cusack or Martha Tilke had added it to the mail.'

'Tilly,' Billy said decisively.

Senga nodded. 'I'm inclined to agree.'

'But why has the focus moved away from your mother to you?' Billy asked.

'Perhaps they – whoever "they" are – feel that they can get at Katherine through her daughter,' Holdstock said softly, 'or perhaps they feel that you know something.' He shook his head. 'It doesn't add up. Your mother's network is both extensive and powerful, and even if she had managed to alienate some of the underworld families she would still be able to call upon some very powerful friends.' The two women were watching him intently. 'So whoever or whatever she's up against must be very powerful indeed.' He leaned back in the chair, tilting it up on its rear legs.

'And it has something to do with the theft of the Crown Jewels,' Senga reminded him. 'Someone doesn't want those jewels found for reasons of their own.'

'Scandal,' Billy said softly, and Colin Holdstock dropped both front legs of his chair on to the floor.

'Scandal,' he murmured. Bits and pieces of the puzzle

fell together. 'I'm going back to London,' he whispered, his breakfast sour in his stomach. He suddenly had a very good idea who didn't want those jewels found.

CHAPTER NINETEEN

'Why?' Senga asked simply.

Colin Holdstock joined the young woman on the balcony. He leaned on the rail, his fingers loosely entwined, relaxed and at ease, looking down into the street below. He was alone with Senga Lundy for the first time, Billy having gone down to find him a cab to take him to the station.

'Why?' he asked, glancing sidelong at her.

'Why did you come to Paris?' she asked, her dark eyes sparkling.

He shrugged. 'I had come over with the intention of bringing you back to London, you and Billy.'

'Think you could have managed us both?' she asked, archly.

'I did have that foolish idea. Now, I'm not so sure. You both seem well able to take care of yourselves.'

'Billy's taught me a few things,' Senga said, meeting his eyes and then looking down into the street below. Billy Fadden appeared out of the shadowed doorway, glanced up and waved once before hurrying off down the sloping, cobbled street.

'So you came to bring us back – what changed your mind?'

Holdstock shrugged again, uncomfortable with her directness, suddenly self-conscious in the young woman's presence. For a brief instant he imagined her naked, as he had seen her when he had stepped into the room a few hours ago, her skin ghost-white, silk soft, the small, dark nipples . . . He looked away quickly and rested his head in his hands, elbows on the metal rail, hiding the blush that coloured his cheeks.

'What changed your mind?' Senga asked again.

'When I saw you both fighting for your lives. When I discovered that one of the men was English. I think I realised then that you would probably be in more danger in England than you are here, although,' he added, turning to look at her, 'your location and identity have obviously been compromised. Those people knew where you were, even down to your room number. I'd say you've a traitor very close to home.'

Senga nodded slowly. She hadn't even considered that. 'What should I do?' she asked eventually.

'You'll have to move on.'

She nodded. 'You remember Graf Rutgar von Mann . . .?'

He nodded.

'He has suggested that we might like to go to Berlin with him . . .'

Holdstock nodded. 'You should be safe there – although there is always the possibility that they might find you there also. It really depends on how many people know about von Mann.'

'Rutgar says he can guarantee my safety.'

'How?' Holdstock wondered aloud.

'His father has estates in the country, secluded, well-guarded estates. No one will ever find me there.'

'Will you go?'

Senga shook her head slightly. 'Doesn't seem as if I have much choice, does it?' She turned to look at Holdstock. 'When will I be safe again?'

He shook his head slowly. 'When the people responsible are behind bars. When the jewels are found. When your mother is dead. Take your pick,' he finished bitterly.

'Not much of a choice, is it?'

'Not really.'

Senga turned to Colin Holdstock, resting her fingertips

on his sleeve. 'Will you help me? Will you release me from this trap? Barely a few weeks ago I was just another, rather ordinary young woman with her future stretching before her, full of promise and excitement. Oh yes,' she added sarcastically, 'it's still full of excitement, but the promises have changed. What have I got to look forward to now? I'm suspicious of everything. I'm seeing assassins everywhere. I've had more contact with the police in the past few weeks than I'd had in my entire life. And what am I going to do? Keep running. Running until they catch up with me . . .'

Colin Holdstock took her into his arms and held her tightly, holding her as the tears came and she sobbed against his shoulder, crying out her frustration and anger, her impotence. He ran his fingers through her long hair, soothing her gently, murmuring softly to her. He could feel the pounding of her heart, feel the swell of her breasts against his chest, her face damp against his shoulder. And he was suddenly very aware of her as a woman, a very beautiful, very desirable young woman.

Colin Holdstock had been married for ten years, and had been divorced for the same number. There had been few women in the past ten years, the ever-present, all-encompassing job, lack of time and even less opportunity contributing to ensure he remained virtually celibate. The job had destroyed his marriage, and had then conspired to ensure that he didn't form another relationship. It had been too long since he had held a woman in his arms.

Much too long.

He bent his head to look into her eyes . . . and suddenly found himself kissing her. Shocked by his own impulsiveness, he was about to pull away when he realised that she was responding . . . her arms moving around his back, pulling him closer to her, her lips opening beneath his. He kissed her with a passion he didn't know he possessed and she responded with an ardour that almost frightened him. He was forty-nine, she couldn't be more than in her early twenties. He was aware that his heart was pounding, and he could feel hers tripping away, her breathing ragged against his face, his hands wrapped tightly into her hair.

A clatter from the street separated them both, and they stood looking at one another almost guiltily, both almost too frightened to speak, afraid of saying the wrong thing. A whistle from below made them look down; it was Billy, a cab trundling along behind her.

Colin Holdstock reached out and squeezed her hand. 'Go to Germany, stay safe. I'll solve this mystery and find your mother. I swear it. The next time we'll meet, you'll have nothing to fear. I promise you.'

Senga leaned forward and kissed him lightly on the lips. 'I look forward to the next time.'

Colin Holdstock squeezed her fingers. 'So do I.'

Billy moved Senga out of the hotel later that day. It was obviously only a matter of time before someone else came looking for them. They had initially travelled light to Paris, but Billy went through the bags, stripping them of all inessentials, leaving only enough to be carried in two small handcases. Both women were armed, Senga carrying the large pistol her brother had given her, along with the small Derringer, while Billy wore the metal-studded, leather greaves on her arms, and the metal plates on her hands, hidden beneath a pair of fine, kid-leather gloves.

'Where are we going?' Senga asked, as they slipped out of the hotel through the tradesman's entrance into a foul-smelling alleyway.

Billy smiled tightly. 'The last time I was in Paris, I had to look after a young woman who thought she was going to be an artist.'

'And was she?'

'Aye, she could paint,' Billy agreed. 'She just couldn't paint very well, so she came to Paris to "discover her talent". Anyway, she rented rooms in Montmartre and then hired herself the best teachers, bought the best paints, brushes, easels, hired dozens of models. But she still couldn't paint,' she added with a wry smile.

'You were minding her?' Senga asked, following the twisting cobbled street which seemed to wind interminably upwards.

'Her parents were paying me to look after her.'

'Did she know?'

Billy turned to look over her shoulder and smiled. 'No. She thought I was a fellow artist and a model. I fancy I painted better than she did and indeed I even posed for her on a few occasions.'

'Nude?' Senga asked with a sly chuckle.

'All her models posed nude,' Billy grinned. 'Sometimes she even painted nude. It made her very popular with the male models.'

'I'm sure it did. What happened to her?'

'Once she realised that she wasn't going to be a painter, she decided she wanted to be a sculptor . . . and then a composer . . . and after that a musician . . . and finally a writer. She even had a collection of her verse published.'

'Was she any good?'

Billy shook her head. 'I discovered later that her father had paid the publisher to produce a limited edition of her poems, and they never went on general sale.'

'What happened to her in the end?'

She returned to London and settled down. She became engaged to be married, but broke off the engagement a few weeks before the event, and the last I heard of her was that she had returned to Paris and was once again attempting to survive as a writer . . . although this time without the support of her parents, who were somewhat put out when she broke off the very suitable engagement they had arranged. Through a mutual friend. I learned that she was writing pornography for one of the smaller presses for a few francs a page.' She turned off into a series of small, twisting side-streets and meandering alleyways, where the houses clustered so closely that the streets below were in perpetual gloom.

'But why were you protecting her in the first place?' Senga wondered.

'I was supposed to keep her out of trouble and, although this was never actually stated, I was supposed to ensure that she remained virginal.'

'And did she?'

Billy just laughed and shook her head. 'She was barely four hours in Paris before she lost that. I think I knew then that she was going to be trouble.' She stopped suddenly before a flaking green door in a tiny street that was so narrow that three people walking abreast would have had difficulty passing. Billy rapped on the door with the palm of her hand, the metal plate ringing hollowly.

Nothing happened.

She had raised her hand to knock again, when the door slowly creaked open, and both women found themselves looking down at what Senga at first assumed to be a child. It was only when the face poked out into the light that she realised it was the wizened face of an incredibly old woman. She looked the two women up and down and then said in a broad Cockney accent, 'What do you want then, eh?'

'You're English,' Senga said in surprise.

'Oh, very good, Miss, very smart, what a trained ear for accents you have,' she snapped disparagingly.

Billy glanced at Senga. 'This is Madam English, sometimes called the English Madam,' she added, her pale, colourless eyes twinkling, 'because of her other activities.'

'But never to my face,' the old woman snapped, squinting up at Billy. And then the lines around her eyes and mouth dissolved into laughter. 'But there are some people I'll allow to call me that, and I think you're one of them, Billy Fadden.'

'Her bark is a lot worse than her bite,' Billy confided to Senga.

'Don't you believe it,' the woman spat. 'I'm eighty-two and I've still got all my own teeth.'

Frowning, Senga looked at Billy.

'She's also mad as a hatter.'

The old woman glared. 'If only you weren't so big, Billy Fadden, I'd have one of my boys talk to you.' As she was speaking a huge Negro wearing a double-breasted suit materialised out of the shadows behind the tiny woman. He folded his arms across a massive chest and stared at Billy, his face impassive.

'Your boys have grown, Madam,' Billy remarked.

'Keep them fed and happy.'

'Like good little dogs,' Billy murmured to Senga. The old woman didn't catch what she'd said, but the Negro's eyes flickered from face to face, and his mouth firmed itself into a thin line.

'American?' Billy asked, looking at the man.

He nodded.

'American Doughboy,' Madam English grinned. 'Decided he liked it here in *Gay Paree*, liked the music, loved the women . . .'

'Loved the music *and* the women,' the man said, his voice surprisingly soft and gentle.

'And no one really cares what colour you are,' Billy added with a grin.

The big man returned her smile, his teeth white against his dark skin. 'Oh, a few do, but they don't matter.' He stuck out his hand and Billy reached for it. 'Paul Bunyan,' he said. Although Billy didn't catch the significance of the name, Senga looked surprised enough for him to notice. 'I'm a third generation Paul Bunyan, so any Bunyan jokes you have, forget it, I'll have heard them.'

Senga smiled. 'I don't know any Bunyan jokes,' she said shyly.

The doorman nodded. 'Then I think vou and I'll get along just fine.'

'Are we going to stand here on the doorstep?' Billy inquired sarcastically. She stood back to allow Senga to precede her into the darkened hallway, and then automatically checked the street behind her.

But she didn't see the shadowy figure in the doorway opposite.

*

197

Senga and Billy were given an attic room at the back of the house, which was dominated by a single window set into the gable end. The view across Paris was spectacular, overlooking hundreds of red-tiled, sloping roofs, while in the immediate vicinity they were looking down on to flat, tar-paper roofs, some of which were decorated with flowers and one of which held an artist's easle and a score of bird cages. The room was bright and airy, the walls painted white, the bare, wooden boards sanded to a mirror gloss that reflected the sunlight back on to the walls and deeply-sloping ceiling. Two enormous skylights had been set into the ceiling, ensuring that, morning or afternoon, the room would be bright with natural light.

'It's a perfect artist's studio,' Senga exclaimed the moment she saw it.

'It's the best room in the house,' Billy agreed, closing the door behind her, and then stooping to ram home a heavy bolt. 'Now, pay attention for the moment.' Senga turned, noticing the series of bolts on the back of the door. Billy grinned at her expression. 'It's also the most secure.' She dropped her bag on to the floor and hit the door with her fist. It thumped solidly. 'The door is solid oak, salvaged from a chateau that was bombed during the Franco-Prussian War. It is held with five hinges mounted into the wall rather than the frame. There are five bolts, and the bolts connect directly into the stone wall rather than into metal hasps.' She pulled back the bottom bolt and opened the door slightly, turning the key for Senga's inspection. The tongue of metal that emerged from the lock was easily four inches long and at least two inches thick. 'The lock was also liberated from an empty chateau. And there is only one key,' she held up the long, antique-looking key. Closing the door, she turned the key in the lock and then crossed to the window. Senga joined her. 'Through this window, you'll see it's a fairly easy escape route across the roofs . . .' She traced the route with her finger. 'And any of the windows in those houses opposite open on to landings which in turn lead directly down on to the street.'

'I take it you've used this room before?' Senga asked.

'Once or twice.' Billy smiled. 'This is one of the most expensive rooms in Paris.'

Senga turned to look around the almost bare room. 'You don't get much for your money, do you?'

The long attic room was practically bare of furniture. There was a long, low bed tucked into one corner, a single rickety stool beside it. Behind the door was a cheap wardrobe, and there was an old table with two chairs up against the window.

'You get peace of mind for your money. And a good night's sleep,' she added with a yawn. 'And I don't know about you, but I could do with a good night's sleep.'

Billy's yawn was infectious, and Senga suddenly realised that she hadn't really slept the previous night. The events of the previous few hours, her passionate encounter with Billy, the murderous attack, Colin Holdstock's appearance, seemed to race in upon her, overwhelming her senses, and she sat down heavily on the hard bed, completely exhausted. Without a word, Billy crossed the room and slid home the five, heavy bolts, the solid sound of them in itself reassuring. Taking the key out of the lock and slipping it into her pocket, she pulled off her gloves and began to unclip the metal plates on the palms of her hands. 'At least we're safe here,' she said.

'Are you sure?' Senga yawned, struggling out of her clothes, her fingers numb.

'I can practically guarantee it.'

The street Arab sold his information to a small, swarthy man in a bar behind the La Rotonde Restaurant. He, in turn, passed on the information for a suitable fee to a small, one-eyed Frenchman who had been contracted to bring the girl back to London at all costs.

His name was Tattoo, and his reputation was formidable.

199

CHAPTER TWENTY

Patrick Lundy met his sister on the steps leading up to the Place de l'Opéra as the Parisian air trembled with hundreds of churchbells tolling noon. Billy remained in the shadow of one of the ornate archways, arms folded across her chest, carefully watching the square and the movement around it. The big woman felt unaccountably nervous. Perhaps it was the very openness of the meeting – designed, no doubt, to afford a measure of security – but Billy would have a preferred a more private meeting in some anonymous hotel room.

Or no meeting at all.

The telegram had come from Patrick to their old address, where it had been collected by one of Madam English's servants and delivered to the safe house. The note itself was succinct and to the point: 'Am in Paris. Meet me steps Place de l'Opéra. Noon today. Patrick.'

'I don't like it,' Billy said softly, reading the note over Senga's shoulder. 'It could be a trap.'

'It sounds like Patrick,' Senga said hesitantly, reading the note again.

'I think you'll find it very difficult to identify someone from a telegram.' Billy remarked with a wry smile. 'And remember, dear, our previous address had been compromised.'

'I'm going,' Senga said firmly.

'Oh, I know that. I'm merely advising you that you may be walking into a trap.'

'But I'll have you with me, I'll be perfectly safe,' Senga

said softly, reaching for Billy's calloused hand, squeezing it gently. 'You'll look after me, won't you?'

Billy kissed her briefly on the forehead, smoothing back strands of jet-black hair. 'Of course, I'll look after you.'

'I wasn't sure if you'd got my telegram,' Patrick said, smiling, coming to his feet, holding out his arms to encircle his sister in them. 'And when I checked at the hotel this morning, they told me you'd checked out.'

'Oh,' Senga kissed her brother's stubbled cheek, tasting the salt from his skin. 'You don't know then?'

'Know what?'

'There was an attempt to kidnap me from the hotel the day before yesterday!'

Patrick looked at her in shocked silence.

Senga nodded, her dark eyes wide and serious. 'Two men, one French, one British. They attacked us in the middle of the night.'

'What happened?' he breathed.

'There's little enough to tell. They knew where we were, they even had a key to the room. They crept in sometime early in the morning . . . and then they met Billy.' She smiled humourlessly. 'The Frenchman's dead, and the Englishman won't be going anywhere for a long time.' Linking her arm through her brother's, she led him down the steps, moving away to the left towards the Café de la Paix which Billy had recommended.

'I'm taking you back to Dublin,' Patrick said decisively.

'No,' Senga shook her head. 'To be honest, Patrick, I'm not sure I'd feel safe there. Someone very close to us is feeding these people information. No,' she took her head emphatically. 'I'm going to Germany with Graf Rugar von Mann. When you've got everything sorted out, I'll come home.'

Patrick stared at her for a moment, suddenly seeing his mother in the determined set of his sister's jaw, the hard-eyed, direct gaze. 'I cannot change your mind?' he asked.

Senga shook her head.

They found seats at one of the pavement tables beneath a striped awning close to the building. Following Billy's instructions, Senga sat with her back to the wall with a clear, uninterrupted view of the street and access to the café through a door a few feet away. 'Now, what brings you to Paris?' she asked, when Patrick had ordered two coffees in surprisingly fluent French. 'You must have news.'

'I've some news of our mother,' Patrick nodded, not looking at his sister, his eyes on the people moving past the table. He was just beginning to wonder where Billy was, when he spotted her across the square, sitting on the top step of the Place de l'Opéra, just another tourist amongst countless others. Without turning his head, he asked. 'How are you getting along with Billy?'

'She's very nice,' Senga said, after a moment's hesitation.

'She's also very dangerous,' her brother smiled. 'Try not to get on her wrong side, eh?'

'Don't worry, I've seen her in action,' Senga smiled. Her hand went to her purse as the waiter reappeared with two, tiny cups of steaming, black coffee. Her hands only returned to the table when he had gone. She noticed, almost sadly, that her brother's hands also reappeared on the table at about the same time. 'Tell me about our mother?' she said softly, moving the spoon around on the saucer.

Patrick nodded. 'As we guessed, this is all to do with the theft of the Irish Crown Jewels in 1907. Now, leaving aside whether our mother was involved or not in the theft, her interest in them had sparked the attention of none other than the British government. Some of its representatives are determined to find the stolen jewels.'

'But surely they wouldn't . . .?'

Patrick held up his hand for silence. 'The theft of the jewels caused the British government a great deal of embarrassment in 1907. The jewels were stolen on the eve of the king's visit to Ireland, and apparently these were the

202

jewels he had intended wearing during the various official functions which had been arranged during his stay. There was a scandal, which brought to light the various private practices of some very public people. Now, most of the sordid details, including the name of the thief, were successfully hushed up, but no one wants to see those old coals raked up again.'

'So it's the British government who is after our mother?'

Patrick shrugged. 'That depends how you define the British government, but certainly at some level, within some department, someone has the file on Katherine Lundy – and intends closing it once and for all!' He sipped his coffee, grimacing at its sharp bitterness. 'Our mother has attracted the interest of the police in several countries, but the police file on her in Dublin – which I've seen – is quite extraordinary. Leaving aside the various petty crimes of receiving stolen goods, running a bawdy house, living off immoral earnings, gambling, the sale of alcohol and narcotics, it also includes supplying girls under the age of consent, procuring girls under the age of consent, we also have accessory to crimes of grievous bodily harm, accessory before and after murder. There is also a charge of attempted murder and actual murder outstanding against her name.' He shrugged and sipped his scalding coffee. 'So it's not as if they are victimising an innocent woman. There's no doubt that she deserves everything she gets. Our problem is that they know of my involvement in the organisation and there are several warrants outstanding against my own name. Obviously, they've tarred you with the same brush, and while they've nothing specific on you they're using you as a lure to bring our mother into their trap. Can't say I really blame them, I'd have done the same myself.'

'Thanks,' Senga said sarcastically.

'Don't mention it.'

'So . . . on the one hand we have our mother's former partners in crime who want her dead. The murder atempt at the party was their handiwork.'

203

Senga drank her coffee, barely tasting the dark, bitter liquid.

'On the other hand, we have the police who want you back in London, and aren't too fussy how they get you there. That was the kidnap attempt the night before last.'

'Do you know where our mother is?' Senga asked quietly.

'Yes and no.'

'Good answer, Patrick.'

'She's in London, last I heard. I gather she's making every effort to buy the jewels, and I would imagine she'll turn them over to the proper authorities if she secures them. She should be able to do a deal which ensures that the police lose interest in us, and then it follows that the other crime families will lay off.'

'How did you find all this out?'

'It seems our old friend Tilly Cusack has kept in close contact with our mother . . .'

'I thought as much.'

'Aye . . . well, that lady has been less than honest with us. But that's for another day. Anyway, our mother is well, looking healthier than she has for a long time. She wants for nothing, she's living rough, but not on the streets, if you know what I mean. However, there is a problem . . .' He finished the last of his coffee in one, long swallow. 'Our mother's partners-in-crime have taken out what is commonly called a contract on her. She has brought their various operations into the public- and police-eye and they are very angry indeed. The terms of the contract call for her to be removed, publicly, bloodily and permanently. But . . . and this is the but . . . they seem to have the idea that the only way to lure Katherine Lundy out of hiding is to hold her beloved daughter hostage!'

Senga could only stare at her brother in horror, numb with shock.

Patrick reached out and took his sister's hand, squeezing the fingers tightly. 'Now, I'm telling you this because I believe that you should know what you're up against. It means that there are two groups actively looking for you. My people are also looking for the jewels and, if I can come up with them before our mother, I'll use them to placate the authorities.'

'And what about our mother's partners-in-crime?'

Patrick smiled coldly. 'They don't present me with such a major problem. They're my type of people, I can take care of them.'

'How?'

'You don't really want to know.'

'How?' Senga persisted.

'I'll make an example of two of them, and then simply let it be known that a similar fate awaits anyone who shows even the slightest interest in Katherine Lundy or her family.'

Senga looked at her brother, looking at the man this time, noting the lines around his eyes, the tightness across his lips. And she found she was looking at the face of a stranger, cold and cruel.

'Are you sure you won't come back to Dublin with me?' Senga looked away, shaking her head.

'We can protect you in Dublin; my organisation can take care of you.'

'I thought your own situation in Dublin was tenuous enough.'

He shrugged. 'The political climate is changing; the heroes of yesterday are becoming the villains of today, the brigands are being called heroes.' The bitterness in his voice was almost palpable.

She reached out and squeezed his fingers tightly. 'What is that saying . . . "History is a fiction agreed upon" . . .?'

'I know,' he attempted a smile. 'History is written by the victors. But Ireland's history is not yet written; there's a few pages left to write.'

'Well, you make sure that Patrick Lundy's name doesn't appear as a footnote in that history.'

'I'll be happy if it doesn't appear at all.' he grinned. He

suddenly sobered. 'I would be happier if you came back with me.'

'No,' Senga said firmly. 'My mind is made up. I'm going to Berlin; Rugar von Mann has family there, I'll be safe there.'

'I think you'd be safer in Dublin,' Patrick said slowly, 'but I have a feeling that's not the only reason you want to go to Berlin.' He looked at her questioningly.

'I want to travel while I still have a chance.'

'I'll not stop you,' he said softly. He glanced back over his shoulder to where Billy sat, still and silent, on the steps. 'Will our Scottish friend accompany you?'

'She will. Does that ease your mind?'

'A little.' He stood up and leaned over the table, kissing her quickly on the forehead. 'I can only advise you, but the final decision is yours. I'm not going to do to you what our mother did to me: you have your own life to lead, your own decisions to make.' He shook his head. 'My baby sister's become a woman overnight. Be careful and stay safe. The next time we meet I hope it will be with good news.'

'You're the second person to make me that promise.' She pressed the back of her hand to her brother's rough cheek. 'Stay safe, Patrick. You're all the family I have, you know that.'

'There's always our mother.'

'That's what I said: you're all the family I have.'

The door opened silently inwards, and Graf Rutgar von Mann found himself staring into the barrel of a large pistol held steadily in two small hands. The face behind the gun was virtually unrecognisable.

'Senga?'

A hand reached out from around the door jamb and pulled him into the room. The door thudded closed and Rutgar turned in time to see Billy slamming home the bolts and turning the heavy key in the lock. When he looked around again, Senga had lowered the gun and eased back the drawn hammer. She attempted a smile, which failed miserably, and her eyes suddenly sparkled with moisture.

'Senga?' he asked, stepping forward, taking her into his arms. Billy moved around behind the young woman to check the windows, and Rutgar looked to her for an explanation.

'We met her brother earlier today,' Billy explained patiently, her broad Scottish accent evident now, betraying her agitation. 'On the way back here, however, there were two attempts on her life.' She lifted her sleeve, revealing the greaves. The dark leather was scored with long, bright marks, the metal studs sparkling. 'You are familiar with the Great Dane hunting dog?'

He nodded numbly.

'It came out of an alley heading straight for Senga. It had obviously been set on her. I managed to get this into its mouth and let it chew on that for a while. Even so, I thought the beast was going to rip my arm off.'

'What happened to the dog?' the German asked.

'I hit it a few times; that took care of it.'

'Could it have been an accident?' Rutgar asked, absently rubbing Senga's long hair, his eyes on Billy's face.

'There's always that possibility. Or there was until a second dog attacked us almost outside the door to this building.'

'I won't ask what happened to it,' he said, attempting to lighten the atmosphere.

'Don't. It's not dead, but let's say it won't be fathering any pups either. And then, when Madam English told us that Graf Rutgar von Mann was here, we knew that it was another trap, since no one knew our address . . .'

'But I only came because you sent me the address.'

Senga's head came up, and she looked from Rutgar to Billy.

'What's wrong?' he asked.

'We didn't send you the address,' Senga said very quietly.

'*Mein Gott . . .!* But then . . .'

'Exactly,' Billy snapped. 'We've got to get out of here.'

There was a long scream from below which ended abruptly in a burst of gunfire.

'Too late,' Billy whispered.

'No,' von Mann said, 'never too late.' He reached into his pocket and produced a Luger. Thumbing off the safety catch, he turned to face the door. 'We can make a stand here. The door is solid.'

Billy threw open the windows. 'The solid door is just one of this room's many advantages. There is another, however . . .' She leaned out of the window and groped beneath the broad sill, returning seconds later with a thick bundle of knotted rope. 'This is secured to a hook beneath the window.' She allowed the rope to uncoil down over the roofs. 'We go down to there, and then we've a choice of escape routes . . .'

The rest of the sentence was drowned in a burst of gunfire that rattled against the door, shaking it in its frame. Billy grinned; they could keep that up all day and they still wouldn't get in. All they were doing now was drawing attention to themselves. She was turning back to the window when a sudden wink of light caught her attention on the roof opposite. Instinct drove her across the room, slamming into Senga, dragging her to the floor, shielding her body with her own.

Rutgar turned . . . and the window exploded inwards, gunfire shredding the frame, tearing chips from the windowsill, biting into the wall opposite. Billy rolled Senga across the floor, glass and wood splintering beneath their bodies. 'A sniper on the roof opposite,' she gasped. They joined Rutgar who was sitting beneath the window, his back against the wall, his legs straight out in front of him, the gun cradled in his lap. He looked at Senga and grinned widely, his eyes large in his pale face. 'I have met you no more than three times, Senga Lundy; and each time my life has been threatened. Is it you or me, I wonder?'

More shots whined around the room, tearing into the wall opposite, ripping plaster from the wall.

'Is there another way out of this place?' Rutgar asked, looking at Billy. She shook her head slowly: now, they were trapped.

Something hard and metallic struck the door. 'Open up. Give us the girl, and we'll be gone.' The intonation was French, but the words were American-accented English. 'Don't make us have to come into the room. Come, give me your answer.'

'We're trapped,' Rutgar whispered. He looked at Billy. 'What do we do now?'

But it was Senga who lifted her gun, pointed it at the door, and sent a bullet into the thick wood. 'That's my answer.'

CHAPTER TWENTY-ONE

'We're trapped,' Billy hissed, crouching below the level of the window. 'The shooter on the roof opposite will keep us in here until the others break or shoot their way in.'

'How much time do we have?' Senga demanded.

Billy shrugged. 'The door is fairly solid. It could be a while unless they try something else, like coming in over the roofs, or burning us out.' She paused and added with a cold smile. 'That's what I'd do if the shoe were on the other foot.'

'And I thought Paris was a romantic city, full of adventure,' Rutgar smiled.

'Is this adventure not enough for you?' Senga demanded.

'It's enough.'

Bill wrapped her foot around a chair and dragged it over. Pulling off her coat, she threw it over the back of the chair and then lifted the chair by its two rear legs into the air above the level of the window-ledge. A series of single spaced shots from the roof opposite cracked into the room, one of them actually catching the edge of the chair, plucking it from Billy's grasp. Nursing a bruised hand, the Scotswoman scuttled back against the wall and drew her knees up to her chin. 'The first shots came from a machine-gun of some type, but he must also have a rifle with some sort of scope.'

'But not a very good shot, eh?' Rutgar grinned.

Billy nodded at the chair which had been carried to the other side of the room. The back bar was smashed where the bullet had struck it. 'Good enough,' she said slowly.

'Open up.' The pounding was unremitting and concentrated, something flat and hard, like a hammer or an axe reverberating off the wood.

'What about the neighbours?' Senga asked.

'They won't get involved, I can guarantee it,' Billy said.

'Do you mean that we could be killed in here and they would say or do nothing?' Rutgar asked in shock.

Billy leaned forward, grinning wolfishly. 'People have been killed in here before and no one has said or done anything. You might say that all law stops outside that door.'

'We need to get out,' Senga said unnecessarily, almost to herself. 'Hello,' she suddenly called. 'I want to speak to someone in charge.'

'I am in charge.' It was the accented English voice, muffled from behind the door. Listening to it carefully, she thought she definitely caught an American intonation to the words.

'What do you want?' She scuttled across the floor on her hands and knees to crouch to the left of the door, with her back flat against the wall.

'I want the English girl. Give her to me and I will be gone.'

'Why do you want her?' Senga eased back the hammer on the heavy pistol and then held it alongside her head, attempting to position the voice on the opposite side of the door.

There was a pause and then, in a tone of voice which implied that the person was smiling, he replied. 'Because I have been paid to bring her back.'

'I will pay you double what you have been paid.'

'Aaah, but I have given my word and I am a man of my word.'

Something nagged at the back of Senga's mind, but she couldn't put a finger on it. 'Would you be one of the . . . the *milieu?*' she asked suddenly.

Again the smile was back in the voice. 'I think one could safely say that I could be so described.'

Senga had positioned the man now. Standing in a

211

crouch she pressed the barrel of the gun flush against the door and wondered if the bullet would pass through the wood at this range. Keeping him talking, making a final check on his position, she asked. 'Would you know the name Katherine Lundy, sometimes called the Madam? I believe her name is not unknown in Paris.'

The silence on the opposite side of the door lasted so long that she was beginning to think the man had gone. When the Frenchman spoke again, there was a curious note in his voice, which, even though it was muffled through the door, sounded almost like fear.

'I am aware of Katherine Lundy. Why?'

'Are you aware that you have been sent to kidnap her daughter?'

'Mademoiselle Senga?' the voice asked in astonishment, the accent suddenly thicker. 'You are Mademoiselle Senga Lundy?'

Startled, Senga stepped away from the door and lowered the gun. 'Yes, why?'

'Answer this then,' the voice demanded, harder, harsher, 'prove to me that you are Mademoiselle Senga Lundy. The last time you met your mother in Paris, she was accompanied by a Frenchman who had one very distinguishing feature. Tell me what that was?'

Senga frowned. 'You mean the small Frenchman with the eyepatch?'

'*Mon Dieu!*' The voice was suddenly closer, and Senga got the impression that the man's head was pressed against the wood. 'Do you mean to tell me that you are Senga Lundy?'

'I am Senga Lundy,' she repeated.

'Aaah, and your hair, do you still wear it so short?'

'If you know me you'll know that my hair reaches to the back of my knees,' Senga smiled, realising the man was testing her in turn.

'Aaah, so I've heard, so I've heard. You must forgive me Mademoiselle Senga. I did not know whom I had been sent to take. I am Tattoo, I am the small Frenchman with the

212

eyepatch! And you must forgive me for having treated you in such a shabby fashion, but truly I did not know whom I had been sent to chase and take.'

'I believe you.' She turned and grinned at Billy and Rutgar. 'But does this change matters? Do we continue shooting at one another?'

'Of course not. This changes everything. Open this door and we will discuss this extraordinary situation.'

Senga looked over her shoulder again at Billy. 'What should I do?' she mouthed.

The Scotswoman darted across the room to crouch beside her. 'It's your decision. How well do you know this man?'

'I met him once, years ago, for about ten minutes. He had just shot a man.'

'That hardly inspires confidence.'

'But he knows my mother,' Senga murmured, 'and that's quite a different matter.'

'Make the decision. I'll back you, either way.'

Senga Lundy faced the door and turned the key in the lock. With a quick glance at Billy, she bent and eased back the two long bolts at the bottom of the door. Billy reached up and slid back the top-most two. Holding the gun flush against her left thigh, Senga worked back the final bolt with her right hand, and then quickly stepped back from the door, allowing it to open silently of its own accord.

With a precise movement, the small Frenchman with the eyepatch over his left eye stepped into the room, turned and closed the door behind him, turning the key in the lock. When he turned back to Senga there was a broad smile on his face.

'Such a pleasure to meet with you again,' he bowed slightly, ignoring the weapon in her hand, and then turned and bowed to Billy. 'I have not had the honour of your acquaintance, Mademoiselle . . .?'

'No, you haven't.'

Tattoo bowed again, his eye locked on Billy Fadden's face, watching her, sizing her up, recognising the type. He turned and bowed in Rutgar's direction. 'But you,

213

Monsieur, I recognise, and you are a long way from home.'

Rutgar lifted the Lugar slightly, pointing it in the Frenchman's direction. 'How do you know me?' he demanded, his accent clipped and hard.

'Your father and I have done business in the past!'

'I think it unlikely that my father would have done business with the likes of you,' the German sneered.

'I know. Disgraceful, is it not? Me, a Frenchman and a Jew too. But necessity often makes strange bedfellows, and your father is, first and foremost, a businessman.'

'He is a German!' Rutgar said proudly.

Tattoo nodded. 'He is a German businessman, but not necessarily in that order,' he said, and then, before Rutgar could reply, deliberately turned back to Senga. 'Now, what shall we do with you, eh?'

'You could try getting us out?' Senga suggested.

The small man's shoulders moved in a shrug. 'I could try. However, there are four more men downstairs, and at least two have been employed by my employer, so I would not put my full trust in them. And they will ask questions if I do not come out with you. As we speak,' he smiled, 'I am supposed to be placing an explosive charge against your door.'

'There is an escape route across the roofs,' Senga said, 'but there is a gunman on one of the roofs opposite.'

'Ah yes. He, too, is in the employ of my employers.' He reached in under his coat and took out a long-barrelled, broom-handled Mauser. Senga recognised the type of pistol because it had once been a favourite of her brother's associates back in Dublin. From beneath the other side of his flapping black coat, he removed a long, wooden stock. With a solid click, the handle of the Mauser fitted to the case, and suddenly Tattoo was holding what looked like a small rifle. The Frenchman smiled at the German's expression. 'A present from your father,' he said with a crooked smile. Crossing to the window, he knelt on the floor and poked the barrel out over the window-ledge.

'Perhaps one of you would be good enough to distract the man?' he said softly, glancing back into the room.

Billy reached over and grabbed the pillow off the bed and then crept over to stand on the opposite side of the window. Standing well back, holding one end of the pillowcase in her right hand, she slowly raised the pillow just above the edge of the sill and then quickly jerked it upwards.

Three shots rang out in quick succession, two of them biting into the sill, one chipping the plaster on the opposite side of the room.

'*Encore*,' the Frenchman muttered.

Billy eased the edge of the pillow up to the level of the window and then held it there. Two more shots rang out, the sound cracking flatly across the roofs. The first shot missed, whining around the room, but the second plucked the pillow from Billy's hand, tossing it into the centre of the room in a flurry of feathers.

And then Tattoo's Mauser barked, four shots in quick succession, shell casings tinkling on to the floor. The Frenchman looked up into the silence which followed, and grinned humourlessly. 'You said there was an escape route across the roofs.'

'But the gunman opposite?' Senga asked.

Tattoo stood up, the stock of the ugly-looking gun resting against his hip. He was standing in full view of the window and Senga joined him without hesitation. She doubted that she had anything to fear from the Frenchman; if he had wanted her dead, he had had plenty of opportunity to kill her so far. She looked out across the roofs and there, almost directly opposite, was the slumped shape of a man, arms and head resting on the sill, a rifle lying in the gutter beneath his outstretched hands.

Billy joined Senga at the window. 'Nice shooting,' she remarked. 'Is there anyone else out there?' she asked.

'Not that I am aware of.'

'Let's get going,' she said. She bundled up the rope and tossed it down over the red tiles, testing it with a firm tug.

'Rutgar first, then Senga, then me.'

With Billy keeping the rope taut, Rutgar climbed slowly and nervously down its knotted length. It was a twelve-foot drop to the nearest roof, but if he fell the German knew that the sloping angle of the roofs below would ensure that he tumbled the remaining thirty feet into the street below.

Senga turned to Tattoo. 'Thank you. You have saved our lives; but what will you do, how will you explain our escape?'

The Frenchman shrugged. 'Do not trouble yourself about that. Now go, go quickly . . .'

'I'll make sure my mother will learn how you put yourself at risk to help us.' Senga kissed the Frenchman on both cheeks quickly, before he could respond. 'Thank you,' she said again, and then turned to sit on the window-ledge, grabbed the rope and swung herself out, her heels clicking on the smooth stones, half-walking, half-climbing down the rope to where Rutgar waited on the roof below. He wrapped his arms around her waist, swinging her around to him when she got close. She staggered, her leather soles slipping on the smooth tiles, and Rutgar's grip tightened, holding her close. She looked up into his deep, blue eyes and smiled. 'Thank you.'

Rutgar bent his head and kissed her lips lightly. 'Thank you,' he murmured, his breath warm against her moist lips.

'For what?'

'For no reason. Perhaps I was thanking God for keeping you alive.'

'God had very little to do with it. It was you and Billy, and Tattoo,' she added, looking up.

Billy paused before she climbed out on to the window-ledge. 'You take care,' she said to Tattoo. 'I'd suggest you blow the door now and discover us gone. Blame the sniper's death on us.'

'Do not worry yourself, Mademoiselle, I had every intention of doing so.'

Billy nodded. She looked into the Frenchman's single eye and smiled. 'I'll look you up the next time I'm in Paris. We'll have a drink and laugh about this.'

The Frenchman bowed slightly. 'Yes, I think I would enjoy that, Mademoiselle. Ask for Tattoo in the Quarter.'

'I will,' Billy promised.

Tattoo watched the two women and the man clamber over the roofs and then vanish through a broken skylight on the roof of an hotel. With a long-bladed hasp knife, he cut away the knotted rope, allowing it to fall on to the roof below where it rattled on the tiles before sliding off into a tiny, enclosed yard. Stooping, he picked up the brass casings from his own shells and pocketed them, then turned back to the room, checking it for a final time. Leaving the room, he pulled the door shut quietly behind him, turning the key in the lock and pocketing it.

Seconds later, as the two dishevelled women and the equally dishevelled man walked calmly out of a doorway three streets away, a tremendous explosion cracked across the Parisian rooftops, sending thousands of pigeons skywards. A rain of fine grit drifted down across the streets, and a pall of smoke rose slowly and majestically into the clear, blue, spring sky.

'A little too much explosive, I think,' Rutgar said gruffly. He looked at Senga and shrugged. 'I am something of an expert on explosives. My father does manufacture munitions.'

Billy turned to grin at Senga. 'But done deliberately, I think. I'd say our friend has taken out most of the top floor with that explosion. Whoever was chasing you will have a hard time finding anything recognisable in the room. If they assume we all died there, it will give us a few hours to make good our escape.' She turned to Rutgar. 'You once offered to take Senga to Germany.'

'The offer is still open. Whenever you want to go . . .'

'Now!'

'I beg your pardon?'

'We want to go now. Immediately.'

CHAPTER TWENTY-TWO

In Dublin and London, Patrick Lundy and Inspector Colin Holdstock received the report of the bombing at roughly the same time; their reactions were remarkably similar, and they both asked the same question.

'Were any bodies found?'

Malachi Thinn shook his head. 'There're all sorts of stories floating around the Paris underworld at the moment. As far as we can determine, a team was sent in to capture the girl. They found them holed up in a fortified room on the top floor of a bordello in the heart of Montmartre. There was an exchange of shots, but when the kidnappers realised that they couldn't shoot their way into the room and, with time against them, they set explosives against the door . . .' he shrugged. 'And that was that. Unfortunately they seem to have used rather too much explosive or – and this is perhaps more probable – there was something flammable or explosive in the room. Two floors of the building were completely destroyed and there was a lot of damage in the surrounding streets. There was some speculation in the press that it was an unexploded bomb from the war. No one has said anything to deny that.'

'And bodies?' Colin Holdstock said tightly, his stare hard and uncompromising.

Thinn shrugged. 'Hard to say. The *gendarmes* are still sifting through the mess.'

Colin Holdstock stared at him and then bent his head to look down at the single-page report on the desk in front of him. His heart was tripping madly, and he was aware of a solid band closing around his chest, constricting his lungs, while something ice-cold and solid settled into the pit of his stomach. Was she dead, her body ripped and torn by the explosion? He tasted bile in his mouth and breathed deeply. His eyes ran down the report, not seeing the badly-typed words, until the last line; '. . . no bodies have been recovered from the wreckage.' There were no bodies, but he took small consolation from that.

The tall Irishman shook his head. 'What I can't understand, Sir, is why should anyone go to all that trouble for just one girl?'

Colin Holdstock looked up at him, his expression closed. Why indeed?

'I'm going to Paris,' Patrick Lundy said, the muscles in his jaw clenching and unclenching to prevent his teeth from chattering.

'That might not be wise.'

Patrick turned to look at the speaker, his eyes like stones, and the man simply nodded and hurriedly left the room, suddenly remembering the stories of Patrick's youth and his reputation as a stone killer. Having looked into his eyes, he could well believe it.

Patrick walked around the desk and turned the single sheet of paper, reading the copy of the police report again and again, and then he turned and walked to the window, looking down on to Bachelor's Walk. From where he was standing he could see most of O'Connell Bridge and the quays down to the Custom House where one of the large Guinness barges rocked at anchor. Gulls wheeled and circled around the barge, and Patrick watched their erratic flight, his own thoughts rising and falling with them. Was Senga dead? Had she been killed in the explosion? No bodies had been found and that was a good sign, although he realised he was probably clutching at straws; he had seen explosions in which the bodies had been flung dozens of yards, to be found hours or even days later.

But by God, if she was dead, he would make sure that her killers paid, and paid dearly . . .

He shook his head savagely, cutting off that line of thought. He knew once the blood lust took him, he would be incapable of careful planning until he had slaked that rage, and that was a luxury he couldn't afford just yet. Right now he needed facts, and he wasn't going to find them sitting here in Dublin.

'Paul,' he said without looking over his shoulder. He heard a slight movement as the bodyguard stood up. 'I'm going to London, and then on to Paris. Will you make the arrangements for me, please.'

'When do you want to go?'

'Immediately.'

'I've never been on a train like this before,' Senga said breathlessly. She was sitting across from Rutgar von Mann in the dining-car of the Paris-to-Berlin express.

'I will take you on the Orient Express soon,' Rutgar promised. 'It makes this train look like a mobile slum.'

Senga stared at him, her expression registering disbelief. She sat back into the leather-backed dining-chair, and touched the silver cutlery, the crystal glassware and the lace napkins, and realised not for the first time just how little she knew, how little she had travelled. Despite all her years – and she was twenty-one now! – she hadn't really travelled. Even though she had lived in London for so long, she knew so very little about it. She had never visited any of the museums or galleries, never seen the changing of the guard, never even been into the Tower of London. She wasn't even sure that she could find her own house in Mayfair! She had seen Paris briefly eight years ago – a few mean streets, taverns, clubs – before she had been taken back to Dublin. And Dublin was so provincial. Now she had returned to Paris, and, once again, she had seen only its mean streets, its backstreets, alleyways and lanes – and its rooftops too, she reminded herself with a grin.

But perhaps all this had changed now.

She was on her way to Berlin with a handsome young man, a member of the German aristocracy, who was obviously attracted to her, who seemed genuinely interested in her. He had promised to show her the city and its sights, had promised to take her shopping, take her into the countryside, make a holiday for her. Perhaps now – away from the very real danger of Paris, London and Dublin – she would get a chance to relax, a chance to experience a little of life. And after that, who knows: perhaps she would be able to travel, see a little of Europe.

'A penny, a franc, a mark for them?' Rutgar said softly.

Senga grinned and rested her hand atop his. 'You must forgive me, I was miles away.'

'You had a homey look to your eyes.'

She nodded. 'I was thinking of home actually. How did you know?'

'A lost, vacant look to your eyes, a certain wistfulness. I've seen the same look in my mother's eyes when she's thinking of home.'

'She isn't German, then?'

'She is from Austria. I think she misses her home, especially in the winter, when the Berlin streets are filthy with melting snow. I can remember her telling me that in Linz, where she was born, when it snowed the snow stayed white and pure until it melted.'

'Is she beautiful, your mother?' Senga asked.

Rutgar smiled, softening the hard lines around his eyes and mouth. 'She is. She is like you.'

It took her a moment to realise what he had said, and she looked away, embarrassed. Beyond the windows, broad, flat, chequered fields flashed by right to left, the flickering appearance of the telegraph poles almost hypnotic. An occasional white road bisected the fields, some of them containing broken or shattered buildings, relics of the war.

'I'm looking forward to meeting her,' she said eventually, to break the silence.

'I think you'll like her. I think she will like you.'

'I hope so,' Senga murmured.

221

'I'm sure of it.' He looked up at a white-coated, white-gloved waiter who had arrived. 'Aaah, food.'

'You could have joined us,' Senga said, sitting patiently in the chair before the small mirror in her cabin while Billy stood behind her, brushing her long dark hair with strong, even strokes.

'Och, but two's company and three's a crowd. And he wanted you all to himself. The last thing he needed was me in the way.'

Senga looked at Billy's reflection in the mirror, the small glass distorting her eyes, making them seem huge and bulbous. 'What do you think of him?'

Billy grinned, and then she leaned forward, her hard hands resting on Senga's shoulders. 'You don't want me to tell you what I think of him. You like him, you like him a lot, and I'm certainly not going to say anything about the first man you've stepped out with.'

'How did you know I've never gone out with a man before?'

Watching Senga's expression in the mirror, Billy kissed the top of her head. 'A girl can tell these things,' she murmured.

Later, much later, when they both lay in Senga's bunk, Senga nestling in Billy's arms, her head against her breast, she said, 'Have you ever had a boyfriend?'

After a long silence, Senga felt Billy move slightly. 'Yes.' And later, much later, when Senga was just nodding off to sleep, lulled by the solid pounding of Billy's heart, which was now keeping time with the train's rhythm, the Scotswoman said, 'He was a client at first. His father owed some people money, and they wanted to kidnap the son, hold him for ransom. Not unlike your own case, actually. I was brought in to act as his fiancée, and to keep him safe. What started out as an act gradually turned into the real thing.'

'What was his name?' Senga murmured.

'Anthony . . . but he allowed no one to call him Tony, except me.'

'Was he handsome?'

'No,' Bill smiled into the darkness, remembering the plain, ugly face, the pale-blue eyes, the strong jaw. 'He wasn't. But he had a gentle personality. And he was kind, and good-humoured, soft where I was hard, strong where I was weak.'

'What happened?'

Billy shrugged, a sudden movement of both shoulders. 'It would never have worked out. Oh, it's easy for me to look back now and see all the obstacles in our way. I was nothing but a hired help, but I thought otherwise, and I thought that he looked at it that way. I think he did too, for a while anyway.' There was a silence, and when she continued her voice was harder, colder, her heart now pounding a different tune to the train's lulling counterpoint. 'I met him, fell in love with him, and loved him. Loved him deeply with that first great love, the *grand passion*. Take it from me, my girl, it will probably only happen to you once, and you'll know it when it arrives, the *grand passion*. For some people it never happens.'

'I think he loved me in return, at least for a while, at least until someone pointed out that I was from the slums of Glasgow and he was a middle-class Londoner, although barely one jump up from the slum himself. But I suppose new money is always jealous of its position. His parents didn't approve, of course, and when they discovered what was going on between us I lost the job, and my wages. There was a huge scene, with Tony present, and I suppose I thought he would come to my assistance, but he didn't; he just stood there, listening to his father berate me, calling me all sorts of names. They were implying that I had seduced their son in order to marry him for his fortune, and yet it was their son who had very definitely seduced me. I listened, and then left.' She paused and then added coldly, 'But I got my revenge.'

'How?' Senga mumbled.

'Two days later the son was kindnapped. Someone must have told the kidnappers where he was. Can't think who, can you?'

'I'm sure I can't.' Senga said very slowly.

'It taught me a valuable lesson, though – work for someone, but don't get involved. Take their wages, but not their problems. And that was fine – until I met you.'

'And then?'

'And then I broke all the rules!'

'Why?' Senga asked into the silence that followed.

Billy moved in the small bed, sliding down until her face was level with Senga's. 'Perhaps because when I looked at you, I found it very easy to remember what I was like when I was your age.'

'Are we alike?' Senga asked, surprised.

'No. I can't even say what it is about you which reminds me of me when I was your age. Maybe your strength, maybe your vulnerability, maybe a combination of both. Maybe I just don't want to see you manipulated by others. I don't want to see you make the mistakes I made.' She laughed, a dry, coughing sound. 'Maybe if I had had someone to guide me, to direct me, I wouldn't be where I am today.'

Senga reached out and held Billy. 'Do you regret what you are, what you've done?'

'Sometimes. Sometimes, late at night. I realise that I'm thirty-two, not married, with no prospects of marriage, and with no real future ahead of me. I can't go on doing this all my life, can I?'

'I suppose not.'

'I have less than ten years left in this business, if I should live that long. And if I do survive, what am I qualified to do? I'll even be too old to walk the streets, although,' she added wistfully, 'I suppose you're never to old to walk the streets.' She moved forward, kissing Senga lightly on the lips. 'I suppose I just wanted to pass on a little of what I knew to someone like you. Just to prove that it hadn't all been in vain. Posterity, I think the phrase is.'

'I think I know what you mean.'

'I didn't deliberately set out to sleep with you either. My

own first experience with a man was not a success, but I think if I had been a little more knowledgeable it would have been a much more memorable experience. I've had relationships with both men and women; I think you'll find that women are a lot less demanding, a lot more gentle and far more understanding.'

Senga nodded, her hair hissing against the pillows. 'I've never slept with a man so I can't make the comparison, but I think I've already discovered how gentle and understanding another woman can be.' She kissed Billy deeply, her hands moving down the woman's naked body. 'What else can you teach me?' she murmured.

'A lot.'

Senga awoke in the cold, pre-dawn light, the train's ever-present clacking now absent, although in the distance she could hear the chugging of steam and the vague sound of voices. They had either stopped at a station, a customs-crossing or to take on water. She looked at the naked woman lying beside her, a little surprised at how easily she was accepting all this. But perhaps the events of the past few weeks had put her in a state of mind which made such things easier to accept. She supposed she should have felt outraged, or upset or defiled or ashamed by the fact that she had slept with another woman. But she didn't. Billy, despite her size and strength, was remarkably gentle, and her large, rough hands were capable of an extraordinary delicacy of touch. She could still feel their tingle on her flesh.

And she didn't regret it; she didn't regret it for a moment.

She had a lot to thank Billy Fadden for; at least now, when she did sleep with a man, she would have some idea what he would do, what he would expect, and that was an awful lot more than a lot of young women of her own age would know on their wedding night.

A single image flashed behind her mind's eye, and she suddenly remembered the farmhouse she and her

225

schoolfriend had hidden out in when they had run away from the Chateau, the Swiss finishing school. The woman of the house, a young French woman, Marie Lieber – she had never forgotten the name – had been very kind to her, too kind perhaps, and had even given her a present of some expensive French underwear, the first silk underwear she had ever worn. She still remembered their flesh-soft touch the first time she had worn them. Senga had a distinct memory of sleeping in the woman's bed, and at some time during the night the woman had rolled over and her hand had found Senga's emerging breast. She remembered thinking it odd at the time and being vaguely embarrassed, almost frightened. Now, it made a little more sense.

Senga looked down at Billy, thinking back over what she had said. It was true: she wouldn't be able to carry on her particular trade for very much longer. Age would slow her down; younger and stronger men were coming along, and common sense would dictate that she move out of the job before she was badly hurt or even killed. And, in any case, who would hire an old woman as a bodyguard? What would she do then, what could she do?

Senga owed her. Owed her more than her life. Billy Fadden had taught her what it was to be a woman. And that was a debt that Senga Lundy would never be able to repay.

CHAPTER TWENTY-THREE

The train had been moving through the somewhat dreary and cheerless suburbs of Berlin for the past hour, and the thin rain that had come on with the dawn made the grey streets look grim and drab.

Senga and Billy were sitting across from one another in the dining car. Rutgar hadn't joined them for breakfast this morning, and they had lingered at their table, drinking endless cups of coffee, watching the countryside roll by, making desultory conversation.

However, Senga found that her boredom gradually changed to apprehension as the first of the small houses began to slip by and their destination became a reality. Suddenly, travelling to Berlin with Rutgar von Mann – who was, after all, a virtual stranger – didn't seem such a good idea.

Billy, sensing her apprehensive mood, reached out and squeezed her hand lightly. 'It can't be that bad,' she smiled. 'Nerves?'

'Is it that obvious?'

'I'd be surprised if it were otherwise. It's natural.'

Senga looked directly into Billy's hard, almost colourless eyes. 'I'm just a little worried about Rutgar and his family. We know virtually nothing about them . . .'

The Scotswoman squeezed her fingers again, silencing her. 'It's all right; you don't think I'd let someone get close to you without checking them out, eh? Now just relax and enjoy the adventure.'

'Billy,' Senga said quickly, 'when all this is over and

everything is sorted out, I'd like you to do something for me . . .'

Taken aback by the sudden change of subject, Billy could only look at her blankly.

'I want you to come and work for me. I want you to be my . . . my . . . personal secretary . . . my aide . . . I don't know . . . give yourself whatever title you think appropriate.'

Billy stared at her in astonishment.

Senga watched her intently. 'You see, I've decided I don't want to lose you. Whatever happens to us, I want us to be together.' She shrugged. 'Perhaps it's just me being selfish, but I want to have you around. I want you there to advise me . . . and my children too, if there are any. I reckon if my mother had had someone like you, she wouldn't be in the mess she's in now.'

In the long silence that followed, the click-clack of the train sounded very loud, and the countless tiny sounds that accompanied it – the gentle shivering of the cutlery and crockery on the table, the buzz of the breeze through half-open windows, the hiss of the rain against the windows on the far side of the carriage – seemed magnified. It was one of those singular moments that live on in the memory for no special reason, and yet can be recalled with absolute clarity in years to come.

'Thank you,' Billy finally whispered, breaking the spell, and Senga was shocked to find that the big woman's eyes were sparkling with moisture. She squeezed Senga's fingers so tightly that they hurt. 'We'll talk about it someday, perhaps.'

'I've already thought about it, Billy. It's what I want. All you have to do is to decide if it's what you want too.'

'You shouldn't make such offers now. You're vulnerable and you're afraid. You've turned to me because I've been there to save you, and it's only natural that you should want me around you; it's your fear talking. But I'm still flattered,' she said sincerely. 'Maybe later, much later, when all this is over and done, we'll talk again.'

'Forgetting everything you've said, all the reaons you've given me, answer me just one question: would you *like* to live with me?'

'Very much indeed.'

'Then that's settled,' Senga said decisively. 'Now, tell me about Graf Rutgar von Mann.'

Billy turned to stare through the rain-spattered window, taking a few moments to compose herself. It took a lot to unsettle her – the last time it had been a small man with a very large shot-gun – but Senga Lundy had knocked the wind out of her sails, and no mistake. It would be lovely to take her up on her offer, but Billy had the idea that once the novelty wore off – or once the girl got herself a lover or a husband – things would change. The offer Senga Lundy had made was the ideal solution to her problems; it was the offer of security and a future, a peaceful retirement. And Billy was old enough to realise what she represented to the girl – a feeling of security, adventure, the forbidden. And what would happen in a year or two down the road, what then?

And yet she knew that Senga Lundy was mature enough to have weighed up all the options before making the decision; but did Senga have the experience to make decisions. She was still an immature, sometimes naive, young woman. Time would tell.

'The von Manns are industrialists,' she began suddenly. 'Farm machinery originally, munitions now.' She shrugged. 'Nothing particularly unusual about that, except that the von Manns have been particularly successful at it. Their business interests are quite enormous, and they are now one of the largest manufacturing industrial concerns in Germany.' She looked at Senga from beneath lowered brows. 'They are also wealthy, wealthy in a way that you or I cannot comprehend. By comparison, your mother is a pauper, Senga.'

'I understand.'

'I don't think you do,' Billy murmured gently. She

stopped as the train slipped into a tunnel, plunging everything into darkness. When it emerged minutes later, the light seemed to have a different quality, as if everything had taken on a graininess, like a bad photograph. It took Senga a few seconds to realise that particles of soot were whirling through the air of the dining carriage. 'These people are wealthy,' Billy continued as if nothing had happened. 'And great wealth, I've found, makes people stupid or arrogant. They believe that their money can buy everything – and I suppose, in many cases, it can. But you'll sometimes find that what they cannot have, they destroy.'

'Why are you telling me this, Billy?'

'I'm telling you this so that you will be careful of Rutgar. While he was out of the country, he was fine, a little ignorant, a little arrogant, but he is a Junker after all, and that sort of behaviour would be almost expected of him. But now he is returning home, into a family situation where he is merely the younger son in a large family. So do not expect him to react or act in the same way towards you. Now, he will be aware of his position, his status, his wealth, and if he forgets for a moment then someone there will be sure to remind him. He will also be under a certain amount of pressure from the family because he has brought you home,' Billy continued. 'So what you will have to do, right from the very start, is to impress your character on your surroundings. Do not let them overpower you; stand your ground, fight them – but always, always, remain a lady. The Germans place a great store on family and title – and because you have none, that will go against you – so it will be up to you to impress them that you are a lady.'

'His father knows my mother,' Senga reminded her.

Billy nodded absently. She was watching a short, stout, bald man a little further down the carriage. He had seemed to be paying attention to them on and off throughout the morning, but now he had taken to staring openly.

'Well, if his father knows your mother, he obviously

230

knows what your mother is. However, for lots of reasons he may not want his wife to know how he came to be acquainted with the Madam of a brothel . . . in fact, from what I know of the Germans, I'm quite confident he definitely will not want his wife to know about that at all. But we have no way of knowing how he is going to react; take your cue from him when you are introduced . . . now sit perfectly still, because a man who has been watching us very intently is heading this way,' she continued in exactly the same tone of voice, without turning her head.

It took a monumental effort of will for Senga to continue to stare at the window. Blinking hard, adjusting her focus on to the rain-streaked glass, she saw the man moving towards them. The Derringer was in the purse on her lap. Without turning her head, her left hand began to move towards it, her heart fluttering wildly in her breast.

'*Fraulein?*' The short, stout man stopped before their table and bowed slightly, his heels clicking together, which betrayed his profession – or former profession – as easily as if he were still wearing his uniform. When he spoke, his English was perfect and virtually unaccented. 'I was wondering if you ladies would care to join me . . .'

'*Nein!*' Billy said coldly.

The man continued smiling, even though his eyes turned glassy. 'I was about to invite you to join my tabl . . .'

'And I said, "no",' Billy snapped.

'I would of course pay . . .'

'How much?' Senga murmured, a mischievous smile touching her bottom lip.

The small man smirked and, placing both hands palm down on the table, leaned forward and smiled at Senga. 'A lot for your company, Miss . . .' he flicked a glance at Billy. 'Not so much for your friend.'

'We are together,' Senga whispered.

The man glanced at Billy again. 'I'm sure we can reach some compromise . . .' he began, and then stopped, slowly becoming aware that something was wrong with his left hand.

231

The pain registered slowly, like a cinder that has alighted on the flesh, and then pain raged up through his hand in a molten flash. The scream caught in his throat, and for a moment it sounded as if he were panting for breath. He looked down at his hand and was almost shocked to find that, at first glance, it seemed to be unmarked, but then, even as he watched, a tiny bead of startlingly-red blood appeared on the back of it. As he watched, the bead swelled and bubbled and then ran in a twisting rivulet down on to the white, linen tablecloth. He looked at the younger woman, puzzled, confused . . . and saw the six-inch hatpin clenched in her right hand. The shining metal was dark and glistening.

'Why you . . .!' His right hand – his uninjured hand – drew back to strike the woman across the face, when the bigger woman slammed her clenched fist into his groin, dropping him to the ground, twisted in agony.

'I have never been so insulted in all my life,' Senga proclaimed loudly for the benefit of the few people in the buffet car. 'This man . . . this man was most uncivil to me, and then actually threatened me with physical violence.' She rounded on the astonished waiter. 'I demand that you call the guard.'

The waiter bowed and backed away immediately, his eyes on the man on the ground. He didn't know what the man had done to these two women, but he could see what they had done to him – and he certainly didn't want to share the experience. He had a good idea why the man had approached the women though. Sometimes some of the street girls worked the trains on the longer routes, and they usually picked up their clients in the buffet car; obviously the man thought they were that type. He looked at the two women again; the younger of the two was certainly pretty, but the older looked more like a man than a woman, but they certainly didn't dress or act like whores. Besides, if there had been whores working the train, he would certainly have known about it.

★

232

'I am pressing charges. I have been assaulted.' The small German was almost incoherent with rage, white spittle flecking his lips, an unhealthy flush to his cheeks. He rounded on the bemused guard. 'I am not without influence. I demand that these two . . . two women be handed over to the constabulary as soon as we stop in Berlin.'

'We will be stopping within the next ten minutes or so,' the guard said, glancing at the large, brass clock above the long bar. Turning back to the two women, he looked at them carefully, not saying anything. They certainly didn't look like some of the prostitutes who sometimes plied their trade on the trains, and he knew all of the usual girls by sight, and, of course, there was also the matter of the small commission he received for turning a blind eye to such activities. They might be freelancers, he thought but then immediately dismissed the idea. The younger one was too pretty – she'd never be working the trains, she could probably command a high price in the brothels – and the older one looked like a man. Their accents were peculiar too, vaguely similar, yet disparate. They were speaking English, but accented English.

Looking at Senga, he said, *'Fraulein,* would you care to tell me what happened here?'

But it was Billy who answered. 'This man propositioned my charge and myself in a filthy and despicable manner. He even attempted to . . . to touch my person,' she added, making sure her voice was loud enough for everyone in the crowded carriage to hear. 'I pushed him away, and he fell.' Billy rose to her full height and looked the guard straight in the eye. 'I am appalled that the German Rail Authority allows such people on to its trains where innocent visitors to your beautiful country can be molested at will. I will lodge a complaint with the highest authority, and I wish to press charges against this perverted beast.'

Beside her, Senga had to chew on the inside of her cheek to prevent herself from bursting into laughter.

'This man . . . this man claims that he was stabbed in

233

the hand, and then punched in the groin,' the guard suggested almost diffidently.

'How dare you!' Billy thundered. 'How dare you speak like that before my charge. I will not permit it.' She turned to glare at the short, bald man, who was beginning to wilt beneath her barrage and the combined stares of the crowd who had gathered to enjoy the spectacle. 'And what, pray, did we stab this man with? Do we look like the sort of women who would carry swords with which to casually stab at passers-by – even perverted, old men? And do I look like the sort of woman who would touch this man's groin – let alone punch him in it? Do I?' she barked.

'No, Ma'am, you do not,' the guard said, although privately he thought she looked exactly like the type of woman who would punch a man in the groin.

The crowd parted and Rutgar stepped up beside Billy. Without saying a word he looked around, taking in Senga sitting calmly with her hands folded on the table before her and Billy standing tall and straight beside her. The guard standing a few inches from Billy's face looked completely bemused, and there was a short, bald man sitting hunched over in the chair across the aisle.

'Would someone like to tell me what is happening here?' he asked quietly, speaking in English for the women's benefit.

The guard came to heel-clicking attention, recognising Rutgar. 'Sir! There was an altercation between this gentleman and these two women. The man maintains that the women assaulted him, they counter with the accusation that the man propositioned them.'

'I think the former is highly unlikely,' Rutgar von Mann said softly, his deep-blue eyes fixing on Senga. 'This woman is my fiancée!'

CHAPTER TWENTY-FOUR

It was raining when they stepped out of the station, a cold, thin drizzle that not only soaked through their completely unsuitable clothing but also dampened their spirits. There was a maroon-coloured Mercedes tourer parked at the kerb, which was without question the longest car Senga had ever seen. Its sleek, metallic-grey exterior was complemented by its luxurious interior, and the car possessed a smell of leather and polish that reminded her of the Long Room in Trinity College Library back home in Dublin.

'Welcome to Berlin,' Rutgar laughed, climbing into the car after her, not bothering to pull the door closed behind him. A tall, silent chauffeur gently closed the door and then climbed into the driving seat. Without waiting for instructions he pulled out into the light traffic.

Billy rubbed her hand to the steamed-up window. The heaters in the Mercedes were notoriously ineffective. 'I'm not sure we're going to get to see much of it,' she remarked, peering out into the murky afternoon.

'No, I suppose not.' Rutgar sat back into the seat, beside Billy and opposite Senga.

'Do you want to tell me what that was all about back on the train?' Senga demanded coldly. Her abrupt tone caught Rutgar by surprise.

'I must apologise for the unfortunate occurrence. The man was a lecher. He unfortunately mistook you for the type of women who often work on the long-distance trains. They usually solicit their trade in the buffet cars, and naturally the man . . .' he spread his hands. 'I'm sorry. It was an unfortunate mistake, but a natural one in the circumstances. These women often work in pairs . . . and when he saw the two of you sitting there . . .' He attempted a smile. 'I don't think he will travel on that train again – at least not in the immediate future, and possibly the inconvenience will teach him a lesson. The next time he might not be so quick to approach a woman in the same manner.'

'That's not what I meant, and I think you know that. You said I was your fiancée. Would you like to explain that?' Her face was set into a hard mask that lent her a sudden maturity, and for a moment Billy Fadden had the distinct impression that this was what Senga Lundy would look like ten years hence.

Two spots of colour touched Rutgar's pale cheeks. 'I felt it was the simplest explanation. Also,' he added, warming to his theme, 'I am not unknown in this city, and I felt sure that it would speed things up appreciatively if the guard knew that you were my companion.' He looked into Senga's stone-hard face and faltered. Finally, he looked to Billy Fadden for some sort of assistance, but found no support there either.

'It was a stupid mistake to make,' Billy Fadden said into the lengthening silence. She turned away from the rain-dappled window and looked into the dusty interior of the car. With the bad light, the roomy interior seemed huge, stretching away to some indeterminate distance. 'We are trying to remain inconspicuous. Now, you are, by your own admission, well-known in Berlin. I am not a gambling woman, but I'd take a bet with you now that your engagement to an unnamed Irish or British girl will be announced in the newspapers.'

Rutgar started to shake his head – and then stopped, realising the truth of what Billy was saying.

'And what are your family going to think,' she continued steadily, 'when they read that their youngest son is engaged to a woman they have never met before? Eh?

What sort of pressure is that going to put Senga under? You profess to have some feeling for her, but this is certainly not the way to show it.'

'Enough, Billy.' Senga said tiredly. She looked at Rutgar, attempting to make out his expression, but in the gloom it was virtually impossible.

'She's right,' Rutgar said quietly. 'I was not thinking.' He leaned forward to look into Senga's dark eyes. 'And perhaps I was only putting into words what I wished was fact.'

For a moment the meaning of the sentence eluded her, and then she suddenly gasped. 'You are asking me to marry you?'

He shook his head slightly. 'I am asking you to do me the honour of consenting to be my fiancée.'

Senga looked at Billy in alarm. 'I don't know . . . I don't know what to say,' she said eventually.

'Say yes,' Rutgar urged.

'Say nothing,' the Scotswoman said loudly. She rounded on the German. 'I think it is unfair, and most ungentlemanly of you, to attempt to force Senga into making a decision like this – especially now, when she is at her most vulnerable; without her family, with no friends, and the only clothes those she is standing up in. You are her only friend – indeed, you are the only person she knows in Germany. You are taking advantage of her.'

'But . . .' Rutgar began, but Billy pressed on.

'Under the circumstances, it would be the most natural thing in the world if she were to consent to become your fiancée, and hence your bride, but that would be out of a misplaced sense of loyalty rather than love. Give it time,' she said, softening her tone, 'allow this thing to develop naturally.'

The silence in the car was broken by the hissing of the broad tyres on the wet roadway, the faint murmurings of the engine.

Finally, Rutgar nodded. 'You are right, of course. I was not thinking. It is something of a fault of mine. I tend to act

237

somewhat impulsively.'

'There's nothing wrong with acting impulsively; that original, impulsive action of yours saved Senga's life remember. But perhaps it is a fault if one acts impulsively all the time. One must learn prudence.'

'I'll try,' Graf Rutgar von Mann said, but without much enthusiasm.

'She's left Paris,' Tilly Cusack told Katherine Lundy. 'There were at least three attempts on her life, and I suppose it was only a matter of time before someone got to her.'

Katherine Lundy sighed, running her fingers through her brittle, grey hair. The two women were wandering through the early morning markets at Spitalfields, lost amidst the surprisingly large crowd, the raucous cries drowning out their murmured conversation. Moving alongside the two women were two bodyguards Tilly had brought down from Scotland. Both men were armed.

'Where is she now, Tilly?'

Tilly Cusack shrugged. Shivering, she turned up the ratty collar of the coat she was wearing, but the icy wind, occasionally flecked with rain, still managed to find her neck, and the scarf wrapped around her head provided little protection from the elements. She felt naked without a hat, but only whores wore hats at this time of day, and they were usually on the way home after a night's business.

'I don't know where she is,' Tilly replied truthfully, 'they left without telling me.'

'Why wouldn't they tell you?' Katherine wondered.

Tilly shrugged. 'I don't know.'

'Don't they trust you?'

'Of course they trust me. But I've a feeling that they were afraid that someone close to us has been leaking news of their movements.' She saw Katherine's expression harden and hurried on, not giving her time to think on the idea. 'Now, I've no proof, nothing solid and I'm not even

238

sure if it's true. But look at it from their point of view: there's been just too many coincidences. Wherever she goes, the people chasing her turn up. And it looks now as if their intentions have changed; they might have initially wanted to use her as a lever against you, but now they seem to want her dead. I don't know why – she's done nothing to them. The only reason is as a way of getting to you, hurting you.'

'They don't know me very well, do they Tilly?'

'They don't.'

'Tell me what to do,' Katherine Lundy whispered. They turned down a rubbish-strewn alley, and the two bodyguards immediately changed positions, one moving ahead, the other coming along behind. 'Your boys?' she asked.

'Glasgow's finest. Convicted killers both of them, but reformed now.'

'How did you reform them?'

'Paid them more than they could ever hope to earn any other way. Gave them complete freedom, with one proviso – that they don't get into trouble with the law and that they come when they're called.'

'Tell me what to do,' Katherine repeated.

'Give up your search for the jewels.'

Katherine shook her head violently. 'I can't. Not now. I'm so close.'

Tilly took two quick steps forward, stopped and turned to grab Katherine by both forearms. 'These people are going to kill your daughter!' she said vehemently. 'Now, if you care for her at all, if you have any feelings for her, if you ever had any feeling for her, you'll stop this right now. No jewels, no pieces of glass and metal are worth this much.'

Katherine looked into Tilly's bright-blue eyes and smiled dreamily, and Tilly was suddenly frightened. She had known that her old friend had been growing increasingly eccentric over the past few years, but this was probably the first time that she realised she was truly insane.

'I can't stop now,' she murmured. 'It's gone too far for

that. I have to find the jewels to save Senga. The people who are chasing her will only stop if they know that I have the jewels.'

'Why, Katherine? For Christ's sake what's so special about these particular jewels?'

'They are the Irish Crown Jewels,' she said simply, as if that explained everything.

'I know, I know. But what would make someone kill to get them, or kill to keep you from finding them?'

'Because I know who stole the jewels.' She turned to look at Tilly, her wide-set, brown eyes blazing, 'And if necessary I'll give the story to one of the newspapers, and I'll name names. And they will not want that; they will do all in their power to stop it.'

'Why?' Tilly asked carefully, watching Katherine closely.

'Because it's too close to the throne for comfort!'

'Paris was lovely. Weather too hot. Gone on tour. Be in touch soon. Love Senga.'

Patrick Lundy read the postcard again, turning it to look at a sepia photograph of the Eiffel Tower, and then rereading the fifteen words again. Lifting his head, he could see an almost identical view through the window of the cheap hotel. The postcard had been sent to Dublin and then redirected to Paris. Leaning forward on the flaking-metal balcony, Patrick allowed his forehead to touch the cool metal between his outstretched hands and wept for the first time in many years. She was alive. Thank God she was alive. He had seen the ruins of the last rooms she had stayed in, and looking at the devastated building, he had found it difficult to imagine that anyone could have got out of there alive. Only a copy of the French police report, which stated that no bodies, or the remains of bodies, had been found in the ruins, had given him any hope.

He reread the simple message for the tenth time. There was nothing about Billy, but he guessed that he must still be with her, otherwise she would have said.

240

But where had she gone?

It could be anywhere in Europe – or out of Europe for that matter, Berlin possibly. He realised that if he started looking for her, he could inadvertently bring other attention to her. She would be in touch when she felt the time was right, and all he could do now was to wait and trust in her judgement. There was nothing he could do at the moment; there was no point staying in Paris either. He would go back to London and attempt to make contact with his mother through Tilly Cusack, and this time he would not take no for an answer.

Inspector Maurice Durffle crossed his legs and adjusted the crease in his trousers and watched Colin Holdstock struggle through the report. The French inspector didn't offer to translate; he knew Colin would be terribly insulted. He had only met the English officer on two previous occasions, both of them business, once in London, the second time in Paris; both occasions had ended in murder, but the two policemen had struck up an instant friendship, which they instinctively knew would last, no matter how infrequently they met.

Colin Holdstock looked up from the report, closed the folder and then looked out through the dirty window across the muddy waters of the Seine. 'No bodies,' he said finally, surprised at how relieved he felt.

'No bodies,' Durffle agreed. 'Your English lady escaped, it would seem.'

'I hope so.' He caught Durffle's surprised look and smiled sheepishly. 'She is an innocent, caught in the middle; she doesn't deserve this.' He turned his attention to the report again. 'What about this person . . . this Tattoo?'

Maurice Durffle shrugged slightly. 'What can I say? He is a criminal, one of the *milieu*, a gangster. A dangerous, vicious man. There are numerous, unsolved murders laid at his door, but with no evidence to convict.' He smiled humourlessly, his thin lips barely parting. 'There's a place for him on Devil's Island, never fear, and we'll fill it one day.' He leaned over and tapped the report with a beautifully-manicured index finger. 'But he is not inexpensive this man. He is *formidable*, and costly. Whoever took out this contract on your English lady has obviously paid well, very well indeed. They must want her very badly.'

Colin Holdstock nodded. 'They do.' He looked up at Durffle. 'I want to meet this man Tattoo. Can I do that?'

The French policeman shook his head. 'Impossible.'

'Unofficially, of course. Not as an officer of the law.'

'Aaah, now that might be possible. Money would have to change hands of course.'

'Of course.'

'And it would be dangerous . . .'

'Of course.'

Maurice Durffle leaned forward and tapped Colin Holdstock on the knee. 'You must know that we – that is the French government – have sometimes used this man for some senstitive operations both at home and abroad.'

Something clicked at the back of the Holdstock's mind. 'So this Tattoo would be known to the French and British governments?'

'*Non*. Certainly not! I would imagine that the French and British governments will never know of the existence of Monsieur Tattoo, but certain departments within those governments would, of course.'

'I understand.'

'I am telling you this so you do not do anything which might embarrass you or me with those departments.'

'You're afraid I might kill this man?' Colin laughed. 'Ridiculous.'

'You might if he had killed the woman you loved!' He laughed aloud at Colin's expression. 'Do not look so surprised my friend. It is in your face, in your eyes, you cannot deny it to me.' He paused, and asked seriously. 'Does she know?'

'No . . . yes . . . I don't know. I think she must suspect.'

'Never underestimate women, my friend. If you think she knows – then she knows. Be sure of it.'

CHAPTER TWENTY-FIVE

Senga leaned on the balcony, looking out into the night. After the Parisian night, Berlin's skyline seemed almost muted, only the brilliantly illuminated Reichstag building across the darkened rain-washed rooftops lighting up the sky above it in a soft, orange glow.

From the cobbled street below, music and voices raised in laughter drifted up, and for a single moment Senga imagined herself back in Paris, with the Eiffel Tower in the distance and Parisian voices and music coming up from the street below. Someone swore in guttural German and the image shattered.

Only the monuments, language and songs have changed, she reflected.

Senga turned back into the room. This was not quite what she had expected. While she had no right to expect anything from Rutgar, she had at least thought that he would take her to his home, or one of the numerous houses he said his family owned across the city – or, at the very least, book her into a good hotel.

Instead, he had left her in this . . . this doss house! If she hadn't felt so numb, she would have found the whole affair hilariously funny.

When the Mercedes had stopped in the narrow rain-swept street, the light had almost completely gone, and it was virtually impossible to make out any details of their surroundings. Senga and Billy had been hurried into a small dark hallway and then ushered upstairs and along a corridor that bore the unmistakable odours of food and disinfectant. They were shown into a shabby room at the end of the corridor.

'Rutgar . . .?' Senga had asked.

'I know it is poor, but it is only temporary. What Fraulein Billy has said is perfectly true: I may have betrayed you by my stupidity. This place is . . . is a private hotel. You will be safe here; it is the last place someone would think to look for you.' He bowed over Senga's hand, pressing his lips to her fingers. 'I will make some arrangements and return later.' He left the room without another word and, although Senga stood in the door watching him as he hurried down the corridor, he didn't look back. That had been nearly four hours ago.

There was a series of taps on the door and then the lock clicked and Billy Fadden stepped into the room. She smiled approvingly at the gun in Senga's hand and then turned the key she had taken away with her and propped a chair against the handle to ensure their privacy. When she turned back to Senga, her broad face was grim. 'I've found out where we are, and I've also discovered that this might be just a poor class of hotel, or it might be a brothel. But I know which I'd put money on.'

Senga turned back to the window, somehow unsurprised. It accounted for the vague sense of familiarity she had felt with the place. She had spent her formative years living in a brothel, and she supposed that one brothel smelt very much like another, a smell which no amount of disinfectant would disguise: an odour of stale sweat and sex. She opened the window a little further and stepped out on to the iron-railed balcony. The voices coming up from below were clearer now, the German sounding guttural and harsh after the fluid liquidity of the French she had been listening to for the past week and a half. She was aware that Billy had come up behind her, she was close enough to feel the radiated heat from the big woman's body.

'What should we do?' she asked, without turning around.

244

'We've a couple of choices,' Billy said quietly. 'We can leave, walk out right now, or we can stay and see what happens.'

'Some choice . . .'

'I don't think Rutgar's going to betray you, if that's what you're thinking,' Billy said softly. 'He's had opportunity enough to do that already.'

'Where is he now?'

'I would imagine he's meeting his family, telling them some story about you, paving the way for your appearance.' Her big hands went to Senga's shoulders, squeezing reassuringly.

'What will happen?'

Billy shrugged. 'They'll talk sense to him, or try to, and if that doesn't work, then they'll remind him of his position, his situation . . . and his inheritance.'

'Will that bring him to his senses?'

'Yes.'

Senga stepped out to the edge of the balcony, away from the shelter of the room and Billy's hands, the rain now sparkling on her long hair, beading her face.

She turned to face the Scotswoman. 'What do you think he'll do?'

'He is a German aristo, and a gentleman, and he is obviously attracted to you. He doesn't love you, although he might think he does; if you were to ask him he would swear his undying love for you.' She smiled tightly. 'And even though he's dumped you in a brothel, he won't abandon you. At least, not just yet.'

'I do seem to have a habit of ending up in brothels,' Senga remarked wryly. 'I'm twenty-one years old and I've experienced Dublin, London, Parisian and now German brothels.'

'Must be something in the blood,' Billy laughed. 'And I don't think you should say you've *experienced* those brothels. Until you've either worked in one or been a client in one, you haven't *experienced* one.'

Senga nodded, turning back to the night, looking down

245

over the street. Three men in some sort of army uniform with tall boots were wending their way drunkenly down the street, two blonde-haired women between them. Even from this distance, she could pick up the false sound in the women's laughter.

'I seem fated to end up in brothels,' she said turning away from the balcony, stepping back into the room. She ran her fingers through her glistening hair. 'Perhaps I'll follow my mother into the trade.'

'If you do, then make sure it's your own choice.'

Senga pulled off her damp coat and flung it on to the bed, and then turned around to allow Billy to undo the buttons along the back of her dress. It slid off her shift and pooled on the floor around her feet. Stepping out of it, she padded into the bathroom and pulled down a thick, fluffy towel from the sagging rail. With her other hand she undid the bands and clips on her hair and shook it loose. Tilting her head to one side, she began to pat it dry. Peering through the tangled strands, she asked, 'So we stay here?'

'For the moment,' Billy agreed. She leaned against the bathroom door, her back straight against the frame, her arms folded across her chest. Without looking at Senga, she said, 'But don't be surprised if you find your fiancé's attitude is somewhat strained when he returns. His family will have encouraged him to look on you in a different light.'

'What'll we do then? Have you any friends in Berlin?'

'None. But not to worry. Between us, we'll work something out. We can always go back to Dublin.'

Senga straightened up and draped the towel around her neck. Holding both ends she shook her head firmly. 'No, I don't want to do that. You know, I've experienced more in the past few weeks than at any other time in my life, except when I ran away from school. And even then, everything I did seemed unreal; it was tainted by fear, the fear of being caught, the fear of having no money, of going hungry, of being alone.

'This is different. I know there are people after me, but

I'm not really afraid – at least, I don't think I am. The *fear* is there, somewhere deep inside me, but I can handle it. I know it's there, and I know it's not going to rear up and overpower me. I've coped with it. You helped me do that, you've helped me cope with the fear. And whatever happens, I've got you.' She reached out and squeezed Billy's hard hand. 'What more do I want? What more do I need? No,' she shook her head again, 'I'm not going back to London or Dublin; if I did, I'm sure I'd feel suffocated. Even if Rutgar von Mann never returns to this room, I'm staying in Berlin . . . or Rome . . . or Vienna.'

'It's your choice,' Billy said quietly, smiling slightly. 'You know I'll back you up.'

There was a sudden tap on the door, startling them both. 'Senga . . . Billy?' a voice hissed loudly. 'It's me, Rutgar.'

Billy swore. 'So now he lets the whole house know our names!' She glanced sidelong at Senga. 'He's not very bright, is he?'

'He's in love!' Senga said wickedly.

'That would account for it, right enough.'

'I'm sorry about the hotel,' Rutgar apologised again as the white-aproned waiter found them a corner table in the Kranzler Café. 'But I thought that if, by some mischance, someone was looking for you, or had followed us from the station for example, it would be the last place they would expect to find you.'

'It was the last place I expected to find me,' Senga said, smiling thinly. She was feeling overdressed and embarrassed by it. Obviously Berlin fashions were at least two seasons behind London, Paris or even Dublin styles, and her own knee-length beaded dress in a soft pastel-pink was obviously the object of some interest. She leaned across the table. 'Where did you get the dress?'

'I bought it in Paris for my brother Maximilian's fiancée, Sieglinde. I thought it might fit you. It does fit you?' he asked anxiously.

247

'It fits me, but it's just a little too fashionable for this occasion, I think. Everyone is staring.'

'They are wondering who you are,' Rutgar murmured. He raised his glass of schnapps to toast a darkly handsome young man across the room. It took Senga a second look to realise that it was actually a woman dressed as a man. Rutgar saw the expression in her eyes and smiled. 'It is the fashion now for certain types of women to dress as men.'

'What is this place?' Billy asked quietly, taking in their opulent surroundings.

'This is one of the most fashionable café's in Berlin.' Rutgar said solemnly.

'It is hardly discreet here, then?' Billy said, her eyes on a table of women dressed as men. She was a little surprised to see two of the women openly kissing one another passionately.

'This place has a reputation,' Rutgar murmured, lowering his voice. 'I think it is hardly the sort of place where anyone looking for Senga might think to search or watch.'

'You are either incredibly naive or grossly stupid.' Billy looked him straight in the face, her lips twisted into something which closely resembled a smile. 'Naivety is charming, but stupidity is not. It would be relatively easy to discover the contact you made with Senga in London, and you may be assured that they know that you met again in Paris, so, obviously, it would be only natural to continue the search here in Berlin. And while our mysterious enemies might know nothing about Berlin, and guess that Miss Senga knows even less, it would not take a genius to realise that it is you who will be under observation. And you, in turn, will bring them to us.' She tilted her head slightly. 'You see . . . simple.'

'But I was very careful when I returned to the house on the Franzosichestrasse,' Rutgar protested.

'I am not denying that. But what did you do then? You brought us here. And would I be right in thinking that this is one of your usual haunts?'

The young German had the grace to look embarrassed. 'Well . . . yes, I suppose.'

Billy sat back into the wire-backed chair with a sigh. 'I rest my case.' Leaning forward quickly, she said to Senga. 'Are you armed?'

Senga nodded, her eyes on Rutgar, watching his colour change.

'You're armed,' he hissed, 'here?'

'I'm sorry,' Billy said, sounding completely unrepentant, 'but you'll find that assassins rarely give you prior warning of their intention.'

'Don't worry, Rutgar,' Senga smiled tightly, 'we'll try not to shoot any of your friends.'

'Rutgar . . . Rutgar . . .!' The woman who sat down on Rutgar's lap was big and broad, with an enormous bosom that was barely contained in the scooped neck of the clinging, black dress she wore. Her eyes were glazed and her cheeks flushed. Her hair had once been blonde but was now streaked with grey and silver, and the deep, purple bags beneath her eyes bore evidence of her life-style. She exuded a palpable aura of alchohol. She spoke in almost unaccented English, obviously attempting to embarrass the two women. 'We don't see you anymore. But I can see why . . .' She focused on Senga, and then her eyes moved on to Billy. 'So, your taste has changed now . . . you prefer twosomes . . .' She leaned forward, pressing her bare flesh to Rutgar's cheek, and continued in a drunken, overloud whisper that they knew they were meant to hear. 'The young one is fine, a little skinny maybe, but I'm not so sure about the big cow. She looks like she could break you in half . . . but perhaps you've developed a taste for the rough stuff, a little domination, eh?' She nudged him so hard in the ribs that the two women saw him wince.

'Rosa, Rosa . . .' Rutgar attempted to disentangle himself from the woman's clinging embrace. 'You are more than a little drunk, and you are embarrassing me.'

Rosa ignored him and turned her attention to Senga. 'Ah, but she is so pretty, and so frail. Perhaps she is ill, do

249

you think, diseased, come to take the waters. She looks diseased to me.'

'And you would be an expert on diseases yourself, *Fraulein*,' Senga said quietly. 'You have the look of someone who has suffered much from diseases.'

The woman stopped, her expression changing. With a drunk's snap-change of humour, her temper turned foul. 'Aaah, she can speak, she bites. Like a trained dog. A bitch.'

'I do not know you, woman, nor do I know why you are angry with me. Perhaps it is jealousy, but then I suppose someone as old and as ugly as you must often get jealous.' Senga smiled coldly.

The woman lunged across the table, her fingers curled into claws. Billy got to her first, her cupped palm coming around to crack the woman across the back of her head. She slumped forward on to the table without a sound. In the mêlée of the café, the scene had gone unnoticed.

'You know some nice people,' Senga said almost casually.

'And you play a very dangerous game!' Fear and embarrassment had made him angry. He nodded at the unconscious woman who was now beginning to snore raucously. 'I once saw her scar a young woman for life, because she had the audacity to sit with a man Rosa desired.' He glanced sidelong at Billy. 'Do you know how close you came . . .?'

Senga opened her hands which had been clasped before her throughout the brief encounter. The tiny Derringer was nestling in them, the barrel barely protruding. 'I knew Billy would take care of her,' she said confidently, 'but if, for some reason, she hadn't, well, then I was prepared to take care of her myself.'

Rutgar von Mann looked at her in horror. 'You would have shot her?' he demanded, his voice barely above a whisper.

'I would have shot her. I would certainly not have sat here and allowed her to "scar me for life." And I would have thought that you were too much of a gentleman to allow that to happen.'

Rutgar stared at her for a few moments longer and then he dropped his gaze. 'You are correct, of course. It is just that I am so used to Rosa's ways that I forget how uncivilised and savage they must seem to outsiders.'

'She obviously feels proprietorial towards you,' Billy remarked.

'Yes . . . she . . . she was a good friend of my father's.'

'A whore then,' Senga observed shrewdly.

Rutgar looked at her stunned. 'Yes, how did you know?'

'Rutgar,' Senga admonished, with a smile, 'you seem to forget that I am not your average, blushing, English rose. I grew up in a brothel, I lived in a brothel amongst the tarts and whores; some of them I called aunty. And, even if you leave aside this woman's mode of dress which, I'll grant, is becoming less and less of an indicator nowadays of a woman's rank or occupation, you mentioned that she was an acquaintance of your father . . . well, so was my mother. And since your father obviously has a taste for certain types of women, it stands to reason that she was a whore.' Tilting her head downwards and watching him from beneath lowered eyebrows, she continued quietly, 'And from the little I know of such things, I understand that it is not uncommon for a father to introduce his son to *his* mistress or whore in order for the boy to be deflowered properly.' Colour blazed in Rutgar's pale cheeks. 'I see that this was true in your case also. Well, that explains why she took such an interest in you.'

The German finished the last of his schnapps in one long swallow. 'You are a very clever girl, Senga Lundy. Perhaps a little too clever. If I might be allowed to give you some advice,' he said formally, 'most men are not attracted by over-cleverness in their women. Smart women make them nervous. Perhaps you might temper your displays of intelligence; I think you will go further!'

'Stop it!' Billy snapped. 'Both of you. You're acting like

251

a couple of schoolchildren.' She turned to glare at Rutgar. 'I think an apology is due.'

The German opened and closed his mouth and then he finally nodded. 'Yes, yes, you are right. I apologise. I am . . . out of sorts,' he admitted. He patted the sleeping woman's head. 'And you must forgive Rosa. It is her way.'

'I take it your interview with your family did not go well,' Senga said, watching him closely. On the opposite side of the room a loud argument had begun. People began shouting comments from all sides of the café.

'How did you know I was meeting my family?' Rutgar asked quietly, his voice barely audible above the noise.

Senga shrugged.

'Never mind; I don't want to know. Yes, you're right. It did not go as I expected. We had words, my mother and I, and she can be intimidating. My father interceded for me with her, but privately he told me that he had to agree with her. I'm afraid I made the mistake of telling him who you were, and I think this alarmed him even more.'

'Rutgar,' Senga reached out and rested her hand on his. 'You owe me nothing. You don't have to do this. Tomorrow morning Billy and I will leave here and cause you no further embarrassment.'

'No!' Rutgar shook his head firmly. 'I'm sure if they were to meet you they would change their minds.'

'Rutgar . . .'

'And so there is to be a small dinner party two night's hence. You shall come with me as my guest and companion.'

Billy looked up sharply.

'I don't think it would be seemly if I arrived with two women on my arm, eh, Fraulein Fadden.'

'Where Senga goes . . .' Billy began.

'It's all right,' Senga interrupted. 'Rutgar has a point.'

'I don't like the idea of you going to a party; it's too open, too many people, you're too exposed.'

Rutgar leaned forward. 'But this will be a private party in our house in the Grunewald Forest. It's about an hour's drive outside Berlin and will be strictly by invitation only. She will be safe, I guarantee it.'

Billy nodded, but looked doubtful. 'It's just that I don't like the idea of Senga being out on her own.'

'But she shall not be on her own; I shall be with her. And I shall take extra special care of her.' He laughed. 'I suppose you will want her home by midnight?'

'I want her home in one piece,' Billy said with a smile, but the threat was plain in her voice.

The argument across the room began to grow heated. Billy reached over and took Senga's hand. 'Let's go before we're caught in the middle of a fistfight.'

Rutgar looked at the two women holding hands and laughed shakily. 'Why, Fraulein Fadden, I think you are taking your job too seriously. One would almost think that you harboured feelings for this young woman.'

'If something happens to her while she is in your care, you'll find out how deep those feelings run,' Billy warned.

CHAPTER TWENTY-SIX

Tattoo had survived for a long time in the vicious Paris underworld for three simple reasons. His reputation was second to none, and he was respected – and feared – by friends and foes alike. He had also developed an innate sixth sense which warned when danger approached. It took the form of an irritating itch deep in the empty socket of his left eye. Occasionally the urge to dig the heel of his hand into his eye was almost overwhelming, but, since he had lost the eye to an old whore's ragged fingernails many, many years ago, he contented himself with rubbing at the shiny, frayed eyepatch.

L'Américan was a bar at the respectable end of Montmartre. The food was unremarkable, the drinks expensive, the decor gaudy and in appallingly bad taste, but the music . . . the music was *different*. L'Américan specialised in jazz – proper jazz too, not this bastardised version that had been coming in lately, but real, black jazz, *le jazz hot*. Tattoo firmly believed that only the Negro peoples could play jazz, and despite its many faults L'Américan boasted one of the best jazz bands in Paris. He knew it was risky for a man in his position to have a well-known habit, a routine like the L'Américan, but the Frenchman believed that there were some things in life worth taking a risk for. And the all-Negro jazz band in L'Américan was one of them.

Wending his way through the small, circular tables, a cognac held lightly in his right hand, he rubbed at his eyepatch, his remaining eye scanning the crowd for anyone or anything that looked vaguely suspicious. But it looked like a normal Friday-night crowd of tourists, all of them confident that they were experiencing the real Paris at last, none of them realising that the real Paris was only two or three streets away, living in squalor and poverty, where crime and prostitution were as rampant as in any other European city.

Tattoo's customary table was to one side of the small, circular room. It put his back to the wall and afforded him a view of the entire room, the stage and – more importantly – the door. It also allowed him access to the back entrance behind the stage. He sipped his cognac and glanced at his watch; the jazz set would begin in a few moments. He was returning his watch to his waistcoat pocket when he sensed movement coming towards him.

A young woman was approaching his table, a hard-faced man on her arm. The man was vaguely familiar . . . something about his face . . .

Tattoo knew the woman – a mid-price street girl who worked the theatre and opera strip – that must be where he knew the man from: he had the hard-eyed expression of a pimp. The small, swarthy Frenchman knew the type – cut you soon as look at you. After a while they stopped seeing people as humans, saw them only as animals with a price on them; so much per hour.

Tattoo thought they were going to by-pass his table, perhaps make their way around the back of the stage. Some of the girls in the chorus also picked up a little money working the streets, but it was only when the girl neared the table that Tattoo saw her eyes flickering nervously in his direction.

The irritating itch in his empty socket disappeared and Tattoo immediately regretted not bringing a pistol with him. He had his knife – an Italian stiletto – tucked into the waistband of his trousers, but little good that would do him if he were faced with a shotgun.

The man stopped a few paces away from the table, his arms folded, watching Tattoo impassively. The woman came nervously forward and sat down beside the

Frenchman. Glancing back at the stranger, she began whispering to Tattoo in rapid, guttural French, with an accent that placed her to the south of the Seine, on the wrong side of the river, her voice barely audible above the first raw notes of a trumpet solo.

'This man comes to see me at my apartment this evening. He knows me. He knows a lot about me. And he knows you. He wants to see you, to speak to you. I refuse. He asks me about Marie, my baby. He tells me he will kill her unless I take him to you, and when I look into his eyes I believe him.' Tears sparkled in the woman's eyes, glistening there, unshed.

Tattoo leaned forward and patted her knotted fists with his right hand; his left was busy with the knife. He had slipped it from his waistband, prised the blade free and then embedded it, point first, into the underside of the table. The mother-of-pearl handle hung straight down, almost brushing his leg. 'Think nothing of it,' he murmured, his eyes on the man's face, his hard, dead eyes. 'You had no choice. I will not hold this against you.' With his gaze still holding the man's, he reached slowly into his inner pocket and removed a pigskin wallet. He passed her a hundred francs. 'Now, go home. You are too overwrought to work.'

The money vanished, and then she grabbed his hand and brought it to her lips. '*Merci*, Monsieur Tattoo. Be careful. This man is death.'

Tattoo smiled benignly. 'Thank you. Now use the back door.' He sat, completely still, not watching the woman leave, his eyes fixed on the stranger. Eventually, the man moved forward and sat down in the same seat the girl had used – after first pulling it around so that his back was to the wall.

'I am Patrick Lundy,' the man said quietly.

Tattoo had been too long on the streets to know the meaning of fear; fear was an old friend, a close companion – always present, missed only when it was absent. But looking at the cold-eyed man sitting beside him, Tattoo felt that curious tingle settle into the pit of his stomach. Adrenalin rushed into his system, and he was almost ashamed when he reached for his cognac to find that his fingers were shaking.

'I am Katherine Lundy's son.'

Tattoo nodded. 'I remember you,' he whispered.

He had met Patrick once, eight years previously, when they had rescued Senga from a would-be rapist. It was a moot point who had actually killed the man – both had fired together. But the Frenchman remembered the look in the young man's face then, remembered clearly the gun pointed in his direction. The Irishman had told him to walk away and he had, never thinking he would ever see the man again. He wasn't surprised he hadn't recognised him: the years had touched him, ageing him beyond his years . . . he would be . . . thirty now, but he looked older. Recalling what he knew of the man, Tattoo wasn't surprised. Patrick Montgomery Lundy had made his reputation as a killer in the Irish Civil War, a fanatic, a mad-dog who had been feared even by his own people. And if the eyes were the mirror of the soul, then this man had no soul. His eyes, dark, indeterminate, were dead, like stones. 'What do you want with me?'

'I am looking for my sister,' Patrick said softly.

Tattoo never even thought about lying. 'She is gone from Paris. I don't know where. Germany, I would imagine. I helped her escape.'

'Tell me,' Patrick said softly. A few hundred francs had bought him the information that the small Frenchman had been involved in a kidnap operation which had gone disastrously wrong, which had ripped out the top two floors of one of the oldest buildings in Montmartre. Aside from that, however, he knew nothing. The rest was conjecture, and he was quite prepared to allow the Frenchman to talk his way in – or out – of trouble. He was also quite prepared to kill him if he didn't like his answers.

The jazz band on stage had finished, and had been replaced by a small troupe of exotic dancers, most of them wearing feathers and little else. Neither man took any notice and the shouts and whistles from the audience drowned out their murmured conversation.

'I was approached through an intermediary to bring a certain English girl back to London. I was told that she had run away from home and that the lowlife she was associating with were attempting to blackmail her parents, although she was not aware of this . . .' he smiled depreciatingly. 'And since I too associate with lowlife, they assumed I was the best man for the job.' He looked up and caught the waiter's eye. Pointing to his glass, he raised two fingers. 'I did a little work, put the word out on the street and discovered that the girl was staying in a house in Montmartre, in the company of another woman.' He shrugged. 'It checked out with what I had been told.'

The waiter brought the drinks and Tattoo waited until he had moved away before continuing.

'I reported my findings and I was given an address where I would find three thugs to assist me in taking the girl. I protested – I prefer to work alone, no witnesses, no complications – but my employer insisted; the men had already been bought and paid for, and if I was not prepared to allow them to accompany me then he would get someone who would. The fee for his job was high, so I agreed.

'So, I organised a raid on the house in Montmartre. Now, I must explain that your sister and her companion had taken residence on the top floor. This particular house has – *had* – a reputation as something of a safe house, and the top floor was often used by people who wished to lie low, or as a neutral ground for aggrieved parties . . . or whatever. It was reputed to be virtually impregnable, but we had brought along explosives, and we knew we would take the room given time. What I didn't know at the time was that my employer had positioned a sniper on the roof opposite to ensure that none of the birds flew the coop.

'There was shooting, but the room was as impregnable as its reputation, so I decided to use a small explosive

258

charge to take off the door. But before I resorted to that I spoke to the people in the room, asking them to give me the girl.

'And you can imagine my surprise, my horror, when I discovered that the girl I had been sent to take was none other than Mademoiselle Senga! Well, naturally, I couldn't continue with the plan. I am indebted to your mother. And I am a man of honour,' he added quite seriously.

'There were three people in the room, Mademoiselle Senga, Rutgar von Mann, the youngest son of Manfred, the German industrialist, and the Scottish woman, whose name I do not remember. I shot the sniper on the roof opposite and helped them to escape across the roof. Then, I used an excessive amount of explosives on the door to ensure that the room was completely devastated.' He stopped and finished half his drink in one long swallow. He paused and added quickly. 'They are not in Paris, and Rutgar has left the city also. It would not surprise me to discover that the two women went with him.'

Patrick stared at him a moment longer than was necessary, and then he reached out and sipped from the fiery cognac. 'I believe you.'

Tattoo visibly relaxed.

'Now, who hired you?'

'I was contacted in a bar near here. A message had been left for me in the usual way . . .'

'Explain, "the usual way".'

Tattoo looked away, his face beginning to tighten into a mask.

'I can kill you,' Patrick said very softly. 'And I can continue my investigations. Your death would be but a momentary inconvenience. Consider this: I am not interested in your secrets . . . but are they worth dying for?'

Tattoo half-turned towards him, his single eye wide and sparkling, the white showing around the iris. 'For what I tell you now, I could be killed.'

'If you don't, you will be killed, 'Patrick said, 'and that is not a promise, it is a simple statement of fact.'

'Are you a Catholic?' Tattoo asked suddenly, surprising him.

'Yes . . . once.'

'I am Jewish, but it has been a while since I have worshipped in a synagogue. But I am still a Jew. You are still a Catholic, no matter how long it has been since you have worshipped in your church. Do you swear to me on your honour, by your god, that you will not reveal what I tell you?'

'I will give you my word,' Patrick said seriously. 'And men have lived or died by that word.'

Tattoo nodded, satisfied. 'Occasionally – very occasionally – I work for certain government departments. Dirty work, illegal, some of it necessary, some of it . . . well, I don't know. But I am well paid and I am immune from prosecution for some of my other sins,' he smiled.

Patrick watched him, saying nothing, sipping his drink, wondering where this was leading.

'When they wish to contact me, they leave a message in a bar near here. "A package has been cleared by customs." The owner and barman think I am smuggling, and I suppose it does my reputation no harm. The message simply means that I am to meet with my government contact.'

'Where?'

'Outside the Bastille, eight o'clock. He will wait every night until I appear.' He grinned and shrugged his thin shoulders. 'He would never have to wait more than two nights since I visit the bar regularly.'

'And that was the message you got?'

'It was. But instead of my contact being alone, there was a stranger with him. My contact introduced me to him, said that I should do as he wished and that he would make his own arrangements for payment, and then he left, leaving me alone with the stranger.'

'And this stranger?'

'He was an Englishman. Tall, elegant, well-spoken, cultured. He gave me a description of the two women, but told me that I need only bring back the girl, unharmed, untouched. I was paid, one-third in advance, one-third on the discovery of their whereabouts and the final third on safe delivery of the girl. When I discovered their whereabouts, I contacted him, received my second portion of money and learned about the thugs he had hired to accompany me.'

Patrick leaned forward, watching Tattoo intently. He didn't think the man would lie – he was too frightened – but he might not deliver the truth, the whole truth, and nothing but. 'And this man, this Englishman, was brought to you by your government contact.'

'That is correct.'

'Have you seen this man since?'

'Only once, when I reported the whereabouts of the girl. He was staying at a cheap hotel in the Rue de Venice, near Les Halles. I was surprised; I would have imagined he would have stayed in one of the larger, grander hotels. But I think he wanted to remain incog . . . incog . . .'

'Incognito,' Patrick supplied.

'*Merci*. He has since left that hotel,' he added.

'Was this man, this Englishman, a civil servant? You know the type?'

'I know the type well. I thought he was army; it was in the way he walked, the way he moved, the way he held himself. I could not tell if he was a civil servant or not.'

'And he has left the country?'

'He has certainly left the hotel; I do not know if he has left the country or not. I would imagine so.'

'Have you any way of getting a message to your government contact?'

Tattoo stared at him for a moment. 'Why?' he said, very softly.

'I think I should talk to him.'

Tattoo started to shake his head. 'I cannot; I could not. I would be killed if I bring you to him.'

'And I will kill you if you don't.' Patrick finished his drink quickly and stood up. Leaning over the table, he glared at the small, swarthy Frenchman. 'Don't worry. I won't betray you. Arrange a meeting; discuss something unimportant with him and then walk away. I will follow him, and ask my questions later, when you have an alibi. I will be back here tomorrow night. I trust you will have the arrangements made by then.' Without a backward glance, Patrick made his way through the crowd and out into the damp, Parisian night.

Tattoo raised his hand and miserably ordered another cognac. It was going to be a long night.

Across the smoke-filled room, Colin Holdstock dipped his head to the glass, attempting to make sense of what he had just witnessed. Whatever it was, the Frenchman looked very unhappy with the arrangement. His lips twisted in a smile. He had the distinct impression that Patrick Lundy was after exactly the same thing he was.

CHAPTER TWENTY-SEVEN

'The last time I went to a party someone tried to kill me,' Senga said lightly. She was standing in the window of the cheap hotel, wearing an over-long man's dressing-gown, towelling her hair dry.

'Don't be surprised if it happens again – but at least the only thing they'll be out to assassinate this time will be your character.' Billy opened the final box on the bed and carefully unfolded a sheer, black silk sheath. It was one of the dozen or so dresses Rutgar had bought for Senga when he had taken her shopping along the Kurfurstendamm, Berlin's equivalent to Oxford Street, or Dublin's Grafton Street. Senga had walked up and down its length at least twice before settling down to the very serious business of choosing a gown for the evening's dinner with Rutgar's family. In the end, faced with an almost impossible choice, Rutgar had bought her all of those she had expressed a liking for, along with matching shoes, hats, gloves and underwear. 'Although,' he had added, like a schoolboy delivering a naughty secret, 'I have heard it said that the modern young women have quite given up the idea of wearing underwear.'

'Rutgar,' she had whispered in the same voice, 'it is quite the custom amongst rebellious young women not to wear underwear. They usually do it for at least one season, and then they develop colds in their chests or in their kidneys and they change their minds!'

'This,' Billy said, holding up the black silk evening dress. 'With your colouring, and your hair, you will be stunning.' She pulled out the shoes and the black silk underwear.

'Rutgar told me that the young women in Berlin don't wear underwear,' Senga remarked. She looked at the dress spread out on the bed. 'And I think I'll be wearing little enough with this outfit.'

'It'll fit you like a second skin,' Billy said doubtfully. 'Here, try it first.'

Senga slipped out of the heavy bathrobe. She stood naked while Billy chose a smooth, black, Foundette girdle and a pair of black, lace-trimmed French knickers. There was a structured brassière designed to go with the girdle, but it was impracticable to wear it with the plunging neckline and off-the-shoulder design of the evening dress.

Senga stepped into the flesh-soft knickers and then stood still while Billy adjusted the girdle on her. When it was in place, Billy stood back and looked at her and then finally shook her head. 'You don't really need it, and it will show through the dress,' she added, running her fingers along the edge of the corset. 'In fact, I wouldn't even wear a garter belt. Use simple garters to hold the stockings.'

Senga slipped out of the girdle and pulled on the black, silk stockings, fixing two garters high on her thighs.

'Better,' Billy nodded. 'Now, your hair.'

Senga sat down in a high-backed, wooden chair, her head tilted back, her long hair trailing over the back of the chair, brushing the ground. Billy knelt on the floor behind the chair and began to brush the hair in long, even strokes until it shone with the same luminescence as the dress on the bed. When she was finished, she stood and came around in front of Senga and stretched out both hands, helping her to her feet. She stared at her face for a few moments, tilting her chin slightly with her strong fingers. 'Make-up,' she muttered.

She applied the barest hint of powder to Senga's oval face, highlighting her strong cheekbones, a touch of colour above her eyes to accentuate them, and finally a deep-red lipstick the same colour as the two dozen red roses Rutgar had sent.

Finally Senga stepped into the dress. The material was

incredibly sensuous, like a caress, sending shivers up along her spine, and Billy's touch, usually so delicate, felt rough and coarse against her skin. Her flesh tingled, and her cheeks flushed, her breath catching.

The Scotswoman smiled at her reaction. 'Aye, silk can do that to you.' She moved around Senga and began to arrange her hair. She swept it back off her face and forehead and then her quick fingers deftly wove the hair into a thick, braided rope. Plucking a single, tightly-closed, red rose-bud, she twisted the rose into the end of the plait. 'The heat will open it for you later,' she said, and then she stepped back to admire her handiwork. 'Aye,' she whispered proudly, 'you look a picture.' She reached over and turned the key in the wardrobe, allowing the door to swing open so that Senga could see herself in the mirror there.

She looked into the mirror and gasped, for one single moment not recognising herself. The simple make-up had lent a depth and maturity to her face, adding years and a certain amount of sophistication. The elegant black dress emphasised her height, her colouring and her svelte figure. The plunging neckline accentuated her bosom and, in a season where short hair was the fashion, her unfashionably, long, braided hair lent her character and a certain mystique. Black court shoes and a slender, virtually flat, soft leather purse completed her wardrobe.

'What about jewellery?' she asked.

'Something solid around the neck perhaps, but since we've nothing we'll just have to make do with nature's best.' Billy Fadden plucked another rose from the bunch and popped it into Senga's hair just above her left ear. The tiny bud was virtually invisible, but, like the bud woven into the end of her hair, the heat of the evening would cause it to open.

'You look stunning,' Billy said admiringly, and Senga had to admit that the total effect in the mirror was quite breathtaking.

'Thank you,' she said simply.

'Don't thank me; thank God for your looks and poise, thank Rutgar for the dress. Now,' she continued in a slightly different tone, 'stand there and listen to me for a few moments.' She reached into her pocket and pulled out Senga's tiny Derringer pistol. Slipping the catch, she broke the gun and eased out the two rounds and then, with a small brush, began to clean out the barrel and works of the gun. 'I'll not deny that tonight is going to be difficult, but that's no reason why you shouldn't enjoy it. Think of it as a game, you against his family, with Rutgar stuck somewhere in between. And remember, he is in a very difficult position. He professes to like you – and I'm sure he does, he may love you, but I don't think even he knows that yet, but there is also the love and loyalty he owes to his family. Always bear that in mind. If he stands with you against his family, that is one thing, but never try to turn him against his own people. You might have a short-term victory, but he will come to resent you for it later on.' She held up the gun and sighted through the empty barrel. 'Now, be pleasant to his family, do not antagonise them. I know you know a little German, but don't let them know that – you'll be surprised what you'll discover that way. Be pleasant, and at all times stress that you're Irish, not English. The Germans have always had a good relationship with the Irish – remember, they even sent them weapons during their Revolution.'

'The Easter Rising, 1916,' Senga said automatically.

'You have to walk a very thin line here. You have to show them that you will not be intimidated by them or their wealth, and yet you cannot afford to argue with them.' She slid the two copper-headed bullets back into the gun and clicked it shut. 'And I wouldn't recommend shooting any of them either.'

'I wasn't going to bring it. I really have no place . . .' Senga began. 'It will show through this thin purse as clearly as if I were carrying it in my mind.'

Billy produced a garter with a loop sewn into one side. 'I made this for you this afternoon.'

'What is it?'

'What does it look like?'

'It looks like a garter . . .' She stuck her index finger through the loop, 'but you've added something.'

'Raise your right leg,' Billy commanded and, as she did so, the Scotswoman took the garter and slid it up along her leg, stopping just above her knee. Positioning the loop on the inside of her knee she popped the small pistol securely into the loop. 'If the pistol was on the outside you would see it through the dress, and at least this way it won't interfere with your walking . . . unless your knees knock together as you walk.'

'I don't think so,' Senga smiled.

Billy lifted the six-inch hatpin from the bed. 'Now, we do have a slight problem with this little toy.'

Senga reached around behind her back and touched the long plait. 'Slide it in here.'

Billy fixed the long pin straight down the plait, until only the tiny rounded end was showing, and that was almost invisible against her mass of hair. 'Now, there you are, beautiful and armed – a lethal combination.' She moved around in front of Senga and gripped her by the elbows. 'Above all, don't allow Rutgar to make love to you.'

She had spoken so casually that it took the younger woman a few moments to realise what she had said. She blinked at Billy, dumbfounded.

'You will be under a lot of pressure tonight. Rutgar will be the only person you'll know, and naturally you will find yourself leaning on him. Perhaps you'll drink, I don't know, I wouldn't recommend it, but don't express your gratitude to him in any way other than a formal good night. German men can't be very much different from men the world over; they like their women liberated, free with their charms, but they rarely marry them. If he gets what he wants he'll lose interest in you. And remember, we are dependant on him for the moment, until our circumstances change.'

'I'll be good, Mother,' Senga said sarcastically.

Billy cupped her face in both hands and kissed her lips lightly. 'Stay safe.'

A sleek, metallic-grey Mercedes arrived to collect her, the driver resplendent in a vaguely military-style uniform, complete with gauntlets, high polished boots and a peaked cap. He escorted Senga to the car, opened the door for her, inclined his head slightly as she entered, and then closed it gently behind her. He walked around the car and climbed into the driver's seat and allowed the car to glide down the street, the noise of the engine barely audible above the hissing of the tyres on the wet cobbles. Senga sat back into the smooth, leather interior and wondered what the driver must be thinking, collecting someone who looked and dressed as she did from a hotel which he almost certainly knew was little more than a brothel. Undoubtedly the driver would be reporting everything to Rutgar's parents – and this was not an auspicious start!

Rutgar's parents had a house in the Grunewald Forest, to the south and west of Berlin, a little more than an hour and a half's drive by car. She found the streets fascinating: some, like the Kurfurstendamm, bright and busy with perhaps far too many young men and women standing on the street watching the traffic for it to be entirely natural, others, across the Alexander Platz, quiet, almost deserted. It had an entirely different *feel* to it from Paris or London or even Dublin. Dublin was quiet, almost provincial, with provincial values, sedate, settled; London was cosmopolitan, vast, sprawling, while Paris was wild and carefree, exuberant. Berlin was different; there was a seriousness about it, a harsh edge she found vaguely disturbing. It was not a city she would like to live in, she decided. Soon they were driving through Berlin's drab suburbs which reminded her of pictures she had seen of the industrialised north of England. The streets were deserted, or so she first thought until her eyes adjusted to the gloom and she discovered that most of the empty doorways held two or three blanket-wrapped, huddled bodies, and once the bright beam of the car's headlights picked out what looked like an entire family cowering in against a shopfront. Senga Lundy decided she didn't care for the modern Germany.

She settled back into the car, closed her eyes and attempted to doze, but the images from the streets kept appearing, upsetting her. She needed to be bright and alert for that evening, and it promised to be a long night. She had intended to sleep when she returned from shopping, but it had taken far longer than she had intended and Rutgar had seemed to take a genuine interest in her clothes.

With a deliberate effort of will she remembered the last man who had bought her clothes like that: Jean Michel Hugo. He had been twenty-three years old, married and very wealthy. He hadn't exactly kidnapped her, but then he hadn't actually allowed her to go free either. He had taken her to fine restaurants, bought her fine clothes, and then he had taken her to his flat overlooking the Seine on the Quai de la Tournelle, close to Notre Dame, and almost directly across from the Tour d'Argent Restaurant. There he had attempted to rape her. And that's where he had died, killed by a bullet from Patrick's pistol and a blast from Tattoo's shotgun.

It had taught her a lesson; no matter how altruistic a man, he always expected payment for a gift. And she couldn't help wondering what sort of payment Rutgar would expect for all of this.

Perhaps he did love her. The thought had occurred to her, and she was sure it had occurred to him, but she wasn't sure she knew what love was. She knew what passion was. She had experienced passion beneath Billy's sensitive fingers and lips, and she had learned so much from the woman. Billy had taught her what it was like to be a woman, how to please a man . . . and a woman; she had helped liberate her from the morality and ignorance which would have been the norm for a girl of her class. Billy had also taught her how to respect her own body; the body was an instrument, the Scotswoman had told her, designed to give and to receive pleasure. Would Rutgar have been able to teach her as much as Billy Faden had? Would she have allowed him? She trusted Billy . . . but did she trust Rutgar? The question brought her bolt upright, eyes wide, staring into the night.

And she realised the answer was *no*.

The hissing of the car's white-walled tyres on the road lulled her, soothed her gently, and eventually she slipped into a light doze. Her dreams were pleasant: she dreamt that she was making love to Billy, but at some stage the woman metamorphosised into Rutgar, and she found she was naked, lying on her back on the cold marble floor of a grand ballroom, making love to him, surrounded by men and women dressed in evening dress and gowns. The semi-conscious portion of her mind rationalised it as nothing more than her confusion about her relationship with both Billy and Rutgar and her apprehension about the evening's party. But the other, deeper, unconscious portion of her mind simply enjoyed the vicarious experience.

Eventually, she slipped into a deeper sleep, and if she dreamt then she had no conscious memory of it.

The chauffeur watched the woman in the rear-view mirror. He was a Russian émigré, and had once held the title *prince* – although such titles were not uncommon in Europe after the Bolsheviks had taken over, with just about every Russian he met claiming to be a prince or a baron or a duke. All he had to do was to look at them, and he could tell – immediately, instinctively, by the way they moved, the way they held themselves – whether they were people of quality. And so few of them were.

The von Mann's now, they were *nouveau riche*, workers who had made money and who took a certain pleasure in having a genuine Russian prince as their driver.

His eyes flickered to the woman dozing in the back of the car. He had been a little surprised when he found that the address Rutgar had given him of the woman he claimed was his fiancée was in one of the less fashionable parts of Berlin, but he had been even more surprised when he had seen the young woman. When he had seen the hotel, he had immediately assumed that she was one of the street girls, but as soon as she had stepped out on to the pavement and smiled at him, he had known that she was a person of quality.

And far too good for Graf Rutgar von Mann.

CHAPTER TWENTY-EIGHT

The smooth hissing of the tyres on wet roadway was replaced by the crunching of gravel, which brought Senga fully awake. For a moment she sat in the warm, comfortable interior of the car, totally unaware where she was. She peered through the window, rubbing her hand against the fogged glass, and found that they were driving up a long, tree-lined, gravel driveway. What looked like ornate lampposts dotted the driveway, shedding an illumination that was more ornamental than anything else. Tendrils of mist or haze wrapped themselves around the lampposts, coiling about the lights, flowing against the car's headlamps, lending the night an eerie, almost frightening aura.

The fear brought realisation flooding back and she took a few moments to check her make-up in a small compact; then she moved her legs together, checking on the small pistol strapped to her thigh. Patting her hair, she touched the long pin, ensuring that it was still in place, and then she smiled: just the sort of preparations any girl would make for a party . . . if her life was threatened, and she was in a foreign country, and feeling very much alone and just a little afraid.

She looked straight ahead, peering through the windscreen as the night sky ahead of her lightened, and then finally the house appeared through the trees with what looked like every light in the house ablaze, all the windows uncovered, yellow light streaming out into the damp night.

271

The car slipped into a tunnel of trees and then swept out into a broad courtyard, complete with ornamental fountain. There were people milling about on the deep, wide steps that led up to the house, and their car had to wait while a Daimler ahead of them disgorged an elegant, elderly couple and an absolutely hideous younger woman, whom Senga took to be their daughter. Their car then moved off, its exhaust puffing whitely on the air, and her own car moved into position.

The chauffeur climbed out and slowly walked around the car to open the door for her. He held up a black-gloved hand which she accepted as she stepped out, and then she stopped, taking a final deep breath before commencing the climb up the steps which, at this angle, looked enormous.

'Good luck,' the chauffeur whispered catching her eye, the corners of his mouth crinkling in a smile, and then he bowed again and stepped back.

Senga stepped forward, glad that she wasn't wearing high-heels, sure she would have stumbled on them. Her heart was tripping in her breast, and there was an almost painful lump in her throat. She moved sedately, but not slowly, abruptly glad of the few months she had spent at the finishing school in Switzerland. She could still clearly hear Madame Royer declaiming in her sergeant-major's voice, 'a young lady does not run, for to do so is vulgar, nor does a young lady creep along, for that is common. A regular sedate pace, with the arms held loosely at the sides, not swinging like some bumpkin, the shoulders relaxed, the head held proud . . .'

Rutgar was waiting at the top of the steps, resplendent in a tailed dress suit, complete with starched shirt, winged collar and bow-tie. He was holding what looked like a pair of white silk dress gloves. His eyes flared in surprise when he saw her, but before he could say anything she extended her hand to him as she approached. Taking her hand, he pressed the back of her fingers to his lips, while bowing over them, his heels clicking together. When he

272

straightened, he looked straight into her eyes. 'I almost didn't recognise you,' he mumured. 'You are stunning, absolutely stunning.'

'I have you to thank for that,' she smiled.

'Clothes are nothing without the wearer. You could put that dress on a dozen, no, a hundred other women, and they would not have the grace to wear it as well as you.' The smile faded off his face as he glanced over his shoulder. 'My parents are waiting. I don't think there will be a problem with my father . . . but my mother . . .' he let the sentence hang. Placing her hand on his arm, he steered her through the crowd on the step towards the open door. He was aware that she was attracting many admiring glances; he found it difficult to reconcile the image of the girl he had driven that afternoon to buy the clothes with this stunning creature on his arm. Senga Lundy was many things, he realised, and he was only beginning to realise just how versatile she was. He was aware how difficult this was for her; he only hoped his mother would be gracious. At least Senga's poise and looks would help. His mother had scathingly commented on 'peasant Irish, bare-foot, living in sod huts, little more than savages.'

Senga would give the lie to that.

Clara von Mann was standing in the circular hallway to receive her guests. A tall, thin, aristocratic woman in her late fifties, Rutgar had inherited his Nordic colouring from her, but, whatever flesh had once covered her large bones, much of it had fallen away with the years, leaving her gaunt, her eyes deep-sunk, cheekbones and chin prominent and sharp. Her temperament was as sharp and acid as her looks.

By now most of the guests had arrived – all the important guests certainly had – and there was no further reason for her to remain at the door. To remain here afforded those latecomers a measure of respect which they certainly didn't deserve. However, Clara von Mann wasn't going to move until she had met this Senga Lundy, this

273

Irish girl whom Rutgar had met in London and again in Paris, and had then foolishly invited here as his guest. She knew the girl was going to be late, because Rutgar had had to send the car into Berlin for her. She wondered where the girl was staying – well, no matter, she would ask Mikhail the chauffeur where he had picked her up.

She spotted Rutgar moving towards her, a woman on his arm, and, although her eyesight was not as good as it once was and modesty and fashion forbade her from wearing spectacles in public, she could see that this sophisticated creature wasn't the woman she was looking for.

'Mama.' Rutgar stopped before her and bowed his head slightly. 'I would like to present Miss Senga Lundy, from Dublin, Ireland,' he said.

Clara von Mann smiled automatically, a smile which broadened as Senga dropped into a deep curtsey.

Taken aback, the woman bowed and extended both hands. Senga came smoothly to her feet and moved into the circle of the woman's arms, brushing her powdered cheeks lightly with her lips.

'Senga,' a very nervous Rutgar, introduced his mother, 'this is my mother, Frau Clara von Mann.'

'I am delighted to make your acquaintance, Madam,' Senga said carefully. 'It was most kind of you to invite me tonight.'

'Rutgar has spoken so highly of you,' Clara von Mann said gently, taken aback and impressed by the charm and elegance of the young woman. 'And of course it is an honour to have you here tonight.' She linked her arm through Senga's and led her into the huge, marbled hallway. 'But your heart is pounding,' she said quietly, slipping from English into French. Her right wrist was resting just below Senga's breast.

'I am a little nervous, Madam,' Senga replied in the same language, wondering if the woman was attempting to gauge her education.

'Why, surely not? We're not ogres. It is always a delight to receive friends of my son.'

274

Senga bowed her head slightly, attempting to hide a smile. 'I think it is only natural that you should be curious about this strange woman your son met in London and Paris and brought with him to Berlin; I know if I was in your position I would be very curious indeed.'

The older woman's smile broadened. 'Aaah, I see you are honest and not afraid to speak your mind. I think we could get along, you and I.' Instead of heading directly into the huge ballroom, from which the sounds of revelry and a jazz band were drifting, she steered her towards a pair of tall, dark-wood doors which were embossed with an ornate coat of arms. A white-coated servant moved ahead and opened the doors as the two women approached, closing them when they had stepped inside.

'We do not wish to be disturbed, Franz,' Clara von Mann said softly as they passed him, and Senga felt sure that if she opened the doors she would find the bulky man standing directly outside, arms folded across his chest.

They were in a library and, like most of the things she had seen in the house, it was built on a grand scale. Perhaps there had been another room above it, but it was long gone, and now the library was lined with books, stretching from floor to ceiling, with a narrow gallery half-way up the room running around the wall. There were numerous small tables scattered around the room, most of them covered with books, and there were further volumes scattered around the floor or piled high beneath the tables and in the corners.

'It is a very fine library, Madam, certainly one of the finest I've seen in private hands,' Senga said truthfully. Her initial reaction was that it was just for show, but it was untidy enough to indicate that someone actually used the room on a regular basis.

'My father was a great collector,' Clara von Mann said softly, looking around the room. 'He built most of this collection himself; I have added a little to it, but not much. After the war it was difficult to buy books, and of course as many books were destroyed during the war, and even

275

more *after* the war as people simply used them for kindling.'
She stepped away from a small, false-fronted drinks cabinet
she had swung out from a section of shelving and handed
Senga a dry, white wine. 'Please sit . . .' she indicated a fat,
overstuffed, leather settee, while she moved around to sit
on a hard-backed, wooden chair before a broad, leather-
topped oak desk.

Realising what the woman was doing, Senga sipped her
ice-cold drink and prepared herself for the interrogation.

'You're not what I expected,' Clara von Mann said
simply.

'What were you expecting?'

The woman smiled. 'Something . . . someone . . . less
sophisticated, less well-educated . . . shall I use that
dreadful phrase: I expected someone lower-class.'

Senga smiled to take the sting from her words. 'I'm not
sure how I should take that, Madam.'

The woman sipped her drink, obviously enjoying herself. 'It was not meant as an insult, but I have met several of
my son's girls. I have been less than impressed. I even tried
to arrange a suitable match with a young woman of his own
class and standing, but he refused even to consider the idea.
So when he told me he had met an Irish girl and was
bringing her along tonight, I suspected that I was about to
be faced with yet another low-class woman. Someone
common.'

'Rutgar has been very good to me,' Senga said watching
the woman carefully. She obviously doted on Rutgar, so
much so that she was even prepared to turn a blind eye to
the young women he brought home, even though she did
not approve of them. Knowing that, it was relatively simple
to gain her attention and her sympathies. 'In London, he
saved my life,' she added conversationally. 'He was so
gallant.'

Clara von Mann blinked in surprise. 'That does not
sound like my Rutgar at all.'

'It is true, I assure you.'

'I am surprised he did not tell me. Why would he not

have told me?' she pressed.

'Modesty perhaps?'

Clara von Mann shook his head. 'It is unlikely. Rutgar has no secrets from me.' She brought her wine glass up to her face and stared at Senga over the rim. 'You will have guessed that I brought you in here so that I could speak to you before you got lost in the crowd outside – or before Rutgar could spirit you away and then contrive to keep you out of my way for the rest of the evening.' She smiled. 'Rutgar can be such a little boy at times; he occasionally does stupid things too,' she added in a slightly harder tone.

'Like inviting strangers home with him?'

'You're a clever girl. I admire your directness, and your honesty. Let me be honest with you in turn. Rutgar is a very wealthy young man. His personal fortune is already quite impressive and he stands to inherit a considerable sum when his father and I die. There are people who would find the fortune a great attraction.'

Senga dipped her head to hide a smile; they had finally arrived at the true purpose of the conversation. 'I am sure there are, Frau von Mann, but I am not one of them. When I met your son in London. I did not know who he was: he could have been a prince or a beggar for all that I cared. He had saved my life and been injured in the attempt. That is how our relationship – if you want to call it that – started. We are friends at the moment, I think Rutgar would like us to be more than friends, but at the moment I don't think we know each other well enough to go that far. He has talked of marriage, but I'm not ready for marriage. I do not want for money. My mother has extensive business interests in Dublin,' she lied, 'which are now looked after by my brother Patrick. Our father was killed in the Easter Rising in 19 . . .'

'. . . 1916,' Frau von Mann supplied. 'Yes; it might surprise you to know that we supplied a portion of the arms used in that unfortunate attempt to free yourselves from British rule.'

'My mother now runs her business interests from an address in Mayfair in London, and I know she had offices in several of the larger British towns.'

'Business,' the German woman said, with a little moue of disappointment.

'It is a . . . private investment and advisory service for young gentlewomen; it involves a certain amount of banking.'

Clara von Mann brightened up considerably. This girl was beginning to look like a better and better prospect; the daughter of a female private banker, obviously wealthy and well-educated, and pretty too. Indeed, she sounded almost too good to be true – either that or she was married. 'But you said that your life had been threatened in London . . .?

'A case of mistaken identity. I had taken my mother's place at a function, and an aggrieved client attacked what he thought was my mother. I was dancing with Rutgar at the time and he protected me from the man's blows. It turned out that the man had been drinking heavily that evening and was not responsible for his actions.' Senga marvelled at how easily the lies came.

'Your French accent is almost perfect,' Clara von Mann complimented her, changing tack.

'I was sent to a Swiss finishing school and after that I holidayed in France. My recent stay in Paris has renewed my ear for the language.'

There was a tap on the door and Rutgar poked his head into the room. 'Aaah, there you are. I've been looking everywhere for you; I thought you might have gone home.'

'You must forgive me, Rutgar, but I just had to take Senga away while I had the opportunity, you know how hectic it will get later this evening.' She stood up and Senga came to her feet at the same time. The regal German woman came around the desk and walked right up to Senga, kissing her on both cheeks. 'I will speak to you again, before you go . . . in fact, I will have a bedroom

278

prepared for you. The journey back to Berlin will be tedious in the extreme. Rutgar, my old room will be prepared for Miss Senga.'

'Yes, Mama.'

When she had gone, Rutgar turned to Senga, his face a delighted mask. 'You've done it! You've passed the most difficult hurdle of all, and you've got her stamp of approval. *Mein Gott*, she's even offered you her old bedroom. That is approval indeed.' He laughed uproariously and then said quickly, 'Why, we could get married in the morning and she'd approve. What do you say, eh?' he asked, half-joking, half in earnest.

'Ask me in the morning,' Senga said, already tired of his chatter.

'I will!' he said, so forcefully that it sounded like a threat.

CHAPTER TWENTY-NINE

In a wharfside café in Dover, Tilly Cusack watched Katherine Lundy wolf down a greasy sandwich with apparent relish. Katherine glanced up at her old friend and smiled. 'Hunger makes good sauce.'

'How long has it been since you've eaten?' Tilly said quietly, glancing around her, turning up the collar of her coat. Katherine had asked her to dress inconspicuously for the meeting, and although she had worn the oldest rags she could find she still felt overdressed for this place.

Katherine thought about it for a moment. 'I left London three days ago, and I haven't really been eating well since then.'

'What happened to make you leave London so suddenly? I waited for you as usual on the bridge; when you didn't turn up, I got very worried.'

Katherine waited while a dozen dockers filed through the café's grimy door into a leaden morning. Cold air wafted into the small, stuffy room, briefly displacing the odours of grease and unwashed humanity with the stench of diesel and rotting fish. The dozen or so people remaining in the café moved like a single organism with the change of air, hunching over their cups, eyes fixed on nothing in particular. The air of hopelessness in the room was almost palpable. Katherine Lundy smiled over a chipped cup of appalling tea. 'Two things happened almost simultaneously which convinced me that it was time to move on.' She sipped some of the tea and grimaced. 'Christ, that's foul!' But she still drank some more. 'I had made contact with an old . . . ahem . . .

acquaintance of mine, a dealer in stones and metals . . .'

'The Greek?'

'Yes, you remember him?'

'I remember him; I thought he was dead.'

'He is now,' Katherine said, her face expressionless. 'A few years ago he offered me the jewels, but before I could get to them circumstances caught up with me . . . that was about the time Patrick ran away.' She shrugged, dismissing that time back in 1919 when her family had fallen apart because of her own greed and stupidity. 'Anyway, by the time I got around to the Greek, the jewels were no longer on offer. He had been acting as a middleman, and the principal had withdrawn the stones from sale.

'I went back to him last week. He is an old man now, into his nineties, but his memory of the stones was excellent, and I suppose it is something of a compliment that he still remembered me. I explained a little of my story to him, told him why I needed the stones, how important they were to me. To be honest I didn't expect him to believe me . . . I was more than a little surprised when he did. However, thinking back on it, I wonder if my story came as a complete surprise to him.' She sighed and shook her head. 'Anyway, it's not important and we'll never find out now. I spoke to him for over an hour, and the only thing of any real importance he could tell me was the stones had been sent to Paris to a jeweller there who specialised in the "re-arrangement" of stolen stones.'

' "Re-arrangement?" '

'Good stones would be removed from a mundane setting and reset to create an entirely new piece.'

'Surely that destroys the value of a piece?'

'Sometimes; occasionally it enhances it. But remember, the Irish Crown Jewels were not of great monetary value, though some of the individual stones were pure and might command respectable prices on their own. If the British Crown Jewels were stolen today, it would be very difficult to place them as complete pieces, though the individual stones would be very valuable, especially if they were reset.'

'Is that what happened here?' Tilly asked. She was watching a large, ugly labourer at a nearby table who was looking at the two women intently. She knew she looked too respectable, but Katherine looked every inch a wharf whore.

'We don't know. We think so. The Greek said he would make some inquiries for me, and I left him my address so he could pass a message on to me.' She paused, realising she hadn't got Tilly's full attention, and then turned to glare at the labourer. The man's smile broadened, and he winked. Katherine ignored him and turned back to Tilly. 'The following night, someone burst into my room and emptied both barrels of a shotgun into my bed.'

'Where were you?' Tilly breathed.

'Oh, I was in the room all right, but I'd taken to sleeping in a chair by the window, while leaving pillows under the covers to simulate a body.' She grinned smugly. 'The only way you'll stay alive in this game is to stay one step ahead of the opposition.'

'What happened to your would-be-assassin?'

Katherine shrugged. 'I don't know. I never saw him, and he didn't wait around to examine the results of his handiwork.'

'The Greek obviously betrayed you. What did you do?'

'I paid him a visit.' She stopped and finished the last of the cold tea. 'He was dead. And he hadn't died easy, so maybe he didn't give out my address without a fight.'

'Was he looking for the jewels for you?' Tilly asked intently.

'He said he would make some inquiries. Obviously those inquiries brought him to someone's attention.' Her face hardened into a mask. 'They tortured an old man for my address, Tilly, and when he gave it to them they killed him.' She looked down at her hands, which had tightened into white-knuckled fists on the table. Tilly reached over and covered the hands with her own. 'What sort of people are they, Tilly?' she asked softly.

'What are you going to do now?' Tilly asked, deliberately changing the subject.

'I'm going to Paris to find the jeweller the Greek mentioned.' She turned her hands on the table, taking hold of her friend's fingers. 'And you better be careful now,' she said seriously, 'just in case someone decides to ask you a few questions.'

'I still have my two Scottish boys.'

'Aye, but these people play rough. And they play for keeps.'

'Don't worry about me; you just look after yourself. Where will you go in Paris, do you know anyone there?' she asked.

'I used to have a very good connection in the Parisian underworld. I'm not sure if he's still alive, but I'm sure I would have learned if he had passed on naturally or otherwise.'

'Tattoo?' Tilly asked.

'Tattoo,' Katherine nodded.

Tattoo walked away from his meeting with the government official bathed in a cold sweat. His reason for seeing the man had been flimsy enough – a report of a shipment of arms coming in through Marseille – but what had really made him nervous was the knowledge that Patrick Lundy was standing in the shadows, a gun trained on his back. And Tattoo had no doubt that the Irishman was more than capable of using it. The small Frenchman passed the tree behind which Patrick had been standing, but the Irishman was gone, and Tattoo heaved a sigh of relief. Turning up the collar of his coat, he hurried into the night; he knew an after-hours club where he could get a cognac or two and some female company, and he reckoned he needed – and deserved – both.

Patrick Lundy followed the tall, thin man Tattoo had met through the deserted streets. The man initially took a few simple precautions to avoid being tailed, but these seemed more from habit than any real fear of someone

283

following him; in any case, Patrick had learned his trade on Dublin's mean streets where he had hunted and been hunted by the IRA. He was dressed completely in black, and with the collar of his overcoat turned up and the brim of the slightly over-large hat pulled down, he was virtually invisible against the shadows. There were two guns in his inside coat pockets, a .45 Browning and a smaller .38-calibre Colt revolver. It had been remarkably easy to buy the weapons on the Parisian black-market, and Tattoo's presence ensured that he had got them at the right price.

As the streets grew broader and busier, the government official obviously no longer felt there was any need for secrecy and now walked along openly, without even bothering to check behind him. Patrick continued to tail him, keeping to the shadows, determined to track him to his home.

And behind Patrick, Colin Holdstock followed discreetly. Who watches the watchers, the Englishman grinned. Who indeed?

The man had evidently decided to walk home – which suited Patrick, since following him in a cab would have been so much more difficult and the chances of being discovered that much higher. Nor was he in any particular hurry, stopping on several occasions to admire the displays in the windows of the larger department stores. Finally, he headed up into Montmartre, and now his interest seemed to be directed more towards the women, and, on two occasions, he stopped and spoke to them, obviously assessing their services or their prices.

Patrick ground his teeth in frustration. He had counted on the man going home, which at least would give him his address and which would allow him to pay the man a visit at some later time – like three o'clock in the morning.

The Frenchman continued deeper into the Quarter, finally stopping outside a dingy three-storey building which bore the legend/'*Hôtel*' in ornate, decorative script above the door. Just by looking at the sign Patrick had a very good idea what type of hotel it was.

The man obviously knew the place, which meant that he probably visited one particular girl, so Patrick decided to wait at least ten minutes to allow the man the opportunity of getting down to business. He stood on the street corner, his hands tucked deeply into his pockets, trying to look as inconspicuous as possible.

Colin Holdstock stood on the next street corner in the shadow of a doorway, and tried to copy him, realising how suspicious they both looked. He had originally been intending to confront Patrick Lundy earlier that evening, after his meeting with the Frenchman Tattoo in the L'Américan, but he realised that with the Irishman's hair-trigger temper it might be inadvisable. He had finally decided to follow him and act when and if the opportunity presented itself.

At the other end of the street, Patrick moved.

With a sigh, Colin Holdstock gripped the revolver in his pocket and started off after him. He had a feeling that his original idea – a straightforward conversation with Patrick Lundy – was not going to work out.

The hotel lobby was far more luxuriously appointed than Patrick had expected. A leather bench ran along one wall, and there were three pretty young women sitting there facing the door. They all looked up expectantly when Patrick entered. Ignoring them, he crossed to the concierge, a slender, rather nervous-looking young man, prematurely bald, one eye in a permanent squint from the curl of smoke from the cigarette that looked as if it might have been grafted on to his lip.

'Excuse me,' Patrick said, playing up his foreign accent. 'My friend . . . the man who came here a moment ago . . . did he . . . that is, he was to choose a . . . young woman . . .'

The concierge looked at him intently, his startled expression unchanging, and Patrick realised that what he had first taken for nervousness was actually a somewhat cruel trick of nature. The man's eyes were wide and slightly protuberant, his mouth was slack and his forehead was creased with permanent wrinkles of astonishment. But there was no sympathy in the man's pale eyes.

'Did he pay? I'm not sure what we agreed; I offered, but he insisted. Anyway, I'd like to pay, so please don't take any money from him.' Patrick opened his wallet and began extracting one-hundred-franc notes. 'You will have to help me . . . I'm unused to this currency . . .'

Something like a smile flickered across the man's face as he lifted four of the large-denomination notes. Patrick continued smiling, and made a mental note to recover the money on the way out. What he had just paid should have bought him the entire hotel.

'First floor, second door on the right,' the concierge said, dropping his eyes to the newspaper in his lap.

There was an elevator, but Patrick ignored it, preferring to use the stairs. He had once killed a man in a hotel elevator, shooting him the moment the doors opened and then sending the lift back up to the sixth floor, while he calmly walked down and out of the hotel. Since then he had never used elevators himself.

At some stage in its past, sometime around the turn of the century, someone had attempted to redecorate the hotel in the style of the period, and it was obvious that quite an amount of money had been spent on it. But whatever tourist boom had been expected in Paris had left this part of Montmartre untouched. Nor had the hotel been rede-corated in the past thirty years. Obviously the only part which had been properly maintained was the lobby, like a tart's make-up – designed to create a good impression, but once you got past that . . .

Patrick stopped outside the second door to the right on the first floor. It was indistinguishable from every other door on the floor, and all of them were without numbers. Taking the heavy automatic from his inside pocket, he stood with the side of his face pressed against the flaking wood. From within he could hear a muted conversation, punctuated every now and again by laughter. Only the man's laughter seemed to be genuine, the woman's rang harsh and falsely brittle.

Crouching slightly, Patrick tried the handle, whilst resting his weight against the wood. The door was unlocked but a bolt had been thrown close to the top. Pressing his face against the door again, Patrick heard the unmistakable sounds of lovemaking. With a grim smile, he threw his weight against the door, springing the cheap bolt, sending it clattering across the room. He strode into the room, the heavy automatice pointing unswervingly at the naked couple on the bed.

'You,' he pointed at the rather plump, blonde-haired woman who was astride the man, 'go away. If you do anything, if you say anything about this, if you call the police, or if you even contact the concierge downstairs, I will kill you. Do you understand?'

Looking into his hard, cold eyes, she nodded.

Patrick ignored the woman while she climbed off the man and dressed hurriedly, wrapping her dressing-gown around herself, bundling her few clothes in her arms, hurrying from the room. Grabbing a straight-backed, wooden chair, he swung it around and then sat astride it, his arms folded across the back, the pistol held loosely in his right hand. Looking at the naked man on the bed, pale, slightly sagging flesh, wide, terrified eyes, he found that he felt nothing. When he had killed for his country and a cause he believed in, he had found that the only way to retain his sanity was to approach each person as a job, a piece of information to be extracted or used, because once you started to think of them as people, with families, wives, children, you lost your edge, you lost the ability to kill.

This man now, he was a job, all Patrick wanted from him was a name, a contact name further up the line, another link. If he gave the name, he would more than likely let him go; if he didn't, he would kill him. But looking at the man, Patrick decided that he would give him the name.

'*Monsieur . . . Monsieur . . .*' the man eventually broke the lengthening silence.

Patrick raised the gun and the man fell silent. 'I don't

287

know you; I don't want to know you. I don't even know your name, and I don't want to know it. But I will ask you a question and you will answer. And you will tell me the truth because you do not know how much I already know, and if you lie to me for any reason, I will kill you. Do you understand me?'

The Frenchman nodded.

'Say it!'

'I understand.'

'You work for a government department . . .' he saw the man's eyes widen slightly, 'and some time ago you introduced a thug named Tattoo to an Englishman. That Englishman wanted him to kidnap an English girl, named Senga Lundy. I want that Englishman's name.'

The Frenchman started to shake his head, but Patrick raised the pistol and worked the slide, sending a round into the chamber, the metallic sound harsh and uncompromising. Pointing the gun at the man's groin, Patrick said very softly. 'You will tell me, because there are many ways to die, and some of them are not very pleasant.'

'I don't know the man's . . .'

Patrick fired at the man's face, the bullet scorching into the pillow alongside his ear. In the absolute silence that followed, the stench of urine was sharp on the perfumed air. Wisps of feathers floated about the room, giving it a slightly surrealistic appearance.

'The man . . . the man worked for one of the English government offices . . . we had dealt with them before . . . but not this man . . . I had never met him before . . .'

'His name dammit, his name?'

'Moore, Colonel Martin Moore!'

Patrick Lundy stopped as if he had been struck. He stared at the Frenchman in absolute astonishment. 'Martin Moore? Are you sure? Describe him!'

'That is the name I was given. He was a tall man with a moustache, into his early forties, distinguished . . .'

Patrick stood up off the chair and stepped back, his

thoughts whirling. Whatever answer he had been expecting, nothing had prepared him for this.

'You know him?' the Frenchman asked.

Patrick nodded. 'I know him,' he said very softly.

'So do I!'

Patrick whirled, gun levelled. Colin Holdstock was standing in the doorway, arms folded across his chest, looking from Patrick to the Frenchman.

'I know you,' Patrick hissed. 'You're that English policeman, Holdstock . . .'

'Inspector Colin Holdstock at your service,' he said with a grin.

'You had better have a very good excuse for being here,' Patrick said ominously.

'I'm here for the same reason you are. I'm looking for the man who's trying to kill your sister.'

'Why?'

Colin shrugged. 'No young woman deserves to be hounded like she is. I swore to her that the next time I saw her, I would have eliminated the threat to her life.'

'Why?' Patrick repeated.

'Because I love her!'

Realising that both men were occupied, the Frenchman decided to make his move. Throwing himself off the bed, he scrabbled for his coat, knocking it off the chair, desperately pulling open the inside pocket, reaching for the small, double-barrelled Derringer. Thumbing back both hammers, he looked up over the edge of the bed . . . and found himself looking into two guns! The Frenchman squealed with fright and dropped the tiny pistol and then stood up, arms above his head.

Patrick looked at Colin. 'Let's get out of here.'

'What are we going to do about him?'

Patrick grimaced. 'Well he knows us, and he knows your name, and he knows we're looking for Martin Moore . . .' He turned back to the Frenchman, smiled, and shot him through the heart! Then, pushing a stunned Colin Holdstock through the door, he hurried him out into the corridor and down the stairs. In the foyer, he stopped and pointed the pistol at the concierge while holding out his left hand. Without a word the man handed him the four hundred francs. Patrick allowed two to drop on to the newspaper on the table. 'You have not seen us. If I discover that you have seen us, I will kill you.' He walked away, shoving the gun into his coat pocket and steered the inspector out into the cold night. Without saying a word, the two men walked down the sloping street, turned to the left, and left again, and found themselves facing the brightly-lit, canopied entrance to La Rotonde.

'Drink?' Patrick asked.

'I need it.'

'One thing first. Tell me how you know Martin Moore.'

Colin shrugged. 'I know of him only by reputation. He is reputed to be one of the officers in charge of British intelligence, with a special interest in the welfare of the Crown. Technically, he would be my boss.' He stopped and then asked. 'How do you know him?'

'Martin Moore is Tilly Cusack's husband!'

CHAPTER THIRTY

Rutgar paraded her like a prized possession.

Senga eventually stopped trying to remember the names. She would bow slightly and smile when she was introduced; and on the two occasions when the introductions were to a prince, she curtsied. Bearing in mind what Billy had told her, she spoke only French and English, and on several occasions as she was moving away from a couple or group, having been presented by Rutgar, she had to bite the inside of her cheek to prevent herself from laughing at the remarks she heard about herself. The majority of them, she noted, were complimentary, admiring her beauty, manners and dress, a few of them wondering where Rutgar had found her, and more than a few commenting that she was obviously too good for him. The few disparaging remarks she put down to jealousy.

'How are you enjoying it?' Rutgar asked, much later that evening. He had drunk far too much and his pale cheeks were flushed, his eyes bright and glassy, his movements just a little unsteady.

'It's a marvellous party,' Senga lied. 'I'm so glad you invited me.' It was quite possibly the most boring party she had ever attended – not that she had attended many.

'Have you seen Mama?'

Senga shook her head. She had seen Frau von Mann on a couple of occasions during the evening and, disconcertingly, she had found the woman had been staring directly at her on every occasion.

'Have you met Papa?'

Senga shook her head. So far this evening, she hadn't

been out of Rutgar's company, and he hadn't even allowed her to dance with any of the numerous young Germans who had almost queued up to offer. Rutgar himself, though, was a very accomplished dancer, although he held her just a little too tightly, and his hands, while not improperly placed, were not entirely correctly positioned. However, as the evening had worn on, Senga had noticed many couples whose hands were anything but properly placed.

'Come and I'll introduce you to Papa. He's in the next room.' Gripping her wrist, he tugged her out into the centre of the room and began to wend his way through the dancers.

Senga pulled her wrist free. 'I'm not a piece of baggage,' she snapped.

'Quite right,' someone replied in perfect French, and whirled her off into the midst of the dance. Senga shrieked with surprise, reaching up to grab hold of her hair, her fingers touching the head of the pin concealed in her plait. She looked up into the laughing face of a young man a few years older than Rutgar, but whose resemblance to him was marked. His face was broader than his brother's, smoother, without the wrinkles around the eyes and the creases in his forehead caused by Rutgar's shortsightedness. And whereas Rutgar was unnaturally thin, his brother was bulkier.

'Forgive Rutgar, drink brings out his possessive qualities.' He shook his head, his eyes mocking. 'Even as a child he was never eager to share.' He grinned broadly. 'But you must forgive me, I am Maximilian, Rutgar's older brother. Call me Max, everyone else does.'

'I am Senga Lundy.'

'Aaah, but I know. Everyone has been asking about Rudi's mysterious Irish companion.'

'Rudi?' Senga asked, as Max whirled her out of the crowd and escorted her to a table set against the wall.

'Yes, Rudi, short for Rutgar. Call him that if you wish to infuriate him.' He grabbed two glasses of white wine from a passing waiter. 'Now sit here for five minutes and talk to me. It will take him at least that long to find us. He's probably going insane at the moment looking for you. He's very proud of you, you know?'

'I didn't.'

'Ach . . . well, he's my own brother, and no doubt he will accuse me of trying to capture you for myself, although that's not the case – my fiancée Sieglinde would certainly disapprove. But allow me to advise – *warn* seems such a strong word – allow me to advise you about Rudi.' He sipped his drink, his bright-blue eyes intent on Senga, his boyish exhilaration replaced by a seriousness that caught Senga's attention. 'Rudi is the youngest of seven brothers, and while the rest of us have gone on and made our way in the world, Rudi seems to have been left behind, tied to his mother's apron strings, I suppose. He had tuberculosis as a child – nearly killed him too – and I suppose our mother has been overly protective of him, and allowed him to get his own way far too often.'

'The favourite son?' Senga asked, raising her eyebrows.

'Definitely. Favourite and favoured. The rest of us went into the army for a spell and then followed our father into his business. But not Rudi. Too weak for that, our mother said, although,' he added with a smile, 'he's by no means a weakling. Anyway, he developed a taste for the playboy life and got himself quite a reputation, first in Berlin and then in Paris and London and Madrid . . .'

'I get the picture,' Senga laughed. This older, much more relaxed version of Rutgar was quite charming, completely lacking his younger brother's often morose seriousness, and she couldn't help but compare the two unfavourably. 'But I thought brothers were supposed to look out for one another. I know I would never talk about my brother in the way you've talked about Rutgar,' she said seriously, picking her words carefully, yet still expecting an outburst of temper.

But Max grinned hugely. 'Aaah, I can see why our mother liked you so. You're like her – direct and to the point, and strong on family, she's like that too.' He finished the last of his white wine and signalled the waiter for two more. A young couple stopped to talk to Max, but he made his excuses, making it obvious that he wished to be alone with Senga, promising to see them later. When the drinks arrived, he turned back to her. 'Actually I don't feel that I'm talking out of turn about my brother. You see I do care for him greatly, and I don't want to see him hurt.'

'I'm not sure I understand you.'

'My brother wants to marry you . . .'

'But I don't want to marry him,' Senga said immediately. Aware of the surprised look on his face, she continued quickly. 'Your brother has this idea that I am his fiancée. I'm not. I like Rutgar, I owe him my life, and I suppose I'm fond of him, but I don't think I love him.'

'Does Rudi know this?'

'I've tried to tell him time and again, but it just doesn't sink in.'

Max shrugged. 'Well, that's Rudi all right.' He sounded confused.

'What were you going to tell me about Rutgar?'

'It seems almost redundant now.'

'Tell me anyway.'

'I was going to tell you that he has quite a reputation with women. He falls madly in love on a regular basis; when it breaks up, he is terribly hurt, confused, depressed, suicidal. Occasionally, when he is in one of his dark moods, he tries to hurt the girl, vent his frustration on them. The doctors say he is really hurting himself, but,' he shrugged, 'he's not the one getting beaten. I was going to warn you about getting involved with him.'

'Thank you for the warning; I don't think you need worry about me, but if you could wean Rutgar off me, that would help.'

Max stood up and, taking Senga's hand in his, bowed over it, pressing his lips to the back of her fingers. 'I'll see what I can do; with Rudi, absence makes the heart grow neglectful.'

294

'Senga? Senga!' Rutgar loomed up out of the crowd. 'Where have you been, I've been looking everywhere for you?' he continued, without waiting for her to reply. 'Where's Max?' he continued. 'I saw him grab out. You'll have to be careful of him; he's quite the ladies' man. Wouldn't be at all surprised if he tried to grab you for himself,' he added seriously, 'although he's engaged to be married.'

'I know. He told me,' Senga said with a smile.

'He told you! You spoke to him?'

'We sat here and had a glass of wine, waiting for you to turn up.'

Rutgar looked around suspiciously. His cheeks were still flushed, but he didn't seem to be as unsteady on his feet as he had been. 'You be careful of him,' he said again.

'Have you many brothers?' Senga asked, deliberately changing the subject. She was tired now, tired of the party and tired of Rutgar. All she wanted to do was go home and sleep. It had been a mistake to come here, she could see that now. She had come out of a misplaced sense of duty or gratitude to Rutgar, but she realised all he wanted to do was to show her off as some sort of conquest, to flaunt her before his brothers and friends.

'Seven,' Rutgar said sullenly. 'Come on; I was going to introduce you to my father.' He reached for Senga's arm, but stopped when he saw the expression on her face.

Senga followed him across the floor. Although it was now a little after one, the floor was still packed with dancers, most of them trying out some of the newer American dances to the sounds of the jazz group. Looking around, Senga realised that only the younger crowd remained in the room, the older people seemed to have drifted away. When they stepped out into the hallway, she found that most of the older generation had gathered in a long drawing room, where they were being served coffee and schnapps, while a string quartet laboured – unsuccessfully – to drown out the raucous jazz. Unlike the ballroom, which reeked of cigarette smoke, the heavier, aromatic odour of cigars and pipes hung on the air here.

Manfred von Mann was the image of his son Max, and Senga realised that this was what the young man would look like if he lived to be seventy. Tall, straight-backed, with a bristling moustache and red-cheeks, he looked every inch the military man. He was smoking a long, thin cigar and punctuated his sentences by stabbing at his listeners with its lighted end.

He looked up when he saw Rutgar approaching, and immediately broke away from the group which surrounded him and strode forward, his right hand thrust out in front of him. 'And you must be Senga Lundy, Katherine's daughter. Rutgar has told us all about you, and when I learned who you were, why I just couldn't believe it. I knew your mother . . . I should say I know your mother.' He snatched Senga's hand and pressed it to his lips. She could feel his moustache scratch along the back of her fingers. 'How is she?' he demanded, speaking perfect, almost unaccented English.

'She was very well the last time I saw her,' Senga answered truthfully.

'Good. Good. I have very fond memories of your mother. And I can see you in her. Aye, you have her shape, her face, her eyes, certainly her determined chin.' Holding Senga's hand in both of his, he leaned forward and murmured confidentially, 'She is a remarkable woman, your mother.'

'When she spoke of you, it was always with the greatest respect,' Senga lied. She had never heard her mother speak of the German; indeed the first time she had ever heard his name had been at that party a little more than two weeks ago . . . was it two only weeks ago? It seemed longer. 'But she never said where she first met you.'

'Oh, my dear, why it was . . . twenty-nine . . . yes it must be twenty-nine or thirty years ago.' Settling Senga's hand into the crook of his arm, he turned and strolled down the long, marbled hallway, leaving the warm, smoky rooms behind him. Away from the noise, the musicians and the crowds, it was remarkably quiet. They strolled out through the high double-doors into the chill night. He breathed deeply, and Senga was glad of the opportunity to clear her head, blinking her stinging eyes. She was sure she would reek of smoke for weeks to come.

Rutgar appeared at her side. Manfred glared at him. 'Go away, find something to do, someone to talk to. Let me talk to this charming creature for a few minutes.'

Rutgar bowed stiffly. 'Of course, Papa.'

When he had returned to the house, Manfred breathed deeply again, looked sidelong at Senga, and said, 'I truly abhor these parties.'

Senga leaned forward and smiled. 'So do I.'

'Ah, but you were asking me where I met your mother. It was in Berlin at the turn of the century, in one of the better-class brothels on the Tauenzienstrasse. Your mother had come over from Dublin on behalf of a famous Madam there called Bella Cohen. She was learning the trade. Ah, she was a beautiful young woman – your age, or possibly slightly younger. I remember I fought a duel for her honour. One of my companions wanted to bed her, and when he learned that she was not for sale grew loud and vulgar.' The old man laughed heartily. 'We fought a duel – with legs of chicken.'

'You won.' Senga said quietly.

'Of course.' He lunged forward, arm outstretched, parodying a sword thrust. 'A lunge to the heart, and he was down. Aaah,' he shook his head from side to side. 'But they were happy days, innocent days. Gone now. And Fritz, the man I fought for her honour, is dead now. Gone like so many of the others. The seasons pass, slowly, sedately, but surely. And eventually, the seasons end, and death claims us, eh?' He turned to face the young woman. 'It's only when I see people like you – the children of friends of my youth, that I realise that age has caught up with me. My season will end soon.' He straightened suddenly. 'But come, enough of this maudlin talk. Tell me about yourself. Tell me what you do, where you've been,

297

where you are going. Tell me about London and Dublin
. . . is Dublin still as beautiful as it once was? What about
the rebellion there back in 1916; has the damage been
repaired? Such a beautiful city. I've always felt a little
guilty about the damage that was caused there, you know.'

'But why?'

'Ah my dear, I'm afraid I was responsible for supplying
many of the weapons that were used then. Your people
bought guns from me and my agents, and if I had had my
way I would have sent far more. Ah well.'

A waiter appeared, a heavy, mink coat thrown across his
arm, a long, leather overcoat across the other. 'Frau von
Mann suggests that you might require these,' he said stiffly.

Senga turned and looked back towards the house,
surprised to find that they had walked quite a distance
from it. Clara von Mann was standing in the doorway and
Senga raised one arm in salute. The woman raised her arm
and then turned back into the house.

Manfred draped the luxurious, sensuous, full-length,
white fur across Senga's bare shoulders, and she was suddenly glad of its warmth. He allowed the waiter to drape the
heavy, leather coat across his own shoulders, and then waited
until the man had backed away. Raising his dead cigar
slightly, he asked, 'Do you mind if I smoke?'

'No.'

Manfred stopped, head bent, features highlighted by
the flame from the lighter. Looking up at Senga, he said.
'You really must have made quite an impression on her,
you know?' He jerked his head back towards the house for
emphasis.

'I wasn't trying to make an impression,' Senga said softly.

'I know. She knows that too. Maybe that's why you
made the impression.'

And Rutgar, standing in the shadow of the bushes, could
barely conceal his glee. He had his parents approval, he
needed nothing else. Tomorrow evening he would ask Senga
Lundy to marry him! No, not tomorrow morning. Tonight.

This very night!

CHAPTER THIRTY-ONE

'Tell me about Martin Moore,' Patrick Lundy said, his voice low, virtually lost amidst the tumult in La Rotonde. A party of what looked like arts students had taken over a dozen tables in and around the door, and were proceeding to hold a drunken court.

Colin Holdstock sipped the *café-au-lait* and shrugged. 'I've told you virtually all I know. You know what an organisation like mine is for gossip – I'm sure yours is something similar,' he added with a wicked grin.

Patrick smiled, liking this rather ordinary-looking man, admiring his nerve. He was a British police officer, having just witnessed a murder, now conversing with the same murderer and a man whose name still appeared on the wanted lists in Britain and Ireland. 'So you do know my reputation?'

'Oh, I know who Patrick Lundy is . . . and was. One of my officers, Malachi Thinn, knows you very well indeed. If he knew I was sitting here drinking with you now, he'd think I'd lost my head . . . and I suppose he'd be right. I have lost it.'

'I thought you were in love,' Patrick grinned.

'I was. I am. Do you object?'

'Senga deserves every happiness she can find. And a man who has done as much for her as you have can't be all bad. It'll be an interesting wedding though. Your boys on one side of the church, mine on the other.'

Colin Holdstock had the grace to look embarrassed. 'Yes well . . . I think that's a long way down the road.'

Patrick raised his coffee cup. 'Here's to it. I'll not stand in your way.'

Colin raised his cup in salute. 'Well, I'll thank you for that. I did think that might be a problem.'

'Not with me. Now, tell me about Martin Moore.'

'There are numerous branches within the service, but you know that already. Some of these branches deal with specific problems, organised crime, vice, the Irish problem . . . that sort of thing.'

Patrick nodded. He was watching the party of students. The majority of them seemed to be thoroughly enjoying themselves, except for one dark-eyed young man sitting close to the door. Patrick couldn't be sure, but he thought the young man was watching himself and Colin closely.

'Well, Martin Moore is reputed to be one of the officers detailed to look after the affairs of the Crown. In other words, he ensures that no whiff of scandal touches them. Apparently he has some vague Irish connection . . . he was one of the officers who alerted the authorities to the Easter Rising in 1916. He served under the famous Major John Lewis.'

Patrick's grin was fixed and icy. When he looked at Colin Holdstock his face was rigid in a death mask. 'Perhaps it would interest you to know that Captain – later Major – John Lewis was my father!'

Colin stared at him in bewilderment. He started to shake his head, when Patrick continued.

'My mother, Katherine Lundy, was a maidservant in the Lewis household. She became pregnant by Lewis who threw her out on the streets on Christmas Eve, 1898. She was discovered by Tilly Cusack and brought to a woman called Bella Cohen, brothel-keeper in Dublin about that time. The woman took her in as a secretary or whatever. That is how my mother got into her particular trade. I was the child my mother was pregnant with at that time. Tilly Cusack was my godmother; Senga and I called her *aunty*. Later, Tilly Cusack met John Lewis's assistant, a young English officer called Martin Moore; she married him following the rising . . .'

'Martin Moore is Tilly Cusack's husband,' Colin Holdstock breathed slowly, still coming to terms with the idea. 'I never knew her married name; I never even knew she had married.'

'Tilly Moore,' Patrick nodded.

'But does she know what her husband does for a living?'

'Of course she knows,' Patrick snapped. 'And now that we know who is looking for Senga, we can start tidying up a lot of loose ends. I did wonder how the first assassination attempt was set up; how the assassin managed to attend an invitation-only party; I did wonder how they seemed to know Senga's every move. I'm not a gambling man, but I'll lay you money that Tilly's the one who has been passing on the information about Senga's whereabouts to the authorities. We were looking for a spy in our camp; we just never thought it was so close to home.'

Colin Holdstock shook his head. He glanced up at Patrick, his eyes flickering to the long glass above the bar, 'You do know that we are being watched?'

'Yes, young man with the students in the corner. He's been there for a while. Do we want him?'

Colin lifted his cup. 'It would be interesting to discover why he's watching us.' He laid down the cup and reached over to rest his fingertips on Patrick's sleeve. 'But please . . . try not to kill him. I would prefer not to leave a trail of bodies all across Paris to mark our passage.'

Patrick grinned. 'I'll try not to damage him.' He raised his hand and caught the waiter's attention, pointing to their cups. The man nodded, and when he appeared a few moments later, two steaming cups of creamed coffee precariously balanced on a tray, Patrick asked him for the men's room. Without a word, the man pointed to the end of the long room. Patrick excused himself and made his way through the crowded tables, adrenalin beginning to rush along taut nerves. He recognised the old feeling, the rush of excitement, the barest touch of fear, the thrill of the chase. For far too many years he had lived on the edge

301

during Ireland's nasty Civil War, too many days with nerves jittering from the previous night's killing, too many nights buzzing with excitement. It was difficult not to become addicted to it: and he'd be lying if he even pretended he hadn't. Now he fought his battles on paper, organising men and supplies, applying pressure in the right quarters, creating the Ireland his fathers, both real and adopted, had died for. But he missed that old excitement, that fatally attractive rush of adrenalin.

Stepping into the cool, slightly sour-smelling toilets behind the bar, Patrick quickly checked beneath the stalls, but they all proved to be empty. Moving into one, he shot the bolt home, and then, standing on the edge of the toilet bowl, levered himself up and over the edge into the next stall.

Seconds later he heard the door opening, and metal-tipped heels clicked over the stained, white tiles. There was a moment of scuffling, and then there was a tap on the door of the stall next to the one he was hiding in.

'Monsieur . . .?'

Patrick eased the pistol out of his pocket.

'Monsieur, I have a shotgun pointed at this door . . .'

'And I have a pistol pointed at the back of your head!'

Patrick hopped down off the toilet bowl and cracked open the door to find Colin Holdstock standing behind the Frenchman, the pistol held tightly in both hands. The Frenchman looked from Colin to Patrick and then carefully placed the sawn-off shotgun on the ground. He raised both hands above his head and attempted a smile.

'Tattoo said you would not be easy to surprise.'

Without a word Patrick stepped up to him and kicked him with the flat of his shoe in the knee. The sound of popping cartilage was clearly audible and, before the man could scream, Patrick had rammed his pistol into his mouth, knocking out one of his teeth. As the man went to the ground, Patrick followed him down, his left hand wrapped around his throat, fingers biting into his windpipe, right hand pressing the gun deeper into his mouth.

302

'You're not from Tattoo,' he hissed. 'He wouldn't be so stupid as to send someone after me with a shotgun. He knows how I'm liable to react when I'm confronted by someone holding a gun.' The man beneath him began to thrash as his brain screamed for oxygen.

'Patrick . . .' Colin said warningly. 'He's all we have. We need him alive.'

Patrick reluctantly loosened his grip on the man's throat, and removed the gun from his mouth so he could breathe. For a few moments, the Frenchman lay there, sobbing breath into his tortured lungs, a tendril of blood running from his mouth, his right knee curled up beneath him.

'Who sent you?' Patrick demanded. He pulled back the hammer on the pistol, the sharp sound emphasising the question.

The man coughed, wincing with pain, spraying blood. 'A commission, a street commission . . . I was told to bring you . . . bring you to a certain place . . . and say that Tattoo had arranged it.'

'And who gave you this commission?'

The man started to shake his head, but Patrick pressed the cold barrel of the gun into his forehead.

'Who?'

'The blind beggar outside the doors of Notre Dame. He is not really blind,' he added.

'And where were you to bring us?'

'To the train station, platform four, at eight o'clock tomorrow night.'

'And?'

'There would be an accident.'

'And who would arrange this accident?'

'I don't know. I wasn't told,' he added hastily. 'There was no need for me to know.'

'That's probably true,' Colin chipped in.

'Probably.' Patrick stood up and looked down at the man, one hand stuck into his pocket, the hand holding the gun dangling loosely. Coming to a decision, he moved over

303

and ripped the towel off its rail. 'Do you have to report back to this blind beggar?'

'Tomorrow night at ten, when I would be paid.'

'Good,' Patrick whispered. Wadding the towel into a tight ball, he pressed it to the barrel of the gun and shot the Frenchman through the head. Dropping the scorched and smoking remains of the towel on to the man's ruined face, he pocketed the pistol and stepped past Colin, who stood frozen in horror at the casual killing.

'Well, I could hardly let him live, now could I?'

'The beggar is only a middleman, an arranger,' Tattoo said nervously. He desperately resisted the temptation to turn around and look at Patrick Lundy's companion who was sitting behind him. 'He was probably hired to set up the hit on you, arrange the messenger, and the muscle.'

'Well, he can give me another name,' Patrick murmured, 'another link in my chain.'

'Does he do government work?' Patrick Lundy's unnamed companion murmured from behind him.

Tattoo shook his head. 'I couldn't say. I sometimes use him myself, however, so it's not beyond the bounds of possibility.'

'How did he come to have your name?' Patrick asked.

Tattoo shook his head again. 'I don't know,' he repeated, his eyes beginning to widen in desperation. He had no doubts that this madman would kill him without a second's thought. 'Someone might have followed you . . .'

'Impossible,' Patrick said simply.

'. . . or they could have followed me.'

'A traitor in your organisation?' Patrick suggested.

'Possible, but unlikely.'

'Or you perhaps?' Patrick murmured. 'Selling us out?'

There was real fear in Tattoo's eyes now. 'No, no, Monsieur, I swear to you, I would not . . .'

The smile on Patrick's face was ice-cold. 'No, I know you wouldn't. You're too clever for that . . . and you know what would happen to you if I found out. Don't you?'

Tattoo swallowed hard and nodded.

'Now, my friend and I are going to visit this blind beggar . . .'

'He's not blind,' Tattoo said quickly.

'So I've been told,' Patrick said pleasantly.

'And he's dangerous too, so be careful.'

'Thank you for the advice. While we're off talking to this man, I want you to find out how he got your name – and mine. And you had better have the answer before I return.' Patrick stood up suddenly, but the Frenchman reached out and plucked at the edge of his sleeve. 'Monsieur. There is something else.'

Patrick subsided into his seat.

Tattoo passed over a single sheet of paper without a word. Patrick looked at it disinterestedly and then slid it back across to the Frenchman. He stood up and headed for the door without another word. Taking a deep breath, Colin tagged along behind, wondering how in God's Holy Name he had managed to get himself mixed up in all of this. He had been told that men did stupid things in the name of love – stupid yes, but certainly not suicidal. And staying with Patrick Lundy had all the hallmarks of suicide.

After the closeness of the bar the night smelt cold and damp, the freshness of the air tainted by the miasma coming in off the river. One of the street women, spotting the single man emerging from the bar, began a casual stroll across the cobbled street towards him. She stopped when she saw the second man emerge from the bar, take the first by the elbow and turn him around, and begin speaking very intently and seriously. A lover's quarrel no doubt. No business for her tonight; their type worked along the banks of the river.

Colin Holdstock gripped Patrick by the elbow and turned him around to face him. Patrick was slightly taller, but Colin was broader. 'Let's try to work out a plan before we rush off and kill someone else.'

'I thought we were going to see this beggar,' Patrick said quietly.

'What was in the letter Tattoo showed you?

'Nothing.'

'You owe me an explanation.'

Patrick turned to look into the Parisian night and then he finally nodded. 'You're right. I do. It was a letter from my mother. She's coming to Paris.'

'Does that present us with a problem?'

Patrick shrugged. 'Possibly. Probably. The only reason my mother's coming here is to search for her precious jewels. And whatever attention the British authorities have been paying to her in London will certainly follow her here. Now we know that a French government department has been assisting a British government department tracking her and me, so it stands to reason that both of these mysterious departments will concentrate all their attention on Paris. In any case, she's probably told Tilly Cusack where she's staying, so the British authorities already know by now. However, while she's here, she'll probably hire herself a squad of armed bullyboys and bodyguards, and these will be watched by a squad of armed police and army.' He smiled humourlessly. 'All I want to do is to make sure that when the firefight starts I'm not around.'

'And Senga?' Colin Holdstock asked.

'Pray she's still in Berlin where she's safe.'

CHAPTER THIRTY-TWO

Senga was frightened.

She stood at the window of the opulent bedroom, wearing the ivory silk nightdress and dressing-gown that Rutgar had bought for her, and shivered with fear and the insidious night chill.

She wished she was back in the cheap hotel in Berlin, safe in Billy Faden's arms.

The small-faced clock on the marble mantelpiece chimed three, the sound coinciding with the roaring of powerful engines and the crunching of gravel as some of the revellers departed for Berlin. Senga wasn't sure just how many were staying over for the night, but certainly she could still hear the muted sounds of revelry drifting up through the house. The slightly tinny sounds of jazz had been replaced by the more solid German drinking songs, and from her room overlooking the lawn to the right of the avenue she could see stray couples wandering across the damp grass, usually entwined in one another's arms, most of them weaving drunkenly.

The young woman wrapped her arms around herself and moved away from the thick, badly-made glass which radiated a subtle chill. The bedroom was cold. A fire had been set in the hearth but it had been allowed to die down to the merest glimmer, and now only the bear-skin rug before it was still warm. Senga crouched on it, resting the point of her chin on top of the bear's snarling head, and stared deep into the glimmering cinders. She attempted to analyse her fear, to break it down piece by piece, and then reduce those pieces even further until they became meaning-less. It was a trick her brother had taught her. A threat is only a threat because it seems so large, so all-embracing, but break down that threat, reduce it into single elements, and then it loses its power.

Standing up suddenly, she crossed to the bed and pulled off the heavy coverlet. Returning to the rug, she sat cross-legged before the fire, the coverlet draped across her shoulders and head, wrapped tightly around her.

Why was she frightened?

Break it down . . . reduce it to its elements. She could almost hear her brother's advice ringing in her head.

She was frightened because she felt alone . . . but that wasn't really true. Yes, she missed Billy and the solid comfort she represented.

Also, this was the first time she had ever been at a grand function like this, the first time she had ever mixed in such exalted company: she had been introduced to so many princes and princesses, dukes and duchesses, counts and countesses that she had quite lost track of them all. And, although her mother had been a famous Society hostess in London, whose balls and fêtes were the social events of the Season, Senga had always been too young to attend.

She was also a foreigner in a foreign land, unused to the mores and customs of the people and entirely dependant on their charity. She was also on the run for her life. Surely that, in itself, was enough of a catalogue of misfortune to entitle her to a little fear.

But against all that she was armed and in good company, and so far all attempts on her life had proved to be in vain. She didn't think she lacked courage, nor did she lack a sense of adventure. Perhaps it was just that she could see no end to the problem in sight. Would these mysterious people who were out to kill or kidnap her continue until she had finally been killed or kidnapped? Would it end when her mother discovered the Crown Jewels, or would it end when they had caught up with her mother? Was it any wonder she felt trapped?

And then, of course, there was Rutgar . . .

Suddenly she had found herself in a situation where she was being married off to this German whom she hardly knew, and whom she had no real feelings for . . . or had she?

Break it down . . . analyse it. Had she had real feelings for Graf Rutgar von Mann?

She was grateful to him, of course, for having saved her life, and she liked him . . . or rather, she had liked him. He had been amusing and witty while they had been in London and Paris, but curiously, the closer they had come to Berlin, the more his character had seemed to change. He had become dour and humourless, harder, slightly crueller –, she remembered his comments about the Negroes in Paris, and abruptly she realised that she knew very little about the young man. However, she did know that he had obviously told his entire family and his host of friends that she was his fiancée, and what was even worse she had obviously been approved of by both his mother and his father. Were they so desperate to see him married off that they would gladly assent to his marrying the first respectable-looking foreigner that chanced along? She had the feeling that they might; his brother Max had certainly intimated that Rugar mixed with a wild, dissolute bunch in Berlin.

A coal fell in the grate, sparks spiralling upwards, disturbing her reverie.

Was this then the real reason for her fear; the fear that she was being forced into a situation that was going to be extremely embarrassing – and possibly even difficult – to extricate herself from? She was in Germany on Rutgar's forbearance; if she should anger him, it would be very easy for him to turn her over to the police, or very simply leave her at the mercy of those hunting her. Whilst she still had him, she still enjoyed his – and his family's – protection. And while she might be many things, she was not stupid, and she wasn't going to throw that away so easily. Perhaps it would be to her advantage to play him along for a few weeks. In the meantime she would try and get a message to her brother in Dublin, asking him to come and bring her home. Failing that, she could always attempt to make her way back to Ireland with Billy.

The only problem was that they had no money. Well, that was a bridge she would cross when she came to it . . . Billy would know what to do . . . Billy always knew what to do . . .

Her head dipped, rose and dipped again. Moments later she was asleep, sitting up before the fire.

Senga Lundy dreamt.

She dreamt she was standing before a broad, silver river, sun dappling its surface. It was late summer and the leaves were falling from the trees with gentle, rustling sounds, whispering against her skin as they brushed against her. She stood on the bank of the river and allowed her ivory-coloured shift to slide down, and then, naked, she inched forward into the water. Its touch was feather-light, warm and inviting like a caress. It rose up along her legs, over her thighs, brushing across her groin, up over her belly, pausing to linger at her breasts. She breathed deeply and attempted to move deeper into the water – but couldn't.

And awoke.

Rutgar was sitting cross-legged before her, wearing powder-blue, silk pyjamas, his hair wild, his eyes glazed. The blanket that had been draped over her shoulders had been peeled back and his hands were on her breasts, caressing them through the thin cloth of her nightdress.

'Senga . . . dearest . . .'

Senga drew back her fist and punched him in the groin.

Rutgar doubled up, curling into a tight ball, hands clutching himself, toppling sideways. Senga slapped him hard across the side of the face, her palm cupped in the way that Billy had taught her, compressed air rupturing his ear-drum. Rutgar lay shuddering on the rug and then he began to vomit in body-wrenching spasms. Senga moved away from him, her face tight with disgust, her

310

own gorge rising reflexively. She smoothed her nightdress across her flat stomach, the silk hissing beneath her fingers, attempting to wipe away the touch of the German's fingers which she imagined she could still feel. Looking at the retching man she shook her head contemptuously. So much for playing him along for a few weeks! So much for all her carefully-laid plans.

However, what was done was done and could not be undone.

Turning her back on the man, she crossed to the wardrobe and removed her dress from its hangers. Shrugging off the dressing-gown, she unhooked the straps of the nightdress from her shoulders and allowed it to slide to the floor, and then, naked, she reached for the black silk stockings and garters. Lifting one leg to the bed, she slid on the stocking, smoothing it up along her calf . . . and was roughly grabbed from behind and flung to the floor.

Rutgar loomed over her, his blue eyes wild, glittering dangerously, flecks of vomit on his chin and pyjama shirt. His flesh was whey-coloured. His mouth worked for several moments before he was finally able to speak. 'How . . . how dare you!' But she didn't hear the words; his eyes held her, the madness behind them burning fiercely now.

For a single moment, Senga Lundy was thirteen again, in Jean-Michel Hugo's apartment in Paris. She had seen that look before, the naked lust, the unnatural rage. She came to her feet slowly, making no attempt to cover her nakedness, facing him as proudly as if she were fully dressed. 'I am not one of your street whores,' she said coldly. 'I am not to be fondled like some cheap piece of fruit.'

'You . . . you . . .'

'I thought you were a gentleman,' Senga said, sounding almost sorrowful. 'And yet you take advantage of a sleeping girl in a despicable fashion.'

Senga's contempt cut through Rutgar's drunkenness, and as she watched she saw some semblance of reason

311

return to his eyes. The character change was so abrupt as to be almost frightening, and she realised that it couldn't be put down entirely to alcohol. She looked into his deep, blue eyes and discovered that the pupils were tiny.

'I don't know what came over me,' Rutgar said quietly, sounding rational, speaking with the slow and careful enunciation of someone who knows that they have had far too much to drink.

'You are drunk,' she said, deliberately keeping the hard edge of anger in her voice. 'Drunk or drugged.'

'Yes,' he said numbly. 'A little medicine.' He attempted to smile, but the muscles of his face were twitching and wouldn't obey him. He licked his lips. 'Just a little something to relax me. This was a very tense day for me . . . I mean, I didn't know how my parents were going to react to you . . . I didn't know how you would react to them . . .' He attempted to smile again, this time with more success. 'I looked into the room to wish you a good night, and I saw you asleep before the fire. I sat down before you, and I just looked at you and then . . . and then . . . and . . . and I . . . I just couldn't help myself. I had to touch you. You are so beautiful, Senga Lundy.' Almost unconsciously his right hand came up, fingertips brushing across her breast.

Senga slapped it away. 'Keep your hands off me!' she snarled.

She realised she had made a mistake when she saw the look in his eyes change. The muscles in his face began to spasm and tighten, his mouth closing, his lips covering his teeth in an almost invisible line. It was like looking at another person. When he looked at her his sharp, blue eyes were hooded. 'That's what you say, but I think you want me to touch you . . . else why would you stand there shameless and naked?' He reached out and tweaked her nipple.

Without blinking Senga slammed the heel of her hand into his mouth, splitting his lip against his teeth. 'I told you not to touch me . . .' she began.

Rutgar hit her, an open-handed slap across the side of the face that set her whole head ringing. She staggered back on to the bed, and then used her own momentum to roll off on the other side. Her heart had begun tripping in her chest and she had come to the realisation that she was dealing with someone who was – temporarily at least – unhinged. She had never experienced such personality changes before: Rutgar was a quiet, somewhat reserved person, but the few glimpses she had had of his other self now made sense. Alcohol – or some other stimulant, probably cocaine, which was the fashionable drug at the moment – was probably responsible for slipping him into his aggressive persona.

Rutgar leaned forward, both hands resting on the bed. His eyes moved across her body, lingering at breasts and groin. 'You forget, my dear, that you owe me.'

The years rolled away and Senga heard another man in another time and another city say almost exactly the same words.

'I owe you nothing,' she said icily.

'You owe me everything,' he said arrogantly, moving around the bed to stand before her. 'Principally, you owe me your life.' His blue eyes drifted up and down her body with insulting slowness. 'And if you must know, I intend to ask my parents' permission to marry you. I am confident that they will acquiesce. You will be mine, Senga Lundy,' he promised.

Senga shook her head firmly. 'No. Rutgar . . . you're not well, you're not thinking . . .'

'Oh, but I am,' he whispered. 'Perhaps for the first time since we've met, I'm thinking properly. You will make a good wife.'

'Go to bed, Rutgar, we can talk about this in the morning.'

'We can talk about it now.'

Senga shook her head. Rutgar's hard fingers locked around her jaw and he tilted her head back, squeezing the soft flesh. 'And I said we will.' His left hand moved up along her body, brushing her thigh, drifting across her stomach, finally coming to rest on her breast.

Senga attempted to kick him in the groin, but he twisted, the blow landing on his thigh but with enough force to make him grunt with pain. She struck out for his eyes with her stiffened fingers, and he flung her away as her nails raked down his cheek. Throwing herself across the bed, she scrabbled at the drawer of the bedside cabinet, finally wrenching it open, and hauling out the tiny pistol she had worn in the garter on her leg. Taking a deep breath to steady her nerves, she gripped the gun in both hands and thumbed back the hammer.

'Don't be a fool,' Rutgar laughed. He dabbed at his cheek with the sleeve of his pyjamas. 'You're not going to use that. Not on me, not here in my parents' house. And let's suppose you did use it, what would you do then, where would you go? You're a long way from home, Senga Lundy. You won't do anything stupid.' He peeled off his soiled pyjama shirt and wiped it across his mouth and torn cheek, and then tugged down his pyjama trousers. Naked, he came around the bed towards her. 'It's time to pay the piper,' he whispered, touching himself, holding himself.

Senga's two shots took him through the heart, the sound of the gun surprisingly quiet in the large bedroom. He was dead before he hit the floor.

Senga lifted the gun and pointed it at the door, expecting it to crash open at any moment and hoards of guests or servants to appear. But nothing happened.

She looked down at the body on the floor and found she could feel nothing for it, no regrets, no remorse . . . no, that wasn't quite true, she was sorry she had had to shoot him, it complicated matters dreadfully. She shivered suddenly; she sounded so cold, so callous; she sounded just like her mother. Anyway, whatever plans had been made, they had just been changed.

Senga dressed quickly, surprised by how calm she felt. Perhaps she would break down later, but at the moment she had never felt so alive in all her life. She could feel her

314

heart pounding, feel the blood rushing through her veins, her breath in her lungs, the touch of the silk on her skin, the coldness of the metal gun against her thigh. Her brother Patrick had spoken of men who enjoyed killing for killing's sake; if this was what they experienced, she no longer wondered why.

She evaluated and re-evaluated scores of plans before finally settling on the simplest. Hauling Rutger's body up on to the bed – she was surprised because there was so little blood – she rolled him under the covers and pulled the blankets up to his head. To the casual observer he was asleep. Kicking his pyjamas under the bed, she gathered up her purse and then sat down before the dressing-table and put on her make-up, almost amused to discover that there was not so much as a tremble in her hand. And then, without so much as a backward glance into the room, she stepped out into the hallway, closed the door and turned the key in the lock from the outside. Half way down the long corridor was a tall, broad-leafed palm, and as she walked past she dropped the key into the soft mulch, pressing it down beneath the soil with one dainty finger.

The long corridors were virtually deserted, although in some of the small rooms off the main hallway and through half-opened doors she glimpsed scores of people lying around drunk and in a state of undress. There were empty bottles everywhere.

The large foyer was deserted and on impulse she turned and headed downstairs looking for the servants' quarters. The kitchens were at the back of the house and still busy – although now beginning to prepare breakfast for the scores of guests who had stayed on. A half-dozen men in chauffeurs' uniforms were playing cards at a long, wooden table. Senga stood in the doorway looking for her chauffeur. Her presence gradually silenced the chattering servants and one by one they turned and looked towards the silent woman. Her chauffeur recognised her and immediately stood and bowed.

'*Fraulein?*'

'Would it be possible for you to take me back to Berlin?'

Although his face remained impassive, she could see the surprise in his eyes.

'Now?'

'Now.'

'Of course, *Fraulein*.'

Senga nodded and then strode past him to pull open the kitchen door and step out on to the large, damp paving stones at the back of the house. A dozen cars had been parked along the verge.

The chauffeur materialised alongside her. Adjusting his cap, he looked down at her and murmured. '*Fraulein* is in some distress?'

Senga smiled at the quaint expression. 'Aye, some distress. Is it so obvious?'

'It is not obvious. It was a guess.' His smile was genuine. 'If I can be of any service . . .'

'If you can get me to Berlin as quickly as possible, that will be service enough.'

'Of course.'

They had driven as far as the gate, gravel crunching and spluttering beneath the car's tyres before the chauffeur glanced in his rear view mirror and said. 'Now that we are away from the house, would you care to let me know what has happened? You can trust me,' he added.

'I suppose I have to trust someone,' Senga sighed. Looking up at the chauffeur's stone-grey eyes in the mirror, she said, 'I've just killed Rutgar von Mann.'

The chauffeur never even blinked. 'He deserved it,' he said quietly and put his foot down, surging the car along the quiet country lane heading back into Berlin.

CHAPTER THIRTY-THREE

When Captain Martin Moore had been posted to Dublin to work with the infamous Major John Lewis, he had sworn that it would only be a temporary posting to the army intelligence unit. When he had met Lewis and worked with him for a couple of months, he had then sworn that no matter how things worked out he would never end up like the embittered soldier.

He was wrong on both counts.

Martin Moore had found love in Dublin – with a woman who had once been a prostitute no less, and although he had had to give up much to marry her he had done so despite his parents', his friends' and his colleagues' wishes and advice. Many people thought that it would be a brief affair and that they would divorce within a couple of months. They also felt that his career in the army had finished.

They were wrong on both counts.

Martin Moore had married Tilly Cusack in 1916, and they had been married for nearly thirteen years now. Although it had been a long time since they had slept together, and perhaps even longer since they had had any real feelings for one another, it was not a loveless marriage. But theirs was not a physical relationship. Martin Moore was not a physically demonstrative person; the son of very strict parents, he still found the act of lovemaking physically repulsive, and Tilly Cusack had found that she had spent too many years pretending to enjoy sex, found that all the barriers and defences she had created between

317

herself and the men who had bought her night after night, were virtually impossible to remove.

But the marriage suited them; it gave their relationship a respectability that they both craved, allowed them to move in polite circles, allowed Martin Moore to begin the climb up the social ladder.

Following the 1916 uprising in Dublin, and the mysterious death of Major John Lewis, Martin Moore had been the most senior officer left in charge. When the week-long rebellion had been quelled, the leaders tried and executed, the reports submitted and resubmitted, read and reported upon, Martin Moore's name had begun to appear with a surprising degree of regularity. Someone in the ministry had remembered that Martin Moore had warned of the impending uprising before it had actually taken place, and he was marked for promotion. And so, when the Special Investigations Unit was being established, Captain Martin Moore was appointed its chief.

The Special Investigations Unit was responsible directly for the protection of the Crown, both in body and spirit. Its duties included the provision of bodyguards – the long-held belief that the monarchy was inviolate had been shattered by the war – and the investigation of all events which might embarrass the Crown.

The theft of the Irish Crown Jewels had caught Martin Moore's attention for a number of reasons, although he had been aware of the theft long before he joined the unit. He had been seeing Tilly Cusack back in Dublin in 1916 when he had accidentally come across a copy of Lewis's report, in which he stated quite firmly that Katherine Lundy had been instrumental in stealing the jewels, probably assisted by Tilly Cusack. The allegations had been unfounded and had never been investigated. He had even gone so far as to remove the file and burn it, but he had been young then, and in love.

That had been his introduction to the Crown Jewel Affair. But with the passage of years the details about the theft had become lost and blurred, until eventually some

318

people didn't know the Irish Crown Jewels had ever been stolen, or indeed whether the Irish had ever possessed any Crown Jewels!

Until Katherine Lundy's greed opened up old wounds, deep wounds, with an enormous potential for scandal.

Suspicion for the theft had fallen on Francis Richard Shackleton, the younger brother of Ernest, the explorer. Francis Shackleton was extremely friendly – perhaps even unnaturally so – with the Duke of Argyll, King Edward's brother-in-law. The theft of the jewels had already caused the royal family some embarrassment – they had been stolen virtually on the eve of the royal visit to Dublin in 1907 – and Martin Moore was determined that the matter would remain closed: he would personally see to it. The stones would never be recovered. There would be no thrilling exposé of the discovery of the stones, no raking over old scores, no whisper of scandal. Katherine Lundy would not succeed in her quest to find the jewels, of that he was quite certain . . . in fact, he would almost guarantee it!

The grey-haired man dipped into his waistcoat pocket and fished out his pocket watch. It was a few minutes to ten: the Dover express was on time. He would be in Paris on the morrow, and he hoped he would be able to see this business to a conclusion once and for all. His Majesty had been most understanding about the delay, but Martin Moore had never failed on one of his special missions, and he wasn't going to begin now.

The feeling was back. The old, old feeling, the feeling she hadn't experienced in a long time. In the old days, *the Dublin days,* as she liked to call them, it had been an almost constant companion, but lately she hadn't experienced its euphoric rush. The feeling was success, power, accomplishment . . . call it what you will. Every winner felt it, every successful man or woman understood it: it was that single moment when you knew that you – *you* – had succeeded where all others had failed.

Katherine Lundy took a deep breath as she stepped off the train and on to the platform of the enormous station. The air was tainted with smoke and fumes, oil and the metallic odour of burnt diesel from the trains, but it still smelt sweet to her.

Katherine Lundy had come to Paris to buy the Irish Crown Jewels.

And once she had the jewels, she would expose the story of their theft and the true identity of the thief . . . or at least she would threaten to expose it. There were certain people who would pay very handsomely indeed for that story not to become public. There were others who would pay to ensure that the Crown Jewel Affair was not brought to the public's attention, and there were still others – people of quite some substance – who would not be happy with the amount of bad publicity the whole story would be sure to engender.

All in all, she wasn't exactly sure how much money she would make from the various parties, both Irish and English, but whatever the figure she would ensure it would more than amply pay for the jewels themselves. And she would keep the stones. She would in effect get the Irish Crown Jewels for free! Well, she had waited nearly twenty-three years for the jewels, and she had been expecting to have to pay dearly for them. But now it looked as if things were going to work out very nicely indeed. The tall, grey-haired woman, veiled and wearing a widow's garb, chuckled to herself as she made her way down the length of the station. Those who heard it shook their heads sorrowfully, pitying her. Katherine saw their snaking heads and averted eyes and laughed all the louder: if only they knew.

She spotted Tattoo at the back of the station, his eyepatch making him easy to spot amidst the milling crowds. She thought he had aged considerably since she had last met him . . . when was that, eight, nine years ago? But then age had a habit of creeping up on you, until one morning you looked in the mirror and discovered that the lines and wrinkles you had been ignoring had settled themselves in permanently. She had grown old in her search for the jewels, but at least she would be afforded the satisfaction of finding them before it was too late. How many people accomplished their life's ambition before they died?

She stopped before the small, dark Frenchman, and he blinked up at her in surprise. Lifting her veil slightly so that he could glimpse her face, her lips twisted into something approaching a smile. 'You're getting slow, Tattoo. In the old days you would not have let someone get this close to you.'

'If you care to look to your right and left, Madame, you will see that I no longer work alone.'

Katherine looked to either side and found two, hard-eyed young men watching her intently, their hands inside their baggy overcoats.

'One of the advantages of age, Madame, is that one gains experience.' He reached for Katherine's hand and bowed over it, pressing it to his lips. 'I have a car waiting outside.'

'Is everything prepared?'

'All is in readiness,' Tattoo said slowly, with just the hint of hesitation that Katherine Lundy was intended to hear.

'There is a problem?'

The Frenchman considered and then he finally nodded. 'There might be.'

'And what is this problem?'

'Who,' Tattoo gently corrected.

'Who?' Katherine asked.

'Your son, Madame. Patrick Lundy has been making something of a nuisance of himself.'

'What's he doing here?'

'I believe that he is here for the same reason you are, Madame. I believe he is looking for the Crown Jewels. I understand he means to bargain for his sister's life with them.'

321

Katherine hissed with annoyance. 'And where is he now?'

'I have no idea, Madame. But rest assured, he will show up. Oh, and there's one other thing,' he added grimly, 'he is accompanied by an English police inspector, a Colin Holdstock.'

Katherine Lundy climbed into the back of the Daimler, her euphoric mood completely shattered. Well, she hadn't come this far to be thwarted at the last moment. Patrick – and his English police friend – would have to be removed from the picture. And she knew just how to do it.

Patrick Lundy and Colin Holdstock had not moved on the blind beggar who sat outside Notre Dame for several reasons. They decided that once he knew his emissary had met with his untimely accident, he would be on the alert, no doubt with plenty of guards in attendance. Both men, dressed as tourists, had taken it in turns to watch the pitiful bundle of rags crouching on the lower steps of the cathedral, a filthy, gauze bandage wound around his eyes, a white stick propped beside him, a wooden bowl by his feet.

Every morning the beggar would be led to the steps by what Patrick had first taken to be a child, but which had later turned out to be a dwarf, and in the evening, following the late devotions of the cathedral, the same dwarf would come to collect the man. Sometimes the dwarf would be accompanied by a second, much larger man, who bore all the hallmarks of a bodyguard, and he would take charge of the numerous bags of change the beggar would pass over.

'He reminds me of a character in a Sherlock Holmes story,' Patrick said to Colin as they stood and watched the blind beggar hobble away into the night, surrounded by his two mis-matched companions. 'It was something about a man who disguised himself to go begging and made such a success at it that he couldn't give it up. Holmes was called in to investigate when the man disappeared.'

'The Man with the Twisted Lip,' Colin Holdstock smiled. 'When did you read Holmes?'

'I started reading him in my youth; one of my great friends worked in a bookshop. And later, when I was on the run, I read a lot.' He grinned suddenly. 'I didn't think it was fashionable for the police to read about amateur detectives.'

'I recommend Holmes to all my young bobbies, if for no other reason than the dictum which Holmes explains to Watson again and again: look, look and then look again. Observe.'

Patrick nodded towards the distant, shadowy figures, 'Well, Sherlock, what do you make of this, eh?'

'I deduce that our blind friend is making a lot of money, an awful lot of money . . . nothing wrong there. Free enterprise and all that. But leaving aside the ordinary visitors to the cathedral who dropped him a few francs, he did seem to have an awful lot of well-dressed benefactors who stopped for a chat.'

Patrick nodded. 'What about the bodyguards?'

'None that I could see. And that bothered me. I watched the crowds come and go, and unless they kept changing the guard constantly he didn't seem to have any guards. But then I started looking for the obvious . . . what was it Holmes said: "When you eliminate the impossible, whatever remains, however improbable, must be the truth," or something like that. So the only two people who remained in plain sight all day were the guards outside Notre Dame.'

'Of course,' Patrick breathed. 'Brilliant. Absolutely brilliant.'

'And then, in the evening there is the dwarf and occasionally the big man. I think he arrives if there has been an exceptionally good day. But have you noticed the four cyclists who appear each evening and head off in the same general direction as the beggar. Two in the lead, two behind. Now, they might have nothing to do with him, but I'll stake my pension they're bodyguards.'

'That's good enough for me.'

'What will we do?'

'We'll take him,' Patrick said decisively. 'I want to ask him a few questions.'

'When?'

'First thing in the morning, when they're still asleep.'

In a small, utilitarian office in sight of Notre Dame de Paris, Martin Moore shook hands with the French official. No names had been exchanged and both men preferred it that way. They spoke French out of courtesy to the Frenchman, but the file Martin Moore presented was in English.

'There are some new facts.'

'So I see.' The Frenchman looked up. 'And what would you like us to do?'

'I would like some assistance to place a twenty-four-hour watch on this Lundy woman, and this Tattoo.'

'We will, of course, do our utmost to assist you. But I should add that we have often found the man you refer to as Tattoo to be extremely useful to us in the past, and no matter how this event turns out we would prefer it if he were not mentioned in your investigation, and under no circumstances should he be charged.'

'Of course.'

'If the woman is with Tattoo, we will find her. We are aware of this man's whereabouts and we know his haunts. It is only a matter of time.' He put down the file and slid it across the smoothly-polished, walnut table. 'However, there are one or two points which you might not be aware of.' He leaned forward and began ticking them off on his long, narrow fingers. 'There have been some killings in the city of late: we believe that Patrick Lundy, Katherine Lundy's son, is responsible. There was a death recently in which Senga Lundy, Katherine Lundy's daughter, was involved – a case of assault, or robbery, or kidnap which went wrong . . . or whatever.' He smiled coldly and continued. 'There is an English police inspector, a Colin Holdstock, also in Paris. He initially kept in touch; but not recently. However we do have a report which places him in the company of Patrick Lundy.'

Colonel Moore blinked. 'Perhaps he's using him as a way to get to Katherine Lundy or the daughter.'

'Perhaps.' The Frenchman folded his hands together and leaned forward across the table. 'I would like to see this business settled soon Monsieur. Very soon. Up to very recently I had never heard of these Lundys, and now a whole family of them has appeared and my life is a misery. Sort out this business and go home, please Monsieur.'

'Don't worry,' the Englishman smiled. 'It's nearly finished now. It's almost done.'

CHAPTER THIRTY-FOUR

Billy Fadden stepped away from the window and back into the shadows when the large car turned the corner and began its slow descent down the street, fat tyres hissing loudly on the wet cobbles. She had been standing by the window for most of the night, the vague, nagging fears that had pursued her throughout the day having claimed her fully as the night wore on. She hated to see Senga going off on her own, not least because she had been hired to protect her and there was damn all she could do to guard her if she was off at a party on the other side of the city.

And of course Senga was going to meet Graf Rutgar von Mann, and Billy was more than certain that he was going to announce his betrothal to her. He had certainly dropped enough hints over the past few days, and he had begun to act with an almost proprietorial air towards her.

And Billy wondered what Senga was going to say – and do – when Rutgar made his announcement.

She closed her eyes, leaning her forehead against the cool glass, recognising the mixed emotions that knotted her stomach: she was jealous and afraid.

Jealous of Rutgar's attraction to Senga, afraid that she might be attracted to him in turn.

Her preference ran to women, she made little secret of it, she had her reasons for it, and she knew numerous other women who shared her Sapphic interests. But she liked to think that she wasn't entirely as them. She liked to think that she could allow her companions to come and go

as they pleased, that she wasn't possessive, domineering
. . . masculine.

Usually, she wasn't. But Senga Lundy was different.
Her feelings for the young Irish girl had been creeping up
on her for the past few weeks and, as she had watched the
long, dark car sweep Senga away, it had dawned on her
that she might never see her again . . . or, that if she did,
Senga might well be engaged to that arrogant, upstart
German.

As the night moved on she found herself restlessly
pacing from side to side in the room, trying to imagine
what they might be doing. She finally came to stop before
the window, her breath coming in great gasps, her
fingernails biting into the flesh of her palms. Forcing
herself to relax, she stared out into the night, watching,
waiting.

Standing in the shadows, she had watched the activity
along the street, the street women, their customers, the
few strolling customers and other, darker, furtive figures
who hugged the shadows and preyed upon the others. She
had intervened only once, and that was when a young
couple – who looked like tourists – were being stalked by a
thin, dark-skinned man, one of whose hands held the
tell-tale glitter of a knife. Billy had thrown a flowerpot
down on to the man, the sudden explosion sending him
scurrying for cover, similarly driving the young couple out
into the broader, better-lit streets.

As the night paled towards dawn, a deep, grim
foreboding settled on to her shoulders, knotting the
muscles, releasing acid into her stomach. Unconsciously,
her broad fingers massaged her troubled stomach, her eyes
never leaving the street.

When the car finally appeared, she knew – deep in her
heart, she knew – that something was wrong. She watched
the driver get out, look up and down the street before
stepping back to open the door. And then Senga,
ashen-faced and hollow-eyed, stepped out on to the street
and ducked into the doorway. The uniformed chauffeur

327

moved back around the car and slid into the driver's seat. There was a single puff of smoke from the exhaust as the engine was turned off.

Billy had turned around and was facing the door, heavy pistol level in her hands, when Senga burst in. Even across the room, Billy could almost feel her desperation.

'What's wrong?' Billy demanded. 'For Christ's sake, tell me what's wrong!'

'It's Rutgar . . .'

'What's he done? Asked you to marry him?' she added, starting to smile. 'Dinnae worry about it.'

Senga shook her head vehemently.

'Worse?'

Senga nodded, her large eyes sparkling with tears.

'What could be worse?'

'I've killed him, Billy. God help me, but I've killed him.'

There had only ever been two times in her life when the big Scotswoman had been truly surprised: when she had first killed a man, she had been surprised to find how easy it was, and the second time, years later, when she had shot a man five times and he hadn't fallen down. Both of these occasions were etched into her memory for various reasons, and she had never forgotten that mind-numbing sense of shock as if everything had stopped – heart, lungs, thought. She experienced it again now.

Whatever she had been expecting Senga Lundy to tell her, it certainly hadn't been this.

Billy wrapped her arms around the younger woman, wondering – desperately wondering – what she was going to do. The door swung open and Billy's arms swung up, the heavy gun pointing directly into the opening. Without ceremony, she shoved Senga to the floor and then stepped over her. Her finger was tightening on the trigger as a tall man-shape moved into the room, when Senga gasped, 'Don't shoot, Billy. He's a friend.'

The shadowy figure turned and closed the door behind him, before moving into the light. Billy helped Senga to her feet, her finger still on the trigger, the gun still pointing unswervingly towards the man.

'This is Mikhail, the von Mann's chauffeur,' Senga said quickly. 'He knows what's happened. He brought me back here.'

The tall, grey-haired, grey-eyed man stepped forward and bowed stiffly.

'He's Russian,' Senga added. 'He speaks English, German and French.'

Billy stepped forward, the gun no longer pointing directly at the man, but with her finger still on the trigger. 'Why?' she asked.

'Why?' Mikhail said, his head tilted slightly.

'Why are you helping this girl?'

'Does there have to be a reason?' he asked, switching from English to French.

Billy answered him in the same language. 'Usually, yes.'

'He was not a good man,' Mikhail said. 'And if any man deserved to die, then he did. It is only justice that he should have died by a woman's hand.' He spread his arms, 'But this is wasting time; you must pack, you must go. I will drive you to the station. If God is with you, you will catch the six o'clock express to the border, and thence make your way back to Paris or London. I would suggest a large city; it is easy to lose oneself in a large city,' he added with the voice of experience.

'Billy,' Senga murmured, 'Rutgar . . . he . . .'

'Sssh. Not now. Tell me later. Mikhail is right. We must pack and go.'

'Is there anything I can do?' the Russian asked.

Senga had flung open the wardrobe and was busily throwing her own articles of clothing on to the bed. The dresses Rutgar had bought her she left . . . until Billy had reached in and added them to the pile. 'If you don't want them, we can sell them.' She looked up and smiled at Mikhail. 'Tell me about Rutgar,' she said quietly, glancing significantly at Senga.

The Russian nodded slightly, knowing what Billy was

doing. He leaned back against the door and folded his arms across his broad chest. 'He was not a nice person. He was . . . what is the phrase . . . a split personality. Like two people. At times he could be charming, gentle and humorous. But later he would be dark and sour. He was unlucky with women, and his reputation in Berlin ensured that no self-respecting family would allow their daughters to go near him. He frequented ladies of . . . of easy virtue . . .'

Both Senga and Billy smiled at his quaint expression.

'. . . but even amongst these, his reputation was for sudden, unpredictable violence. I drove too many young women out to him, and then later drove them to the private hospital on the outskirts of the city that tended to their wounds. Drink or opium usually precipitated these dark moods.

'He went away about a year ago, and only made infrequent visits home. I know he did some work for his father, selling munitions and armaments abroad.'

'I thought Germany was not supposed to have any munitions manufacturing?' Senga asked.

'It's not. But there are many things which Germany is not supposed to have, but it does.' Mikhail grinned, and Billy Fadden suddenly found herself attempting to put an age on this elegant man. She had initially thought him to be in his late fifties or early sixties, but he looked and spoke like a much younger man. 'I'll just get my own case,' she said, moving into the adjoining bedroom.

Mikhail spoke directly to Senga. 'Recently, reports began to trickle down to the servants' quarters that Master Rutgar was returning home with a foreign bride. The story later changed to a fiancée, and I assumed that you were that fiancée.'

'So did a lot of people,' Senga murmured, 'including the entire von Mann family, and especially Rutgar.' She paused and then added, 'But in all fairness, both Manfred, his father, and Max, his older brother, came very close to warning me about Rutgar, especially Max.'

'He is the best of them,' Mikhail agreed.

Senga snapped the claps shut on the single suitcase, just as Billy reappeared with her own, battered suitcase. Mikhail moved away from the door and lifted both cases without a word. 'Ladies . . .?' he asked.

Billy checked her gun and then slipped it into the pocket of her coat and Senga, suddenly realising that the Derringer was empty, dug it out of her handbag and broke it open, ejecting the two spent shells and reloading with two rounds from the small box Billy held open to her.

Mikhail watched them both without a flicker of surprise. He had guessed that Senga was an extraordinary woman the moment he had laid eyes on her . . . but just quite how extraordinary he was only beginning to realise. 'Ready?' he asked.

They both nodded. Without another word, Billy cracked open the door and peered out into the hall. She nodded briefly and allowed the door to open of its own accord and stepped quickly out into the corridor, her hand on the gun in her pocket. Mikhail was next, followed by Senga, who turned and pulled the door closed behind her, turning the key in the lock.

They moved down the stairs quickly, Senga between Billy and the Russian, conscious now that every moment spent in the hotel increased their chances of capture.

Billy stepped out into the street first, head moving, feeling the electric tingle of excitement along her nerves. It felt good to be working again – working properly. Her eyes roved up and down the street, checking the shadows, the movement of the wind-carried dust, the disposition of the countless pigeons that every building in Berlin seemed to possess.

Mikhail appeared behind her, went to the car, dropped the cases to open the door, and then quickly threw both suitcases inside. On Billy's instructions, he left the rear passenger door open, and then moved around and climbed into the driver's seat. The engine growled and then purred to life. When it was running smoothly, Billy stepped back

331

into the shadows and, taking Senga's arm, hurried her down the steps and into the open car door, stepping in behind her. The car was moving before the door had closed.

As the car hissed through the deserted, early-morning streets, Billy kept twisting in her seat to watch behind them.

'There's no one there,' Mikhail said quietly.

'I know. It's just force of habit.'

'What will happen to you, Mikhail?' Senga asked.

The big Russian smiled. 'Nothing.'

'But they'll know you drove me back to Berlin.'

'True. But I did not know that Master Rutgar had come to an untimely end, did I? I will tell them that I drove you back to your hotel in Berlin, and I left you there . . .'

'No,' Billy said quickly. 'Someone might have seen us leave with you. Better if you stick to the truth.'

The big Russian nodded. 'I drove you back to your hotel. I waited while you packed your bags and, accompanied by your companion, I drove you to the station. You were talking excitedly about Italy, perhaps?'

'Italy,' Billy nodded. 'That would be perfect.'

'But whatever you decide, wherever you decide to go, I would advise you to leave Germany this day. The von Manns are powerful with many friends. They also have contacts with many foreign governments, so you would be wise to take care. You would be wise perhaps to head to Paris, which has a large international community, or perhaps make your way to London where the German influence is not so strong.'

Senga leaned forward and rested her hand on the man's shoulder. 'Thank you for your advice. Perhaps you might heed it also. Come with us to Paris or London.'

Mikhail shook his head sadly. 'Would that I could. But I am under contract to the von Manns. Indentured, you might say. I fled Russia after the Revolution – I was the last of my family, the rest had died in the fighting. When I arrived here after the war I had nothing. But the von

332

Manns wanted a title amongst their servants, and so they hired me . . .'

'What do you mean, they wanted a title amongst the servants?' Senga interrupted.

Mikhail's eyes glanced into the mirror, smiling at the young woman. 'It is quite fashionable now in Berlin, especially amongst the *nouveau-riche*, to have former nobility as servants.' He paused and added softly, 'In Russia I was a prince . . . oh, it is not such a rare title there, but here, in this modern country, it still has the power to impress.'

'Why can't you leave?' Billy asked, not looking at the driver, her eyes on the few stragglers along the deserted Friedrichstrasse close to the station.

Mikhail shrugged. 'Because I signed a contract. Because I gave my word.' His eyes found Billy's in the mirror. 'Why have you remained with Miss Senga?'

A bitter smile twisted her lips. 'Because I gave my word,' she whispered.

The car stopped outside the ornate entrance to the railway station. The Russian twisted in his seat to face them both. 'Like me, your choices have been limited by circumstances. We do the best we can within those circumstances. And if you can keep your conscience happy – then what more can you ask for?' He stepped out of the car, coming around to open the door for them both. Billy stepped out first, stopping to check, and then holding out her hand for Senga to follow. Together the two women walked quickly into the shadow of the station, Senga carrying both bags, leaving Billy's hands free. They stopped briefly at the door and turned to wave to the Russian, but the car had gone. Vaguely disappointed, they both hurried on, wondering why he hadn't waited. But as they were turning away, they saw the black police car move down the road in the same direction the Daimler had taken. They didn't know whether it had been following the car or not, but they didn't wait to find out.

The train to the border was virtually deserted, and they

had a compartment to themselves. Neither woman spoke; they were both too tense and tired, and the reaction following the night's events was beginning to set in. Senga nodded off eventually, although, judging from the play of her facial muscles and the trembling of her eyes beneath the closed lids, it was neither a restful nor an easy sleep.

Billy wouldn't allow herself to sleep – at least not until they were over the border, and even then there were no guarantees that there wouldn't be a police squad waiting for them with warrants for their arrests. And Billy had no illusions about how they would be treated. This wasn't France where a crime of passion was looked upon slightly differently; Senga had killed a German Junker. She wondered if they still had the death penalty in Germany.

She settled back into the seat, feeling the comforting weight of the pistol in her pocket. Well, Germany hadn't worked out the way she had hoped it might. And now, back to Paris, and thence to Dublin, where Patrick's organisation should be to able to afford them a measure of protection. But first they had to survive the journey to Paris. And Billy couldn't help the feeling that they might be jumping from the frying pan into the fire.

CHAPTER THIRTY-FIVE

The tourist looked and dressed like an American, and the camera hanging around his neck was also of American manufacture. He was tall and thin, and the right sleeve of his jacket was empty and tucked into the coat pocket. He might have been a veteran from the Great War returning to Europe for a holiday. He stopped in front of the blind beggar who sat on the steps of Notre Dame cathedral and dropped a few coins into his bowl.

'*Merci, Monsieur,*' the blind man whispered, his bandaged head turning in the direction of the sound.

The tourist turned to look at the cathedral. 'Say . . . can you tell me a little about this place, eh? I'd pay, of course,' he added hastily in an atrocious French accent.

'Of course, *Monsieur*. What would you like to know?' The beggar's face turned towards the tourist questioningly.

'Do you know a lot about this place?' he asked.

'I know everything about the Cathedral de Notre Dame de Paris,' the man said proudly, smiling, displaying surprisingly white teeth in a filthy, seamed face.

'Well, I thought you might. Be my guide, then. Show me around the sights.'

'I am blind, *Monsieur,*' the man murmured.

'Then you'll be able to show me things which other guides might miss.' The tourist paused and then added. 'I lost my right arm in the Dardenelles, and people treat me as if I'm some sort of invalid. They don't realise that my left arm has more than compensated for it. So, I'd say

335

you'd know more about the beauties of this place than anyone else.'

The beggar groped for his long, white stick and shuffled to his feet. His clothing, which had once been of good quality, had been patched so often now that whole sections of it were nothing more than a threadbare patchwork. Incongruously, his shoes were brand new and highly polished. His face was thin, the cheekbones pronounced, his eyes hidden behind heavy-lensed dark glasses. Holding tightly to the rail with his right hand, his left tapping the steps with his stick, the man began the climb to the great double doors. 'Is this your first time in this country?' he asked.

'I was in the services and I served over here during the Great War. I billeted in Paris for two nights, but I never managed to see the sights. I made a promise to myself when I was invalided home that I would return here one day and see all those sights that the war prevented me from seeing.' The man's bad French accent made his sentence structure unwieldly, but the beggar seemed to have no difficulty in following him.

'Are you enjoying it? You have come with your wife perhaps?'

'Well, it's sure a lot quieter this time than the last time I was here. Still a lot of foreigners here, though. And no, I'm not here with my wife. She passed away two years back.'

'I am sorry to hear that. A man should have a woman to care for him.'

'True enough.'

The two guards on the doors looked at one another as the two characters passed into the cool, shadowy interior of the cathedral. They watched them chatting amicably together and they then turned back to their bored perusal of the early-morning crowd. Later perhaps there would be some young women to look at and ogle, but for the moment there was nothing.

'Notre Dame de Paris is one of the finest cathedrals in Europe,' the blind beggar began . . .

'Personally, I couldn't give a damn,' the tourist said, pressing the cold barrel of a revolver into the man's side. 'This weapon is silenced, and I will shoot you down without a second thought.' The appalling French accent had disappeared, replaced by almost flawless French. There was still the hint of an accent and the beggar desperately attempted to identify it.

'I am but a blind beggar, *Mon* . . .'

'And if you lie to me, I might just kill you anyway.'

'Who are you?' the beggar asked, straightening, reaching up to pull off the dark glasses, pale, grey eyes blinking in the dusty, cathedral light. He looked around at the man holding the gun on him, and frowned: he didn't recognise him. 'I don't know you, *Monsieur*.'

'Ah, but you do. I am Patrick Lundy.' He watched the man's expression change and added grimly. 'Ah, I see my name is not unknown to you. Now, I have some questions for you, and it would be in your best interests to answer them. Lie to me and I will hurt you. Continue to lie to me and I will kill you.' With the gun in his ribs, Patrick manoeuvred him into one of the small side chapels, forcing him to sit in one of the small, wooden pews. He slid in alongside the man, the gun still pressed into his side.

'Do you have a name?' Patrick asked.

'Do you need a name?'

'I suppose I don't. But what do I call you?'

'Most people call me Notre Dame. It's as good a name as any.'

'I want to know who put out the contract on me and my companion,' Patrick said very softly, his eyes locked on to the man's face.

'If I tell you that, I will die,' Notre Dame protested mildly.

'And if you don't, you will die. You are caught, as the expression is, "between a rock and a hard place". I want to know.'

'I do not think I can tell you,' Notre Dame smiled tightly. 'But I should say that it was nothing personal. It was simply a job. It is what I do.'

Patrick took out a large, white handkerchief and dabbed at his forehead with it, and then he simultaneously rammed the handkerchief into the man's mouth – and shot him in the foot. Notre Dame's eyes widened in explosive agony and the small chapel was suddenly suffused with the ammonia smell of urine.

'I won't ask you again,' Patrick hissed, his face close enough to the beggar's to smell the sweat masking the urine. 'I've got five more rounds in this gun, and I'll shoot you to hell and gone – and you'll still be alive. I guarantee that. Maybe I'll even take your eyes, and then you'll really be a blind, crippled beggar. Eh?' he spat.

Large tears had welled from the man's wide, frightened eyes, and the handkerchief was bloody from where he had bitten into his tongue.

'Tell me.'

'I . . . I don't know . . . I don't know who. I never ask names.'

Patrick dug the gun deeper into the man's side.

'But I always . . . always make it my business to find out.'

'I thought you might.'

'It was an Irishwoman . . . she came to me through one of the Parisian whoremasters . . .'

And Patrick Lundy knew of one woman who fitted the description. He was surprised . . . or was he? His mother had taken out a contract on him once before and had even accompanied the four hired killers to Dublin to ensure that they carried out their contract. He wasn't surprised . . . only puzzled. He didn't think that he and his mother would ever be friends, but he didn't think they were enemies – although with Katherine Lundy one could never be too sure. Patrick hadn't been too sure of his mother's sanity for a long time now.

'Did you learn the reason why this woman wanted me dead?'

'I didn't. It was something to do with some stolen

jewellery. You were coming too close to the truth about their theft and the truth would hurt certain people.'

Patrick shook his head quickly. It didn't make sense. His mother wanted those stones; she didn't give a damn about the truth and certain people getting hurt.

'And that's it . . . that's all? There's nothing else you want to tell me?'

'I did have the impression that if this attempt on your life didn't work, her husband would devise something which would!'

Husband?

During his years on the run Patrick had been betrayed more than once, and he remembered the sick, cold feeling in the pit of his stomach he always experienced when he discovered that people he had once trusted had sold him out.

'The name,' he said very quietly, 'give me the name of the woman who hired you.'

'Mrs Martin Moore.'

'Tilly Cusack!' Patrick whispered aghast. And shot Notre Dame in the head.

'Keep walking,' Patrick said urgently, walking smartly away from the cathedral.

Colin Holstock glanced behind him, in time to see one of the guards on the door turn to enter the shadows. 'You didn't . . .?' he asked, although he had already guessed the answer.

'He knew too much,' Patrick said crisply. They rounded a corner and he shrugged out of the jacket, fitting it on properly, pulling the camera strap from around his neck and dropping it into the small bag Colin was carrying. 'He could have betrayed us . . . and more importantly, he could have tipped off our enemies that we were on to them.'

'Surely shooting him would have much the same effect?'

'But now we know who our enemy is,' Patrick grinned coldly, and the English inspector shivered suddenly at the ruthless expression on his face.

'Who is our enemy?' he asked.

Patrick turned to the left, heading down on to the quays. A hundred yards further on he stopped and leaned over the edge of the waist-high, stone wall that separated the path from the river. All the nervous energy seemed to drain out of him. He pressed the heels of his palms into his eyes, wiping away the gritty exhaustion that had abruptly washed over him.

'It's been a set-up since Tilly Cusack first approached Senga and myself back in Dublin. She's obviously been working with Martin Moore to trap either Katherine or myself – and possibly kill us too – and she's been using Senga as the bait. I'm inclined to think that she's also after the jewels – otherwise she could have taken me in Dublin. Possibly they're the whole reason for this.' He shrugged. 'Anyway, she betrayed us to the beggar . . . and he said something to the effect that if this attempt on our lives failed, then her husband would devise something which would succeed.'

'I would imagine Martin Moore is in Paris then,' Colin said quietly.

'Can you check that?'

'I don't know. I'll try. I'm just wondering how much they know.'

Patrick glanced sidelong at him. 'If they know you're running with me, then you're in trouble.'

Colin nodded. He rubbed the toe of his boot in the dust and then looked directly at Patrick. 'You realise that if – no, *because* Tilly Cusack has betrayed us, then she knows where Senga has gone . . . or at least she would have a very good idea. I think we have to get Senga back to Paris where we can guard her.'

'She has Billy . . .' Patrick said slowly.

'Well then, at least warn her. She trusts Tilly Cusack. If Tilly captures her . . . what then?'

Patrick nodded slowly. 'You're right. We've got to try and make contact with her. But how?'

'We know she's a guest of the von Manns; it should be

340

possible to get a message to her through them. And we should be able to make contact with them through the German police.'

Patrick nodded. 'Do it then. And pray to God that she's safe.'

Across the city the numerous church bells began to toll noon. To both men the usually joyous peals sounded leaden and ominous.

Senga reset the tiny hands of her wristwatch to noon and then pressed her wrist to Billy's ear. 'Is it ticking?' she asked.

'It is,' the Scotswoman said shortly. She was feeling tired and slightly hungover, even though she hadn't been drinking, but she knew that their first priority was to get off the streets until she had assessed the situation. In her present, exhausted state, such assessment was plainly beyond her.

Senga was relieved to be back in Paris even though she knew the city wasn't safe. The last few hours had been fraught with danger, and there had been numerous heart-stopping moments, especially when they had been crossing over the border and the German police and border guards had come aboard to check papers and tickets. The two women were counting on the fact that the guards would not have been alerted to Rutgar's death, but even so Senga had watched the silent guard read through the papers without breathing. He had looked first at Senga and then at Billy with almost colourless eyes, expecting them to look away, but both women outstared him. Usually these English women wilted . . . he checked the papers again, and discovered that one was Scottish and the other Irish. Well, obviously they were made of sterner stuff. Bowing slightly, he had backed from the carriage. When he had gone, Senga remembered to breathe.

There had been a similar moment when they had stepped off the train in Paris and found that the platform had been swarming with guards. Billy had immediately dragged Senga back on to the train, and the two women had waited in the corridor until the police had moved to the next carriage, surrounding a uniformed officer and his bride. In the resultant confusion, the two women managed to sneak away unnoticed.

'Any suggestions?' Billy asked.

'How about Tattoo?'

Billy shrugged. 'Do you know where he lives?'

'No. But we know where he frequents. It should be just a matter of asking questions.'

Billy laughed softly. 'My dear, always remember that asking the wrong questions in the wrong place is liable to lead you into a lot of trouble.'

'There's nothing else we can do until we get a message to Patrick.'

'I know,' Billy sighed. 'Come on then . . .'

'Shall we get a cab?'

Billy looked up and down the rank of black taxis and then shook her head. 'Better not. If there was an inquiry someone might remember two women travelling together off the early morning train. We'll walk.'

They walked in silence for a while and then Senga turned to Billy, her eyes dark and shadowed, her forehead creased. The exhaustion which she had so successfully kept at bay was now washing over her, making her thought processes sluggish. 'Billy . . . Billy, why did Rutgar do what he did?'

It took a moment or two for the Scotswoman to register what Senga had said, and she finally shook her head. She too was almost too tired to answer. 'I don't know. He was . . . he was sick, I suppose. Two people living inside him; one was good and kind and gentle . . . the other, well the other was not a nice person.' She smiled gently. 'I've seen it happen before. Sometimes it is a trait that runs in families.'

'Bad blood,' Senga remarked.

'Something like that.'

Did that explain the enigma of her own mother, Senga

342

wondered. She had mixed memories of her parents. She barely remembered her father, Dermot Corcoran . . . and when he had died in the ill-fated 1916 rising, her mother had refused even to speak his name in the house. She had changed the family name at the time, claiming it was for security reasons, but Senga had realised a long time ago that it was more than that. But Senga did remember how her mother had been: a cheerful, smiling woman and, with equal clarity, she remembered how the woman had changed, how she had become cold and embittered. She remembered too how when Patrick had left home back in 1919 her mother had refused even to mention his name, and Patrick later claimed that his mother had organised a squad of killers to hunt him down in Dublin. It was hard to believe . . . no sane woman would have done that, but was she sane, could she be sane . . .?

And was that to be her own fate, she wondered. Would she eventually descend into some sort of paranoid madness? Was she not already on that slope? She had killed Rutgar with barely a thought, but what terrified her was that she did not regret it at all. She felt nothing, no remorse, no shame, no guilt. And surely she should feel guilt? What sort of person could kill another and not feel anything about it?

A mad person.

Was she then already going insane? She didn't think so, she didn't know . . . but then if she was going insane, surely that would be exactly how she would think? She squeezed her fingers into the soft flesh of her palms, using the pain in an attempt to clear her head.

She had never wanted this wild adventure. It had been thrust upon her; her whole way of life had been uprooted, her schooling upset, her life threatened. She was twenty-one years old; she was at that age where she should be out meeting people, enjoying herself, not on the run for her life with the threat of the noose – or its German equivalent – hanging over her head. She grinned inanely at the unintentional pun. She should be meeting young people of her own age, but curiously that didn't appeal to her; she had spent most of her life in the company of older people: mother, brother, 'aunts' and now Billy, and she didn't consciously think of herself as being twenty-one, and obviously other people didn't perceive her as being that age – she was particularly thinking of Colin Holdstock now – but sometimes she thought it would be nice to be twenty-one, with all the minor emergencies and upsets peculiar to that age. It would be heaven.

And boring.

The Black Cat nestled on the very edges of Montmartre and looked disreputable enough. Senga waited outside, her hands in her pockets, a weapon in both hands, while Billy went inside with what remained of their money in her pockets. When she emerged a few moments later, she shook her head slightly.

'The barman told me he'd never heard of anyone called Tattoo, but when I asked him again, he told me.'

Senga bit the inside of her lips to keep herself from smiling. 'And what did he say when you asked him the second time?'

'He told me where he was.'

'Just for argument's sake,' Senga said quietly, not looking at her friend, 'how did you ask?'

'I pinned his hand to the bar with a fork!'

'A little indiscreet that,' Senga remarked, turning her head away to conceal the smile.

'True. But I wasn't prepared to spend the next hour talking nicely to him.' She touched Senga's arm and they walked a dozen yards down the street, when Billy suddenly turned into another bar which was incongruously named Le Club. 'He sometimes drinks in here.'

The interior of Le Club was dark and foul-smelling, the smoke which clung to everything stinging their eyes and throats. Billy was moving through the crowd, heading towards the barman, when Senga suddenly touched her arm and pointed to a one-eyed man standing at the end of the bar. 'There he is.' She broke away from Billy and moved lithely through the crowd, stopping in front of the one-eyed Frenchman. 'Tattoo . . . Tattoo . . .' she said into the startled man's face, and then she turned to apologise to the man he was talking to . . .

And stopped.

The man reached out a hand and took one of hers in his, pressing it to his lips, his eyes locked on her face. 'You're a long way from home,' he murmured.

'So are you,' she mumbled, attempting to make sense of it all.

'Are you going to introduce us?' Billy asked, coming up behind Senga, her right hand in her pocket.

'Of course. Of course,' Senga said, distracted, obviously confused. 'Bil . . . Miss Willimena Fadden, may I present my uncle, Colonel Martin Moore!'

CHAPTER THIRTY-SIX

'She's wanted for murder.' Colin Holdstock came down the steps of the police station, white-faced, his teeth clenched tightly to prevent them from chattering.

'Mistake . . .' Patrick breathed.

'I double-checked. And then checked again. I've seen the warrant.' He turned to the left, heading down the brightly lit street. He remembered seeing the striped awning of a café somewhere . . . yes, here . . . and he needed a drink.

'Cognac, two,' he said, holding up two fingers and sliding into one of the metal seats which was tucked away in one corner, cut off from the rest of the street by a wall of shrubbery. Patrick sat down beside him, his back to the wall. He said nothing, simply watching this man he had come to admire and like. They might never be friends, there were too many years, too many experiences, too many prejudices between them for that. But they were both – in their own way – professionals, and they both held the other in high regard. And Patrick also respected Colin's feeling for his sister: Senga could do far worse than this man.

When the drinks arrived, Colin drained half of his in one long swallow.

'Do you want to tell me what happened?' Patrick asked softly.

Colin wrapped both hands around the small glass and stared into its warm depths. 'Senga is wanted by the German police for questioning in connection with the investigation into the death of Graf Rutgar von Mann.'

Patrick sipped his cognac and said nothing.

'She was the last person to see him alive, and he was found shot dead in her room. There were two rounds in his body, both from a small-calibre pistol. Senga Lundy was seen to leave the von Manns household in the Grunewald Forest in the early hours of the morning, and she quit her cheap lodging rooms in Berlin the same day. She was seen to board a train for Rome, but the German police strongly suspect that she will make her way back to Paris, and I would be inclined to believe them.'

'Did she kill the German?' Patrick murmured.

'It looks that way. All the evidence is against her.'

Patrick finished his drink. 'Well, we shall worry about that later, eh? Our first job is to find her, and get her to a safe place. Agreed?' he asked harshly, hoping to snap Colin out of his daze.

'Yes . . . yes, most definitely.'

'So, we'll work on the assumption that if she is not already in Paris, then she's on her way here. But first we'll determine if she's in the city or not. Agreed?'

'But who . . . where?' Colin asked and then he turned to Patrick, a name forming on his lips . . .

'Exactly,' Patrick said with a smile. 'Let's find Tattoo.'

Something was wrong, Senga realised, something slightly out of true. All she had to do was to identify what was awry. She had been surprised to find her uncle – although he wasn't really her uncle – in Paris. But the more she thought about it, the less surprising it became: he travelled quite extensively in his work as . . . she stopped, frowning, realising that she wasn't quite sure what he did exactly. He worked for some government department, map-making or something like that.

But what was he doing with Tattoo?

The question – ice-cold and absolutely chilling – slipped into her consciousness, and she stopped, her glass of white wine poised in mid-air. With an almost conscious effort of will, she pressed the rim of the glass to her lips and sipped the cold liquid, not tasting its tartness, her mouth suddenly sour.

What did she know of Tattoo? Little enough. He operated on the fringes of Parisian society, a villain certainly, a friend of her mother's too, which meant that his contacts went deep into the French underworld. She had once watched him kill a man, and he didn't look as if he was a stranger to it. From the little Senga had managed to pick up, she understood that he had once worked for her mother, and, if he had done that, then he had been involved in prostitution . . . and that begged the question, how did her uncle know him?

Watching Martin Moore carefully, she asked him.

The older man smiled, tiny wrinkles forming around his eyes. 'Your mother always said that the next time I was in Paris I was to be sure to meet Tattoo. She told me that no one could show me Paris like he could.'

The small Frenchman smiled tightly. 'Certainly no one else can show you the Paris I know,' he said proudly.

'You never said what you were doing here, Uncle Martin,' Senga persisted.

'There is an international cartographers conference being held here,' he said softly, glancing from her to Billy, who was now watching him carefully, Senga's persistence having alerted her to the fact that something was wrong here. 'It's very boring really, but someone had to represent my department, and I'm afraid I drew the short straw.'

'Is Aunt Tilly with you?' Senga asked.

'No, she's not. The last I saw of your aunt, she was heading down Oxford Street promising to buy herself a little something . . .' he shrugged. 'I suppose I had better bring her back something nice, eh? Any suggestions?'

'Lingerie,' Senga suggested.

'Clothes,' Billy nodded, 'definitely clothes.'

'Clothes and lingerie it is, then. And perhaps you two ladies will do me the honour of joining me, help me to make a choice?'

Senga looked at Billy and then nodded doubtfully.

Billy shrugged.

'Fine then,' Martin Moore smiled broadly, 'that's settled. Tomorrow perhaps? Tomorrow afternoon; my last lecture finishes around noon or so, and I'l be only too glad to escape for the afternoon in the company of two delightful young women. And now,' he continued, 'since meeting you is such a pleasant surprise, and you have brightened an otherwise dull day, I shall insist that you have dinner with me, tonight. No, not tonight – *now!* And you too, of course, Tattoo,' he added, looking at the Frenchman.

'Thank you, *Monsieur*, you are most kind, but I am afraid I have a prior engagement . . .'

'A pity,' Martin Moore said, and then proceeded to ignore the man. Moments later, the Frenchman stood up and excused himself, and then vanished into the crowd.

'An interesting character,' Billy remarked, watching Martin Moore over the rim of her glass. Both she and Senga had drunk lightly, although Tattoo had downed a seemingly endless supply of cognac without any apparent complaint. She was trying to decide what she didn't like about this man. He looked like a favourite uncle, grey-haired, grey-eyed, distinguished and charming, with an easy grin and a surprising number of his own teeth. It wasn't unusual for her to form instant likes or dislikes – she tended to follow her instincts and her instincts had kept her alive through too many turbulent years for her to dismiss the warnings lightly.

'Yes quite,' Martin Moore said lightly, 'quite a rogue, it seems.' He shrugged and then added with a deprecating smile, 'But then, he is French.' He finished his drink. 'And now dinner, what do you say?'

'Well . . . it would be nice,' Senga said doubtfully.

'But we don't want to impose on your busy schedule,' Billy said quickly, coming to her rescue.

'Nonsense, nonsense, I insist. Now, I suppose you'll want to change first eh?' Although he was speaking to them both, he was looking at Senga. She nodded slightly. 'Well, you go and change, and I'll have a car pick you up in . . . what, an hour?'

'Make it an hour and a half,' Senga said.

'Of course, an hour and a half it is then. Now, if you'll just give me the address where you're staying, I'll send the car around . . .'

Katherine Lundy stared at the small Jewish jeweller in absolute disbelief. 'You know where the jewels are?' she asked slowly and distinctly, unsure if she were hearing him correctly.

The small, gnome-like man stared at her over the rim of his spectacles and nodded vigorously. 'It is no real secret.'

'I want to buy them,' Katherine said decisively.

The jeweller shrugged, the movement indistinct in the dimness of his cluttered backroom. He had closed up his shop for the afternoon to receive this important client. She had come very highly recommended to him. He was also aware that she had money to spend and, much more importantly, the desire to spend it. He didn't know her name – although he had a very good idea who she was, and her interest in the Irish Crown Jewels virtually confirmed this – but she did not know his name. Nor the location of his shop. She had been brought to this shop through the back streets by one of Tattoo's hirelings and he had passed her on to one of the jewellers' apprentices a few streets away. For the final stage of the journey, she had been made to wear a bandage tied tightly across her eyes.

'These stones, these jewels,' the jeweller said slowly, 'they are nice, but not of any great value. If you have the desire to spend money as I understand you have, then I could perhaps show you some other pieces which are of greater, intrinsic value.'

'I'm not interested,' Katherine snapped, 'I want the Irish Crown Jewels.'

'I have access to some of the jewellery of the Russian royal . . .'

350

Katherine stood up, both hands resting on the silver handle of her umbrella. 'Take me out of here. It is obvious that I am wasting my time. You evidently know nothing about the Irish Crown Jewels.'

The jeweller sighed audibly. 'The Irish Crown Jewels,' he sighed again, slowly shaking his broad head from side to side. He looked up at Katherine from over the tops of his spectacles. 'I have in my possession a diamond star composed of brilliants consisting of points issuing from a centre enclosing a cross of rubies and a trefoil of emeralds and sky-blue enamel. Also, a diamond badly set in silver, containing a trefoil of emeralds on a ruby cross, surrounded by a sky-blue, enamelled circle with text cut in rose diamonds in a circle of large, Brazilian stones, surmounted by a harp in diamonds and a loop.' He turned away from Katherine in an attempt to hide his smile. He had caught her attention. 'Furthermore, there are five collars of the Knights Companions of the Order of St Patrick, which I also have. They are of gold with roses and harps alternately tied together with knots of gold, leaves enamelled and an Imperial jewelled crown surmounting a harp of gold. There is a badge of the order composed of Brazilian stones and a Cross of St Patrick in rubies in a blue, enamelled circle with the motto picked out in rose diamonds, the whole enclosed in a wreath of trefoil in emeralds on a gold ground enamelled in colours.' He paused and took a deep breath. 'They were stolen in 1907, the theft being discovered virtually on the eve of Edward VII's visit to Dublin. No one was ever charged with the theft, although suspicion fell on many of the people closely associated with the jewels. One of the people whom the police suspected of having organised the theft was the notorious Madam Kitten, a brothel-keeper in Dublin at that time.'

'How did the jewels arrive in France,' Katherine asked, ignoring the gibe, wondering if she would have to kill the man to ensure his silence. However, she was sure he would build certain safeguards into the sale of the jewels to ensure his own safety.

The Frenchman shrugged. 'The stones were taken to London by . . . by one of the principals, shall we say. It was a prank which had gone disastrously wrong and he suddenly found himself in a very embarrassing position. However, in London he discovered that none of the dealers, either legitimate or otherwise, would touch them. And so circumstances forced him to bring them here to Paris, where he eventually made contact with me. I bought them off him for a nominal sum – although at that stage he freely admitted that all he wanted to do was dispose of them.' Looking around the interior of the tiny shop he shrugged again. 'I am a businessman, I was not going to turn away a profit, so he did not fare well out of me. But he fared better than he would have done from some of the less scrupulous dealers.'

'And?' Katherine asked impatiently, 'What happened to the jewels then?'

'I offered them for sale to the Irish government through an intermediary.' He stopped and looked at her, his eyes wide in astonishment. 'They refused to buy them!'

'Did you offer them to the British government?' Katherine demanded.

'No, Madame, no, I did not.'

'Why?'

'Because I believed that such a move would be unhealthy,' he smiled gently.

'What did you do then?'

'I offered the jewels – either individually or collectively – to several dealers and collectors of my acquaintance. But with no success. Unfortunately, they have little intrinsic value – the last official valuation before their disappearance put them at between sixteen and seventeen thousand sterling; they might be worth upwards of twenty thousand now, and as Crown Jewels go, that is nothing. Nor are they pretty stones, neither are they of noteworthy design. They stayed with me, or kept returning to me. Certain jewels are like that. It is almost as if they are waiting for the right person to come along and claim them.'

Katherine nodded. 'Yes, I think you're right. And I think the right person has come along.'

The jeweller nodded, his round spectacles catching the light, turning them into twin mirrors, reflecting some of the greed and madness in Katherine Lundy's eyes at that moment.

'Have you got them?' she asked.

The jeweller reached down beside him and took up a tall, rosewood box, inlaid with mother-of-pearl panels, with gilt hinges and clasps. Opening the two, tall 'doors' he revealed four horizontal boxes. Taking the tiny knobs between thumb and forefinger, he gently tugged the box open . . . triangular brilliants of light danced around the room, rainbow-edged, shivering delicately . . .

. . . And Katherine Lundy realised a twenty-year dream.

'Your uncle is a handsome man,' Billy remarked, sitting back in the hotel bedroom's only chair, watching Senga dress.

The younger woman shrugged. 'I suppose you could say so. I can't really see it myself.'

'You've known him too long. But I would imagine he was one of those rather plain young men, who have only become distinguished as they grew older.'

Senga stopped and looked at her reflection in the mirror, and then nodded, 'I think you're right, I don't ever remember him as being handsome.'

'He would be younger than your Aunt Tilly?'

'Oh much. Sometimes,' she added, 'I'm surprised they've stayed together. They're so unlike.'

'Possibly that's what keeps them together,' Billy remarked. She continued watching Senga, admiring the flow of her muscles as she dropped her dress over her shoulders. 'Tell me,' she asked very quietly, 'what makes you so suspicious of him today?'

Senga glanced sidelong at her. 'I didn't realise it was so obvious.'

'Just a little.'

'I suppose I was just surprised to find him with Tattoo.'
She shrugged. 'I suppose I was just surprised at finding
him in Paris at all.'

Billy nodded.

'Why?' Senga stopped and turned to face her. 'Did you
think there was something wrong?'

Billy nodded slowly and reached into her coat pocket for
the heavy pistol. 'I'm no great believer in coincidence.'
She snapped open the cylinder on the heavy pistol and
checked that it was fully loaded. 'What do you know about
him?'

Senga turned back to the mirror and continued
dressing, stepping into her shoes, dragging her fingers
through her thick hair, pulling it back off her face. 'Very
little,' she said eventually. 'I've told you he met my aunt in
Dublin sometime before the rising, they married and
moved to Scotland. We stayed with them a couple of times
– but he was usually away on business, so we saw very
little of him. When we did see him, he was always very
nice to us, gave us presents, and he seemed to be very
loving towards Tilly.' She looked at Billy and frowned.
'Something's not right,' she whispered.

Billy stood up and dropped the pistol on to the chair.
She went around behind Senga and straightened the collar
on her dress, and then wrapped her arms around the
younger woman, folding them across her stomach, resting
her head against her lustrous hair. Senga placed her own
hands over Billy's and leaned back into her friend. 'Tell
me that everything is going to work out all right?' she said
very softly, her voice barely above a whisper.

'It will be,' Billy promised.

There was a knock on the door and both women broke
apart, glancing at the clock on the mantelpiece.

'Uncle Martin, right on time,' Senga said, reaching for a
pearl choker as Billy went to the door.

'Who is it?' the Scotswoman asked.

'Colonel Moore's driver, Ma'am . . .'

Billy Fadden opened the door.

354

The shotgun blast at point-blank range lifted her right off her feet and threw her across the room. She crashed to the floor upsetting the chair, toppling her gun to the floor, and as she scrabbled for the pistol a man stepped into the room and shot her again.

It was as if time itself had slowed . . .

Senga heard the bang – the long, rolling detonation – that shocked her senseless and then Billy Fadden's bloodied body tumbled almost at her feet. Senga was bending to her, aware that something was desperately wrong, unable to comprehend what had happened, reaching for her, touching her fingers. Pearls were falling from her nerveless fingers, tumbling to the floor, the string breaking, white beads splashing into the blood . . .

. . . And the blood was everywhere . . .

Billy's hand touched the butt of the pistol, and then her body spasmed and twisted as another explosion rent her flesh, her nails tearing strips of flesh from Senga's hand before they relaxed. Blood – hot and salty – splashed across Senga's face.

There was blood on Billy's face, on her tongue, her lips, dappled across her cheeks. Her mouth worked, air hissing through her lips . . . and then the light behind the eyes died, turning them to stone.

There was a rushing, roaring sound as Senga's vision began to spiderweb, darkness creeping in from the edges. There was sound, a distant banshee wail of grief that thrummed deep in her bones and tore at her throat. She looked up.

There was a pistol pointing in her face. She focused on the weapon, not seeing the figure behind it, smelling the cordite and powder, the hot metal.

'Nothing personal,' the man said, and rapped her across the side of the head with the gun.

Martin Moore looked at the two bodies lying in a bloody pool on the floor and then shook his head in disgust: blood had splashed on to his new shoes.

CHAPTER THIRTY-SEVEN

She had vague memories of having screamed until her throat had been raw; she remembered vomiting until there was nothing left to retch; she remembered crying until she had been cried out, but it was as if the memories belonged to someone else. Initially she had refused to accept them, had refused to dwell on the fact that Billy Fadden was dead, suddenly, brutally and absolutely dead. The crusted, red-brown stains on her black dress bore mute testament to that.

But when the truth finally sank in, she experienced all the anguish anew, relived the final seconds of Billy Fadden's life in minute and graphic detail. Her fear, the horror, the terrible loss had transmuted, however, had mutated into a terrible, raging hatred. She had taken that loathing and examined it, cherished it, clung to it with a passion because that was all she had left now. She would avenge Billy's murder, or she would die trying.

But was it really Martin Moore she had been standing over her with a gun in his hand? Her memories were vague, confused, and the pounding in her head didn't help. There was a straight gash down along the side of her face, running across her temple and up into her thick hair. There were flakes of dried blood on the side of her face and in her hair, and she imagined that it was only the thickness of her hair that had saved her from a cracked skull. She remembered the gun-barrel, its metallic, oily smell, the heat from it . . . the pain when it had struck her.

Her last, truly conscious memory had been of a man –

whom she had first thought to be Martin Moore . . . but it couldn't have been Uncle Martin, could it? No, surely not. The shock of Billy's terrible death and then the blow to her head had confused her. She wondered how long she had lain unconscious; long enough anyway for her to have dreamt, hallucinated, and . . . and . . . and . . .

Senga Lundy opened her eyes, fully conscious and alert. She lay back on a rough, hard pillow, her eyes taking in the tiny room around her and, satisifed that she was alone, she closed her eyes again, attempting to still the pounding in her breast; the throbbing matching the agony in her head.

She wished her brother was here, wherever he was.

She even wished her mother was here.

Breathe, breathe evenly, calmly and think. Think. Think.

Lying on the bed she attempted to sort out the options open to her. She had always been able to reason incisively; such an unusual trait in a young woman, one of her lecturers had so condescendingly remarked that Senga had never returned to his classes. What she needed to do now was to analyse her situation.

Physically – with the exception of her pounding head – she seemed to be unharmed, although she was stiff and bruised along one arm and leg, as if she had been thrown down at some stage. She was still wearing the dress she had put on to go to dinner – and with absolute tactile clarity, she remembered Billy Fadden doing up the button at the back, resting her hands across her stomach, her head on her back . . .

Taking a deep, shuddering breath she forced herself away from the image. Later, there would be time enough to grieve later – if she survived this, a perverse voice whispered.

Touching her hair, she discovered that the two, six-inch, razor-sharp and pointed hatpins were still in place, so at least she wasn't completely defenceless.

Opening her eyes, she eased herself upright in the bed

and then stopped until the pounding in her head had moderated enough for her to see properly. She was in a small, stark room that had obviously been unused for a long time. It wasn't exactly dirty, but a thin patina of dust covered everything, and the hard bed she was lying on smelt faintly musty and was damp to the touch. The roof was steeply slanted on both sides and the only window was a skylight that showed nothing more than a patch of blue sky. With the exception of the bed and a small, covered chamberpot in the corner, the room was bare.

She slid carefully off the bed and was surprised to find her shoes tucked beneath her bed. She took a moment to put them on and then walked slowly and carefully across the bare floor and tried the door. Unsurprisingly, it was locked. Turning and resting her back against the flaking wood, she looked around the room. It was not entirely unfamiliar and she had a vague memory of two men holding her down on the bed while another – a doctor – had injected her . . .

She pushed up the sleeve on her left arm and found the tiny bruised puncture in her flesh . . . so it hadn't been a dream. So, did that validate all that she had experienced, all that she had thought and imagined . . .?

Shaking her head – and immediately regretting it – she concentrated on the room again, and her gaze kept fixing on the skylight. Returning to the bed, she attempted to shift it. It had a cast-iron base and rattled thunderously on the bare floorboards as it moved.

'You're wasting your time!'

Senga whirled, and then swayed as the blackness and the pain in her head threatened to engulf her. She sat down heavily on the bed.

'There really is now way out of here,' Martin Moore said, stepping into the room and closing the door behind him. The key was turned from the other side.

'It was you!' Senga breathed, horrified.

Martin Moore stared at her, his eyes hooded, watching her without expression. 'Never think of them as people,' his old mentor, John Lewis, had said, 'think of them as problems, objects, cattle. You'll find it easier to handle that way.' And Martin Moore had been thinking of people as cattle for so long that he found it difficult to think of them in any other way.

Senga stared at this man whom she had thought she knew, looked at him as if she were seeing him for the first time, impressing his face, his features, his eyes – especially his eyes – into her memory. She swore that she was going to kill this man; she would kill him with as much mercy as he had shown Billy.

'Why?' she asked, wondering why he had had to kill her, but Martin Moore chose to interpret the question differently.

'You are only the bait. It is nothing personal. Your mother has, or will have, something which we want. We know she won't sell, so we have been forced to trade, shall we say, with her. When the transaction is complete, both you and she can go free,' he lied.

'Why did you have to kill Billy?' Senga persisted.

The man paused for a moment before considering. 'Willimena Fadden was a dangerous criminal. We knew the woman was armed and a decision was taken to ensure that she would not have the opportunity to harm any of my men.'

'You murdered her in cold blood.'

'If Willimena Fadden had been tried by a British court of law for her numerous crimes – which included multiple murder – she would undoubtedly have gone to the gallows.' His lips moved in a smile. 'I merely saved the British taxpayer the expense of a trial.'

'What are you?' Senga hissed.

Martin Moore's smile was more genuine this time, 'Me? Why, I'm nothing more than a civil servant.' He rapped on the door with his knuckles and it opened immediately. Senga caught a glimpse of two men standing outside in the dimly-lit corridor. One was tall and well-built and seemed to be holding some sort of rifle; the second was smaller, darker . . . with an eyepatch over his left eye!

Martin Moore paused in the doorway. 'We will be passing a message on to your mother shortly. We'll tell her just how safe you are – and just how safe you're liable to remain.'

'And if she won't deal with you?'

'She will deal with me,' Martin Moore said in a tone which brooked no argument.

Inspector Maurice Durffle watched his English friend closely as he broke the news. The colour had drained from Colin Holdstock's face initially, but it was now suffused with rage.

'And you're sure of this?' he demanded.

Durffle turned and leaned on the low wall, and looked down into the murky waters of the Seine. When the weather was good, the water could be any colour under the sun, an inspiration for the scores of artists which lined its banks, but today the sky was grey and overcast, threatening rain: the colour of excrement, he thought. And smelt like it too.

He spoke quickly, keeping his voice carefully neutral, the same tone of voice he used when speaking to a superior. 'I examined the corpse myself in the morgue. I can arrange for you to do so too, if you wish. It has been identified as the body of a woman known as Willimena or Billy Fadden, a well-built female in her mid-thirties known to have been in the company of Miss Senga Lundy. The woman had been shot in the chest at very close range by a sawn-off shotgun. This was deduced from the burn marks on her clothing and the spread of the shot. From the disposition of the room, we have determined that she was flung across the room by the blast, upsetting some items of furniture. Remarkably she survived the shot although it should have killed her outright. She was obviously reaching for a gun when she was shot a second time by a pistol at point-blank range. The bullet entered her forehead and death was instantaneous.

'Blood was smeared across the carpet as if something

had been dragged through it, and we found a partial bloody footprint close to the body. I would speculate that something – or someone – had been pulled across Willimena Fadden's body.'

'Senga?'

Durffle turned his head to look down the quays to where Patrick Lundy leaned against the low wall, his arms folded across his chest, his eyes fixed on the distant Eiffel Tower. 'Miss Lundy's purse was found in the room.' He reached into his pocket and passed across a small, silver Derringer. 'This was in the purse; it is loaded but unfired.'

Colin Holdstock dropped the small gun into his pocket.

Speaking directly to the Englishman now, the French police inspector continued, 'There was a report on my desk a couple of days ago from the German police – you know that there is a limited co-operation between us, although their own arrogance sometimes militates against them. They were looking for a young woman, named Senga Lundy or Landy, who was a suspect in the killing of a German national, Graf Rutgar von Mann. He had been shot at close range by a .22 Derringer.' He glanced sidelong at Colin and smiled slightly. 'But I know what these German aristos are like, and I made some inquiries and discovered that this young man enjoyed an evil reputation. I am sure the weapon was used in self-defence.' He paused and added diffidently, 'However, I thought it best if the gun were not found amongst her possessions.'

Colin looked at him in astonishment. 'You . . . you concealed evidence . . . for me? Why?'

Maurice Durffle shrugged and managed to look embarrassed. 'For no special reason. I think a woman would be good for you, and if you like this woman, then obviously there is much to be admired about her. The more I hear of her, the more jealous I become of you. She is a woman of character.'

Colin nodded. 'She is that.'

'Perhaps I could come to the wedding,' Durffle suggested slyly.

Colin laughed uproariously and then suddenly sobered. 'Have you any idea where she is now? She's obviously being held by Billy Fadden's murderers.'

'I have made certain discreet investigations.' Maurice Durffle raised his small fingers and began ticking off points. 'The Englishman Moore is in Paris. Katherine Lundy is in Paris. Weismann, a jeweller who was known to us as a dealer in stolen stones, has disappeared. Tattoo is no longer about his usual haunts. Tattoo has worked for all three. He is the key.' He reached out his hand and Colin shook it.

'I want to thank you . . .' he began.

'Don't. Just try not to leave too many bodies for me to clean up. And make sure you and your lady walk away from all this.'

Colin nodded. 'One thing,' he said as the French police inspector was about to walk away. 'I once made you a promise that I would not harm Tattoo. I might not be able to keep that promise.'

'I realise that.'

'Do you have any idea where we might find this man?'

Maurice Durffle smiled and handed Colin Holdstock a slip of paper. 'Katherine Lundy is staying at this hotel. He will undoubtedly make contact with her there.'

Colin took the paper and folded it into the breast pocket of his coat. 'Tell me,' he said suddenly, 'have you ever been best man at a wedding before . . .?

Katherine Lundy listened to the report in stony silence, her face a mask, her eyes hooded. She had spent far too many years concealing her intentions and emotions to start revealing them now. Furthermore she had spent far too many years lying to other people not to know when she was not being given the whole truth. Something was wrong here. Very wrong.

'So . . . Billy Fadden is dead,' she murmured. 'It's hard to believe, she seemed so indestructible, and her reputation was superb.'

'I do not think reputations and human flesh are much

proof against a twelve-gauge shotgun at close range,'
Tattoo said slowly. He was sitting across from Katherine
Lundy at a small table in the room she was staying in. In
one corner her bags were packed and she had been about
to pay her bill and sign out when the Frenchman had
arrived with the news that Senga had been taken.

'How is Senga?'

The Frenchman shrugged. 'I do not know. But I would
presume she would be well taken care of until they
determine whether you and they will do business.'

'And if I don't want to deal with these people?'
Katherine asked.

'They will cut off her ears and nose and send them to
you as tokens of their integrity.'

Katherine nodded.

'Should that fail to convince you, they will then cut off
her fingers and toes. Indeed should you fail to deliver an
appropriate response to them within the hour, they will
send you the little finger of her right hand as an incentive.'

Katherine turned to look as the small hatbox on the bed.
Within it lay the culmination of a lot of dreams, a lot of
pain. The jewels were hers, by rights they were hers . . .
and she had paid twenty thousand pounds sterling for
them into the bargain. It was more than they were worth,
but she had wanted the stones so badly and the Jewish
jeweller had known it. The jewels meant more to her than
just precious stones and their monetary value. They meant
so much more; they were part of her past, an integral part
of her history, they had shaped her life in ways that few
people – even those very close to her – could comprehend.
When the jewels had been stolen in 1907, it had been the
catalyst that had brought Dermot Corcoran back into her
life . . . it had brought John Lewis back into her life too,
but that was of little consequence. That was the year she
had fallen in love, the year Senga had been conceived on
that wonderful, never-to-be-forgotten holiday in Galway
during that glorious summer.

Katherine had loved Dermot, loved him deeply, loved

him deeply enough to betray the Irish uprising to the British authorities in exchange for her husband's life. But even as she had betrayed her husband's precious cause, so too had she been betrayed in turn. And Dermot had died, fighting for a cause he passionately believed in, betrayed by the woman he loved.

The Crown Jewels had brought Dermot back into her life, had been instrumental in giving her nine of the happiest years of her life, and now those same jewels could save her daughter – *their* daughter's – life. Katherine Lundy stopped abruptly, realising that she was actually trying to work out some way of keeping the jewels. Trading with her daughter's life. True, she had not been close to either of her children, and although she liked to think that it was not entirely all her own fault, she knew, deep in her heart and soul, that it was. She had been too wrapped up in her twilight world of sex and money, of crime and pain, to spend any time with her children. She had tried to manipulate them as she manipulated the people she employed, and she should have realised that she could not do that. They were both too independent for that. And why should that come as any surprise: both of their fathers, Patrick's and Senga's, had been strong-willed in their own way. And, if she had given anything of herself to her children, it had been her own iron determination.

She looked at the hatbox again. Not bad for a girl whose first job had been in a teashop in Blackpool. Perhaps that was part of the attraction of the stones: how many other ill-educated servant girls would be able to say that they had owned – albeit briefly – the Crown Jewels?

'Your decision, Madame?' Tattoo asked.

'Let's go.' Katherine stood up and reached for the hatbox. 'What choice do I have . . .?' she turned to ask, and the door to the room swung open and Patrick Lundy stepped into the room, a heavy pistol pointed unerringly at Tattoo's head.

'There is always a choice, Mother,' Patrick said coldly. 'And Monsieur Tattoo here is about to help us make ours!'

CHAPTER THIRTY-EIGHT

The house was in the Paris suburbs, a twenty-minute walk from the Champs Elysées but set in a completely pastoral surrounding. It had once belonged to the British High Commission, and during the Great War had acted as a safe house for agents returning from the front line. It was sold after the war and had lain idle for a number of years before being purchased by a London bank acting on behalf of a client. The 'client' was the British government.

Martin Moore leaned against the low balustrade that led down into the large, overrun garden. He was smoking a cigarette without any real enjoyment; he had run out of Turkish and had been forced to smoke the rancid French tobacco, which caught at the back of his throat and stung his eyes, contributing to his foul temper. There was, however, some consolation in the fact that this affair would soon draw to a close and he would be able to return to England and the pleasant niceties of civilisation, like drinkable tea and smokable cigarettes.

Wisps of early morning fog twisted slowly across the overgrown lawn, coiling around the statuettes of Greek gods and goddesses, blanketing the unused, leaf-clogged fountain, lending it an almost dream-like athmosphere. Martin Moore blew out smoke and breathed in the damp, foggy air; it would burn off soon and the day promised to be good. Very good. Tattoo was bringing Katherine Lundy at noon.

'We need him,' Patrick insisted. 'Moore will need to see

him and then you, otherwise he'll know something is wrong and we lose the element of surprise.'

Katherine Lundy glared at the Frenchman and then shook her head. 'I say kill him and be done with it. He has betrayed all of us, me, you and Senga.'

Tattoo looked imploringly at Colin Holdstock. 'Please, Sir, you are a police officer, how can you allow this . . . you cannot . . .'

Colin Holdstock leaned so close to the Frenchman that Tattoo could actually feel his breath on his face. 'If it was left up to me, I'd kill you too,' he whispered.

Tattoo's single eye rolled in his head in terror. What had started out as a simple deal – find the girl and deliver her, and a bonus if he turned up with some stolen gemstones – had disintegrated into an absolute shambles. He was tied to a chair in Katherine Lundy's room, surrounded by three insane people. He knew Katherine Lundy's reputation, he had experienced it first hand when he had worked for her, and he knew of Patrick Lundy's exploits. He was a hardened killer and Tattoo had no doubts that he would kill him without a second thought. But the policeman, Inspector Holdstock, he would have thought he might be able to help him . . . But it looked as if he was just as deranged as the other two.

So all that remained for him to do was what he did best – survive, and he survived by making the best of a bad situation. In all his years, though, he doubted if he had been in worse.

'I'll do what you say,' he mumbled.

Patrick patted the Frenchman's shoulder. 'We know you will.' He glanced sidelong at Colin. 'Why don't you ask him what we want to know? You are the skilled investigator,' he added with a wry grin.

'I think your methods would be more effective here,' the Englishman said softly, watching the Frenchman, seeing the fear in his face.

Patrick Lundy pulled up a chair and sat directly facing Tattoo. Reaching into his pocket he pulled out his pistol and with great care unsnapped the chamber and shook out the six copper rounds into the palm of his hand. He made a deal of picking up just one bullet, placing it in the chamber and then snapping the cylinder shut. Turning the cylinder by hand he positioned the bullet next in line to the hammer.

'Now, you will be aware of the game known as Russian Roulette, I believe it is quite commonplace amongst drunken artists. Well, you and I are going to play a slightly different version of that game.' Tattoo stared at the gun as if mesmerised. 'This is Russian Roulette without the chance. The next time I pull the trigger the gun will fire. We want to know where Senga Lundy is being held, how many men are guarding her and what their security arrangements are.'

Tattoo started to shake his head.

'And if you refuse to tell me, then I will shoot you. Probably in the fleshy part of the thigh, or through the shoulder blades . . . yes, the shoulder blades I think. This will cause you great pain, but it will mean that you can still accompany Madam Lundy to the rendezvous with Colonel Moore. I knew a man back in Ireland who could put ten rounds into a man and still keep him alive,' he added conversationally.

Tattoo looked in Patrick Lundy's stone-hard eyes, reading the truth therein, and then his head slumped. 'They are in a safe house in the suburbs, I am not sure of the name, but I can take you there. I have only ever seen six guards, and they are all armed with pistols and shotguns. Martin Moore is there and he carries a pistol; his wife is also present.'

'Tilly?' Katherine asked in horror. 'Surely not Tilly?'

Patrick looked down at his mother. 'If you're looking for a traitor, then she's the one you should blame. Martin Moore was only doing his job, but she betrayed everything and everyone for this.'

'I blame the war,' Katherine said cryptically and the three men turned to look at her. She looked up in surprise and attempted a smile. 'The war changed people, it changed their attitudes, their morals. Even the trade I was in changed after the war. Soldiers came back from Europe with all sorts of diseases and they passed them on to the girls: it gave whoring a bad name. They started looking for more and more perverse erotica and exotica, and some of them had been so traumatised by what they had seen and done during the war that they were not able to distinguish between what was right or wrong anymore. This *disease*, this selfishness, affected people from all walks of life. People no longer care about right or wrong, duty or obligation, friendship means nothing to them; they care only about themselves. God help us if we ever have another world war – the very fabric of society will be completely destroyed.'

Katherine's eyes had glazed as she spoke, and when Patrick placed his hand gently on her shoulder it took them a few moments to visibly refocus on the room and its occupants.

Colin leaned over the Frenchman's shoulder. 'What does Moore want?' he demanded.

'He wanted the girl, Senga Lundy, and he wanted her because he hoped that she would bring Katherine to him. At least Tilly, his wife, had led him to believe that Katherine would not allow her daughter to be harmed. He wasn't so sure, but she reminded him of the time you, Madam, came to Paris to find your daughter.'

'I would never allow any harm to come to Senga,' Katherine said suddenly, and then she looked up at Patrick and added quickly, 'nor you.' She reached up and squeezed his hand tightly, her eyes sparkling, and Patrick nodded briefly, remembering the time she had hired four men to kill him. The sudden fluctuation of her moods had taken him slightly off balance and he found it difficult to hate this woman with the passion that he once had. He had stopped loving her a long time ago, but he had the terrible feeling that he still cared for her . . . and what was caring but love?

For one brief moment Patrick Lundy wished he was

back in Ireland in the early twenties, on the run, when all his decisions had been simple enough, kill or be killed, and the orders he received were explicit, with no room for interpretation. But then that too had changed, the lines of demarcation had become blurred, and there had come a time when he had found it difficult to accept his orders, when he found himself questioning his superiors, when he found it difficult to hate the old enemies.

And if circumstances could change, surely poeple could change also.

Tattoo was continuing. 'Martin Moore knew that Katherine would buy the jewels from that Jewish jeweller who has the shop behind the fish market. The man had been attempting to dispose of them for some time, but only to selected parties – and at the slightest sign that something was awry, he would clam up. Madame Lundy's reputation would assure him that she was genuine, and it was a certainty that he would sell to her.' He attempted to shrug, but his bound hands prevented that, so he contented himself with tilting his head slightly. 'So, it would then be a simple matter of exchanging the jewels for the girl.'

Katherine leaned forward. 'Why does he want the jewels so badly?'

'I do not know, Madame.'

'I think I do,' Colin said quietly. 'Moore works for a particular department that is concerned with all things royal; part of their brief is to ensure that the royal family remains untouched by scandal. I believe that Moore has been instructed to retrieve the jewels to ensure that the story of the theft receives no further publicity, especially since some of the principals were very close to the crown.'

'What will happen to the jewels?' Patrick asked.

'It's not the jewels I'd be worried about,' Colin smiled, 'it's all those people associated with the affair. If Moore has gone to all this trouble to tie up some loose ends, he's not likely to leave any others around . . . like you and Madam Lundy here, and Tattoo of course. And Senga,' he added in a bitter whisper.

Patrick looked at the clock. It showed a few minutes to ten. Less than two hours to go. He turned back to Tattoo, a death's grin fixed to his thin lips.

'Why, Aunt Tilly?' Senga asked, looking across the breakfast table at the grey-haired woman.

'A lot of reasons,' Tilly Cusack said shortly.

'Such as?' Senga persisted. She was watching the older woman intently, aware of her discomfiture, her annoyance. Through the open doors she could see Martin Moore standing on the patio, smoking. Tendrils of fragrant smoke trickled back into the room. She found herself seriously wondering if she would be able to get to the pins in her hair, lunge across the table and plunge them into Tilly Cusack's throat without making any noise.

'Why did you have to kill Billy?' she asked.

'I wasn't there,' Tilly said shortly.

'But you're involved. You've been involved in this whole affair from the very beginning. Haven't you?' Senga demanded, her raised voice making Martin Moore glance over his shoulder. After a moment, he looked away again.

'Yes,' Tilly said suddenly, her blue eyes blazing, 'Yes, I was involved in this from the beginning. I was the one who actually suggested the plan to Martin, and do you know something? – when he returns with the Crown Jewels to England, he may well get a title, or at the very least a knighthood. And that's the key that opens the doors to London Society. Not bad for an old whore, eh?' she asked, the bitterness in her voice almost tangible.

'That's not what this is all about, is it?' Senga asked cautiously. 'There's more to it than this. This is some sort of revenge on my mother, isn't it?'

Tilly ignored her. She poured another cup of tea from the silver teapot, and added a tiny amount of milk.

'And I thought you were my mother's friend,' she added bitterly.

The older woman looked up, her expression closed and unreadable. 'I was. I found your mother on the streets of

Dublin, remember? I was the one who brought her to safety, who found her a home, and then later, when she was being hunted all over Dublin by Patrick's father, I was the one who ensured that she remained safe and hidden. And do you know how she repaid me? She stole everything that was mine. I would have been the Madam of that house if your mother hadn't intervened and turned Bella Cohen against me. Everything your mother has now – everything she threw away in her search for the stupid, worthless jewels – should have been mine. And I would not have wasted them as she did. I should be one of the wealthiest women in Ireland . . . and instead, what am I?' she asked bitterly.

Senga had been watching Martin Moore come in through the open windows and stand behind his wife. He rested both hands on her shoulders, making her start, and murmured softly, his eyes fixed on Senga's face. 'It's not what you are now, my dear, it's what you will be soon. Soon, you will have a title, you will be Lady, or possibly even Baroness or Countess . . . who knows. Your King will be extremely grateful for the return of the stones, and you will be well-rewarded. Very well rewarded indeed.'

Tilly reached back to pat her husband's hands.

'I've never heard you speak like this before,' Senga said quietly. 'When did you begin to think this way?' she asked Tilly, although her eyes were on Moore's face. She saw a smile curl his lips. 'This is your doing, isn't it?' she said very quietly.

Moore's smile broadened. 'It is easy to allow a supposed friendship to confuse things. I will admit that I spoke to my wife and enabled her to see things a little more clearly.'

'You tricked her into betraying her friend.'

'My dear, you are overwrought and hysterical.' His smile twisted into a smirk. 'Tilly wasn't tricked into betraying her friendship with your mother. But once she saw how your mother had used her, betrayed her – as indeed she betrayed her own son and you too – then my wife made her own decision.'

371

'As far as I can see, the only one who will gain out of all this will be you. How much are they paying you for this dirty work?'

Moore spread his hands. 'I am a civil servant. I am paid a salary, no matter what the outcome of this matter.'

'And the title from your grateful King of course, and what will that get you – a place in the House of Lords, and a huge salary?' She looked at her aunt. 'Can't you see that he's used you? Used you to betray the only woman who cared for you?' she laughed bitterly. 'You know, I used to envy the relationship you had with my mother. I was jealous of the amount of time she spent with you; I envied the way she seemed to relax when you were there. And when she was in trouble, where did she go, who was the first person she called upon?'

'That's enough!' Martin Moore snapped. 'Guard!' he called, and a young man, shabbily dressed with a shotgun on one shoulder, hurried into the room. 'Take Miss Lundy back to her room and lock her in. No one, and I mean no one, is to be allowed in to see her. Disobey me in this and I will have you shot.'

The man looked at him, nodding quickly, clearly in awe of the cold-eyed Englishman. He reached for Senga's arm, but she shook it off. She came slowly to her feet and then, resting both fists on the tablecloth, she leaned across the table and glared at Tilly Cusack and Martin Moore. 'The next time I see you both, I hope I shall be looking at your corpses,' she spat.

'Take her away,' Moore snapped and Senga was dragged from the room.

'Martin . . .?' Tilly began.

'Did you know the girl is wanted for murder?' Martin Moore asked suddenly, shocking his wife into silence. 'The report arrived today. She killed the young man she had gone to Germany with . . .'

'Rutgar . . .? Tilly started to shake her head.

'Yes; Graf Rutgar von Mann. Shot him twice at point-blank range. Oh, she's her mother's daughter all

372

right.' Moore spun on his heel and strode from the room. He still had some arrangements to make. There would be some bodies to dispose of later. Katherine Lundy's, Tattoo's and Senga's of course. He hoped he wouldn't have to add his wife's to the list.

CHAPTER THIRTY-NINE

The guard had stamped down the uncarpeted stairs ten minutes previously and she hadn't heard him return. She had attempted once again to work on the lock with one of her hair pins, trying to catch and work the levers on the large, antiquated mechanism but without success. It was too heavy and the thin steel in her pins had started to bend out of shape, and she didn't want to risk damaging her only weapon. There was one other alternative, however, but she would have to wait until she was sure that her mother was in the house.

Senga checked her watch again. It was a few minutes before twelve. And Katherine Lundy was arriving at noon.

At precisely twelve o'clock, as Tattoo was chauffeuring Katherine in through the wrought-iron gates, Patrick Lundy and Colin Holdstock were making their way through the thick privet hedge that separated the garden from the muddy stream at the back of the house.

Neither man had any illusions about what would happen if they failed. They both knew that Martin Moore, despite the fact that he was ostensibly working for the British government, would leave no witnesses alive, and he had already demonstrated his willingness to kill.

There were two men patrolling the back of the house. They looked like hired help from the backstreets of Paris, and both were carrying shotguns. They stamped to and fro across the lawn, looking bored, chain-smoking an indescribably-foul tobacco that tainted the damp, morning air . . . and which helped to pinpoint their positions amongst the shrubbery. Neither were paying much attention to the grounds.

Colin knelt in the mud with Patrick beside him and parted the leaves on a low bush. 'What I wouldn't give for a London bobby's truncheon,' he muttered.

'Can't help you there, but will this help?' He passed Colin a short, leather sap which was surprisingly heavy for its size. 'Lead weighted,' he added.

'It'll do.'

'I'll take the one on the right,' Patrick continued. 'You work your way around through the bushes and take the one on the left when he's closest to you. And remember, this is no time to be gentlemanly. These people are killers. If they manage to get off one shot, Moore'll have killed Senga and my mother before we can get to them.'

'You take care of your man, I'll take care of mine,' Colin advised. He moved off through the bushes, the sap clutched tightly in a white-knuckled grip.

Katherine had been ushered into the long dining room, where she was confronted by Martin Moore standing behind Tilly Cusack who was seated at the far end of a long, highly polished table. She looked around the otherwise bare room, but there was no sign of Senga.

'Where is my daughter?'

Martin Moore came forward. 'Please sit. Your daughter is safe . . .' he said calmly, as if he were speaking to a stranger.

'I would like to see her,' Katherine stated flatly.

'Business first,' Martin Moore began.

Katherine reached up and pulled off her mannish-style hat. When she lifted her hand again she was holding a small short-barrelled Derringer, and it was pointing unerringly at Martin Moore. 'My daughter.'

'This is a mistake, Madam.'

'Possibly.'

A man stepped into the doorway, a shotgun at shoulder level; a second appeared at the French windows, his shotgun also pointing directly at Katherine.

Martin Moore laughed. 'Put down the gun; you don't have a chance.'

Katherine thumbed back the hammer on the small pistol. 'But I think I could take you with me, couldn't I? I shot your old boss with this gun, it seems almost fitting that I should shoot you with it too.'

'Pull the trigger and neither you nor your daughter will leave this place alive,' Moore said coldly.

'Let me see my daughter alive and well, and we will negotiate for the jewels.'

Moore looked past Katherine. 'Bring the girl.' He waved both guards away. When he turned back to Katherine, his whole attitude had changed, confident that he was regaining control of the situation. 'There will be no negotiation. I will give you the girl, you will give me the jewels. A swap. Oh, and there's also a codicil that you will never speak of this incident or the theft of the Irish Crown Jewels again. My employers wish to forget this incident.'

Katherine nodded, reading between the lines. 'You will have my word.'

'Good. And I know that your word is your bond,' he added, turning away, but Martin Moore intended to make sure that Madam Lundy never again spoke of the jewels.

Colin Holdstock was so close to the guard that he could hear the man's harsh breathing. Although the Frenchman was facing out into the garden, he was obviously interested in what was going on in the house, and all his attention was focused in that direction. The shotgun was held loosely in his left hand, his fingers wrapped around the stock, nowhere near the trigger, Colin noted. The Englishman moved a few inches closer and then suddenly rose up out of the bushes and cracked the guard across the side of the head with the lead-weighted sap. The man slumped to the ground without a sound. Colin dragged him into the bushes and immediately handcuffed his right wrist to his left ankle. He broke the shotgun and checked the loads, and then, taking a deep breath, he continued on towards the house. He caught a brief glimpse of the dining room, and he could see the tableau of Katherine Lundy holding the gun on Martin Moore.

He wondered where Senga was.

Marcel was highly amused by the whole affair. He usually plied his trade in the backstreets of Paris, but, he noted, whether it be slum hovel or upper-class mansion, emotions were similar. Human beings were human beings, and all of them were controlled by greed or lust or anger . . . but mostly greed.

He climbed the bare stairs, humming softly to himself. He had a good idea that this little affair today was going to end in bloodshed. All he had to work out was the number of bodies. The old woman downstairs certainly – the hard woman with the small gun. Marcel had looked into the eyes of killers before and knew the type, but he also knew that she wasn't going to walk out of this house today.

And this young bint upstairs. Unconsciously, he nodded. No, he didn't think she would make it out of the house alive either. Ah, but she was a fine thing. And young too, just the way Marcel preferred them. Perhaps if he was nice to the Englishman, he would allow him to have her for a little while before he killed her.

He was still smiling at the thought as he opened the door – and the razor-sharp pin tore into his face, missing his eye by a fraction.

The Frenchman staggered back, one hand briefly pressing his lacerated cheek, and then he brought the shotgun up, thumbing back the hammer on the heavy weapon. 'You . . . you will pay for that,' he hissed vehemently. The young woman backed into the room, the bloody pin clutched in her hand. 'Maybe I should kill you now, eh?' Marcel grunted in French.

'You can't kill me,' Senga said quietly, in perfect

English. 'That's not going to be your privilege.'

The Frenchman looked at her for a moment and then reached for his belt. 'Well, perhaps you might be taught a lesson before I bring you down. Now put the pin on the floor. Do it!' he snapped when she ignored him.

Senga reluctantly dropped the pin to the ground and then put her hands on her hips, touching the second pin which she had stuck into her dress. She watched the man open his trousers, and then begin to tug up his dirty shirt.

'There are two ways we can do this,' Marcel continued. 'You can struggle and get hurt, or you can relax and enjoy it.'

'It is very probable that I shall vomit with the smell of you,' Senga said carefully, almost abstractedly.

'You are a funny girl. I like a girl with a sense of humour. Do you like this . . .?' he continued, exposing himself.

'Do you like this!' Colin Holdstock suddenly stepped into the room and smashed the cosh across the man's head with all his strength. There was the audible sound of something breaking and the Frenchman collapsed without a sound. Colin stepped across the body avoiding the pool of blood which was snaking from one ear, and smiled at Senga. 'I told you I would come back for you.'

Senga Lundy felt her breath catch in her throat and she sagged into his arms. 'I can see you're a man of your word.'

Colin kissed her lightly on the forehead. 'I always keep my word.'

'You also told me that the next time we met I would have nothing to fear.'

'We're working on that,' he said, kissing her again.

Katherine looked at Tilly Cusack. 'Somehow I'm not surprised,' she said coldly. 'I knew it had to be someone close to me, someone who knew my every move . . . and the only one I was in contact with was you. But you know,' she said very quietly, 'I refused to accept that it could be you. Not you, not Tilly Cusack, my best and closest friend. Shows how wrong you can be,' she said abruptly.

Tilly looked at Katherine, meeting her eyes for the first time since she had entered the room. 'I didn't betray you . . . you betrayed me, you betrayed yourself.'

Martin Moore smiled and sat down in one of the hard-backed dining chairs. He rested his elbow on the polished table and cupped his chin in his hand, staring at Katherine Lundy with an almost dreamy expression, a smile twisting his lips. This woman, this servant girl turned whore turned thief, this *nothing*, would be the instrument of his greatest triumph. So many others – including the King himself – had failed to discover the whereabouts of the Crown Jewels, and yet here he had them almost in his hands, and the thief before him. At the very least, he would have earned a knighthood.

'Tell me how I betrayed you,' Katherine said calmly, playing for time, looking from Moore to Tilly. She had to allow Patrick and Colin time to make their way into the house and free Senga; only when she was safe would Katherine be able to make her move. Once Senga was safe, they would come for her, they said, but Katherine had other ideas on that score. As soon as she knew her daughter was safe she was going to put a little plan of her own into effect.

'You took what was rightfully mine,' Tilly snapped, her eyes, once so bright and blue, now clouded with age. 'I should have been the Whoremistress of Dublin . . . I would have been, until you came along and ruined it all.'

Katherine couldn't help smiling. 'That's some ambition isn't it – to be the Whoremistress of Dublin? Not a very respectable occupation, eh?' she asked sarcastically.

'Everything you had, everything you threw away because of your stupid involvement with the Easter Rising and the Crown Jewels should have been mine. I earned it.'

'The only thing you ever earned, you earned on your back with your legs open,' Katherine snarled, attempting to provoke a reaction. 'You were nothing until I came along. You were a street whore, with nowhere to go but down. Given time you'd have ended up a shilling tart, gin-sodden and diseased. I took you off the streets. Yes, me,' she persisted when Tilly opened her mouth to protest. 'Oh yes, you saved my life when I was in trouble, but how often after that did I save yours? I took you off the streets, arranged it so you never had to work for your living again. You never became pregnant and you never got a dose. Can you say that would not have happened if I hadn't taken you off the streets? And remember when Captain Lewis – this man's superior, the man who trained him – took you and tortured you, remember when he took you, who came and rescued you? I gave up everything when I went into his house then. He didn't even know I was alive. He didn't know who Madam Kitten was. I had worked for years to preserve my cover. And I threw it all away for you, for my friend,' she spat.

'Enough!' Martin Moore surged to his feet, sending the chair toppling backwards, not liking the way the conversation was turning, unhappy with the doubtful look in his wife's troubled blue eyes. He looked towards the door, 'Marcel! Marcel! Where is that man? What's taking him so long?'

Patrick peered into the kitchen window at the two men who were drinking red wine from dirty glasses. They were both in their shirt sleeves, their shotguns lying across the table. To his right another guard stood on the patio, obviously half-listening to the conversation in the dining room.

Faintly, from off to his right, Patrick heard an English voice calling, 'Marcel . . . Marcel . . .'

Moments later a shotgun blast ripped through the morning silence.

The two men in the kitchen grabbed for their guns and one glanced up – directly into Patrick's face. He shouted unintelligibly, spraying wine as he pointed.

Patrick lifted his pistol and calmly shot him in the head through the glass window. He shot the second guard in the back of the head without hesitation, the force of the blow lifting him across the table, dropping him on top of the body of his companion.

Cursing, Patrick turned to the right – only to find that the guard on the patio had disappeared into the room. There was another explosion, and dark, greasy smoke drifted out on to the lawn.

'Jesus!' Patrick sprinted towards the dining room, his only thought for his mother.

Colin Holdstock moved cautiously down the stairs, the gun in his hand, while Senga followed on behind. Her earlier fears had turned to excitement, and she felt safe and secure in this man's presence . . . much the same as she had felt in Billy's presence. The thought slipped into her mind – ice-cold and numbing – and she suddenly felt sick. She reached forward and pressed her hand to Colin's left shoulder, causing him to turn his head. 'Thank you,' she murmured.

'For wha . . .?' he started to ask, when the guard appeared on the stairs.

There was a moment of shocked immobility and then both men fired together!

The sudden explosion of sound brought Martin Moore to his feet, his hand going to the inside pocket of his morning coat. But Katherine's hand came up rock-steady, the tiny pistol levelled in both hands, and the smile that stretched her lips was anything but pretty.

Seconds later two single pistol shots sounded from outside the house.

And then the guard was in the room.

He had appeared in through the French windows, the shotgun levelled. He stopped at the tableau and looked to Martin Moore for direction, and in that instant Katherine shot him in the face. His body spasmed, his fingers jerking on the trigger, blasting off both barrels.

*

381

Pellets tore into the plaster, stinging Colin's face, drawing blood along his cheek, plucking at his hair and the heavy cloth of his coat, but leaving him otherwise unharmed. His own shot, however, took the man squarely in the chest, lifting him up and back, punching him over the banister and down into the hall below.

The Frenchman twisted as he fell, one hand clawing at his face where Katherine had shot him, not even aware that he had fired his own gun. The lead charge tore into Tilly Cusack's back at almost point-blank range, killing her instantly.

Katherine fell to the floor and fired her single remaining shot at Martin Moore. The shot took him high in the shoulder and she saw him stagger and then straighten. With a terrifying grin on his face, he slowly and deliberately removed the heavy service revolver from his inside pocket and advanced towards her.

'You have thwarted me at nearly every turn, Whoremistress. You have mocked me and the office I represent for years, laughed at the police in their attempts to bring you to book.' He thumbed back the hammer on the ugly-looking weapon and then levelled it at her face. 'Well the last laugh is on you. Justice is mine . . .'

The sound of a pistol shot thundered around the room.

Colin Holdstock ducked into the room with Senga by his side. Patrick swivelled to face them, his pistol held in both hands, his face an implacable mask. He took a deep breath and his shoulders slumped, but when he saw his sister his eyes suddenly sparkled with moisture. Stepping across the carnage, he wrapped his fingers around Martin Moore's sodden collar and dragged his almost headless body off Katherine Lundy's. She opened her eyes. Her face and hair were covered in blood – all of it Moore's, where Patrick's hollow-nosed bullet had exploded through the man's head.

Patrick knelt on the ground beside his mother and used

his handkerchief to wipe most of the gore away, while Senga knelt on the opposite side and tore off a section of her dress to wipe the blood from her mother's neck and hands.

'My children,' Katherine Lundy said simply.

'Mother.'

'Mama.'

Colin Holdstock lifted a blood-soaked cardboard box off the floor and peered inside. Sparkling reflections ran across his face and he turned to look at the woman on the ground with her children on either side of her.

Katherine Lundy had waited more than twenty years to claim the jewels, and yet she had still been prepared to give them up for her daughter.

And Patrick Lundy's first concern had been for his mother.

And Senga Lundy?

She had lost and gained also. Lost a good friend, and gained a lover . . . and a mother once again.

He walked to the window and stared out into the brilliant sunshine. There was a touch of summer in the air: a new season was beginning.

EPILOGUE

Against the naked skin, the jewels scintillated with an inner fire. The heavy collar lay across her breasts, concealing the nipples.

'They look good on you.' Colin Holdstock moved into the light, smiling at his wife. He was naked, unselfconsciously so.

Senga Lundy-Holdstock sat up in bed and allowed the jewels to slide down her flesh, the coolness sensuous, like a lover's touch.

Colin came and sat down on the bed, running his hand up along his new wife's thigh, picking up the Badge of the Order of St Patrick which had come to rest on her groin.

Senga covered his hand with hers. 'I didn't think you'd take them,' she said quietly, attempting to make out his face in the gloom.

'Well your mother had bought and paid for them. And you'll never be able to wear them in public, never be able to display them. It's unlikely you'll even be able to sell them. They're pretty baubles.'

'A lovely wedding present,' Senga murmured, and Colin nodded in agreement. 'A lovely wedding present.'

'Something to pass on to our children,' she whispered, wrapping her arms around her husband's neck, taking him to bed for the first time.

'Are there going to be children?' he asked, his voice muffled against her breasts.

'Lots.'

384